My Father's Secret

Kim

Kim,
I hope you enjoy it :)
Happy reading!
Jen McConnel

Happy reading!
Philisenue

My Father's Secret

JEN McCOMBS

TATE PUBLISHING
AND ENTERPRISES, LLC

The opinions expressed by the author are not necessarily those of Tate Publishing, LLC.

Published by Tate Publishing & Enterprises, LLC
127 E. Trade Center Terrace | Mustang, Oklahoma 73064 USA
1.888.361.9473 | www.tatepublishing.com

Tate Publishing is committed to excellence in the publishing industry. The company reflects the philosophy established by the founders, based on Psalm 68:11,
"The Lord gave the word and great was the company of those who published it."

Published in the United States of America

ISBN: 978-1-62854-206-6
Fiction / General
13.10.31

$\mathcal{D}$edication

To my grandmother, and in loving memory of my grandfather.
Thank you for a wonderful life, full of
so much love and happiness.
I am the luckiest girl in the world!

ℭonfusion

Campus is buzzing with activity as I finish my last final. Breathing a sigh of relief, I glance at the clock and realize I need to hurry. I gather my things, make my way to the front of the room, and place my exam on top of the stack sitting on the corner of Professor Martin's desk; he grunts. *Merry Christmas to you too!*

As I step outside, I look to the sky and let the warm sun kiss my face, soaking up the last bit of California heat before heading back to the cold Midwest. Another semester in the books. And this has definitely been the most difficult semester by far. Not because of my classes but because of *him*.

No. I can't go there right now. I'm late.

Shaking the thought of him from my mind I turn to head back to the dorm when I am nearly run down by some idiot on a bike as he speeds past me in front of the economics building. *Jackass!* Everyone is in such a hurry to leave for the holidays.

Thousands of students are rushing around, saying good-bye to friends and loading up their cars. As I make my way back to the dorm, my scalp begins to prickle and every inch of my body starts to tingle. I can sense it; he's following me again. I can feel his eyes on me with every step I take. He never lets me see him, but I always seem to know when he's there—at least I think I do—my mysterious guardian.

The very thought of him is exhilarating but annoying all at the same time. I wish he would show himself to me, talk to me so I know what I'm feeling is real—so I know I'm not crazy. Instead, all I get are random notes left on my pillow, always saying the same thing.

Alex,

Everything is alright. You're safe.
I'm watching over you

—Seth

Safe from what? From whom? Who would want to hurt me? And why does this Seth person feel it's his job to protect me? For the past three months since my nineteenth birthday, this is all I've been able to think about. Every car backfire, every bump in the night, makes me jump out of my skin. I have nightmares and wake up in a cold sweat almost every night. I can't eat, I can't study—I need a break. I can't wait to get out here and go home for the holidays. But will he follow me there? Back home to Michigan? Or am I only in danger when I'm here at USC? Is going to school in California a mistake? So many questions. But deep down, I know California isn't the problem. I can't explain it, but for as far back as I can remember, I have always felt as though someone or something was there, in the background of my life, watching me. And now that someone has a name—Seth.

Who are you? I have spent hours and even days unable to study, unable to function, unable to think of anything else. I've thought about all the people I've met since I've been in California, but I know I've never met someone named Seth: not in any of my classes, where I spend most of my time; not at a party or at a bar, where I spend very little time. And I definitely don't know anyone with that name back home. All I do know—whoever the hell this Seth is—he has me so freaked out I will be lucky if I pass any of my classes this semester. Thank God most of my classes have been art classes. My constant state of distress has actually enhanced my creative juices. Who would have thought?

Professor Sullivan has definitely noticed. He told me my work this semester had taken on a dark but fascinating tone. He especially liked the last piece I submitted. It was a charcoal drawing of a small mouse trapped in a dark corner by a faceless black cat—paw raised, claws exposed, ready to strike. And that was how I intended to turn it in, but at the last minute—in the middle of the night, after one of my nightmares—I changed it. I added the soft shadow of a hand reaching down to rescue the small, helpless creature. Sullivan described the drawing as "hope in the darkness of despair." He also said it was my best piece all term and he wanted to enter it in competition. Reluctantly, I agreed.

I've always had a hard time showing my work. It makes me self-conscious to have strangers critiquing and picking apart something I've put my heart and soul into–especially that piece. It's very personal to me because it is me. I'm the mouse. And the cat is the faceless person or persons who want to harm me. And the hand—the hand is Seth, also faceless but poised and ready to save me. But why?

Ugh! A trip home is definitely what I need to clear my head.

My roommate, Julie, is all packed and waiting for me as I walk through the door of our dorm room. She is lying on her bed, feet in the air, ankles crossed, reading one of her favorite trashy tabloid magazines. She loves to stay current on who is sleeping with whom and who has just broken up with whom. She feels pop culture is much more important than anything else that is happening in the world and much more interesting. Celebrity baby making and whose in rehab will always rank higher than the economic crisis or global warming on Julie's list of "must know."

I toss my bag on my bed and smile at her. Julie is lovely: tall—several inches taller than my five foot four—and thin, with perfect skin and hair. Men love her, and she knows it. As she flips the page, I notice she is wearing a short denim skirt and a purple cotton t-shirt. Her dark-brown curls are pulled back into a ponytail except for one perfect spiral that hangs softly down the side of her face. I'm a little jealous of how she always seems so put together no matter what she is wearing. She's quite the fashionista.

"You have another *mystery* envelope on your bed," she says to me without looking up from her magazine. I glance over at my pillow, and sure enough, there's another note from Seth.

Julie had been the one who noticed the first note Seth left for me on the afternoon of my birthday. I've never asked her, but as far as I know, she has never read *it* or any of the other notes that have followed. She's asked me several times to tell her who the notes are from and what they say, but trying to spare her from sleepless nights and horrible nightmares, I just laugh and tell her they say nothing important and that they aren't signed so I have no idea who they are from.

My standard answer seems to annoy and appease her at the same time, and eventually she just stopped asking. Now she just calls them "love letters from your secret admirer." Julie, a Southern belle with a flair for the dramatic, loves nothing more than a good love story—hence her addiction to tabloid magazines, so I let her believe whatever will keep her from the reality of it all. We're very close, and we talk about everything, but I haven't felt comfortable telling her that my mystery-note dropper is actually my guardian from some unknown danger. She would probably think I was full of crap anyway.

"I bet it's from your secret lover, letting you know how much he's going to miss you over break." She emphasizes *lover*, and I can hear a hint of jealousy in her voice.

"Something like that, I'm sure," I joke, rolling my eyes at her and snatching the envelope off my pillow.

"Seriously, when are you going to tell me who this mystery man is? It's killing me!"

"Honestly, Jules, I don't know who keeps leaving me these notes. I am here in our room every night. If I had a secret lover, don't you think you would have noticed by now? Not that *you're* home every night." I throw her a wink and flip the small white envelope around in my fingers but I don't open it.

"Well, the fact that we've had our locks changed twice and notes keep magically appearing on your bed kinda weirds me out," she replies wryly.

"Come on, you know we don't keep our door locked all the time. So maybe whoever it is just gets lucky and sneaks in whenever we are downstairs or doing laundry or something." I try to sound convincing, but I know he's been in our room at other times. "Or maybe Jeff lets him in. You know that guy will do anything for money."

Our resident advisor, Jeff, has been known to shave off his own eyebrows to win a bet, so I was sure a little B & E for twenty bucks wasn't out of the realm of possibilities.

Julie giggles. "Yeah, you're probably right. Well, finish packing and read your love note. I'm going to say good-bye to Chris, then we have to haul our ass to get to the airport, or we're going to miss our flights." Before I can respond, she tosses her magazine on her desk and is out the door.

Chris is her new quasi boyfriend for the month of December. No one went through men faster than my roommate and it's rather fascinating to watch.

Julie and I were matched up together through the random dormitory lottery freshman year, and on the very first day I met her, she informed me that her plan was to "kiss" as many frogs as she could before settling down with her six-figures-a-year prince. Seeing as I was actually attending college to study and graduate with a degree in advertising, I made her promise that all her "kissing" would be done at the "frog's" place unless I was out of town—and then my bed was off limits.

Unlike Julie, I have only had one true boyfriend, and we had dated all throughout high school, but I'm single now, and school is my priority. Oh, sure I've gone out with a few different guys over the past year and a half, but I am perfectly happy just to hang out with my friends and get good grades. There will be plenty of time for a serious boyfriend later.

I already packed most of my stuff the night before, so I quickly change into clothes more appropriate for a Michigan winter and dig out the winter jacket I had stuffed in the back of my closet. We have less than two hours to get to the airport, and with security tightened for the holidays, that is going to be cutting it close. I grab the rest of the things I need and throw them into my messenger bag along with my laptop and my latest mystery note. I'm ready. I pull the door closed behind me and make my way down stairs to meet Julie.

We jump into a cab and make it to the airport with barely enough time to race to our gates. I give Julie a hug, tell her I'll call her, and we go our separate ways. She is flying home to Georgia, hence the short skirt and t-shirt; it's still warm in Georgia. I am on my way back to Michigan. I can't wait to leave the stress of these past few months behind, and my grandma has promised to make my favorite dinner—spaghetti and garlic bread—in honor of my first night home. *Ahh, comfort food is exactly what I need!* I have only been gone four months, but every time I come home on break, my grandparents make such a big deal you'd think I'd been gone for years fighting the war or something.

My parents died when I was three, and my grandparents are all I have in the world. Going to school across the country has been hard, and even though this is my second year, it hasn't gotten easier. I miss home. I miss my room, the smells of Grandma cooking in the kitchen, my dog Sam, my friends, and I really miss watching hockey with my grandpa—hockey in California just isn't the same. I miss everything! As much as my grandparents wanted me to go to school in Michigan, they encouraged me to go out of state to have new experiences and to see the world outside of our little suburb. Apparently, vacations didn't count.

The preflight routine seemed to last forever, but once we were in the air and the flight attendants had passed out the first round of drinks and peanuts, I leaned my seat back the two inches it would allow and stared out the window for a while, grateful that on this flight, I'm not stuck next to someone who really should have been required to buy two seats but instead has *squeezed* themselves into one and is now spilling over into mine, forcing me to pretend like it's no big deal. *Sure, coach is spacious, I don't mind at all if you share my seat for the next four hours.* Nor am I stuck next to someone who is overly chatty and wants to tell me their entire life story while I am trapped next to them with nowhere to hide. *Of course the story about your infected toenail isn't grossing me out. Please tell me more.* Both scenarios I have experienced on my many flights across the country.

I bought a new book for this flight, to help pass the time, one of those new vampire books that seem to be all the rage these days. Pulling it out of my bag, I begin reading the first few pages, but my eyes are heavy, so I decide to just put in my earbuds and listen to my iPod and maybe get a short nap in. With the time change, it will be evening at home, and I know my grandparents will want to know all that has been going on over the last four months. Plus there is a hockey game on, so I know I will be up late. A nap is definitely a good idea.

The last song I remember playing as I begin to drift off to sleep is "Jane" by the Barenaked Ladies. I know every word by heart, and I am singing along to it in my head.

The song is no longer humming softly in my ears; the music is coming from somewhere else, somewhere in the distance, and I'm drawn to it.

As I follow the sound of the music, I suddenly realize that I'm alone and walking through the park where Julie and I go when we want to, as she would say, "get back to nature." I am walking in the clearing where we have picnicked so many times, and I can hear the music coming from somewhere in the woods off to my right. It beckons to me, drawing me to its melody. Unable to stop myself, I head toward the call. With each step, the trees around me seem to grow thicker and thicker, engulfing me.

The farther I walk, the louder the music becomes, and it feels as though I have been walking for hours. Lost and confused, I stop, and it appears I am standing directly in the heart of the music. I glance around as the voices sing to me, but there is nothing, no one—just a never-ending audience of ghostlike trees staring down at me, studying me.

My heart pounds in my ears, and my breathing has become shallow. I stand motionless. I struggle to listen beyond the music for other sounds. Then without warning, it's gone—no more music. As a matter of fact, there are no sounds at all. No birds chirping, no crickets, no wind rustling through the leaves, just eerie silence.

I'm panicking! My breathing accelerates, my throat is dry, and it feels as though my heart is going to beat right out of my chest. I stare into the shadows and struggle to find my tongue.

Finally, I manage to choke out in a low, shaky voice, "Hello? Is anyone there? I like your music! Hello?"

Nothing.

Wide eyed and apprehensive, I wander a bit further into the dense trees that surround me. By now the sun has set, and it's becoming difficult to see where I am going. Holding my arms out in front of me, I feel my way through the fading light. I walk aimlessly, changing my course when it feels as though I am going too far in one direction. As it grows darker, a more intense panic sets in. I'm shaking. I change my direction again, trying desperately to make my way back to the clearing, but at this point, I have no idea where I am going. Suddenly there's a sound. The sound of someone stepping on a twig. Someone is behind me. My spine stiffens, and I stop breathing completely. I slowly turn to see who or what is there. I stare into the blackness.

"Hello? Who's there?" I ask in a tone that makes it quite clear I'm frightened. There's no answer.

Self-preservation kicks in! I turn and begin rapidly walking away from where the sound came from. *Faster!* Someone is following me. *Run!* The trees have swallowed me up. They are so thick. Branches scrape against my face and tug against my hair. Leaves rustle under my feet. Snapping twigs and exposed roots make it difficult for me to elude my pursuer, but I keep going.

The clearing is nowhere in sight. *Run, idiot, run!* I scream at myself. But the faster I run, the faster the sounds behind me become. In my frantic pace, my toe catches on something. *Ugh!* I'm on all fours in the dirt. I try desperately not to cry out, even though my knee has landed on a gnarled root that has pushed its way to the surface. *Oh God, I'm hurt!* Tears begin to roll down my cheeks. *Stop crying, and get the hell out of here!* I scold myself, knowing if I stay where I am, whoever or whatever is out there will find me. I stand slowly, trying desperately not to make any noise. Before I am able to take another step, I hear—

"Hello, Alex."

My scalp prickles, and I gasp softly. *It's him.* I spin around with so much momentum I nearly fall down, again. I stare into the darkness. There is just enough moonlight streaming through the trees that I can see the faint image of a man.

"Seth?" I whisper.

"We are making our descent to Detroit Metro Airport," a sharp, braying voice comes over the loud speaker. "Please make sure your tray tables and seat backs are in their upright position."

Ugh! What a way to wake up from a dream!

"Are you all right, sweetie?" the lady seated next to me asks. "You seemed to be having a pretty intense dream. I thought about waking you, but the flight attendant beat me to it."

"Oh. Thanks, I'm okay," I answer, a bit embarrassed and visibly shaken.

As I rub the sleep from my eyes, I notice a moist sensation on my fingertips. I've been crying. The dream had been so vivid it spilled over into reality. That has never happened before. All the nightmares I had over the past few months never pushed their way through like this. How strange. My knee even feels sore.

"How long was I out?" I ask my neighbor, wiping my fingers on my jeans and rubbing my knee.

"You fell asleep about a half hour into the flight. You must have been pretty tired."

"I guess so. My last final exam must have taken it out of me. I didn't…um…say anything, did I?" I ask, a little self-conscious.

"No, just a few moans here and there, but you were shifting around a lot. I thought you might wake yourself up. Was it a bad dream?"

"No, not bad, just intense, I guess. I'm glad I didn't start talking. I do that sometimes. My roommate finds it comical."

"I would have woken you up if that happened. Well, unless if what you were saying was interesting, then I might have let you finish." She smirks then winks at me. I smile back.

My traveling companion is a middle-aged woman with shoulder-length chestnut-brown hair that looks as though she had just gotten it done before she caught the flight. You know that look—

fresh highlights with no hint of root and just enough hairspray so when she turns her head, not a single strand moves out of place. She's pretty, the way I always thought my mom would have looked at her age.

"So what brings you to Detroit?" she inquires, taking advantage of my newly conscious state.

"I go to school at USC, and I'm coming home for Christmas break." I answer stuffing my iPod and my vampire book back into my carry-on. "How about you?"

"My daughter is getting married on Saturday."

"Congratulations!" I respond, sounding a bit surprised seeing as it is December and there is about two feet of snow on the ground, at least from the last weather report I had gotten from my grandma. "A winter wedding in Michigan, that's unusual. Most people tend to wait for warmer weather."

She smiles. "My daughter loves the snow. We moved out to California when she was thirteen, and she always said when she was old enough she was going to move back. And she did. She went to college at U of M and has been here ever since. She's my little snow angel." Her face lights up as she talks about her daughter, and I can't help but smile at her.

Our plane lands right on time, and as we taxi down the runway, I can see from my window Grandma's last weather update was correct. Everything is white. I have to admit I miss the seasons in Michigan. I miss fall the most. Driving up north to Mackinac, the highway lined with trees so red they appear to be on fire. Wearing warm wool sweaters to the cider mill, eating sugary donuts and drinking hot, fresh apple cider, running through corn mazes, and enjoying hay rides, there really isn't anything like a Michigan fall. Now everything is covered with snow, but it is also quite beautiful.

"Well, have fun at your daughter's wedding," I say to my neighbor as we stand up and prepare to exit the plane.

"Thank you," she replies with a toothy smile. "It was nice talking with you. I wish you would have been awake longer to keep me company."

"Yeah, me too."

"Well, take care." She gives me a little wave then turns to join the procession of people in the aisle.

As I make my way down to baggage claim, I start thinking about my dream. About Seth. Then it hits me—I haven't read my latest note. I begin scrambling through my bag, and just as I get my fingers on the envelope, I hear—

"Alex!"

I recognize the voices immediately. I look up, and standing about twenty feet in front of me are my grandparents, holding their arms out and grinning from ear to ear. I drop the note back into my bag and run to them, wrapping my arms around both of their necks.

I'm home!

Home

Being with my grandparents again makes me completely forget about the bizarre past few months. I feel safe again.

As we drive home, I can't help feeling like a little girl, smiling and pointing and oohing at the Christmas lights glowing against the white blanket that has covered everything. Christmas in California is much different. Palm trees covered with twinkle lights and surfers dressed up like Santa Claus are a bit more than I can take.

When we pull into the driveway of our modest two-story house the first thing I see is Sammy, the most beautiful black Lab you have ever seen, with her nose pressed up against the front window, barking and wagging her tail excitedly. Jumping out of the car, I run through the back door, drop everything, and bend down to hug her. Before I can stop her, she lays a big wet, slimy doggie kiss right up the side of my face. But I didn't mind.

"She sure did miss you." Grandpa chuckles. "She sleeps in your room every night. It doesn't matter that it's your second year away from home. To that dog, it's like you left yesterday."

"I missed her too. I wish I could have her with me in Cali, but I don't think it would be very easy to hide an eighty-pound dog in my dorm room. I'm pretty sure someone might notice." I nuzzle my face to hers and kiss her on the forehead.

I take a deep, relaxing breath, and my stomach growls. "It smells so good, Grandma. I'm starving."

"Well, let's sit down and eat, and you can tell us about your finals. Your last one was today, wasn't it?" Grandma asks, walking into the kitchen. We all follow, Sam included.

As we eat dinner, I tell them about my art classes, how Mr. Sullivan thinks my progress this semester is miles ahead of last year and how I really have begun to unleash my talent. I do, however, neglect to tell them my classes that were not art related had fallen off a bit. It wasn't my fault, though; I was distracted. We talk about Julie and my other friends, and they, of course, ask about boys. I remind them I am there to study. I'm not there to get my MRS degree like Julie seems to be.

"What's an MRS degree?" Grandpa asks, looking puzzled.

"You know, 'misses' degree—girls who only go to college to find a husband. Getting an actual degree is their second priority. I'm pretty sure Julie is on that plan. I don't think she has even chosen a major yet."

"Oh!" Grandpa says, raising an eyebrow, then casually changes the subject. "Well, the hockey game is starting. Do you want to watch it with me?"

"Let me help Grandma with the dishes first, then I'll be right in."

"No, no, that's okay. You go watch the game, and I'll take care of the mess," she insists.

"Are you sure?"

"Of course, he's been dying for you to come home and watch with him. I'm a poor substitute, he tells me." She kisses my hair and takes my plate over to the sink. "Go, go. I'll do this."

I walk up behind her as she stands at the sink rinsing off dishes and put my arms around her shoulders, giving her a squeeze.

"Love you."

"Love you too. Glad you're home." She smiles then starts loading the dishes into the dishwasher.

I make my way into the family room and plop down on the floor in front of the TV. Grandpa is in his usual spot, sitting in his black leather La-Z-Boy, soda in one hand and the remote in the other. Sam comes over, lies down next to me, and nudges my hand with her nose so I'll pet her. I'm happy to, and I run my hand over the top of her head.

"So it's Detroit vs. Chicago tonight, ah, Grandpa?"

"Yep! A good Original Six matchup," he answers, staring at the TV, waiting for the puck to drop.

We spend the entire game throwing out stats and commenting on who is playing well and who is playing poorly, who we thought was going to win The Cup this year and who we wanted the Wings to play in the first round of the playoffs. Grandma brings us each a bowl of ice cream in between the second and third periods, as she always did, and she sits and drinks her coffee while Grandpa and I squabble over whose favorite player is better.

I am so happy and content. All the stress and confusion of the last few months is gone. It doesn't even cross my mind. I'm home with the people that have loved and protected me my entire life. Nothing can hurt me here. I still can't even fathom who would want to hurt me anyway. I lead the most boring normal life in the world. What could anyone possibly want with me?

By the time the game is over and the three of us are all talked out for the night, it is well past midnight. I kiss them both good night and climb the stairs to my room, Sam right on my heels.

With the time change, I'm still a bit wired, so I decide to take a shower and unpack before going to bed.

I stand in the shower and let the hot water run over me for a while. It feels good. My blood must have thinned being out in California, and the Michigan chill has gotten to me. Once I feel my fingers get pruney, it's time to get out. I wrap myself in a towel and ring my hair out with another. Throwing on the pajamas Grandma laid out for me, I shake the towel from my head and start brushing my long wet blond hair. As the fog begins to evaporate, I stare at myself in the mirror.

Throughout my life, people have always told me I was "cute," but it always seemed to come out in the way someone thinks kittens are cute or the way a cooing baby is cute. I considered the comment as a compliment, but it never gave me the self-confidence you get when people tell you you're beautiful or even pretty for that matter.

I guess I always did have a youthful look. Throughout high school, my friends used to tease me about being the baby of our class. It never really bothered me though. I just figured when our twenty-year reunion rolled around, everyone else would look old and haggard and I would still look fresh as a daisy. I take satisfaction in that.

Something changed, however, since I've been away at school. My looks have started to mature. I still look younger than I am, but my face has thinned and my skin has smoothed. I'm still quite thin, but my body no longer looks like a twelve-year-old boy. My figure has started to round out; I have boobs, and my jeans fit snugger to my butt. I've stopped wearing my corn-silk hair in a ponytail all the time and started to style it more. Julie gave me some makeup tips and showed me how to make my blue eyes "pop." I'm becoming a woman. Maybe even a beautiful woman. At least I can tell that the boys are noticing me more.

I don't have too much to unpack because most of my winter clothes are still in my closet. There isn't too much use for them in Southern California even in winter, so I didn't have to bring too much home with me. After putting everything away that's in my suitcase, I grab my messenger bag, which is lying on the floor next to my bed and pull out my laptop and some drawings I want to work on for next semester.

As I open up my sketch book, out falls my unopened note from Seth. I had completely forgotten about it again. I snatch it up off the bed, tear open the envelope, and slowly pull out the note. I look down at the folded paper in my hand for a long moment, contemplating. I'm not sure I want to know what it says. I'm home now. I can't possibly be in danger here.

Just get it over with, I growl at myself then unfold the note. I take a deep breath and read.

> Alex,
>
> I hope you enjoy being home with your family. Don't worry. I will be there to make sure you're safe.
>
> Merry Christmas!
>
> —Seth

This is making me absolutely insane! Angry, I throw the note on my nightstand, turn off the lights, and lie back on my bed. *Ugh!* I glance toward the window, and I can see it has started snowing again. Too amped up to sleep, I get up, grab a blanket, and go curl up in the pillow-filled window seat, like I've done so many times growing up. I love this spot. I used to sit here for hours to do my homework or talk on the phone or take a nap with the warmth of the sun shining in on my face. Pulling my knees up to my chin, I gaze out the window. I watch as the snow falls, sparkling in the glow of streetlamps and twinkle lights. It is so peaceful and still. I slide the window open a little and breathe in the cool, crisp Michigan air. It makes me shiver, but it feels nice.

My room faces out the front of our house, and I can see my best friend Barb's house across the street, decorated top to bottom with Christmas lights, like almost every house on our block, including ours. I have plans to have lunch with her tomorrow (or today, since it's after two in the morning now) so we can catch up. She stayed in Michigan and goes to Michigan State along with a bunch of our friends from high school. She keeps hoping that I'll hate USC and transfer home to MSU and be her roommate. Yeah, that's not going to happen.

Even though we make a point to talk on the phone at least once a week, I haven't told her about my strange notes or about the faceless Seth and the unknown danger I'm in that has completely consumed my every thought over the past few months. Maybe I will at lunch. I have to tell somebody. It's making me crazy keeping it all to myself. And if there is anyone I can confide in, it's Barb.

My mind drifts with thoughts of what we will do after lunch tomorrow and the Christmas gifts I have left to buy. I try to think of anything else but Seth's note, but I can't stop the thoughts from flooding my mind. His words, *I will be there to keep you safe,* keep flashing in my mind.

There is a streetlamp a couple of houses down from Barb's, and as my eyes wander towards it, I can see that there is someone standing beneath it. It's dark, and I'm tired, and the snow is obscuring my view a little, so I rub my eyes and look harder. *There is someone there.*

I gasp and a small whisper escapes my lips, "Seth?"

I immediately jump to my feet. I have to see him. Talk to him. I creep down stairs as quickly and quietly as I can, trying desperately not wake my grandparents. Throwing on my winter coat and boots, I slowly open the back door, which always creaks no matter how slowly or quickly you open it, and step out into the cold, snowy night. *Yikes, it's cold!* I make my way around the side of our house and, as stealthily as I possibly can, walk down to the end of the driveway. I don't want him to see me and take off.

It has snowed about an inch or so since we got home from the airport, and it's still coming down pretty heavy. Quickly, I begin to walk down the sidewalk, but by now I can no longer see the shadowy figure that had been standing beneath the streetlamp. I start to run, hoping he has just walked out of the light and I can catch up with him, but by the time I reach it, I know there's no hope. He's gone. The only trace that he was even there are the footprints he left behind, and they are quickly being covered up by the freshly falling snow.

Taking about ten steps away from the light, placing my feet over the prints he left behind, for one brief and insane moment, I think about going after him, but I know it's no use. If he doesn't want me to see him, I won't. That has been pretty evident over the past three months, maybe even over the past nineteen years. Besides, my hair is still wet and I'm wearing my pajamas, which are just thin cotton shorts and a tank top. I grab the collar of my coat and pull it tightly around my chin. It's too cold, and I'm certainly not dressed to start tracking someone in the snow. I must look pretty silly standing there in a pair of shorts, a winter jacket, and brown UGGs. I know I feel silly. I'm sure wherever Seth is now, watching me, he is having himself a good laugh at my expense. Reluctantly, I turn around and head back to my house.

As I walk back towards the streetlamp, I see something lying in the snow – something I hadn't noticed before: a single long-stemmed pink rose with a note attached to it. Shivering, I bend down and pick it up.

I glance around one last time to see if I can see him, to see if he's watching me but I appear to be alone even though I know I'm not. I raise the rose to my nose and inhale its heavenly aroma. It smells wonderful. With trembling fingers I unfold the note that is tied to the stem by a thin pink ribbon. It reads…

My Dear Alex,

You're safe. I'm here. I know how much you love pink roses. Merry Christmas, beautiful girl.

–Seth

My heart surges in my chest, and as I stand there clutching the note, I feel exhilarated, almost turned on. I know he's close. I desperately want to see him and hear his voice.

I whisper, "Seth."

There's no answer, and he doesn't show himself to me.

I reread the note. His words burn into me. This is the first time he has written anything personal. They are usually just messages letting me know I'm safe—for the moment—and that he is watching over me. But in this note, he wrote "My Dear Alex" and called me "beautiful girl," and how does he know I love pink roses? They are my favorite.

Ever since I came to live with my grandparents, once a month, my grandfather would come home with a dozen long-stemmed red roses for my grandma and three long-stemmed pink roses for me. My grandfather is very romantic, and he loves my grandmother very much, and he always wanted me to know how much I am loved as well. Even while I've been away at school, every month, I get three pink roses delivered to my dorm room. Maybe that's how Seth knows I love pink roses. Maybe he saw them when he has been in my room. I don't remember getting any notes when I had roses, but I could be wrong.

A cold gust of wind rushes through me, making me shiver and snapping me back into reality. I'm standing in the snow half naked, and my hair is starting to freeze. *Give it up.* I tell myself as I run my fingers through my hair, and it crunches between them. Pouting and freezing, I walk back to my house and quietly sneak back up to my room. I am so cold, so I jump back into the shower to warm up and get the ice out of my hair, then I put on a fresh pair of pajamas and curl up in my bed with Sammy next to me.

I toss and turn, unable to fall asleep, unable to stop thinking about him.

"Seth," I utter out loud into the stillness of my room, his name like a prayer from my lips. I have to turn my mind off, so I switch on the television, hoping it will distract me from my thoughts and I will doze off.

Apparently, it worked. I wake to the smell of bacon permeating from the kitchen. It's about eight in the morning. My grandparents have always been morning people; however, since I have been away at school, I made it a point to never schedule any of my classes before 11:00 a.m., so 8:00 a.m. is a bit early for me these days. I roll out of bed, throw on my robe, and sluggishly walk down stairs. Sam had smelled the food before I did and was already sitting at Grandpa's feet under the kitchen table. I sit down in my chair, and waiting for me is a big glass of orange juice. I take a sip.

"Good morning, sleepy girl. We were wondering if you were going to join us," Grandpa says with a chuckle.

"How can I sleep in with the smell of bacon to wake me up?" I reply with a half-awake grin.

"Well then, here you go." Grandma places a plate of French toast and bacon in front of me then kisses my forehead.

"Thank you," I say with a yawn, picking up my fork. "I'm going to get fat if you keep feeding me like this every time I come home."

"Well, Lord knows how you eat while you're away. Pizza delivery and dorm food can't be very nutritious, so I have to make sure you're eating right while you're home," she retorts as she picks up Grandpa's empty plate and takes it to the sink.

"I don't know. Look at what your nutritious cooking is doing to Grandpa over here." I lean over and pat him on his rather large round belly and giggle.

"Hey, that just means I'm well loved," he insists.

"I'd say so." I throw him a little wink then dig into my French toast.

"So what are your plans for today?" Grandma asks as she sits down at the table with a steaming cup of coffee.

"Barb is coming over to pick me up, and we're going to go to the mall to have lunch and do a little shopping. I'm not quite finished Christmas shopping yet."

"Don't spend your money on us, Alex. You know just having you home is present enough." She smiles her warm "I love you" smile and takes a sip of her coffee.

Old Routines

Barb comes over around noon, and after a few minutes of chatting with my grandparents, we head to the mall.

"What time did you get in last night?" Barb asks, keeping her eyes on the road. She has her dark-blond hair pulled back into a ponytail and puffy blue earmuffs covering her ears. I glance at her and giggle to myself. She looks silly but totally cute.

"Around seven," I reply. "Just in time to eat dinner and watch the game with Grandpa." Barb and I have been best friends since we were in the first grade, and she too refers to my grandparents as Grandma and Grandpa. "What did you do last night?"

"Danny and I rented a movie and ate pizza at his new apartment on campus."

Barb and Danny have been together since we were freshmen in high school. Danny had always been a hard core U of M fan growing up, so when Barb decided to go to State instead of Michigan with him, it made for some interesting challenges in their relationship. But they seem to be doing okay, even though Barb vowed never to step foot on the Ann Arbor campus unless Michigan and Michigan State were playing against each other in some kind of sporting event.

"I thought you said you'd never step foot on U of M soil unless you had a pack of Spartans with you?" I tease.

She snickers. "Yeah well you gotta do what you gotta do for some nookie."

I roll my eyes and shake my head. "Okay, that is enough information for me. Thanks."

"Chase was asking about you last night. They're having a party tomorrow night, and he's hoping you'll come. It's a fancy Christmas party, and we have to get all dressed up. I need to buy something sexy to wear while we're shopping. We're going to get you something hot to wear too." She pulls into a parking spot and looks at me with a devilish grin.

"I don't know, Barb. I don't think I want to see Chase."

Chase is my ex-boyfriend, and I haven't seen him since we graduated. He's also Danny's roommate and best friend. We broke up a week after graduation because he told me he didn't want to have a long-distance relationship and if I didn't change my mind and go to Michigan with him, then our relationship was over. So I told him it was over, and I walked out. I've never been very good with ultimatums.

"Come on, Alex! You told me you're not dating anyone out in Cali, and Chase really misses you. He said he tried to call you a couple of times out there, but you never answer your cell phone, and you never seem to be home when he calls your dorm. He's sorry about the way things ended, and he wants to make it up to you." She smiles—her "I'm not going to leave this alone until you agree" smile.

I know he's tried to call. More than a couple of times, try almost *every* day. I always hit the Ignore button on my cell when his number lights up the screen, and I always tell Julie to tell him I'm not there when he calls our room. And every time I'm home on break and he calls my house, I make sure my grandparents relay the same message. It was so hard getting over him, so I know talking to him and hearing his voice would be too difficult. It's easier for me to just ignore him. Childish, I know.

Barb looks at me with a pleading look in her eyes. "Please come! Please! It's going to be a lot of fun! A bunch of people from high school will be there too, so it's not like you won't know anyone. Pleeeeeease!"

"Don't beg." I hate it when she begs because I always give in. "If I can find something I want to wear, I'll go. If not, then I'm staying home." It has been a year and a half. Maybe it won't be so bad seeing Chase again—well, as long as I look hot when I do.

We decide to have lunch first before hitting the stores. We get our food and sit at one of the tables in the food court. As we eat, Barb rambles on about how things are going with her and Danny and how she's thinking about changing her major to elementary education. She asks about my art classes and why I don't have a boyfriend. I try hard to concentrate on our conversation, but my mind drifts, and I start thinking about Seth.

Even though Barb and I try to speak at least once a week while we're at school, with the time change and our busy schedules, most of our conversations don't last very long, so we still have a lot to tell each other—her more so than me, well, except for...

"So what else is going on with you? You seem a bit distracted, like you have a lot on your mind. What's up?" She knows me better than anyone, and her tone sounds concerned.

Do I really look like I'm hiding something? I always have had a terrible poker face.

"There is something I want to tell you, but it's a bit strange, and I'm not really sure what to make of it myself." I pause.

"Okay? You have definitely piqued my curiosity. Tell me what's going on," she insists, looking puzzled.

I take a breath and wonder if it's a good idea to bring Barb into the bizzaro world I have been living in for the past few months. But I know I need to talk to someone, or I am going to go completely insane. *Here it goes...* "Okay. It all started the day of my birthday."

My birthday was on a Monday this year, September 13th, and I began the day like I did every Monday by going to class. In the afternoon, Julie and I met for lunch, and we decided to skip our afternoon classes and head to the beach to enjoy the beautiful day. We stayed at the beach until about six o'clock and then headed back to the dorm to get ready to go to the bar. A bunch of our friends were meeting us at Chiller's, our favorite local watering hole, to celebrate my birthday.

When we walked into our room, Julie noticed an envelope lying on my pillow, and she called my attention to it. We always made sure to lock the door when we were both out of building, and we had been gone the entire day together, so it concerned us that someone had been in there while we were out.

There was nothing special about the envelope. It was plain white, and all that was written on it was my name. So I turned it over, opened it, and pulled out the note. It read

Alex,

I'm here to keep you safe. You have nothing to worry about. I won't let anything happen to you.

Happy birthday.

—Seth

Barb interrupts me immediately. "Wait! What? Keep you safe? From what? And who the hell is Seth?"

"I have no idea," I say, holding my hand up.

"Wait, it gets weirder."

The content of the note at first confused and then scared me. The first thing I thought was, *why would I be in danger*? From whom? From what? And who the hell was Seth?

Julie stared at me as I sat on my bed looking stunned and bewildered. Concerned, she asked me what was wrong and what the note said. I told her it was just a birthday note. I didn't want to scare her, and I didn't want her to think that because she was my roommate, she might be in danger too. You know, in case I was murdered in my sleep or something, I didn't want her to think she would be next. She had already been freaking out a bit because someone had been in our room while we were gone. And even though I told her there was nothing to be concerned about, she still called Jeff, our RA, to see if he had let anyone in our room, but he swore he didn't.

After that night, the notes started appearing once a week. Never on the same day or at the same time, but still, every week I would receive another note left on my pillow. We even had Jeff change the lock to our room twice, but without fail, every week there was a new note waiting for me. I even started leaving notes for him asking him questions like who he was and why was I in danger and why he wouldn't show himself to me. He never answered any of my questions, but my notes were always gone when a new note appeared.

I tell Barb about my nightmares and how I feel like someone is following me everywhere I go. I tell her about the last note I received just before I left for home, and about seeing someone standing in the snow under the streetlamp by her house and the note with the rose that was left in the snow.

"Oh my God, Alex! Who is this guy?" She's frightened for me.

"I don't know. I've been racking my brain trying to figure this out for three months. I've come up with nothing," I tell her.

"Did you get mixed up with some crazy crowd at school or something? It is California, the land of fruits and nuts."

I smirk. "No way! All I do is go to class and hang out with my friends who are just as boring as I am. Except for Julie, who has a different boyfriend all the time, the rest of us are pretty vanilla," I explain. "And you know how my life is around here."

"Yeah, there's not much to get in trouble with around here." She laughs.

"Right! Can you see why this is making me crazy?" I ask her.

"Um, yeah!"

"I feel safe now that I'm home though. Even though he's felt the need to follow me here, I don't feel afraid." And it's true I don't.

"Aren't you afraid of this Seth guy? I mean you don't have any idea who he is. What he looks like. He could be the one you should be afraid of." Her voice has genuine concern in it, and it warms my heart.

"To be honest, no. Seth doesn't scare me. I can't explain it. There is something about knowing he's out there that helps me function day to day," I admit.

"But if it wasn't for him, you wouldn't know there was something to fear." Her voice is angry now. "If he won't tell you what to be afraid of, then why did he have to tell you anything at all? It's not like you can watch your back if you don't know what to watch out for."

She's right. Why couldn't he just watch over me without letting me know he was there? Maybe he's just some guy trying to scare me. That thought makes me angry.

"I don't want to talk about this anymore," I say, shaking my head annoyed. "Let's go shopping. Let's buy something hot to wear to the party tomorrow." I get up and dump my tray. Barb is right behind me.

"Hell yeah! That's my girl." Barb now has an excited tone to her voice. She's getting her way, and it has made her very happy.

I'm such a sucker!

We spend the rest of the afternoon going from store to store picking out dresses and shoes and jewelry for Danny and Chase's party. I also manage to finish up the rest of my Christmas shopping in the process. It's amazing how easy it is to fall back into old routines.

I spend the entire next day with a sick feeling in the pit of my stomach about the party. Barb calls twice and sends me numerous text messages to make sure I am not going to change my mind. I promise her I won't, but now that the party is only two hours away, I am beginning to change my mind a little—a lot.

I'm exhausted. I didn't sleep very well because I was up most of the night staring out my window to see if the shadowy figure would return, but he never did. Grandma had me running errands with her the whole day, and I really just want to go to bed early, but I know if I bail, Barb will use it against me for the rest of our lives. She's good at that.

Giving into my fate, I jump in the shower around seven so I can start getting ready. I have to admit I am excited to wear the dress I bought—a sexy, little, black dress I look pretty damn good in if I do say so myself. If anything, it will make Chase eat his heart out. And that thought gives me quite a bit of satisfaction.

I finish doing my hair and makeup, and as I stand in the mirror putting on my dress, I catch a glimpse of my rose sitting on the nightstand behind me. I turn around, walk over and sit on the edge on my bed and stare at it. I pick up the note Seth had tied to it, and I keep reading the line "Merry Christmas, beautiful girl" over and over again.

"Who are you? And why am I not afraid of you?" I whisper to myself. It really is true. I'm not afraid of him. There is something about knowing he's out there that is exhilarating.

Ever since I told Barb about him, well, since yesterday, she has been referring to him as my stalker. "Any notes from your stalker today?" She asked both time she called me and once in a text message. "If I see him outside my home, I'm going to kick his ass!" She always prided herself on not being afraid of anyone or anything. I can see her now, hiding in the shadows of her house, standing guard with a baseball bat waiting to confront my "stalker."

The doorbell rings, and I hear Grandpa say hello to Barb. I slide on my too-tall shoes and take one last look at myself in the mirror. *Let's get this over with.* I grab my purse, and just before I turn to leave, I take one last whiff of my rose.

As I reach the bottom of the stairs, I see Barb, with her shoulder-length dark-blond hair pulled back into a sleek updo, striking a little pose for Grandpa, showing off her sexy blood-red dress. She looks amazing. I can't help but giggle a little. Barb always did like to get dressed up, and tonight she went all out. Danny's going to love it!

As I approach, Grandpa turns to me and smiles a proud-papa smile. "You look beautiful, Alex," he says helping me with my coat and kissing my cheek. I blush. *Beautiful...that's a first.* "Thanks," I respond, a little embarrassed by the compliment. "I'm not sure what time I'll be home, and if it starts to snow, we might just stay in Ann Arbor, so don't wait up for me, okay."

"Okay, just be careful," he replies, not too happy with the idea, but he knows I'm too old for him to object. I blew him a kiss and say good night then head out to the car with Barb.

"Chase is so excited that you're coming tonight. Danny said he wouldn't stop talking about it all day."

"Great!" I reply, oozing sarcasm . "I haven't seen or spoken to him in a year and a half, why is seeing me so important to him? You can't tell me he hasn't had plenty of women to occupy his time. I don't get it."

"I think he feels like you were the one he let slip away. He wants to see if there is still something between you. He knows you're not dating anyone out in Cali so he feels like this is his chance to show you he's sorry. He still loves you, Alex." She has a look on her face like she wants this to happen just as much as Chase does. "Plus, the way you look tonight, you are going to have him eating out of the palm of your hand."

Yeah, right.

Chase and Danny have been best friends for about as long as Barb and I have, and when we were in high school, the four of us did everything together. We went to every school function together and spent practically every weekend together. Chase and Danny were on the hockey team, and Barb and I never missed a game. I think everyone thought we would have a double wedding, buy houses next door to each other, and raise our kids together. But once I told Chase I was going to go to USC, everything changed. He started wanting "space," and then when we were together, he kept trying to change my mind, and finally, it was just *over*.

"So does he think we're going to get back together or something?" I ask.

"Come on, Alex! Don't get all worked up about this. He has no expectations. He just misses you and wants to see you and see what happens. Give him a chance. He's a good guy." She smiles her "Trust me" smile, a smile I have seen too many times before. *Crap!* "Yeah, yeah!" I say, giving her my "Back off" smile in return.

She pulls the car into the parking lot and turns off the engine. Adjusting the rearview mirror so she can see herself, she applies a fresh coat of lip gloss and smacks her lips. She turns to me, beaming with excitement, "Okay, here we go. It's going to be a blast. You'll see!"

It's too late to change my mind, so I take a deep breath and get out of the car, prepared to meet my fate.

𝒯𝒽𝑒 𝒫𝒶𝓇𝓉𝓎

With no elevator in the building, we begin to climb the three flights of metal stairs to the top floor, our heels clanging loudly with each step.

Why did I let Barb talk me into buying these shoes? They are way too tall, and ugh, my feet hurt already.

At the top of the stairs is a huge steel door. Barb enters a code into the keypad on the wall, and when it buzzes, she pulls the door open.

"Ready?" she asks, sounding a little too excited.

No! I roll my eyes at her, give her a half-hearted smile, and, like an obedient puppy, follow her through the door.

"Wow!"

Walking through the door is like stepping into a Christmas wonderland—and we are only in the hallway. Garlands laced with hundreds of twinkle lights are strung from one end of the hallway to the other, and hanging on the wall, about every ten feet or so, are uniquely decorated wreaths. One in particular catches my attention.

"You had to be represented too," she giggles.

Hanging there in front of me is a wreath covered in cardinal and gold, and in the center are three large sparkling letters spelling out USC. It makes me smile. Then I realize each wreath represents a different school. There is, of course, a Michigan State one, covered in green and white with little Sparty ornaments. There is a Ferris State one with a big bulldog in the center, a Grand Valley, Duke, Florida State, Arizona State, etc. There is one for pretty much everyone we knew who went to school somewhere other than U of M.

"What about Ohio State?" I ask. "Sean's at OSU, doesn't he get one too?"

Barb rolls her eyes recalling the argument she had with the boys regarding that very subject. "Yeah, the boys wouldn't allow an Ohio State one. Besides, I don't think Sean's going to make it anyway."

"Lizzy's still going to be here though, right? Even without Sean?"

"Yeah, she's coming. She can't wait to see you."

Good! I'm sure Barb will be running around playing hostess all night, so if things start to get uncomfortable with Chase, I know Lizzy will help rescue me. She's a dear friend, and I haven't seen her in forever, and I'm pleased she's coming to the party.

Standing guard on either side of the apartment door are two large beautifully decorated Christmas trees, lights twinkling, as if they're saying, "Welcome to the party." If this is what it looks like on the outside, I can only imagine what the inside must look like.

I give Barb a little poke in the back with my index finger. "Did you do all this? Because I know the guys sure as hell didn't," I ask with a smirk already knowing the answer.

"Of course, I did. The only decoration the guys wanted was a red trash can to hold the keg."

"Right! Classy!" I roll my eyes, and we both have a good laugh at the boys' expense.

Without knocking, Barb opens the door, and we head inside. We arrive early to help with the final preparations, but as we walk in, neither of the guys are anywhere to be found. Barb takes my coat and purse and heads back toward the bedrooms. "The guys are getting ready. I'm going to put our stuff in Danny's bedroom. We're keeping both bedrooms locked, but if you need to get something out of your purse, let one of us know, and we'll let you in."

Left alone to admire my surroundings, I can't help but smile. The apartment is so Chase. Twenty-foot ceilings, with a gigantic living room and kitchen, hardwood floors, and floor-to-ceiling windows that cover the entire east-facing wall. And completing the room is an enormous flat-screen TV. It's the ultimate man den. Chase's dad is a bigwig for General Motors, and he likes to dabble in real estate, so last year, he bought an abandoned warehouse, converting it into lofts. Chase and Danny moved in at the beginning of the semester, and the other seven apartments were rented out by either their fraternity brothers from Sigma Phi Epsilon or teammates from the hockey team. I doubt there is very much studying that happens in this building.

Millions of Christmas lights cover every inch of the apartment, creating the perfect ambiance. In addition to the two Christmas trees in the hallway, there is an enormous eighteen-foot tree covered in maize and blue ornaments that separates the living room from the dining area. It's the perfect focal point.

There is a DJ set up in the center of the enormous wall of windows, and all the furniture has been pushed to each side opening up the room so people can dance. A bar is set up on both sides of the huge room, with a bartender at each, and there are three cocktail waitresses setting up trays of hors d'oeuvres in the kitchen. It's amazing. Barb has truly out done herself.

While standing in the middle of the living room taking everything in, I hear a familiar voice say my name. I turn, and as I do, my dress swirls around in a very Marilyn Monroe–type fashion. When I come to a stop, there is Chase.

I had almost forgotten how cute he is. All six foot three of him, with his broad shoulders, light-brown hair, and chocolate-brown eyes. He is standing there in a perfectly tailored suit that looks so good on him it makes my heart flutter just a bit. As he smiles at me, I can't help the rush I get.

Oh hell! This is going to be harder than I thought! Damn, he looks good!

"Wow! You look incredible!" he says, bringing his hand up to his mouth in awe.

"Thanks," I reply, doing another spin just for effect. "You look pretty good yourself. You always did clean up nice," I compliment, throwing him a little wink.

"I'm so glad you came. I've wanted to see you for so long. How come you never returned any of my calls?" he asks.

I hold up a hand in protest. "Let's not get into that right now. It's a party. I'm here. Let's just have a fun and save that conversation for another time. Okay?"

"Okay," he agrees and walks toward me, making my heart race. "Can I at least have a hug?" he asks, holding his huge arms open.

"Of course."

He wraps his arms around me, lifts me off the ground, and spins me in a circle.

When he sets me down, he doesn't let me go right away. Instead, he kisses me on the cheek and whispers in my ear, "I missed you. I'm sorry." Releasing me from his embrace, he turns and shouts towards the bedrooms. "Danny, Barb, get your asses out here! People are going to start arriving soon, and we need to make sure everything is ready."

"So this is quite the setup you guys have going on here," I say wryly. "Did Barb do all this, or did you guys have a say?"

"Well, my dad and Danny's dad chipped in the cash, and once Barb got word that we were throwing this thing, she insisted that she be in charge. You know how she is. There's no stopping that girl once she gets going. It was a good thing really. Hockey practice and finals were keeping us way too busy, so if it were left to us, we would have ended up with a couple of kegs, some chips and salsa, and a boom box. This is a little classier, don't you think?" He smiles, extending his arms like a game-show host.

"Definitely," I answer with a giggle. "Well, is there anything I can help with?"

"Ask your girl. But I don't think so. I'm just so glad you're here." He throws me a hopeful smile.

"Okay, you two, let's get this party started!" Barb exclaims, emerging from around the corner, Danny in tow.

The DJ starts spinning, and the music fills the entire building. People begin arriving around 9:30, and by 10:30, the place is packed. There are many people I have never seen before, obviously U of M students, but there are also a ton of people I do know, friends from high school. I'm so glad I decided to come.

Every once in a while, I catch a glimpse of Chase, looking at me, smiling. I'm okay with it. I actually feel very comfortable being around him. I don't know if it's because we are surrounded by a hundred other people or because I have finally let go of what happened between us. Whatever it is, I'm enjoying being here and happy to see him as well.

As I stand at the bar waiting for the bartender to pour me a glass of red wine, I feel a soft tap on my shoulder. I turn to find a very pretty dark-haired girl in a burgundy dress smiling at me.

"You're Alex, right?" she asks.

"Yes, I am," I answer, puzzled.

"I'm Sarah. I have been dying to meet you for such a long time. I used to date Chase," she says rather casually then turns to the bartender. "Glass of white, please."

Shocked and a bit defensive—not wanting some kind of cat fight—all I can say in return is, "Oh."

"Don't worry, its way over. And I'm not here to get into some kind of pissing contest with you. Actually, our relationship ended on pretty good terms. The reason I wanted to meet you is because I wanted to meet the girl who still has his heart." She takes a sip of wine and waits for my reaction.

Still confused, I just stand there and stare at her.

Realizing I am not going to reply, she goes on. "Chase is a great guy, and we had a lot of fun together, but there was always something missing. After a few months of not being able to figure out what it was, I just came out and asked him. And the first word that came out of his mouth was *Alex*." She takes another sip of her wine and then giggles a little.

Her giggle shakes me out of my bewilderment, and I finally speak, but all I can say is, "I don't understand."

She smiles at me with her perfectly painted red lips and continues. "When he said the name *Alex*, I thought that meant he was gay, which definitely would have explained why there was something missing, so I just blurted out 'Oh my God, you're gay?' I couldn't believe I was dating a gay guy. But after I calmed down, he told me Alex was short for Alexandra. I wasn't sure if the fact that you were a woman was better or worse than him being gay, but I let him explain.

"He told me you were his high school girlfriend and you broke up because he demanded you stay here to go to school and you rightfully told him to stick it. Good for you by the way." She pauses and holds her glass up to me, giving me a silent "Cheers," then takes another sip. "After he told me the whole story and how he was still in love with you, he apologized to me and hoped he hadn't hurt me, and he hoped I'd meet someone who would love me the way I deserved to be loved.

"I have to admit that at the time I was pretty pissed and thought he was making up some lame story just to blow me off, but he wasn't. I know for a fact he hasn't dated anyone since he and I broke up, and whenever anyone asks him why, he says 'Alexandra.' He uses your whole name now. He wants to make sure no one thinks he's gay." She winks at me, and we both laugh at the thought. "I just thought you should know he's never gotten over you, and maybe if you knew, then you might give him a second chance. He really is a good guy."

Sarah and I continue to talk for a while about Chase and school. She asks a ton of questions about California, and she tells me she wished she had the courage to go to college out of state, instead of staying so close to home. I like her. She's bubbly and flirty, smiling at every man that walks by us. I think given more time together, we could become friends.

Chase notices us deep in conversation and quickly makes his way over, looking pale and panicked. "Okay, you two, you're making me nervous. What are you girls talking about?"

"Don't worry about it," I say and threw a little wink at Sarah. "Just a little girl talk, that's all."

"Well, do you mind if I pull you away for a little dance?" He takes me by the hand, and without any objection, I follow him to the center of the dance floor. Just as he puts his arms around my waist and pulls me close to his chest, the DJ starts to play "I'll Be" by Edwin McCain.

Our song.

Even in heels, I am much shorter than he is, and I have to tilt my head back to look at him. "You didn't plan this at all, did you?" I squint my eyes at him trying to appear annoyed.

"Absolutely not," he replies with a sheepish grin. "How random the DJ would choose this very moment to play our song." He pulls me in tight, and I rest my head against his shoulder. We spend the rest of the song and the next holding each other close, saying nothing. It feels nice, comfortable.

As the last slow song ends, he kisses me on the forehead then takes my hand, leading me over to where Barb and Danny are standing. They are surrounded by a bunch of our high school friends, and they all seem to be having a great time. When we reach the group, Barb and three of our other girlfriends abruptly whisk me away to the other side of the room.

"So?" Barb asks with an excited quality to her voice.

"What?" I snap back, annoyed, knowing exactly what she wants to know. She folds her arms across the chest and just stares at me.

"Come on, we watched you two dancing," Lizzy chimes in. "What's going on?"

"Christ, we just danced. It was nice. What do you want me to say?" I'm irritated by the interrogation. What do they think, that we would resolve all that had happened in one dance? "Take it easy, guys. Let's not get ahead of ourselves."

"Okay, okay, but tell me, did you feel anything?" Barb asks, hopeful.

Knowing she wouldn't let this go until I give her something, I indulge her—a little. "It felt nice, comfortable. We didn't break up because I stopped loving him or because he was a bad guy. He didn't want a long-distance relationship, and I wasn't going to let him bully me into staying here." I pause, and they keep staring at me like I haven't completely answered the question. "What else do you want?" I ask, aggravated. "How's this? If he calls me, I'll take his calls, and if he asks me out, I might just go. Okay?" I snap. It's all the answer I'm going to give them so they need to back off.

They all smile and shriek like little girls, and I can't help but laugh at them.

Just then, Kristy comes running up to our little group. "Hey, do any of you know that guy over there?" She points to a tall dark-haired guy wearing a perfectly tailored black suit that looks very expensive. He's standing at the bar with his back to us, so we can't see his face. "He is the best-looking guy here, and no one seems to know who he is."

"Maybe he's one of the Sig Eps," I volunteer.

"No, he's not. None of the brothers know him," Kristy replies.

"So go up and talk to him," I encourage. "You've never been shy. What's the problem?"

"Catherine tried, but she said he wasn't very talkative. She said he just kept looking around the room like he was trying to find someone. She did say his name was Seth."

As soon as his name came out of her mouth, the DJ kicked up a new song and the whole room irrupted and ran to the dance floor. He's lost in the chaos. I'm not sure if it's panic or excitement, but I grab Barb's arm, and we try to push through the crowd. By the time we reach the bar, Seth is gone.

"Alex, are you okay?" Barb asks, grabbing me by the shoulders and shaking me a little. "You are white as a ghost!" I don't answer her. I just stand there, trying to look through the sea of people in all directions, but I can't find him.

Was it him? Seth?

Leaving Barb to just stare after me, I run to the door and out into the hallway. No one! Where could have he gone? A few seconds later, I feel a hand touch my shoulder. My heart jumps, and I whip around to see who it is. It's just Chase. *Crap!*

"What are you doing out here?" he asks.

I hesitate. "I thought I saw someone I knew walk out the door. I wanted to say hello."

"Well, come back inside, I'd like to dance with you again." He smiles sweetly, taking my hand. I follow him back inside and onto the dance floor, but all the while we're dancing, I keep surveying the room looking for *him*.

The party starts winding down around two in the morning, and eventually, there is just a handful of us left in the apartment. I'm sitting on the sofa staring out the window when Chase sits down next to me and offers me one of his sweatshirts, a large blue fraternity sweatshirt with big yellow ΣΦΕ letters across the chest. I thank him and put it on over my dress. It smells like him.

Once they've said good-bye to the remaining guests, Barb and Danny came over and sit in the oversized leather chair next to the sofa, Barb sitting on Danny's lap. She flings her shoes off, and they make two loud thuds as they hit the hardwood floor.

"Why don't we just stay here tonight?" Barb suggests. "It's late, and I'm pretty tipsy, and I don't feel like driving home."

I shoot her a heated look to let her know I'm not happy with the idea and to stop pushing so hard. Before I can respond, Chase chimes in. "You can sleep in my bed. I'll sleep out here on the couch."

"I couldn't do that. I'll sleep out here. I don't want to take your bed," I object.

"No really, it's okay. I've passed out on this couch more times than I care to remember. It's pretty comfortable. I'll be okay." He put his hand on the back of my head and strokes my hair for a moment then gets up. "It's late, and it's starting to snow again. You shouldn't be driving now anyway," he says then goes to the closet and grabs a blanket and a pillow.

I reluctantly agree then go to Chase's bedroom to change. I put his sweatshirt back on and hang my dress up in his closet. Chase is six three, and I am only five foot four, so his sweat shirt reaches down to my knees. As I stand there alone in his room, I catch a glance of myself in the mirror. Wearing his sweatshirt and being among his things feels very easy to me. Too easy.

There's a soft knock on the door, and Barb walks in. "Hey, I just wanted to see if you were okay and to make sure you weren't mad at me." She flops down on the end of the bed and smiles at me sweetly.

"I'm not mad. I do think you're pushing too hard to get Chase and me back together though. Don't forget I'm going back to California in a few of weeks, and that was his big issue, me being so far away. Our situation hasn't changed, even though his feelings about it may have. Let me go at my own pace, okay?"

"Okay, I'll stop pushing. But I really didn't want to drive all the way home tonight anyway. If you really want to go, you can take my car." She holds out her hand and dangles her car keys from her index finger.

"No, it's okay. I'll stay, but trust me, Chase *will* be sleeping on the couch." We both laugh, and I sit down on the bed next to her.

"Okay, so can we talk about the mystery Seth guy Kristy pointed out and about the fact you sort of flipped out. You don't think it was actually him, do you?" she asks.

"I don't know. But it does seem like more than a coincidence," I answer, trying not to sound freaked out, even though I kind of am. I can't stop thinking about him, wondering if it really was him and if it was, why was he here, in a suit, mingling with my friends? And why didn't he talk to me? And where did he go? It was like he vanished into thin air.

"Well, if it was him, at least we now know he's hot. Catherine and Kristy weren't the only ones talking about him. I heard a few girls gushing about the hot guy nobody seemed to know." She nudges me with her elbow.

Too distracted to truly appreciate her comment, I ask, "You haven't told Danny about any of this, have you?"

"No way! He would have told Chase, and then they would have been on some mission to find this guy and kick his ass. It would have ruined the party," she replies, sitting up straight and pulling her now messy hair back into a ponytail. "I wasn't going to let that happen," she adds with a laugh.

"Gee, thanks. So it had nothing to do with the fact I told you all of that in confidence—you just didn't want to spoil the party." I smack her on the leg and stand up. "I don't want to talk about it right now. I'm kind of hungry. Let's go see what's left to eat."

She agrees, and we make our way out to the kitchen. The boys must have had the same thought because they were already there picking at the leftovers.

By the time we are all ready to go to bed, it is almost four o'clock in the morning. I ask Chase one more time if he's sure he doesn't want to sleep in his own bed. I am happy to sleep on the couch, but he insists I take the bed. I thank him, kiss him on the cheek, and head back to his room and curl up under the covers.

I close my eyes and try to drift off to sleep, but my mind is in overdrive. Now that I'm alone, I'm able to really start thinking about Seth. After he disappeared and I could break away from Chase, I went to find Catherine and ask her some questions about the gorgeous guy Kristy was talking about.

Catherine told me how he was very quiet and didn't say too much. She had to ask him twice what his name was before he finally answered her. When she asked him who he knew at the party, he took out his cell phone and excused himself to take a call.

I asked her what he looked like, trying not to sound too interested. She described him as very tall and lean with dark-brown hair, which I could tell myself just by seeing him from behind. She said he had a small dimple on his left cheek and a warm, sexy smile. Then pausing for a second, she got a very serious look on her face and said, "He had *the* most amazing blue eyes I have ever seen—they were almost hypnotic."

I lay there staring at the ceiling, trying to picture his face. Seth. My Seth. My mysterious protector from unknown danger. "Who are you?" I whisper.

Suddenly the silence is shattered by the sounds of Barb and Danny doing God only knows what in the next room. Feeling like an unwilling voyeur, I decide to get up and go into the other room. I can't sleep anyway, and I like watching the snow fall at night and the view from the apartment is breathtaking.

I tiptoe into the living room, trying not to make the hardwood floor creak under my feet and trying even harder not to wake up Chase. I move across the room and sit on the rug that is on the floor in front of the window. Bringing my knees up under my sweatshirt and wrapping my arms around my legs, I stare out the window.

The snow is falling very softly, and everything outside is once again covered in a fluffy white blanket. As I look out into the early morning darkness, there he is, standing in the snow across the street in the shadows. There are no lights on in the apartment, so I know he can't see me sitting there, but it's like he knows I'm watching him. Slowly, he takes one step forward—he looks like an angel under the glow of the streetlamp.

He lifts his head and looks up toward the window where I'm sitting, unable to take my eyes off of him. I can feel his eyes burning into me, even though he cannot possibly see me. My body tingles with excitement, and I want to go to him. He's like a magnet pulling me to him. He takes one more step forward, and I let out a delighted gasp.

"Alex? Are you okay? Is there something down there?" Chase asks, groggy.

He startles me, and I quickly turn my head toward the sound of his voice. A second later, without answering him, I turn back toward the window. Seth is gone.

I gasp again when I realize Seth has vanished. Concerned, Chase comes over to the window to see what I'm looking at but he sees nothing, just as I do now.

"There's nothing there, Alex. What did you see?" His voice sounds anxious now.

"It's…nothing. I thought I saw something, but it must just be my eyes playing tricks on me. I'm so tired and Barb and Danny are having a sex marathon so I came out here for some quiet.

How do you sleep with those two back there?" I ask with a hint of exhausted annoyance in my voice. "The walls are so thin."

"Tell me about it. I wasn't kidding when I said I passed out on this couch a lot. I wasn't only referring to nights of drunken foolishness. Every time Barb comes down for the weekend, I end up sleeping out here to get away from the porno sounds coming from Danny's room. Half the time, *I* need a cigarette when the two of them are done." He laughs.

He walks back over to the couch, sits down, and pats the cushion next to him. "Here, come sit with me. No funny business, I promise."

I take one last glance out the window, and when I still don't see Seth, even though I know he's there, I get up and join Chase on the couch.

We sit alone together in darkness, and after a moment of uncomfortable silence, he turns to look at me, and I know he wants to have "the talk," but before he can open his mouth to say anything, I blurt out, "Can we not talk about anything tonight, please? I'm so tired. It was a good night. Let's just leave it at that for now, okay?"

He shakes his head in agreement, conceding defeat. Grateful, I put my head on his shoulder, lean my body into his, and fall asleep.

Getting Close—Again

It's been a week since the party, my pink rose has died, and there hasn't been any more Seth sightings and no new notes left for me, either. I've actually spent most of the week with Chase, but Seth always lingered in the back of my mind.

Before heading home the morning after the party, the four of us had breakfast, and Chase asked me if he could take me to dinner and a movie that night. I said yes.

He did most of the talking over dinner, telling me how sorry he was he tried to force me into choosing our relationship over having the college experience I wanted. He told me that the first year I was in California he kept really busy with hockey, pledging his fraternity, and he tried not to think about me. He also admitted he dated *a lot*, trying to forget, but there was always something missing, and that something was me.

"I couldn't seem to connect with any of them. They were all great girls, a couple of them were kind of crazy, but there was always something off. Sarah was the only one who had enough nerve to ask me what the hell was going on with me."

"Yeah, she seems pretty direct." I had to agree.

"That's for sure." He paused for a moment and took my hand. "It was you, Alex. None of those girls were you."

I blushed. He was embarrassing me a little, and I think he noticed, so he quickly changed the subject.

He asked me a bunch of questions about USC and how I liked California. He asked if I had been dating anyone.

"You know me. I really want to graduate at the top of my class, so dating isn't a top priority for me."

He asked about my grandparents. He wanted to know everything that had been going on with me. It was like he was trying to catch up on everything in one night. It was sweet but a bit exasperating.

I could tell he was hoping I would say the reason I wasn't dating anyone was because of him, but I didn't want to lie . I think being away from home and away from the people that knew us helped me forget. There wasn't a constant reminder of him, and it helped me put what happened out of my mind for a while. At least until he started calling all the time. I know Julie was getting sick of taking the messages.

Changing the subject yet again, I told him how much I loved USC and that my art classes were going really well. I told him I liked California for the most part but I really missed home and being away from my grandparents was really hard. I told him about crazy Julie and her mission to play the field before settling down. The only thing I didn't tell him was about Seth and the mysterious danger I apparently was in.

We ended up talking for so long we completely missed the movie. So we decided to take a walk and look at all the Christmas lights and take in how lovely everything was.

"I miss how beautiful everything is all covered in snow," I told him. "California is beautiful too, but it always looks the same."

"I've missed how beautiful you are, Alex." He kissed my forehead, and it gave me butterflies in my stomach. He was always so charming.

We held hands as we walked, and when he could tell I was starting to get cold, he put his arm around me and held me close. It was nice. I was happy being there with him.

When he took me home, he asked if he could come over the next day and take me to see the movie we missed. I said yes. He kissed my lips softly then said good night, and as I watched him walk to his car, I wished he would have stayed and kissed me some more.

We spent pretty much every day together the rest of the week leading up to Christmas day. We had dinner with my grandparents and watched hockey one night. Then a couple nights later, we did the same with his parents. We went out with Barb and Danny a couple of times, and everything felt the way it used to be. I had fallen back into my old home routine, and to be honest, I was enjoying all of it.

On Christmas morning, I wake to the smell of breakfast permeating from the kitchen, and underneath the smell of bacon is a hint of turkey too. Grandma already started cooking dinner. Our entire family comes to our house for Christmas dinner, usually between thirty to forty people, depending on who is in town, and the three of us have a lot to do to get ready.

It has been a family tradition ever since I came to live with my grandparents that we have breakfast together and then open the presents that have been left under the tree by "Santa." Even though I stopped believing in Santa when I was seven, every Christmas morning, my grandparents always had tons of presents waiting for me.

Around noon, we start scrambling to get ready for the party. Grandpa and I put out the extra tables and chairs while Grandma is hard at work in the kitchen. By five o'clock everything is ready and people are starting to arrive.

By the time the party is in full swing, I have aunts and uncles, cousins and longtime family friends I haven't seen in a year asking me questions and wanting to know about school, California, and if I've met any celebrities—being so close to Hollywood. They are all the same questions they asked me last year, but I answer each one with a smile and try to make all my responses sound exciting.

After everyone has eaten until they can't eat anymore, and we have all praised the chef for her fantastic meal, it is time to open more presents. As the snow falls softly behind foggy windows the adults sit around, talking and drinking coffee or adult beverages of some kind, while the kids sit on the floor covered with discarded wrapping paper and play with their new toys. It's nothing short of a Norman Rockwell painting, and it's beautiful. I stand in the opening between the kitchen and the family room and just watch my family as they talk and laugh, and I can't help but think how lucky I am.

I feel Grandma come up behind me, wrap her arms around me, and give me a squeeze and a kiss on the cheek. "It's so good to have you home," she says. "It's just not the same around here without you."

"Don't worry, Grandma, the next two and a half years will fly by. Look how fast the first year and a half went." I turn around and give her a big hug. Just then, the doorbell rings, grabbing everyone's attention. "I'll get it," I announce, going over to see who it is. When I open the door, standing there all wearing Santa hats and grinning like idiots are Chase and Barb and Danny.

"Merry Christmas!" they all shout in unison.

"Merry Christmas!" I answer with a laugh. "Come on in."

Spending Christmas evening together had been a tradition for the four of us the entire time we were in high school. But since Chase and I weren't together last Christmas, Barb came over without Danny so she and I could have some girl time. She told me no matter how much she loved Danny, I was her best friend and Christmas was for us. Danny got New Years.

As I hang up their coats, the three of them go around and say hello to everyone and I overhear a few people telling Chase it was good to have him back with the family. I just shake my head and smile a little. *Christ, not the family too.*

After he's made his rounds, Chase asks me if we can go up to my room for a minute. I say, "Sure," and we make our way upstairs. Chase seems nervous and fidgety, which is unusual. For as long as I've known him nothing intimidates him. Nothing. His extreme confidence was kind of a turn on. But now I'm seeing a different Chase, an unsure Chase. Sitting down on the edge of my bed, he pats the empty spot next to him, silently asking me to sit. As I do, he slides a small box from his pocket. Immediately my eyes widen, and I become very nervous.

"I didn't want to give this to you in front of everyone because I didn't want to make a big deal out of it," he says in a shaky voice. "It's just something to let you know how important you are to me and how much I love you." He places the small box in my hand and gently kisses the corner of my mouth.

That was the first time I had heard him say "I love you" in almost two years. I didn't know how to respond.

"Go ahead. Open it," he insists.

I slowly and tentatively start to tear off the wrapping paper, not sure what I am going find beneath the safety of its cover. My throat is dry, and I can see my hand shake a little. *Oh God, please don't let this be what I think it is!*

Chase sits quietly next to me, waiting for me to make my next move. For a few moments, all I can do is stare at the small velvet box I have balanced in the palm of my hand. *Oh no!* Unable to breathe and with my eyes closed, I open it. When I hear the snap of the hinge, I take a deep breath and open my eyes. Inside is a teardrop-shaped pink sapphire pendant hanging from a sparkling white-gold chain. It's exquisite, and I'm able to breathe again.

"Oh my God, Chase! It's so beautiful!" My voice cracks a little, and I blink back a tear. "But why did you do this? We've only been spending time together for a week. I don't know where this is going, and I can't make you any promises. I don't think I can accept—"

Chase places his fingers over my lips and cuts me off midsentence. "Alex, I told you, this is just a little something to show you how much you mean to me. I'm not expecting us to get back together and for things to be the way they were after only a week, but I want you to know that I love you and I'm willing to do whatever it takes to make this work." He stands up and removes the necklace from its box then places it around my neck. "This is so when you're back in California and you look in the mirror and you see this hanging around your neck, you will think about me and know I'm always thinking about you."

I look down just as a tear escapes the corner of my eye, and I rub the stone softly between my fingers. Chase does make me happy; maybe this can work. Maybe I really do want it to work. I look up into his sweet, boyish, and hopeful face then smile; I can see how much he really does love me. I push up from the bed and throw my arms around his neck. "Thank you, Chase, I love it." I whisper. He kisses me.

We spend the next couple of hours hanging out with my family, and as people slowly start trickling out and heading home, the four of us decide to go see a late show. There is always something new playing at the movies on Christmas day, and my grandparents always insist that we go and they will clean up the mess.

After two hours of mundane, slapstick humor (the boys picked the movie) we head to Sally's, a local diner that is always open on Christmas night. Barb and I have coffee. The boys order food, even though they each had eaten dinner with their families and then ate more when they got to my house, and to top it off, they each had a large popcorn and soda at the movies; apparently, they were still hungry. We stay at the diner and talk until they kick us out, and by this time, it's almost two in the morning. So we pile into Chase's car and head back to my house.

"Oh my God! Alex, I have a great idea!" Barb shrieks, grabbing my shoulder from the backseat of the car. "We are all coming to LA for spring break! We'll rent a little condo on the beach somewhere, and you can show us LA! What do you think?" Knowing Barb the way that I do, this was less of a question and more of a "We're coming, so just say yes" kind of statement.

It really was a good idea, so with a big smile, I reply, "Definitely! That would be awesome!" Knowing in the back of my mind I'm going to have to learn my way around LA and find out where the hot spots are, I'm not too concerned, because I'm sure Julie will be more than happy to help me out. She's much more familiar with LA than I am.

"Awesome! I will be in charge of finding the condo, and Chase is paying, of course," she says with a giggle and a wink. "And all you have to do is get a hot bikini and plan some fun things for us to do."

"Hey!" Chase grunts, chiming in now. "Why do I always get stuck paying?"

"Because you are the one with the rich daddy," Barb retorts, tapping him on the back of the head and laughing.

"Oh yeah, that's right," he says, letting go of my hand and sarcastically giving her the finger.

"Don't worry, man, we'll kick in for the food and beer," Danny throws in, trying not to sound like a freeloader.

"Deal!" Chase agrees.

When we reach my house, Danny walks Barb across the street and Chase escorts me to my door. "Thank you again for the necklace. It is so beautiful. I love it so much, but you really shouldn't have." I slide my arms around his waist and squeeze him tight.

Pulling away from me just a little, he looks into my eyes, kisses me gently on the lips, and then says softly, "I really do love you Alex. I always have, and I always will. I will spend the rest of my life showing you how much you mean to me." He kisses me again, and this time, his kiss is more passionate than any of the other kisses we've shared over the past week. It's a kiss of love. And here in this moment, I know he means it, and I begin to remember what it feels like to love him back.

After we say good night, I quietly go inside and upstairs to my room. I'm sure my grandparents have been in bed for hours, and I don't want to wake them up.

I walk into my room, turn on the light, and find Sam lying on my bed wagging her tail. When she jumps down to greet me, I notice a small present. There's a note next to it.

Alex,

This was under the tree after everyone left. Not sure who it is from. See you in the morning.

Love you,
Grandma

That's strange. I had opened all my presents from my family, and Chase had given me his gift, so who could have left this for me? The box is wrapped beautifully. The paper is white with silver snowflakes, and a perfect white satin bow sits on top. There is a small card slid under the bow, and all it says is

For Alex

It's a little bigger than the box my necklace came in, maybe Chase left me another surprise. It is wrapped in such a way that all I have to do is slide off the ribbon and lift the top to see what's inside. As I do, I find another card, and beneath it is a small charm in the shape of a key.

I'm not surprised to find the key, but I am confused by my grandmother's note. Of course, she knows who this is from. It's from her. Isn't it?

I look down at my left wrist.

Every day, since my thirteenth birthday, I have worn a charm bracelet that my parents had left for me. And every year since, on my birthday, I receive a new charm—a new key. I have nineteen keys.

When my grandparents gave it to me, they explained to me my parents had the bracelet made the day I was born, and every year on my birthday, they were to add a new key. Every key is made of white gold, and every key has a number engraved on it and a sapphire set into it. This key is different, however. It still looks to be made of white gold, but instead of a sapphire, it has what looks to be a diamond set into it and it doesn't have a number. It is more antique looking than my other keys.

Mesmerized by its elegance, I am completely transfixed on it. *But why I am getting a key for Christmas? And why didn't my grandparents give it to me with the rest of my gifts?* Maybe the note I forgot I'm holding can solve the mystery, It is a small silver card with a snowflake embossed on the front, matching the wrapping paper perfectly. Perplexed, I unfold the card and notice the very familiar handwriting.

Alex,

This key is the final charm to your bracelet. Your parents left it with my father in the hope it would remain just a charm and not be used for its original purpose. Before my father's death, he gave this key to me, and I vowed to him I would keep you safe and help you understand the importance of all your keys and the power they hold if and when the time came. The time has come, and very soon we will meet and I will explain everything to you. I know you must be confused, and your first instinct will be to confide in your grandparents or Barb. I ask you not to do so. To them, it is just a bracelet, and that is the way it should stay to keep them out of danger. I don't want you to be afraid. I will come to you very soon, and you will understand everything.

Merry Christmas, beautiful girl.

–Seth

I can't breathe. I just stare into the box at the mysterious key, frightened and confused. I take off my bracelet and lay it in front of me on the bed with all the keys lying flat so I can examine each one. What is so special about them? What kind of power can they possibly have? My head starts to spin.

This is getting too weird. I start to get angry. *Why won't Seth just leave me alone? I don't know any secrets someone would try to hurt me to learn. If someone wants these keys, they can have them. They are very important to me because they came from my parents, but if it's my life or the bracelet, I'll give them the damn bracelet!*

Could any of this be true? My anger turns back into fear the more I let my mind wonder. I grab the bracelet and the box with the new key and slam them on my nightstand. This gets Sam's attention; she stares at me with her ears perked. It is well past three o'clock in the morning, but I'm not tired. I turn off the lights and go to sit in the window hoping to catch a glimpse of Seth.

As I stare out my window, the snow starts to fall again. Sam has curled up on the floor below me, and I can hear her snoring just a little. My breath begins fogging up the glass, and it makes it hard for me to see out. Sliding open the window, the cold air rushes across my face. I pull the blanket up around my shoulders, lean back, and slowly drift off to sleep.

As the sun comes up and the smell of breakfast slowly wakes me from my sleep, I suddenly realize that I'm in my bed. Abruptly, I sit up and look around the room. I immediately notice the window is closed. *Weird.* I know I fell asleep in the window seat with the window open. Why don't I remember getting up, closing the window, and crawling into my bed?

I lift my arms to pull my hair back into a ponytail and feel my charm bracelet softly slide down my arm. It startles me. Now I know I took it off and put it on my nightstand last night. I shake my arm until the bracelet slides softly back down to my wrist, the first key I see is the one from Seth.

He's been in my room. He carried me to my bed and put my bracelet on me. How did he get in the house? We have an alarm system, and I know I set it when I came in last night. The alarm doesn't cover my bedroom window because it's on the second floor, so unless he's Spiderman, there is no way he could have gotten in that way.

Seth is like a ghost. He comes and goes as he pleases: in and out of my dorm room and now, in and out of my house.

The New Key

I should probably be freaking out knowing Seth had been in my room while I slept, but the thought of him touching me, carrying me to my bed, is kind of *hot*! But how the hell did he get in? I check the window, and it's locked, so he couldn't have gotten in and out that way; he had to have used the door. But why didn't Sam bark at him? She always barks at strangers. Is he not a stranger to her? Maybe he's been in here before!

I look around, trying to find some other evidence that Seth had been there, but there's nothing. I pull open my closet door to grab a sweatshirt and double check just to make sure he isn't hiding out in there, but who am I kidding? This guy is a freaking ninja, and if I find him hiding out in my closet, well, that would definitely kill the allure and excitement of it all.

Accepting the fact that Seth is gone, I head downstairs to join my grandparents for breakfast. When I reach the kitchen I find Grandpa sitting at the table, reading the paper and sipping his coffee, Sam lying under his feet.

"Good morning," he says with a smile, taking another sip. "How was the movie last night?"

With all the drama I had experienced in my own room, I almost forgot I saw a movie last night. "It was pretty stupid. We let the boys choose." I roll my eyes, recalling the crappy movie, then pick up my fork and dive into the plate of food Grandma places in front of me. "Did I set the alarm when I got in last night? I can't remember. It was late, and I was pretty tired."

"Yes. I had to disable it to go out and get the newspaper this morning," Grandpa replies, flipping the page.

I knew it! I did activate the alarm when I got in last night. So how did Seth get in the house? Does he know the code? He couldn't have deactivated it from outside or the alarm company would have been notified. "Did you come up and close my window this morning?" I ask, probing a little further. "I fell asleep with it open, and I don't remember closing it."

"Nope. You must have done it yourself. You must have really been out of it when you got home. Were you drinking last night?" he asks with a bit of a smirk on his face.

"Not unless somebody spiked my soda," I answer, sticking a piece of bacon in my mouth.

"So what was in the box I left on your bed last night, and who was it from?" Grandma inquires as she joins us at the table with her steaming cup of coffee.

"Just a little something from Barb." I don't know what else to say. I'm not allowed to tell them the truth.

"That necklace from Chase sure is pretty," she says, reaching over and touching the stone with her index finger. "He seems to be trying awfully hard to win you back. How are things going with him?" She has always liked Chase, so I think she's secretly hoping we will get back together.

"It's good. I'm having fun spending time with him, but we're keeping it casual. I'm going back to Cali in two weeks, so we'll see what happens when things become long distance." With my mind still trying to figure out how the hell Seth got into my house, I don't have much of an appetite, so I get up and take my still half-full plate over to the sink and rinse it off. "I'm going to go up and take a shower. Barb and I are going to hit the mall and return some stuff and see if there are any good sales. Thanks for breakfast, Grams."

Barb and I spend the afternoon shopping, and by five o'clock, we've had our fill of standing in line and pushy people, so we decide to pick up something for dinner and then head over to the boys' apartment.

"You've seemed distracted all day. What's up with you?" Barb asks once we're back in the car. "Are you freaking out about the necklace? Or is it because he told you he loves you?"

Barb knows me better than anyone, but this time, she couldn't be more off-base. The only thing I've been able to think about since I woke up is Seth and my new key. The key I've been trying to hide from her all day. The key she's caught me staring at more than once. Chase is the last thing that has crossed my mind .

"No, I'm just tired. I didn't get much sleep last night," I lie.

She eyes me with suspicion. "Well, let's have some dinner and just chill out tonight. How does that sound?"

I just smile and nonchalantly rub the new key between my fingers.

When we walk in the apartment, both boys are sitting in front of the television watching football.

"Hey, baby!" Danny yells over his shoulder as we came through the door. "What did you pick up for dinner?"

"We're going to make chicken alfredo with garlic bread and salad. Why don't you make yourself useful and open a bottle of wine?" She blows him a kiss, and we start unloading the bags. I smile at Chase as he watches me from the big leather chair.

Danny's dad has always been a bit of a wine collector and never seems to have a problem supplying his under-aged son with alcohol. Danny never abuses the gesture, though. That is one thing the four of us have always had in common; while all of our friends were getting drunk at parties, we usually had a beverage or two and then called it quits.

After dinner, we spend the rest of the evening watching television—Barb and Danny snuggling up together on the sofa and Chase and I laying quietly next to each other on the floor. By eleven o'clock, I am ready to go home. I can't stop thinking about Seth, and I still don't feel comfortable spending the night with Chase, even though I know he really wants me to stay.

"Come on, Alex, just stay. I don't want to go home tonight, and my parents aren't expecting me to, and you know your grandparents won't care as long as you call them. Please!" Barb pleads.

"Barb, leave her alone," Chase chimes in. "I'll drive you home, Alex. I don't mind."

"Fine. Thank you, Chase," Barb snaps, annoyed.

"Yeah, thanks. I didn't sleep very well last night, and I just want to go home and get a good night sleep. You really don't mind, do you?" I ask, knowing he will say that he doesn't, but deep down, I know he does.

"No problem," he says, grabbing his keys. "Let's go."

It only takes about twenty minutes to get back to my house because for the first night since I've been home, it's not snowing. I try to make idle chitchat with Chase as he races down side streets well above the speed limit, and I can tell by his one word responses that he's upset with me. Even though we have spent almost every day together, I haven't spent the night with him other than on the night of his party. And then we slept on the couch, so that doesn't really count. And I knew that it's bugging him.

Flying into my driveway and throwing the car into park, he sits and waits for me to get out. Now I'm annoyed!

"Chase, I can tell you're mad at me. I'm sorry. I just don't want to start something that we won't be able to finish. It's only been a little over a week, and you are pushing things along way too fast."

He keeps his focus on the steering wheel and has no response to what I just said. *Whatever!* I reach for the door handle.

"Wait. Please," he says, putting his hand on my shoulder. "I'm sorry. I know I'm rushing things, but you're going to be back in California before we know it, and I just want to make every minute we have count."

"I know you do. You just have to let things happen at my pace. And you should know me well enough to know that I'm not going to do anything I don't feel comfortable doing, and right now, that is spending the night with you." I have a hard tone to my voice, and I feel bad that I am hurting his feelings, but it's the only way I can get him to understand. After last night and all the other things I have whirling around in my head like a tornado, dealing with Chase is last on my list.

"Fine. I'll call you tomorrow," he says bitterly.

I lean over and kiss him on the cheek. He doesn't respond to my touch so I get out of the car. "Get over it!" I growl as I walk to my door. Chase never takes it very well when he doesn't get his way, but he knows me well enough to know that I wouldn't give in to him just because he's pouting.

Once in the house, I toss my coat on the rack and kick off my boots, completely pissed with what just happened. Then I notice Grandma sitting at the kitchen table, playing solitaire—something that has been her nightly routine for as long as I can remember—and Grandpa sound asleep, snoring like a buzz saw in his chair.

"Hey, sweetie, how was your night?" Grandma asks, looking up from her cards.

"It was fine."

"What's wrong?" She knows me better than anyone, even better than Barb, and she can tell just by the tone of my voice that I'm annoyed.

I have always had a very open relationship with my grandma. I feel comfortable telling her pretty much anything. When Chase and I started going out in high school, she and I had many conversations about sex and intimacy, and when it came to the point when I was ready to take that next step with Chase, I confided in her. She, of course, being a parent, asked me to reconsider and wait until I was married or at least a bit older, but she knew me and knew Chase and knew that if we made the decision to have sex, we would act responsibly. So I have no problem talking to her about why I'm upset. I need to vent, and with as hard as Barb is pushing for Chase and me to get back together, she is definitely not the right person to talk to. I know Grandma will give me good advice.

"Chase is mad at me," I grumble, reaching into the refrigerator for a soda. "He's mad because I won't stay the night with him."

I sit down across from her at the kitchen table and, for the next hour, piss and moan to her about how I'm feeling and about how everything is happening so fast and that I don't know if I can trust that the distance wouldn't end up being a problem for Chase again. I tell her how Barb is pushing just as hard as Chase and how she wants the three of them to come out to LA for spring break. She sits quietly and listens to every word, and after I get everything off my chest, I take a drink of my soda and wait for her response.

Calmly, she places her elbows on the table and leans forward. "What are you really afraid of, Alex?" she asks in a soft voice and with a face that makes me feel safe.

"I don't know" is all I can say.

"You have always guarded your heart so closely, and it takes a lot for you to let people in. Hell, I think you were about six before you really let your grandfather and me in. Losing your parents at such a young age made you afraid to get close to people. I know Chase let you down, and you feel abandoned, but giving him a second chance may be good for you. That is if you still care about him." She reaches across the table and puts her hand over mine. "He loves you."

"I know he does, Grams, and I still love him, I think. It's just I'm a different person now, and I don't know if things can be the same again with Chase." I look down at the table and can feel the tears starting to well up in my eyes.

"Who says things have to go back to the way they were? You are both older and have had new experiences—why can't things be different and maybe even better?" She pats my hand. "Look at me, sweetie. You can't go backward. You can only move forward, so if you want to give it another go with Chase, then put the past behind you and start fresh. Your mistakes are things to learn from, not run away from." With that, she leans back and picks up the deck of cards sitting in front of her. "Now how about a hand of gin?"

We stay up for a few more hours playing cards and talking, and finally around two o'clock in the morning, we are both having a hard time staying awake. She had sent Grandpa to bed shortly after I got home, so the two of us clean up the kitchen and head off to bed. Just as I'm halfway up the stairs, Grandma calls up to me. "Alex, I almost forgot. This envelope came in the mail for you today."

I walk back down and meet her at the bottom of the stairs, and she hands me a large white envelope. "It looks like it may be a late Christmas card or something. Well, good night, sweetie. See you in the morning."

"Good night, Grams."

Once in my room I toss the envelope on my nightstand, turn on the television for some background noise, and flop down on the bed. I'm way too tired to bother putting on pajamas, so I just pull off my jeans and crawl under the covers in just my T-shirt. Within minutes, I'm sound asleep.

I wake the next morning with the TV still on and a news program of some kind going on about the unemployment rate and the increase in crime. I switch it off immediately. I don't think I so much as turned over during the night. I even managed to sleep through breakfast. It was after noon.

I stretch my arms to the ceiling, letting out a loud yawn then get out of bed. I can't believe my grandparents let me sleep so late. I make my way downstairs and find that my grandparents aren't home. I go the refrigerator for some OJ and there, stuck to the door by a USC Trojans magnet, is a note letting me know that they would be home around three and they would like to take me to dinner if I don't already have plans. *Nope, no plans.* And knowing Chase, even though he said he would call today, I know he won't. That's the way he has always been. It takes him at least a day to cool off after a fight. Besides, I've been spending so much time with him I really should spend some quality time with my grandparents.

Taking advantage of having the house to myself for the next few hours, I turn on the stereo and kick up the volume. I brew a pot of coffee and toast myself a bagel. I make a couple phone calls, calling Julie to see how her Christmas went, and then I talk to Barb for about an hour. She tells me the boys are at hockey practice and she is *sure* Chase is going to call me later. If he does, he does; if he doesn't, I'm not going to concern myself with his childishness. He will call eventually; that I'm sure of. She informs me that the boys' fraternity is having a New Years Eve party and Chase is going to ask me to go with him. She knows perfectly well that I spend every New Years Eve with my grandparents and that it is our family tradition, but she still hopes this year I'll make an exception. I tell her I'll think about it.

After we say good-bye, I realize it is already 2:30 and I haven't even showered yet. I turn off the stereo and run upstairs. I spend more time in the shower than I intend to, but when I get out, the house is still silent. Wrapping my wet hair in a towel and throwing on some sweats, I lie back down on my bed for a few minutes and enjoy the silence.

Staring at the ceiling fan as it slowly spins in hypnotic circles, my mind begins to wander. It's then I remember the envelope. I roll over and snatch it from the nightstand and examine its outer shell. It is addressed to Ms. Alexandra Shelley. No one calls me Alexandra, not even my professors. There is no return address on the front, so I flip it over. On the back is a black wax seal and an emblem I don't recognize. It looks to be two swords crossed with a skull in the center—not very Christmassy. I tear it open and pull out an engraved invitation.

The very expensive black paper has a metallic silver border and silver lettering. The calligraphy is very formal, and it almost looks like a wedding invitation. It reads

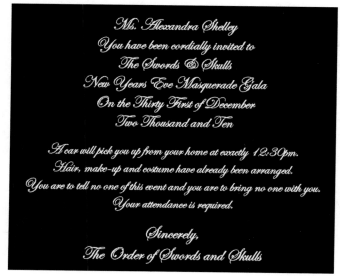

Ms. Alexandra Shelley
You have been cordially invited to
The Swords & Skulls
New Years Eve Masquerade Gala
On the Thirty First of December
Two Thousand and Ten

A car will pick you up from your home at exactly 12:30pm.
Hair, make-up and costume have already been arranged.
You are to tell no one of this event and you are to bring no one with you.
Your attendance is required.

Sincerely,
The Order of Swords and Skulls

What the hell! I stare at the black sheet of paper with complete and total confusion. What is The Order of Swords and Skulls? And why have I been invited to their Gala? Why is my attendance required? And why can't I bring anyone with me?

I power up my laptop and Google *The Order of Swords and Skulls*. There are several results but very little information. All any of the sites say is The Order of Swords and Skulls is a secret society that originated at an Ivy League University. But not one of the sites names the university. I find one site that claims The Order was founded in the 1700s. It is an all-male organization and elite members of American society, which includes past presidents, congressmen, Supreme Court justices, important members of the CIA and FBI, Fortune 500 executives, media moguls and other wealthy members of American royalty. The site also claims this organization is responsible for starting and ending wars, electing the nation's government, and shaping American society as we know it.

Now I'm really confused. I have been invited to some secret society's super-secret New Year's Eve Gala? *What? Why?* This has to be some kind of joke. Maybe it's from Chase's fraternity, and this secret-society thing was the "theme" of the party. That's the only explanation.

When I hear my grandparents come through the back door, I close my laptop, toss the invitation on top, and go down stairs. Both of them have their arms full of shopping bags. It appears they have been shopping the after-Christmas sales and have really cleaned up.

"Alex, there are a few more bags left in the car. Can you go out and get them please?" Grandma asks as she set her load down on the dining room table.

"Sure," I reply, surprised there are still more bags, then head out into the garage.

When I return with the rest of the bags, I notice Grandpa has made his way to the family room and is reclining on his chair while Grandma is busy going through all the bags. "Good grief! Did you two buy out the mall?" I ask with a laugh.

"Just about," she says, winking at me. "They had some really good deals, and your grandfather and I are going to head down to Florida for about a month in February, and we both needed new clothes for the trip. Here, we got you something too." She tosses me a bag and continues organizing her bounty.

Inside is a beautiful black Prada handbag. "Oh my God!" I shriek. "This is amazing, but it must have cost a fortune. You already gave me so much for Christmas. You have to take this back," I insist.

"No, no," she says, putting her hand up. "We got it for a steal, and you have always wanted one, so you keep it and have fun with it."

"But—"

"You heard me."

I know there is no use arguing with her; she is just as stubborn as I am. So what can I do? I give her a big hug. "Thank you. I love it."

"We have dinner reservations for seven o'clock at The Whitney, and then we are going to the theatre so go up and get dressed. Wear something nice, and tell your grandfather to get his butt out of that chair and get in the shower or we're going to be late." She turns, and with her arms full of clothes, heads back to her bedroom, and I turn to do as I am told.

"Grams said you better get in the shower or we're going to be late. I didn't know we were going to the theatre. What show are we going to see?"

"I got your grandmother tickets for the last night of the *Nutcracker* as one of her Christmas presents. Thought it would be nice to do something fancy as a family. We haven't done that in a while." He clicks off the TV and stands up, stretching his arms out. "Okay, I guess I better do as I'm told." He winks at me then disappears down the hall.

While both of them are downstairs getting ready, I climb back up to my room and pull out my favorite dress from my closet. As Maroon 5 plays softly from my iPod dock, I dance around rummaging through drawers, trying to find the right earrings, hoping I didn't leave them at school, and transferring the contents from my modest Target purse to my fancy new Prada.

I finish curling my hair and applying makeup, but even the excitement of the evening can't stop my mind from thinking about the invitation sitting on top of my laptop. I don't know what to make of it, and I don't know if I should go, even though it clearly states that my attendance is required. Who do these people think they are to demand I attend an event hosted by people I've never heard of? What will happen on Friday when some strange person shows up at my door? If I refuse to go, what then? Will they be instructed to take me against my will, or will they comply with my decision and just leave?

I have to admit, though, I am a bit curious to see what this hoity-toity Gala thing is all about. It's all so mysterious.

By six o'clock, Grandma shouts up to me that it is time to leave. I slip on my shoes, grab my new handbag, and run downstairs, not giving the invitation a second thought. Grandpa helps me with my coat, and we load into the car. It's another snow-free night, which I am very grateful for because I decided to wear open-toed shoes. They go best with my dress.

We arrive at The Whitney at exactly seven o'clock, and we are seated right away. Dinner is delicious and the atmosphere festive. The moment our dishes are cleared from the table, our waiter serves us each a plate of chocolate-covered strawberries and chocolate raspberry cups, both of which are my absolute favorites.

"Grandpa, did you order these?" I ask, picking up a strawberry.

"No, I didn't. Excuse me, waiter, can you tell me who ordered these?" Grandpa inquires, perplexed.

"I'm not sure sir. I was just told to bring these out as soon as you had finished your meal," our waiter replies. "Is there something wrong?"

"No, no I just wanted to thank whoever sent them over. They are my granddaughter's favorites. If you can find out who it is, could you let them know we would like to thank them?"

"Of course, sir." He nods and then heads back towards the kitchen.

"Do you have any idea who ordered these, Alex?" Grandpa asks me. "Does Chase know we're here?"

This is exactly the kind of gesture Chase would make, but he doesn't know we're here. No one does. "No, Grandpa, I didn't have time to tell anyone we were coming here. It's a mystery to me."

As soon as the words escape my mouth, I know exactly who ordered our desert. It was Seth.

Is there anything he doesn't know about me? He knows what my favorite flower is, and now it seems he knows what my favorite desert is. That was *not* something he could have picked up in LA. I don't think I have eaten a chocolate-covered strawberry or a raspberry cup *ever* while I have been out there. It's not like that's standard dorm food.

Finally, having given up on the desert mystery, my grandfather pays the bill, and we are off to the ballet.

Walking into the Fox Theatre always makes me feel like a little kid; all the paintings and the sculptures and the gold—everything is so beautiful I can't help but be in awe at the magnificence of it all. We enter the theater just as the lights start to flicker, letting everyone know that the show is getting ready to begin. An usher hands us each a program and leads us to our seats. *Wow!* Grandpa really went all out—fifth row center. After settling in to my seat, there is still time to glance through my program to find out who the cast is, not that I know one ballet dancer from another. When I open my program, something drops into my lap. It's another envelope. It looks like one of Seth's envelopes.

I glance at my grandparents, but neither of them noticed. Before I can pick it up the lights dim, the orchestra begins to play and the curtains open. I slide the envelope into my purse and sit back to watch the show.

As soon as the curtains close at intermission, I stand up quickly, too quickly, startling my grandparents, to go to the bathroom. The line has already reached out into the hallway, but fortunately, I just want to read my note, so I head to the corner of the ladies' room meant for women to touch up their makeup or sit and chat if they feel the need.

There is a dark-haired woman standing in the mirror, adjusting her too-tight dress and applying a fresh coat of bright red lipstick as I enter. Ignoring her, I sit down on one of the small faded sofas, pull the envelope from my bag, and open it.

The note reads:

> *My Dear Alex,*
>
> *You must attend the Gala on Friday. Make up any excuse you can to anyone who asks you what you are doing for New Year's Eve. The Order will not take no for an answer. You will attend the event voluntarily or by force. Don't be afraid.*
>
> *I'm always here to protect you.*
>
> > *Love,*
> > *Seth*

Don't be afraid? Are you kidding me? Thanks to you, now I am afraid!

My thoughts about being kidnapped if I refuse to go are true. Are the things I read on the internet true? Are these the kind of people who have so much power no one dare say no to them? I start to hyperventilate, the woman staring at herself in the mirror notices.

"Are you okay, sweetie?" she asks.

No! I stuff the note back into my purse and rush out of bathroom, bumping into people as I try desperately to get some air.

My eyes watch as the dancers twirl and glide across the stage, but my mind sees none of it. All I can see are the words Seth had written, "You will attend the event voluntarily or by force." *By force!*

After the ballet ends, we drive home, and I hardly say a word. My grandparents chat away about how beautiful the show was and try to include me in the conversation, but my panicked thoughts keep me from hearing what they're saying until finally I hear my grandmother's voice loudly call me name.

"Alex? Are you okay? You haven't said a word since we left the theatre." She sounds concerned. "Didn't you enjoy the show?"

"Yes, I did. It was wonderful. I'm just tired. I haven't been sleeping very well is all." I can't tell her the truth. Besides, this story is getting so outrageous she won't believe me anyway. No one will.

Old Love

Relieved to be home, I say good night to my grandparents and head straight up to my room. I throw on my pajamas, toss my dress on the floor of my closet and quickly scan the room to see if there is anything out of place or anything new that may have been put there while I was gone. Nothing. It's well past midnight, and I am exhausted. I crawl in bed and call Sam up to lay next to me. She puts her head on my stomach, and I play with her ears. I feel safe having her next to me, even though, apparently, she lets Seth come and go as he pleases without even so much as a whimper. Some guard dog.

It takes me a while, but I finally doze off. I wake several times during the night because of one nightmare or another, and when the last nightmare wakes me at 7:30, I can't fall back to sleep. So I get up and go downstairs for the usual breakfast routine, but I find my grandpa sitting at the kitchen table alone.

"Where's Grams?" I ask, pouring myself a cup of coffee.

"Oh, she joined a bowling league a few months back. I'm left making my own breakfast on Tuesdays. They took last week off because of Christmas, but they are back at it this week." He turns the page of his newspaper. "So what are your plans today, kiddo?"

"Nothing, so far. I think I might just lie low today. Maybe I'll just hang out and bug you all day." I joke, poking him in the arm.

"Sounds good to me. It's been a long time since the two of us had some quality time together." He folds up his newspaper and tosses it aside. "Want to go watch Jon play hockey? He's got a game today."

"Sure, that would be great." My cousin Jon has been skating since before he could walk. The whole family is expecting him to go pro one day. And he just might. He is really good. My grandpa loves to brag about his "superstar" grandson.

Spending time with my grandpa is when I learned the most about my father. My grandparents are my father's parents, and from all the stories I've heard over the years, the two of them were very close. I want to ask my grandpa some questions about my father to see if I can get any more information about this secret order and if what is going on has anything to do with him. Spending the day together is the perfect opportunity.

We head out around one, and as we drive to the ice arena to watch Jon play, I know this is as good a time as any to start probing. I need to word my questions carefully however because if he doesn't know anything, I don't want to put him or Grandma in danger by telling him too much.

"Grandpa, didn't my dad go to some Ivy League school on the East Coast? Isn't that where he met Mom?" I'm hoping that's the best opener.

"Yeah, he did. Why do you ask?" He looks puzzled.

"I don't know. I was just wondering why you didn't suggest I go to the same school."

"You didn't show any interest in an Ivy League education, so we never brought it up. We wanted you to make the decision on your own. You could have gone anywhere you wanted to, and we would have supported you." He's right. Going to an uptight Ivy League school was never something I even thought about.

"You never really talked about his school and what he did there. He did graduate, right?" I ask, only half-joking. To be honest, I have just always assumed he did.

"Of course, he did. He made the dean's list and everything. Your mother too."

"Did he join a fraternity or join any clubs that you know of? What about Mom? Did she?" These are fairly innocent questions, and he shouldn't think twice about answering them.

"No fraternity, but he did join a few clubs. I'm not really sure which ones. It's been a long time," he replies. "I'm not sure about your mother. What's with all the questions?"

"No reason, it's just I'm in college now, and I want to know more about what my parents did while they were in college." *Are my questions strange and out of the ordinary? I don't think so.*

My answer seems to ease his suspicion. "Oh, okay."

"Did you always spend New Year's Eve together as a family with dad and Uncle Pete before they got married?" I press a little further.

"Up until your father's last year of college. He didn't come home for the holidays that year. He never said why. And after he married your mom, they always had other plans. And you know Uncle Pete and Aunt Mary come over with the kids every other year or so." He pulls into the parking lot and turns off the engine. He looks relieved to end my inquisition. "Ready? Jon will be happy to have you here to watch him. He tells everyone you're his biggest fan."

During the game, I try to ask my grandpa a few more questions, but he is too involved in the game to concentrate on what I'm asking him, so I give up and get into the game myself. Jon is the star of the game with three goals and two assists. I swear that kid can skate circles around anybody. He is only a freshman in high school, but he already has colleges all over the country chomping at the bit to get to him. Afterward, we hang around to congratulate Jon on a great game and then head back to the house. Grandma is already home when we get back and is in the kitchen making dinner when we walk in.

"How was the game?" she asks.

"Great!" I answer. "Jon was the hero as always. That kid has a bright future."

"Good. Well, wash up for dinner. It's almost ready." She's made grilled cheese and tomato soup. Apparently, she doesn't do much cooking at all on the days she bowls.

As we eat dinner, Grandpa gives Grandma a play-by-play of Jon's game, and I try to think of the best way to tell them I won't be home for New Year's Eve. I couldn't tell them that I'm going to be with Chase because they are going to see him and ask him about it. *Crap!* I have to figure out what to tell Chase too. I know I will probably hear from him, finally, after dinner and he's going to ask me to go to his frat party. That is unless he's still mad at me.

Here goes nothing. I take a deep breath, and trying to sound believable, I give it my best lie. "I have to tell you guys something. A friend of mine from school who lives here in Michigan has invited me to a New Year's Eve party, and I promised her I would go. She lives about two hours from here, outside of Grand Rapids. I told her I'd help her set up too, so I'm going to have to leave in the afternoon to get there. Are you mad?" I hold my breath and wait for their response.

"Of course not. You're an adult now. We can't expect you to spend every New Years with us. Don't be silly," Grandma answers.

"Thanks for being so understanding about it. I'll be here with you guys next year for sure. I promise." I breathe out a small sigh of relief, relax, and finish my dinner. *One down.*

Now that I have my grandparents taken care of, it's time to deal with Chase. Just as I predicted, shortly after dinner, my cell phone rings. It's Chase.

"Hey Alex, can I come over?" he asks.

"Yeah, sure." It's going to be harder to lie to him face-to-face, but if I act sweet and affectionate, it might soften the blow a bit.

A half an hour later, I hear Grandpa answer the door. "Hi, Chase, come on in, Alex is upstairs."

I have to chuckle. That is a sentence I have heard a thousand times over the years. I can't believe how easily things have shifted back to the way they used to be. As soon as Chase reaches the top of the stairs, Sam jumps up and runs over to greet him tail-a-wagging. He's carrying roses. *Crap, this isn't going to be easy.*

"Alex, I'm sorry for being an ass the other night. Will you forgive me?" Handing me the flowers, he leans down and kisses me gently on the cheek. My heart flutters.

"There is nothing to forgive, Chase. I was never mad at you. You just need to relax a little." I reply, emphasizing the word *you* and jabbing him in the shoulder with my finger. "We are both stubborn and don't give in easily, so we just need to take everything one day at a time, okay?"

"Okay. So can I have a kiss?" he asks, flashing his irresistible boyish grin that he knows always gets to me. All I can do is shake my head, then taking him by surprise, I throw my arms around his neck and kiss him quite passionately. I have to admit to myself I still love the big pain in the ass. Now I just need to decide when to make him mad at me again.

I turn on the TV, and we curl up on my bed and start watching the hockey game that had already started. Chase starts getting fidgety halfway through the second period, and I know he is about to tell me about the party.

"So I wanted to ask you about New Year's Eve. I know you always—" I cut him off midsentence before he can start his sales pitch and dread what will happen next.

"I already know about the Sig Ep party. And before you ask and before you get mad at me again, I have to tell you I already have other plans. A girl from school who lives a couple hours away from here invited me to a party, and I already promised I would go."

Before I can say any more, Chase jumps in, "I'll go with you."

"I don't think that's a good idea." I reply, panicking a little. "I already told her that I'd be coming alone, and I promised her I would show up early and help her set up. Besides, you can't no-show your party. Your brothers would kill you." I add that last part hoping it's true.

"How come Barb didn't mention any of this to me?" he asks, annoyed.

"Because I didn't tell her. I don't tell her everything." I answer with an equal amount of annoyance.

"Yes, you do," he snaps.

"Look, Chase, I'm not going to fight with you about this. I'm going to go to my party, and you are going to go to yours, and that's just the way it is. If you're going to get angry, you can just leave."

"Do you want me to leave?" he asks with a rude tone.

"No, I don't want you to leave. I want to lie here with you and watch the game, but if you're going to pout and be nasty to me, then maybe you should leave." I fold my arms across my chest and give him a dirty look.

"Okay, okay, okay! I'm sorry. You're right. I can't expect you to change your plans just because you and I are back together. But for the record, I reserve the rights to next New Year's Eve." He leans forward and kisses me on the forehead. "Okay, let's watch the game."

Just to avoid another argument, I decide to let the comment about us being back together go for tonight. But I *will* pick that back up another time. So I lay back against his chest, and we watch hockey.

The next couple of days, Chase did everything he could to convince me to change my mind and spend New Year's Eve with him. And every time I said no, he took it and didn't get angry.

He's been so great about not spending New Year's Eve together that it really made me fall in love with him even more, and I've decided that I will stay with him on Thursday night, the night before New Year's Eve.

Chase and I spend Thursday evening with Barb and Danny hanging out in the apartment, talking and laughing and eating pizza, and when it comes to that time in the evening when I usually go home, I get up and announce to everyone, "I think I'm going to stay the night."

Chase's face lights up, and it makes me smile. Barb jumps to her feet, and with a girlish giggle, she grabs my hand and drags me back to Danny's bedroom.

"Oh my God, I am so excited for you!" she bellows. She starts rummaging through her bag and pulls out a small Victoria's Secret box. She hands it to me and gushes, "I have been waiting for two weeks to give this to you." Inside the box is a pale-pink negligee. "Merry Christmas!" she squeals.

"This is what you bought me for Christmas? Are you crazy?!"

"I just wanted you to look sexy on your first night being with Chase." She smirks.

"It's not like this is our first time or something," I remind her.

"I know, but it should still be special. Now go put it on," she insists. "I'll go tell Chase to meet you in his room in ten minutes." Before I can object, she is gone.

Once in Chase's room, I close the door behind me, take a deep breath, and slide the pink nightgown from its box. It's lovely and exactly what I would have chosen for myself. Barb knows me so well. The soft satin slides down my skin and feels amazing. It makes me feel sexy and a little bit nervous. It has been a long time since Chase and I have been together. I take one quick look at myself in the mirror, run my fingers through my hair, then without so much as a knock, the door slowly opens, and Chase walks in. *So much for ten minutes.*

Chase locks his eyes on mine and, without saying a word, walks across the room, wraps his arms around me and kisses me. As we stand there kissing, my heart races and my knees feel weak. For a moment, it does feel like this is our first time. Sweeping me up into his arms, he carries me over to the bed. But before setting me down, he whispers softly in my ear. "I love you, Alex."

And for the first time in almost two years, I say, "I love you too." That night, Chase and I make love.

To the Island

As the sun begins to rise on Friday morning, I am already awake. I didn't sleep very well again. My mind kept running with thoughts of what will happen to me once I get into a car with a complete stranger. Where will they take me? And once there what will *The Order* do with me?

Chase is sound asleep next to me, and I don't want to wake him up, so I slide quietly out of bed, got dressed, and write him a note.

> *Chase,*
>
> *I didn't want to wake you, but I have to get home. Have fun at your party tonight. I will try to call you at midnight.*
>
> *Happy New Year!*
>
> *Love,*
> *Alex*

I lay the note on his night stand and gently kiss him on the cheek. He stirs at my touch but doesn't wake. I take one last look at him sleeping there so peacefully, and I know in my heart that

I do love him and a huge part of me wants to slide right back in bed next to him and forget all about what is going to happen today, but I don't.

Sam greets me as I enter the back door of my house. It's quiet. It's still so early that my grandparents aren't even up yet. I toss my things on the sofa and decide that today I will make breakfast. I've been feeling pretty guilty about not only disappointing Chase but my grandparents as well, but I am too afraid not to follow the strict instructions from my invitation and also from Seth's note. Breakfast is as good a way as any to suck up a little.

I've decide to make pancakes and sausage because it's Grandpa's favorite, but first I need to make a pot of coffee to help me perk up a little. I'm tired.

Once the coffee starts percolating and the sausage is sizzling in the pan, I know it wouldn't be long before my grandparents join me, and sure enough, as I turn to grab a plate from the cabinet, Grandma appears in the doorway.

"Good morning," she says. "This is a surprise."

"I thought I'd give you a break from breakfast duty this morning. Have a seat. I'll pour you a cup of coffee," I say, flipping a pancake onto the plate.

"Are those pancakes I smell?" Grandpa's booming voice startles me a little. He's behind me, trying to swipe a pancake from the stack.

"Chocolate-chip pancakes actually," I reply, swatting his hand away.

"Oh, my favorite," he says, grinning.

"I know. Now go sit down. They are almost ready," I instruct.

We sit at the table and eat and talk for a while. I ask them a few more questions about my mom and dad, about some of their college activities, trying to find out if they know anything at all about The Order without asking them outright. They give me nothing. I hate keeping them in the dark, but I have to keep them safe. If my father never told them, then I know there had to be a good reason, so I'm going to keep my mouth shut too.

After cleaning up breakfast, I reluctantly climb the stairs to my room to get ready. I read over the invitation again; it doesn't say what I'm to wear when I'm picked up, so after I get out of the shower, I just throw on jeans and a sweater. I pack a small bag with a change of clothes and a few toiletries, and I make sure my cell phone is fully charged. As the time grows closer, I begin to get nervous. I pace back and forth across my room, looking out the window whenever I hear a car getting close to the house. And as time ticks on, I have a deep-seeded ache in the pit of my stomach. I need to make sure I tell my grandparents how much I love them because I fear that I may never get the chance again.

Grandma is in the kitchen, and I can hear my grandpa singing loudly and off key, so I know that means he's in the shower, the only place where he is allowed to sing.

"What time are you leaving for your party?" Grandma asks, handing me a cup of coffee.

"Around twelve thirty. She's having another friend of hers stop by and pick me up," I answer, trying to sound believable.

"Well, you have a little time then. Want to play some cards?"

"Sure."

Playing cards has always been when we had some of our best talks, and there isn't anything else I'd rather do at this moment. I need to do something that makes me feel safe and normal.

Grandpa joins us at the table a little while later. He reads the newspaper that he didn't read at breakfast, while Grandma proceeds to kick my butt at cards. Without being too obvious, I stare at both of them taking in every feature of their faces. I think about how lucky I am to have been raised by such wonderful people and how I will do everything I can to get back here to them, to my family.

At exactly twelve thirty, the doorbell rings. I gasp and spring to my feet.

"I'll get it," Grandpa says, putting down the paper.

When he opens the door, I hear Sam bark then a male voice. "Hello, Mr. Shelley. My name is Patrick. I'm here to pick up your granddaughter."

"Come on in, Patrick. Alex, your ride is here," he yells to me.

I pick up my bag and walk to the door, Grandma right behind me. Standing there is a short, stocky man who looks to be in his forties. He's wearing what appears to be a chauffeur's uniform and is holding a black hat in his hand. I'm shocked to see him dressed that way as are my grandparents .

As I approach, he smiles at me and says, "Hello, Ms. Shelley, I am Patrick, and I will be escorting you to your party this evening." He reaches out for my bag. "May I?"

Still stunned, I hand him the bag.

"I will wait for you outside. Take all the time you need. It was a pleasure meeting you, Mr. and Mrs. Shelley. Happy New Year." He smiles politely then turns and walks outside.

"I thought you said your girlfriend, what's her name again, was sending a friend of hers to pick you up?" Grandma asks, looking at me very confused.

Forgetting that I had not given them a name for my make-believe friend, I blurt out the first name that comes to mind. "Amber...told me she was sending a friend. Let me call her and see what's up," I reply.

I grab my cell phone out of my purse and pretend to make a phone call. After my fake conversation with my fake friend, I explain to them that she said her friend couldn't make it, so she hired this Patrick to pick up me and a couple other friends she has down here in this area. That way, we don't have to worry about driving drunk tonight. I'm such a horrible liar. I hope they buy it.

"Oh, well, that was nice," Grandma says, sounding a bit skeptical.

I give both of them big hugs and try desperately to hide my fear from them. "I love you both so much. I've been the luckiest girl in the world to grow up with you. I just wanted you to know that. Happy New Year!" I turn around just as a tear rolls down my cheek and quickly walk out the door.

"Happy New Year." I hear both of them say as I head toward the car.

When I reach Patrick, he is standing in front of a black town car, holding the door open for me. As I slide into the backseat, I see a glass of champagne waiting for me. Patrick closes the door then climbs in behind the wheel. He turns the key, and the engine comes to life, but before putting the car in gear, he turns to me and politely asks, "Is there anything you will need before you begin your journey, Ms. Shelley?"

"No, I don't think so, but can you tell me where we are going?" I ask.

"I'm sorry, miss, I cannot. Please sit back and relax. This portion of the journey is a short one." He smiles slightly then turns around, putting the car in reverse and backs out of the driveway.

As we pull away, I look back and watch as my house grows smaller and smaller until I can no longer see it. I try hard not to, but the overwhelming fear and confusion takes over, and I begin to cry just a little. I am scared. *Where am I going? Will I ever be coming back?*

A short twenty minutes later, we arrive at the airport. But not a part of the airport I have ever been to before. This area appears to be for smaller planes, maybe even private jets. The car comes to a stop, and Patrick gets out and opens my door. He holds out his hand to help me from the car. I take it.

"Are we getting on a plane?" I ask, my voice cracking just a bit.

"Yes, miss, we are. Please follow me."

With my bag hanging over his shoulder, I follow Patrick as he leads me into a hangar that houses a large, sleek silver jet. Waiting for us is a young blond woman standing at the bottom of the stairs leading into the plane. She's lovely. Every hair is in its place, and her uniform fits her to perfection.

As we approach, she smiles a warm, welcoming smile that showcases her perfect white teeth. "Hello, Ms. Shelley, my name is Emily. We are so pleased you could join us today. If you would please follow me, we will be taking off shortly."

She climbs the steps of the plane, and not knowing what else to do, I follow behind her. She seems harmless enough, and I'm pretty sure Patrick could catch me if I tried to run. *Suck it up, Alex.* I growl at myself.

Entering the aircraft, I am immediately greeted by another young woman who is equally as lovely as Emily every part of her perfect. The only difference between the two is that this woman has dark hair. She hands me a glass of champagne and smiles sweetly. I notice a bit of an accent as she leads me to the heart of the plane. "Welcome. My name is Sophie. Please make yourself comfortable. May I take your coat?"

The interior is like nothing I have ever seen before, well, except for maybe in a movie. It feels as though I'm in someone's living room—granted a really rich person's living room—but it definitely doesn't feel like an airplane. There are leather armchairs and a leather sofa, plush carpeting, a flat-screen television, and a wet bar. Rich people don't usually intimidate me because Chase's parents have a lot of money and they like expensive things, but this is different. Overwhelmed by my surroundings, I sit down in one of the armchairs and take a sip of champagne. I hadn't touched the glass that had been waiting for me in the town car because I don't care for champagne much, but now that I am in this plane and they are closing the door, I need a little something to calm my nerves.

I hear the click locking the door in place, and at the same moment, Emily appears in front of me. "We will be taking off shortly. Is there anything I can get for you? Are you hungry perhaps?" She pauses for a moment, and before I can answer, she continues. "The flight will be a little over an hour. We have a selection of DVDs if you would like to watch something, or we could play some music for you if you prefer."

I am a little hungry. I hadn't eaten much at breakfast. "What is there to eat?" I ask.

"We have caviar, shrimp cocktail, duck pate, anything you like," she replies and then waits for me to answer—as if those are totally common, everyday meals.

"Wow, that all sounds delicious, but how about something a little simpler? Do you have any fruit or maybe cheese and crackers perhaps?" I ask, trying not to sound too unsophisticated.

"Of course," she replies. "Once we are safely in the air, I will bring that right out to you, Miss Shelley." She turns and walks to the back of the plane then disappears behind a curtain.

I take another sip of champagne, hoping it will stop my stomach from doing flips, but it doesn't help. I grab my Prada and take out my iPod. Maybe some music will calm my nerves. I put in my earbuds, press Shuffle, then lean back in my chair and close my eyes. Al Green croons about staying together as I feel the plane start to move. I feel it slowly taxi into position, then it sit motionless for a short time. Suddenly it begins to pick up speed. Before I know it, we're in the air.

Once the plane is level, I set my glass of champagne down on the small table next to me and notice an envelope with my name on it. I examine it closely and notice it is written in the same calligraphy as my Gala invitation, and on the back, it too is sealed with wax and stamped with The Swords and Skulls insignia. I crack the seal and pull out a small note card. It reads:

Dear Mrs. Shelley,

We hope you are enjoying your trip. Please let Emily or Sophie know if there is anything you need. We look forward to meeting you this evening.

Sincerely,
The Order of Swords and Skulls

While I am reading, Emily appears, holding a tray with a sterling-silver cover. "As you requested, Ms. Shelley." She lifts off the cover and places in front of me the most beautiful display of fruit and cheese I have ever seen.

This is not your everyday cheddar or Swiss cheese and some of the fruit I don't even recognize. I'm speechless. All I can manage to say is, "Wow."

"All of our fruit is flown in fresh daily from all over the world, and the cheeses are aged to perfection and brought to us straight from France. Please enjoy. Let me know if there is anything else I can get for you." She pauses a moment and then adds, "I see that you are listening to your iPod. Would you like me to plug it into the cabin's sound system?"

"Um, sure. That would be great." I unplug my earbuds and hand her my iPod then stare down at my plate. "Could I have some water please, Emily?" I ask, without looking up.

"Of course, Ms. Shelley. Would you like still or sparkling?"

Overwhelmed again, I answer, "Still. Thank you."

Emily disappears again, then a few moments later, she returns carrying a bottle of water—it's label written in French—and a glass that I can only assume is made of crystal. She places the glass on the small table and pours the water until the glass is half full. She places the bottle next to the glass and then pulls a small remote from her uniform pocket. "This will control the music. Just push Play and your iPod will begin. Can I get you anything else, Ms. Shelley?"

I smile and take the remote. "No thank you, Emily. This is wonderful. But please call me Alex."

"Of course, Alex." Her tone sounds motherly. "Please press the button there on the table if you need anything at all. We should be arriving at our destination within the hour." She gives me one of her perfect smiles then quickly retreats behind the curtain.

With a deep breath, I press Play on the remote, and just as Emily said, the entire cabin fills with music. Now it's Bruno Mars to serenade me. I look down at the plate of food, which is almost too beautiful to eat, and it makes my stomach growl. Everything tastes amazing, and before I know it, I've eaten almost everything. I take a drink of water and, with a little chuckle, say out loud to myself, "I really need to go to France."

I can feel the plane begin to descend a little, and suddenly Sophie appears. "How was everything, Ms. Shelley?" she asks, reaching down to collect my plate.

"It was delicious. But, Sophie, please call me Alex."

"Certainly. We will be landing in about thirty minutes, so if you need to use the ladies' room or if you would just like to stretch your legs, please do so now. Is there anything else I can get for you, Alex?" She smiles as she says my name.

"No, thank you," I reply.

"Very good."

It feels as though I have been sitting for days, even though it has only been about an hour, so I decide to get up and look around. Everything on the plane looks as though it must have cost a small fortune. There is gold trim on everything, the leather is so soft it feels like silk, and the wet bar is stocked with the most expensive liquor money can buy. *Pretentious.*

I lean over the back of the sofa and glance out the window. I can see the ground now, but there is nothing I can see that can tell me where we are. Not that I can tell one state from another from the air, and there is no use trying to guess. As I stand admiring the impressive DVD collection next to the flat screen, I run my fingers across the titles—*The Godfather, Some Like it Hot, The Dirty Dozen, American Pie, Speed.* I chuckle. "Interesting selection."

"Alex, we're getting ready to land. Please take your seat." Sophie's voice startles me.

"Oh, okay. Thanks, Sophie." I walk back to my seat. Hesitating for a moment, I turn to Sophie.

"Alex, is everything all right?" she asks.

"Sophie, can you tell me where I'm going?" I ask, trying not to sound frightened.

"I'm sorry I can't. Not that I don't want to, it's just, I don't know." Her voice is sweet. I like her. She places her hand on my shoulder. "But wherever it is, we're going to be there soon, so let's get you buckled in."

I lean back in my seat and once again shut my eyes. I have never been a great flyer, no matter how many times I fly back and forth across the country. I feel the plane getting lower and lower until the jolt of it touching down lets me know it's okay to open my eyes. Once we come to a stop, both Emily and Sophie appear. Sophie hands me my iPod, and Emily walks towards the door and retrieves my coat. The stairs are lowered, and I can tell by the echoing sound they make that the plane has taxied into a hangar. I turn to thank at Emily and Sophie for their hospitality and both are smiling at me as if none of what is happening is in the least bit unusual. *Sure I'm totally used to being flown in a private jet to an undisclosed location. Who isn't? This happens every day.* I think to myself.

I give the ladies a halfhearted, nervous smile in return.

"There is a car waiting for you at the bottom of the stairs," Sophie tells me. "We hope you have a wonderful time during your stay. It was such a pleasure meeting you, Alex."

"Thank you both so much." I give them a little wave and make my way down the stairs. At the bottom, waiting for me, is Patrick.

"Hello, Ms. Shelley. I trust you had a good flight?" he asks, escorting me to the car that is waiting for us a few yards from the plane.

"Yes, it was great. Thank you. Patrick, please call me Alex. Everyone is so formal, and it's not necessary. I'm just Alex, I'm no one special," I explain to him.

"Very well, Alex it is." He motions for me to get into the car. This car is not a town car like the one he picked me up in at my house—this one is a full-blown limousine. This is absurd! I feel like I'm going to the prom or something, but I take a deep breath, slide in, and Patrick closes the door.

"Hey, Patrick?!" I yell, rolling down the partition that divides the front seat from the back. "Can you at least tell me what state we're in?" I beg.

"Ms. Alex, you will be given all the information you need once you reach your destination. We will be there shortly, I assure you." The man is a steel trap. He's not going to tell me anything, and it's annoying me.

Within ten minutes, the limo comes to a stop. He wasn't kidding about the "shortly" part.

Patrick climbs out from behind the wheel and opens my door, again offering me his hand. As soon as I step out, the cold air hits my face and makes my eyes water. I blink a few times to clear my vision, and I can see a small boat at the end of a long pier.

"Please follow me," he insists and begins to walk toward the boat carrying the small bag he had taken from me at my house.

Waiting for us at the end of the deck is a tall, skinny man with salt-and-pepper hair, wearing a long black overcoat, a black scarf around his neck, and black leather gloves.

Patrick shakes the man's hand and introduces us. "Toby I'd like you to meet Ms. Alexandra Shelley. She prefers to be called Alex. Ms. Alex, this is Toby. He will be escorting you over to the island this afternoon. I am leaving you in good hands."

"Ah, Ms. Shelley, I mean, Alex." Toby smiles shyly as he corrects himself. He's handsome. "It is such a pleasure to meet you. We have been expecting you. Please allow me to help you into the boat." He holds out his hand, and as I step down into the boat, it rocks slightly. I stumble a bit, trying to catch my balance, but Toby never lets go of my hand. Once he can tell I'm stable, he lets go, and then he steps down into the boat as well.

"Please have a seat," he says politely.

Nodding, I turn to say good-bye to Patrick, but he's already gone.

I take a seat and Toby hands me a blanket. "It's a short ride, but it will be quite chilly. May I offer you some hot coffee or tea perhaps to help keep you warm?" he asks.

"Some coffee would be great. Thank you," I reply.

He turns swiftly to a large wooden box sitting behind the driver's seat, and lifting the lid, Toby is immediately consumed by an enormous cloud of steam. My eyes widen as I watch him. It looks as though his face is on fire, but instead of screaming in pain, he lets out a delighted "Ah!" With as cold as it is outside, I assume that the sudden rush of warm air feels quite nice on his face, and it makes me laugh. He lifts out a tall black mug and hands it to me. He then reaches back into the box and retrieves a sterling-silver coffee pot that appears to be, to my untrained eye, antique.

"I hope French vanilla is to your liking, Alex." He says as he begins to pour the warm dark liquid into my mug.

"That's perfect. Thank you. It smells delicious." I reply, holding onto the mug with both hands.

"This should help keep you warm as we make our way to the island." He turns and returns the pot back into the steaming box and drops the lid. "Now sit back, wrap up in the blanket, and relax. We will be there in about twenty minutes."

I do as he instructs. Unfolding the large blanket, I wrap it around my shoulders and cross the ends over my lap. Then I pull the hood of my coat up around my ears, lean back, and take a sip of hot coffee. As the boat begins to move slowly across the water, my stomach turns. I have no idea what state I'm in or even if I'm still in the country. The flight had been just little over an hour, so the furthest they could have taken me outside of the United States is Canada, and that is a little reassuring.

Even though we are moving at a fraction of the speed that the boat is capable of, due to the ice chunks floating in the water, the wind is still very cold. It feels as though it might cut into my face. I never would have thought I would be on a boat in late

December, but here I am. I pull my hood tighter around my face and take another sip of coffee, which was getting cooler by the minute. My eyes have started to water again, but my surroundings are so incredibly beautiful I don't want to miss them. I gaze across to our destination, and everything on shore is covered in snow and ice. It's a cloudless day, and the sun is shining bright in the sky, and it makes everything sparkle like it's covered in white glitter. It is truly breathtaking.

"Toby, does the water ever freeze over completely here?" I inquire.

Without turning to look at me, he shouts over his shoulder, "The current is too strong for the surface to freeze completely. But there have been times we have not been able to take the boats over to the island and we had to fly everyone in by helicopter."

I want to ask him more questions, but seeing as none of my other questions were answered by Emily or Sophie or even Patrick, I figure it would be the same with Toby.

"How are you doing back there, Alex?" Toby asks, finally turning to look at me.

"I'm great. Everything is so beautiful I forgot all about being cold," I answer. And for the most part, that's true. The twenty-minute ride went by much faster than I thought it would.

"Good to hear," he says with a smile and then slows the boat even more.

As we approach the dock, I can see a redheaded woman in a long white fur coat waving to us. Toby pulls the boat into the slip and turns off the engine. He takes my coffee cup and my blanket and sets them aside, and with one swift movement, he is standing on the dock, offering me his hand. Once I am safely standing next to him, he turns and smiles to the redhead.

"Darling! So good to see you!" the redhead exclaims in a thick British accent, throwing her arms around Toby and kissing him on both cheeks. "It is blistery cold, isn't it, my love? Thank goodness for the sun."

"Indeed," Toby replies.

Finally stepping away from Toby, the woman turns to me. "I'm sorry, my dear, how rude of me." Blushing just a bit at her faux pas, she offers me a glove-covered hand. "Ms. Shelley, it is such a pleasure to finally meet you. I am Yvette. I will be your hostess for the evening. Welcome to Swan Island," she announces, holding her arms up as though she was a model at an auto show.

Yvette is stunning—perfect makeup, fiery red, curly hair, green eyes, and a smile that would make any man swoon, I'm sure. I can tell that Toby fancies her.

Swan Island? I've never heard of it. I'm completely confused and even more frightened now. Where have these incredibly polite, but incredibly secretive, strangers taken me, and why have I gone along with all of this? For all I know, they're going to lead me into the woods and sacrifice me to some pagan god and serve my blood to go along with this evening's meal.

"Come along, deary. It is freezing out here, and we must get you ready for this evening's festivities. Toby will take care of your bag. Please follow me." She turns and begins walking down the long dock. Without knowing what else to do, and knowing I won't be able to swim for it, reluctantly, I follow her.

Waiting for us at the end of the dock is what looks to be a souped-up golf cart equipped with snow tires. Yvette holds the door open for me and says, "Come now hop in, lovely." Yvette hops in behind the wheel and steps on the pedal. With a swift jerk, we're off down a small path leading into the woods.

"Since this is your first time to the island, Ms. Shelley, allow me to give you a little tour and some background history." Just then, we drive through an opening and out of the trees. "The island was purchased in the late 1800s by The Order of Swords and Skulls as a place for the men to retreat and get away from day-to-day life. Many meetings are held here as well as special events such as the one this evening. The island remains free of telephones, internet, and television, and the only buildings with electricity are the Overlook and, of course, the amphitheater there to your right. All other buildings are lit by gas lanterns and heated by fireplaces.

"To your left, you will see the old farmhouse and barn. There we house a stable of horses should anyone wish to take one out for a ride around the island. There are many paths leading through the woods and along the shore, which are quite beautiful and scenic on horseback. Just behind the barn, under the snow, are a series of tennis courts, and down a little bit further, also covered in snow, is the baseball diamond. If we were to follow the path up here to the left, it would lead through the woods to a large stone fireplace, which is on the northernmost part of the island. In the summer, when the water is warm, the men will have late-night swims and bonfires up there."

Yvette continues to drive down a long path leading us back into the woods, still going on about the different sites of the island, but by now, my panic has caused me to tune her out. *No phones, no internet, seriously?!*

Nestled among the tress are several small stone cottages , each unique and picturesque.

"Here we are, Ms. Shelley," Yvette announces, stopping in front of one of the cottages. "Let's head inside. We have a lot to do before this evening's festivities." She gets out of the cart and begins walking up to the door, and like an obedient puppy, I follow.

As we enter the cottage, I can hear the sound of a crackling fire. The main room is filled with flickering candles and oil lanterns, and the entire cottage smells of cinnamon. Everything is very rustic but elegant. All of the furnishings look to be antiques and very expensive. I'm afraid to touch anything.

"Your bag is in the bedroom straight through the door on the left. The loo is the door there to the right. It is about three o'clock, and the Gala begins at eight, so we have some time if you would like to take a bath or have something to eat." Yvette pauses and waits for me to answer, but I think the overwhelmed look on my face is what makes her ask, "Do you have any questions, Ms. Shelley?"

I drop down onto the sofa. "Yvette, please call me Alex."

"Of course," she replies. "You look a bit exasperated. Is everything all right, my dear?"

I doubt I will get any more answers out of Yvette than I had gotten out of Patrick or Emily or Sophie or Toby, but I have nothing to lose at this point. So I take a deep breath and give it a shot. "Yvette, where am I?"

"As I said, Swan Island," she answers.

I try again. "Yes, but where is Swan Island?"

"It is a small island between New York and Canada," Yvette replies in her pronounced British accent.

"Okay. And why am I here?" I press.

With a big grin and tons of excitement in her voice, she answers, "For the Gala!"

She's not giving me what I want so with increasing frustration I keep going. "But why was I invited to the Gala?"

Without skipping a beat, she replies, "Why, Alex, you are the guest of honor."

What? Guest of honor? Me? Why? Now I'm really confused. Some secret order I have never heard of in my life has practically kidnapped me to an isolated island in the middle of nowhere to attend a party where *I* am the guest of honor? When am I going to wake up from this bizarre dream? It's almost too much to process. I'm spent. I place my face in my hands, and I begin to cry.

Yvette sits down and puts her arm around me. "There, there, Alex, why are you crying?"

Without any hesitation, I blurt out, "I don't know why I'm here, and I don't even know where *here* is. No one will tell me anything, and I wasn't even allowed to tell my family and friends where I was going. I'm scared!" I cry harder.

"Shhh, come now. It's all right. You have nothing to be afraid of," she says, trying to reassure me. "You're here for a party. You're among friends. The Order takes very good care of its own." She hands me a tissue.

"But what is 'The Order,' and what do they want with me?" I ask, wiping my eyes with the tissue.

"Do you not know anything about The Order of Swords and Skulls?" she asks, looking surprised.

"No," I whimper.

"The only people allowed here on the island other than the staff are the Swordsmen themselves, their spouses, and their children. So judging by your age, I am going to assume that you are not married to a Swordsman, so you must be the daughter of one. Is that correct?"

"I don't know. My parents died when I was three, so I don't have any idea if my father was a member of some secret group." The anger in my voice is more apparent now.

"Oh dear, I'm sorry, Alex. I can see now why you must be confused. Let me pour you a cup of tea. Maybe it will help you relax a bit." She gets up, goes to the buffet, and pours two cups of tea. "Sugar?"

I nod, not really wanting any tea, but I figure since I'm here and there is nothing I can do about it, I might as well try and relax a little.

Transformation

For the next couple hours, we sit in the warmth of the cottage, sipping tea as I listen to Yvette give me a brief history on The Order. She tells me how she has been the manager of the island for about fifteen years now and it is her job to accommodate the needs of the Swordsmen. The island isn't used as frequently as it had been in the past, but the "special" events are still a tradition and are held exclusively on the island each year. The Gala is by far her favorite event to organize because it is the most elaborate and elegant. There are three other events held on the island annually throughout the year, but the Gala and the spring solstice are the only two that spouses and children are invited to attend.

Each graduating class holds their 10th, 20th, 30th, and so on reunions on the island, and depending on the class, spouses and children will occasionally attend. Yvette is in charge of arranging it all, from the menu to the decorations to the accommodations. She goes on to tell me that she does not live on the island, but she will stay on the island for days at a time, especially when setting up for an event. With no real form of communication to the outside world, all of the planning has to be done off-site.

At this point, my mind is reeling with information, and I have a feeling that if uninterrupted, Yvette could go on for days about her duties and how much she loves her job, but fortunately, she is interrupted midsentence by the chiming of a small clock hanging on the wall.

"Oh dear, is it five o'clock already? There is so much to do to get you ready for the Gala. We mustn't dawdle. Come, deary, let's get you bathed, so we can begin." Getting up from the sofa she walks over to the bathroom and opens the door. "Everything you need is in here. Take a nice warm bath or shower, whichever you prefer. There is a robe on the back of the door. Slip that on when you are finished, then we can begin hair and makeup."

I step into the bathroom, and Yvette closes the door behind me. *Jesus, even the bathroom is beautiful.* To my left is an antique oak vanity that stretches the length of the room and has a deep copper sink in the center, and above that is the mirror that also covers the length of the room. I stand there for a moment looking at myself and wondering what the hell I am doing here. In the mirror behind me I notice a lace shower curtain. I turn around, pull it back, and there is the *most* beautiful bathtub I have ever seen. It is a deep claw-footed copper tub with one side higher than the other and slightly slanted back. It looks like a tub you would see in an epic Victorian-style movie. I'm half-expecting to hear Yvette knock on the door and tell me she is bringing the first pot of hot water in to start filling it. But thankfully, there is a faucet at the short end. There is even a shower head above it.

Ordinarily, I am a shower person, but when will I ever get a chance to soak in a tub like this again? I reach down, turn on the faucet, and it begins to fill. Next to the bathtub is a small table covered with an assortment of bath salts, bubble baths, soaps, and shampoos. I pick up the bottle of bubble bath labeled Strawberry Sensation and pour some in. It begins to foam at once. The smell and the heat coming from the water are very inviting, so I slip out of my clothes and slide in. I don't know if it is the warmth of the water or the stress or just the fact that I wish I was at home with my family and friends, but all of a sudden, it becomes too much for me to handle, and I begin to cry again. I'm scared and lonely and confused. I want to go home. All of the information Yvette has given me is great, but it does not help me figure out what I am doing here. And it sure as hell doesn't help me understand why The Order has invited me here as "the guest of honor."

I'm beginning to question who my father was. All the stories my grandparents told me about him didn't sound like someone who could be a member of some powerful and elite secret society. I wonder if my grandparents even knew who my father really was. What would they think if they knew I was here and that my father was the reason?

Before I know it, I hear Yvette knock softly on the door. "Almost done in there, love? We need to get started."

The sound of her voice snaps me out of my deep train of thought. I sit up abruptly, splashing a bit of water onto the floor, and answer her, "Just finishing up. Five more minutes, please." I snatch the shampoo bottle off the small table and begin washing my hair.

After I'm finished, I wrap myself up in the plush white robe that is hanging on the back of the door. I notice a lovely pair of pink lace panties lying on the vanity with the French label still attached, and I assume since everything else here is for me, so are they. I slip them on. I take one last look at myself in the mirror, sigh, and open the door.

"Are you ready my dear? It's time to transform you into a princess." Yvette's voice is full of excitement. She walks over and opens the door to the bedroom. "After you."

I walk through the door, and it feels like I have walked into a dream. A dream that has whisked me away from the nightmare of my reality. The first thing I see is a king-size sleigh bed that consumes most of the room. All of the bedding is white, trimmed with lace, and there are at least twenty decorative pillows of all shapes and sizes aligning the headboard. The comforter is so plush and inviting I can't help myself and I dive on top.

"Seriously, where am I? This place is amazing. Is this a dream?" I ask Yvette, trying not to sound like a child with a new toy.

"Alex, we just want you to feel comfortable and at home here. I was instructed to make the cottage into a place that you would adore. How did I do?" she asks, smiling and holding her arms out.

"You did an amazing job, Yvette. Everything is beautiful," I reassure her then quickly stand up. "Okay, what's next?"

Finally conceding to the fact I probably cannot leave even if I want to, I am just going let things happen and try to enjoy myself. To this point, it doesn't seem like what is happening is meant to harm me in any way; it just seems like a party, and who doesn't enjoy a good party? Scared or not, I need to make the best of my situation, so I decide to roll with whatever Yvette throws my way.

Just then, there is a soft knock at the door, and two ladies walk in, each holding a purple bag.

"Alex, this is Cynthia and Helga. They are here to help get you ready for this evening. Take a seat, and we'll get started," Yvette instructs. "We have no time to dawdle. We have to do your hair, your makeup, and your nails then have you dressed and ready by no later than eight o'clock, so take a deep breath. Here we go."

Yvette takes a step to her left, and behind her is a vanity with more makeup and hair products than I have ever seen in my life, so much that I think Julie would even be jealous. I take a seat, and immediately Cynthia begins brushing my hair and Helga begins filing my nails.

Within an hour, Helga is finished with my fingers and my toes. Next she begins to do my makeup, while Cynthia is busy curling, pinning, and spraying my long blond hair into place. I feel like a celebrity getting ready to walk down the red carpet for a big award show. Not even for my senior prom did this much fuss get made. To be honest, having a makeup person and a hair stylist for everyday life would kind of rock!

By quarter to eight, every hair is in its place and my makeup is flawless. Both ladies step back, and I look at myself in the mirror. I can't breathe. I barely even recognize myself. In a few short hours, I've gone from being an ordinary girl into, well, a princess.

"Oh my goodness, it is almost eight o'clock!" Yvette exclaims from behind me. "Let's get you into your gown."

Yvette sashays over to the armoire that is to the right of the bed and flings open the doors. Hanging inside is without a doubt the most gorgeous dress I have ever seen. As she carries it over to me, the light creates millions of tiny rainbows as it bounces off of the soft pink and white stones that cover the entire bodice. In awe, I stand there with my mouth wide open and cannot believe this amazing dress is for me. Hurriedly, Yvette instructs me to remove my robe and step into the dress. Slowly, I feel Yvette slide the zipper up my back then fluff up the skirt. She then places her hands on my shoulders and spins me around until I am facing the mirror. I'm completely speechless. *Who is this person staring back at me?*

I feel like Cinderella and Yvette is my fairy godmother, but I am pretty sure I will turn back into a pumpkin at midnight. But for now all I can do is stare at myself and feel, well, beautiful.

I run my hands down the heart-shaped bodice, feeling each stone with my fingers, coming to a point just below my bellybutton. It is completely covered with white and pink stones shimmering with every ray of light that hits them. Finishing off the top of the dress are sheer white drapes of silk that fall softly over my shoulders, adding a touch elegance that makes me feel very grown up. The white silk A-line skirt flares out from my hips and is lined with pale-pink tulle. The stones that adorn the bodice continued down the skirt in delicate patterns, bringing the whole dress together.

I take a handful of dress in each hand, lifting it up a bit, and begin to spin around. As I come to a stop, Yvette places a stunning pair of pale-pink heels, matching the dress perfectly, in front of me. I step into them, and they add about four inches to my height. My transformation is complete, or so I thought.

"You are absolutely lovely, my dear. How do you feel? Does everything fit all right?" Yvette asks, looking very pleased with herself.

"Yes, everything fits perfectly, and it's so beautiful. But how did you know my size?" I ask, even though by now I should have learned not to. Apparently, these people know everything.

"It's my job to know, lovely," she replies with a smile. "Now for the finishing touch." She turns and walks back to the armoire and takes out a large flat box.

She lays the box on the bed and lifts off the top. As she reaches into the box, I cannot fathom what more I need to complete this amazing look, and just then, she holds up an incredibly beautiful feathered mask.

"You cannot attend the Gala without your mask," she exclaims, holding it out to me.

The mask of feathers and stones, of course, coordinates with my dress perfectly. It is fastened to a long decorative stick that will allow me to hold it to my face and remove it whenever I please.

Taking it from her, I hold it to my face once again, looking at myself in the mirror.

"Perfect!" Yvette exclaims, clapping her hands together with delight.

Interrupting Yvette's celebration is a knock at the cottage door. Yvette glances down at her watch and gasps. "On my, it is eight fifteen. That must be Toby. He will be escorting you to the Overlook. Let me take one last look at you, my dear."

She spins me around and, with a look of complete satisfaction, says, "There will not be a person there this evening who will be able to take their eyes off of you. Alex, you are stunning!"

I blush and look down at the floor. Yvette places her hand under my chin and raises my face to look at her. "Never doubt your beauty, my dear." She smiles at me sweetly then ushers me towards the door.

Just as she reaches for the door handle, Cynthia calls from behind us, "Ms. Yvette, what about the jewelry?" In her hand, she holds a large velvet box.

Jewelry? Isn't there enough bling on the dress? I already feel like a disco ball. Won't jewelry be overkill?

"No, I think the lovely pink teardrop that she is wearing now is exactly perfect," she answers. "Thank you, Cynthia."

I gasp and reach up and touch the sapphire hanging around my neck, and I immediately think about Chase. I haven't thought about him all day. I haven't called him either. He is probably freaking out.

"My cell phone!" I say in a panic. "I need to take it with me."

"Oh, I'm sorry, my dear. It will be of no use to you. No one can get cell phone reception on the island," Yvette reminds me. "Now it's time to go."

The Gala

As the cold night air hit my face, I look out the door, and there is a long red carpet leading out from the doorway, and waiting for me at the end is Toby, standing in front of a horse-drawn carriage.

"Oh come on! You have to be kidding me!" I exclaim. "You have really pulled out all the stops, haven't you?" I turn and glare at Yvette. "The carriage is a bit much, don't you think?" I add.

"Well, you have to get to the Gala somehow, and your dress wouldn't fit into one of the carts, so I figured, why not?" she says, laughing. "Here, wrap this around your shoulders." She holds up a white fur stole. "Now hop to it. You are already late." I feel her give me a little push, and down the carpet I go.

As I approach Toby, I feel my stomach turn again. I do not know a soul at this party. It's obvious Yvette is not coming with me, and I doubt Toby is going to stay with me all night. I have never been comfortable in a room full of strangers, and I'm pretty sure this will be no exception, especially seeing as how they have practically abducted me to get me here. I take Toby's hand and step into the carriage, and as I do, I feel my charm bracelet slide down my arm. I look down at it, and once seated, I begin to swirl it around my wrist like I have done a million times before. I stop when I come to the key that Seth had given me. I run my fingers over and over it, thinking about him. I wonder if he's here on the island with me. He's followed me everywhere else I've gone; is he here too? I hope so.

The carriage ride only lasts a few minutes. Toby opens the door and offers me his hand once again. My hands are shaking, and I can hardly breathe. The nervousness and the fear froze me in place. I look at Toby. He smiles and waits patiently. A gust of cold air blows through the carriage, sending a chill through my body and snaps me out of my comatose state. I reach out and take Toby's hand.

With a tender tone, Toby says, "Miss Alex, you look so lovely this evening. You are going to be the hit of the Gala. Allow me to escort you inside and introduce you to the chairman."

"The chairman?" I ask.

"Mr. Wellington," Toby replies. "He is the current chairman of The Order. He and his wife are expecting you. Shall we?" Toby holds out his arm, and I slide my hand in and take hold.

The Overlook's grand entry is made entirely of marble, and each step we take echoes down the long hall. Enormous Christmas trees line the foyer on either side; each appears to be decorated with a different color and theme. All of the nervousness that I have been holding in the pit of my stomach still burns there, but the beauty surrounding me distracts me from thinking about it if only just for a moment. While I admire my surroundings, Toby leads me down the long foyer towards two huge oak doors with large copper handles. The doors are opened for us by two men dressed in tuxedos, and as we walk through, both men smile, and in unison they greet me, "Welcome, Ms. Shelley."

I am surprised to hear them say my name, but I really shouldn't be at this point. Apparently, everyone knows who I am, but why? The man closest to me holds out his hand and asks if he can take my wrap. Trying to appear sophisticated—and acting as if I attend this kind of event all the time—I smile softly and slide the fur stole off my shoulders handing it to him.

"Well, Alex, what do you think?" Toby asks, guiding me into the enormous ballroom.

I am absolutely speechless, and my entire body begins to shake.

The enormous room is filled with at least a hundred men and women all dressed for the occasion. The men are dressed in tailed tuxedos and white gloves, and all wear black masks tied to their faces with black ribbon. A number of the men have their masks pushed up onto their foreheads so you can see their faces, but others do not. Each of the women wears unique and exquisite gowns that compliment their features perfectly, and all are carrying feathered masks to match. And like the men, some of the ladies hold their masks to their faces and others do not.

Grasping tightly to Toby's arm, we weave around tables perfectly set with china and crystal and beautiful floral centerpieces, and we try not to interrupt the guests as they socialize. The men are shaking hands, the women are giving hugs and kisses, and everyone seems to know each other.

As we make our way across the great room, I try very hard to take it all in. Not just the people and the beautiful decorations but the enormous room itself. I survey the layout. The east-facing wall is made entirely of glass, with a set of French doors in the center leading out onto a terrace overlooking the water. The large oak doors where we had entered face the west. Another set of French doors on the northern wall appear to lead outside, and there are two sets of service doors that I assume lead to the kitchen. I didn't know how I would get off the island, but if I need to, I want to make sure I can get out of this room.

Beautiful people swirl around the room, and the band softly begins playing Gershwin in the background. The music makes me think of my grandparents, and I feel sad. I miss them. I wish I was with them instead of here among strangers. As amazing as all of this is—and as much as I love my fairytale makeover—I'm still afraid and confused, and I want to be at home where I feel safe and loved. But here I am on an island in the middle of

God knows where, surrounded by people I don't know and fearing someone here wants to harm me.

Before the panic can overwhelm me, Toby suddenly comes to a stop. Standing in front of us is a tall dark-haired man with his back to us. Toby taps the man on the shoulder, clears his throat, and says, "Excuse me sir."

The man turns to face us. He is wearing his mask, and all I can see are his dark eyes staring down at me. I shiver. He turns his attention to Toby. "Ah, good evening, Toby," the man says with a pleasant tone in his voice and holds out his hand for Toby to shake.

Toby reaches out and takes the man's hand. I am extremely nervous at this point I do not let go of Toby's arm as he does so. Toby makes me feel safe, and I am not about to let him go.

"I would like to introduce you to Ms. Shelley," Toby says, reaching his left hand over and placing it over the hand I have gripping his arm. "Alex, this is Mr. Wellington."

"Of course, Alexandra Shelley, it is such a pleasure. We have been expecting you," Mr. Wellington says sliding his mask up onto his forehead. He's quite handsome for an older man but intimidating at the same time. He smiles and offers me his hand.

Too nervous to speak, all I can do is return the gesture, and I place my hand in his. He raises my hand to his lips and gently kisses it. Without letting go, he takes a small step back to admire me.

"You look absolutely beautiful, my dear," he says, still holding on to my hand. "Thank you, Toby. I will take care of Alexandra from here."

With a surge of panic, I turn and stare at Toby with a pleading look. Why does he have to leave? *Please don't go!*

Toby leans in and kisses me softly on the cheek and whispers in my ear. "Don't worry, you are in good hands." He looks to Mr. Wellington. Both men nod to each other, then Toby is gone.

"Come, my dear, I would like to introduce you to my wife and my children," Mr. Wellington says, placing his hand on the small of my back and urging me forward.

We make our way toward the tables that line the giant wall of glass. Seated at the table in the center is a lovely dark-haired woman and an average-looking gray-haired older woman. The dark-haired woman is very elegant and graceful as she stands to greet us. "There you are, my darling. I was wondering where you ran off to. And who do we have here?" she asks, giving me the once-over.

"Darling, this is the lovely young lady I told you about. This is Alexandra Shelley," he replies.

"Yes, of course, Alexandra. It is a pleasure to meet you. I have heard so much about you. I am Clare Wellington," she says, holding out her hand limply for me to shake. "We are so pleased you were able to attend our little get-together this evening. And my, look at you. You are positively lovely. Yvette did a fabulous job. I must be sure to tell her so." Her polite tone sounds a bit phony, and I can sense she is not pleased at all that I'm here, but I smile appreciatively at her anyway.

"Thank you, Mrs. Wellington. It is a pleasure to meet you too," is all I can manage to say, but apparently, that is not enough to hold her attention. As soon as the last word escapes my lips, she has turned her attention to another woman who is passing by.

"Susan! How are you my dear? It's been ages..."

"Please excuse my wife, Alexandra. She prides herself on being the ultimate hostess. That will be the longest conversation *I* have with her all evening I assure you," Mr. Wellington says with a sigh.

Not knowing how to respond, I just smile.

"Can I get you something to drink, Alexandra?" he asks.

"No, thank you, Mr. Wellington. I'm fine." My hands are shaking so much, and I'm petrified to get anything on my dress, so I think I'd better stay away from any and all food or beverages until I calm down.

"This is your first visit to our little island. Are you enjoying yourself?"

"It is so amazing. I wish I could see it when it's not all covered in snow."

"Well then, you must come back for the spring solstice in May. It is quite lovely when everything is in bloom." Mr. Wellington holds out his arm for me to take. "Now, my dear, come with me, there is someone else I would like you meet."

As we make our way toward the back of the room, we are politely stopped every few feet so someone can say hello to Mr. Wellington or, as most of the people call him, Mr. Chairman. Being the gentleman that he is, Mr. Wellington makes a point of introducing me to everyone he speaks to, several of whom know who I am. A couple of gentlemen even comment on how they knew my father and how they were sorry for my loss. It's all so surreal. My head is spinning, my heart is racing, and my hands are shaking. I feel like I could either pass out or throw up at any moment.

I really wish I was at home with my grandparents and Chase.

Oh God, Chase! His name flashes in my mind, and I begin to panic just a little. I'm sure he has called my cell phone at least a hundred times and has left just as many messages. If I ever make it back to him, I am going to have a hard time getting him to forgive me for this one.

My mind is still on Chase when suddenly I hear Mr. Wellington's voice again. "Alexandra, I'd like you to meet my daughter, Nicole."

I blink a few times, trying to snap out of my Chase daze, and once my vision clears, standing in front of me is a lovely dark-haired girl who looks roughly to be my age. Smoky eye makeup makes her light-blue eyes sparkle, and her plum-colored dress hug all of her curves perfectly. I smile.

"Oh my God! I am so glad you are here! I've been looking forward to meeting you all week. You and I are going to have so much fun tonight. I'm going to introduce you to all the cute boys, and I will give you the 411 on everyone! This is your first S & S event, so there is so much good stuff to tell you. You look beautiful by the way. That dress is—" She is cut off mid sentence by her father.

"Good lord, Nikki, would you slow down? Alexandra is probably very overwhelmed, and she doesn't need you ranting at a hundred miles an hour," he scolds her in a stern fatherly voice. "And I don't need you filling her head with all the gossip you girls get into."

"Okay, Daddy. You don't have to be so uptight about it. I will behave like a proper young lady as I always do. Now would you please allow me take my new friend to our table? Dinner is going to be served soon," she retorts, taking me by the arm. And with a smile that I am sure she has used on her father a time or two to get her way, she adds, "I love you."

"All right. You two have fun. Alexandra, if you need anything please, do not hesitate to come see me. I am at your disposal." He grins at me and places his hand softly on my shoulder.

With a swift tug, Nicole begins leading me away from her father. "He can be so stuffy sometimes, especially now that he's 'Mr. Chairman,'" she says, making the quote-unquote motion with her fingers. "Please, the whole thing is so much bureaucratic bullsh- ." She pauses, putting her hand to her mouth. "Sorry, that wasn't very ladylike. Here, we just met, and already I'm cussing around you."

"That's okay," I tell her. "I'm not offended."

"Oh good. I get so tired of having to be on my best behavior at these things." She sounds relieved. "I can't wait to introduce you to Melissa and Sasha. We are all around the same age and grew up together in this circus. If your father hadn't died, you would have grown up with us too." She pauses, knowing she has put her foot in her mouth yet again. "God, I am so sorry. That was so insensitive of me. I tend to let whatever is in my head come right out of mouth. I hope I didn't hurt your feelings." She has a sympathetic look I can tell is sincere.

I smile at her. "That's okay, Nicole. My parents died so long ago I barely remember them. My grandparents did a wonderful job trying to keep their memory alive, but honestly stories are all I have." I hope that didn't sound cold. I know my parents loved me and they were great people, but losing them at such a young age makes it easier to cope with comments like hers.

"I can't imagine what it would have been like growing up without parents. Mine bug the crap out of me most of the time but I can't imagine life without them." She chuckles but I can still see sadness for me in her eyes.

"I have parents, but they are my grandparents. I was like any other kid growing up." I want to reassure her that I wasn't an orphan who was passed around from foster home to foster home. I have the best life ever.

"Wow, that's great! Well, here we are." She says, sounding happy to change the subject. "Girls this is Alexandra Shelley. The one I told you about. Alexandra, this is Melissa and Sasha."

Melissa has short blond hair and is incredibly thin and gangly looking. She has on quite a lot of makeup and seems to be trying harder than the other girls to appear elegant. She also appears to be younger than Nicole and Sasha. Under all the makeup, however, I can tell she is quite pretty.

Sasha, on the other hand, is very elegant. She has very long and very dark brown hair, and unlike most of the women at the Gala, Sasha's hair is down and straight. She has it parted down the middle and tucked behind both ears. She has dark-brown eyes and perfectly sculpted eyebrows. Sasha is also thin, but not too thin like Melissa. Honestly, she has the figure of a model and the face to match. Her gown is jet black and fits her like a glove, and as she stands up to greet me, most of the men around us turn to watch her. She is without a doubt the most beautiful woman in the room.

Sasha holds out a hand covered with a long black satin glove, and as I shake it, she says in a pleasant voice, "How do you do, Alexandra? I'm Sasha. We are so happy to finally meet you. Please have a seat."

"Thank you," I reply, happy to finally be able to sit down. My toes are going numb from wearing the too-high heels for so long. I take a seat and immediately kick them off under my table.

The rest of the crowd is also making their way to their tables, and taking seats at our table are two other girls and three boys. They all looked to be about the same age, my age, but it's hard to tell because everyone looks much older and sophisticated all dressed up. As they take their seats, they all smile at me and say hello, but before they can officially be introduced to me, the sound of Mr. Wellington's voice booms throughout the room. All other conversations cease, and everyone turns to look at him. Even the staff stands along the walls perfectly still, giving him their full attention.

"Swordsmen!" Mr. Wellington booms with a deep strong voice that is much different than the tone he had when he spoke to me.

With that one word, almost all of the men in the room stand, including the boys at my table, and in unison reply, "All here!"

Again Mr. Wellington booms, "Swordsmen!"

And again in unison, the men reply, "Above all others!" And without missing a beat, they are all seated.

"Good evening, everyone. On behalf of The Order, I am pleased to welcome you to our 2010 New Year's Eve Gala." Mr. Wellington's voice is softer now, but still very powerful. Everyone in the room is drawn to his commanding presence. It feels as though he is the president or a celebrity; all in his presence are mesmerized and captivated by his every word. "Dinner is going to be served in just a moment, but first I would like to introduce to you our special guest of honor. She is the daughter of one of our Swordsmen who was taken from us far too soon. Alexandra, if you would please stand."

What the...?!

I feel as though I may die right here on the spot. Panicking, I look to Nicole; she is grinning from ear to ear and nodding her head. "Go ahead, you're okay," she says, taking my hand.

Not letting go of Nicole's hand, I slowly rise to my feet. I can feel the entire room's gaze shift to me, and I begin to shake. My face is very warm, and I know I must be blushing. I fake a small smile, trying to appear as though I'm totally comfortable being gawked at. Then I hear Mr. Wellington's voice again.

"Everyone, this is Alexandra Shelley, daughter of Benjamin Shelley, Swordsmen class of '85. This is Alexandra's first Order event, so please make her feel welcome."

A soft rumble fills the room as everyone stares at me. I'm unsure what to do next, then suddenly I feel a soft tug on my hand from Nicole, signaling me to sit back down as Mr. Wellington continues to speak.

"You did great," Nicole whispers to me. "You don't seem like the kind of person who likes to be the center of attention, so I'm glad you didn't pass out or something. That would have been embarrassing."

"No, I don't," I growl. "A little advanced notice would have been nice. How come no one told me he was going to do that?" I ask, hoping the whisper masks my annoyance.

"That's my dad. Full of surprises." She smiles at me again and then nods her head in the direction of her father.

All eyes are focused back on Mr. Wellington and what he is saying. The way he captivates an audience is really quite impressive.

"Now please everyone enjoy your dinner." And with that, he sits down, and the room begins to buzz with chatter.

The wait staff begins vigorously moving around the room, serving the first course. I remove the napkin from the center of my plate and place it in my lap just as a salad is set down in front of me.

"Thank you," I say softly to the waiter.

"So, Alexandra, what do you think of our little club?" I hear a male voice ask me.

I look up from my salad to find one of the boys sitting across the table smiling at me. He is an average-looking guy. He has dark hair slicked down and parted to one side and cold-looking dark-brown eyes. He is pretty dorky looking actually, but you can tell *he* thinks quite highly of himself.

"This whole experience has been a bit surreal if you want to know the truth. I'm still not sure why I'm here. And please call me Alex," I reply.

"Well, Alex, maybe I can help you understand." His speaks in a very stern, self-important voice that made me feel uncomfortable. "*I* am Marcus Wellington, Nicole's older brother and a member of the Swordsmen Class of 2011. The eight of us here at this table, and the seven seated at the table to your left are the children of the Swordsmen class of 1985."

I turn my head and seated at the other table are three girls and four boys. They are all busy chatting and eating, and two of them look as though they may be a couple. A pretty brunette and a really good-looking blond guy are sitting very close, and he keeps leaning in and whispering in her ear, which makes her giggle. I think I may have even glimpsed an engagement ring as the brunette takes a sip from her glass.

I look back to Marcus and ask, "Are those two engaged?"

"Yes," Marcus replies, raising his glass to them, with the blond guy returning the gesture. "They are Amy and Nate, and they have been together since we were kids. They just got engaged over Christmas. The Order is very pleased. We are encouraged to marry within The Order."

That sounded incredibly creepy, and what was even creepier was the way Marcus looked at Sasha when he said it.

What is this Order? A breeding ground for elitist Ivy League snobs? The thought makes my skin crawl, and I begin to feel very uncomfortable.

"Marcus, cut it out!" Nicole snaps. "You're going to make the poor girl think we've abducted her into some kind of cult." She pats me on the thigh. "Don't mind him, Alex. He takes this stuff way too seriously. Just think of us as your extended family."

"So why haven't I heard of you or any of this until now?" I ask.

"Due to your parents' untimely deaths, and the fact you were raised by people who are not privy to The Order, you were kept in the dark until you reached a proper age," Marcus replies, sounding very pompous. "My father, the chairman, felt it was time that you were introduced to our organization. The Order has been keeping tabs on you all these years and is very impressed with your upbringing and the choices you have made as an adult. You will fit in well."

I feel my gag reflex kick in. The sound of Marcus's voice and the way he speaks to me makes my skin crawl.

I spend the rest of dinner pushing my food around the plate and silently trying to make heads or tails of everything in my head. I listen to Marcus spout out more snooty details about The Order, and by dessert, I am mentally exhausted. I really want to get the hell out of here. I glance around at all the exits I had made mental notes of when I first arrived and wonder how easy it would be to duck out.

I can't wrap my head around *why* my father would be a part of such an establishment. And *why* did these people feel the need to include me in it now, after all these years.

Midnight

As the last of the dessert plates are removed from the tables, the band begins to kick up and people start to dance. Nicole and the other girls are looking around, trying to find guys hot enough to dance with, but Sasha looks like she is looking for someone in particular.

"Sash, come on. His chair was empty all night. He's not here. You can have your pick of any guy in this room I don't know why you keep holding out for him. Dance with Marcus. You know how much he adores you," Nicole pleads.

"I'd rather die than dance with your brother," Sasha hisses, sounding disgusted.

"You need to give in to the fact you're going to end up marrying him if you don't find another suitable Swordsman quickly. It's already been arranged," Nicole counters coldly then gets up and walks over to the bar, leaving Sasha and I alone at the table.

"Sasha, can I ask—"

Before I can finish my question, Sasha grabs my hands and cuts me off. "Oh Alex, this is a nightmare. My parents have been pressuring me to marry Marcus for years. I find him arrogant and rude and just all around vile. I can't even stand being in the same room with him, and to make matters worse I've been in love with someone else for as long as I can remember." Looking as though she may burst into tears, she lets go of my hands and raises hers to her face.

"Sasha, you are so beautiful I can't imagine any man not instantly falling in love with you at first sight. If the guy you're in love with doesn't love you back, he must be an idiot." I say, hoping it will make her feel better. "And as for Marcus, I've only known him for a few hours, but I know you can do much better than that jackass."

She looks up at me with tears in her eyes and smiles. "Thank you, Alex. You are very kind."

"Isn't there anyone else you could be interested in? From what I can tell, when they have their masks off, there are some pretty good-looking guys here."

"Yes, I suppose you're right. If I don't want to marry Marcus, I need to start opening my eyes to other opportunities." She dabs her eyes with a napkin, then she stand up abruptly and smoothes out her dress. Grabbing my, hand she insists, "Come on, Alex, let's mingle."

I follow Sasha as she gracefully twirls her way through the crowd. Occasionally, someone stops us so they can introduce themselves to me and ask me questions. Several people compliment me on my dress, and one man seems to take a particular interest in my charm bracelet. If it wasn't for Sasha pulling me away, I would have been stuck talking to him all night.

After turning Marcus down twice for a dance, Sasha finally accepts an offer from a very good-looking guy she introduces as Sage. I stand at the corner of the dance floor with Melissa watching Sage and Sasha spin around as if they were Fred Astaire and Ginger Rogers. Sasha actually appears to be enjoying herself.

I feel a soft hand touch my shoulder, and I turn to see Mr. Wellington standing behind me. "Alexandra, might I have the pleasure of this dance?" he asks.

"Of course, Mr. Wellington, I would be honored." I reply, taking his hand, allowing him to lead me on to the dance floor.

At this moment, I am grateful to my grandfather for insisting on twirling me around our living room as often as he could while I was growing up and teaching me "the proper way to dance," as he put it.

I follow Mr. Wellington's lead as we waltz around the dance floor in perfect time to the music. "You dance very well, Alexandra," he compliments me, but he also seems surprised.

"Thank you, sir. My grandfather loves to dance, and he started teaching me when I was just a young girl. Who knew it would come in handy one day?" I laugh a little, trying not to lose my count and fall out of step.

He chuckles and then spins me away from him, pushing the limits of my dancing skills. "So are you enjoying yourself, my dear?" he asks, spinning me back into his embrace.

"Yes, sir, I am. Nicole is great and so are Melissa and Sasha. Although I must say Marcus is a little intense." As soon as the words come out of my mouth, I immediately wish I could take them back. But much to my relief, Mr. Wellington smiles.

"Yes, my son can be a bit much at times, but Nicole does a pretty good job of putting him in his place."

I smile and nod.

The song concludes, and everyone praises the ensemble with a thunderous round of applause. The band takes a ten-minute break, and with the music gone, the room fills with chatter.

"Thank you for the dance, Alexandra," Mr. Wellington says, taking hold of my left hand and lifting it closer to his face as if to kiss it. "I've been meaning to tell you how lovely your bracelet is, my dear. Wherever did you get it?"

"It was a gift from my parents," I explain to him.

"Keys are such an unusual choice. Do they have some kind of significance?" he asks.

"My grandparents have always told me they are the keys to heaven, and one day, I will use them to see my parents again."

"That is a beautiful sentiment. I'm sure you cherish this gift very much." He spins the bracelet around, examining each key individually. "I particularly like how each key is a different style. Old fashioned to modern...very interesting."

I stand there staring at him as he goes on about each key's unique quality. He asks why each key is numbered and if I know whether or not they actually unlock anything. I don't understand why Mr. Wellington is so interested in my bracelet, but I explain to him how each year on my birthday I receive a new key and as far as I know, they are just charms and unlocked nothing.

"If I am not mistaken, you are nineteen years old. Is that correct, Alexandra?" Mr. Wellington asks with a note of perplexity in his voice.

"Yes, sir, I am," I answer.

"May I ask then why do you have twenty keys?" he asks, still sounding puzzled.

Before I can reply, the band's brief intermission has ended, and music fills the room once again. I am pleased because I am not sure how to explain the mysterious twentieth key I received at Christmas.

"Well, Alexandra, that's my cue. It's almost midnight, and I need to find my wife and prepare for the countdown. We will speak again later, my dear, after everything calms down. Please enjoy the rest of the Gala." He kisses my hand, and then he's gone.

I can see Nicole and the other girls gathered over by the bar, so I make my way over to join them.

"He's here, Sash. I heard Michael say he saw him come in." I overhear Melissa saying as I approach.

"I don't care. I'm over it. He's blown me off for the last time. Besides, I'm enjoying spending time with Sage this evening." She looks in Sage's direction and smiles. "If you'll excuse me..." she says with a huff and a toss of her hair.

We all watch as Sasha saunters over to rejoin Sage. I silently laugh to myself. So much drama. It's all a bit exhausting.

"What was that about?" I ask, turning my attention back to the other two girls.

"Oh, just the latest in the Sasha-and-Seth drama, nothing new," Nicole says, rolling her eyes.

Oh my God! Seth? My Seth? Is that who Sasha was in love with? Was he the empty seat at the other table?

With so many questions racing through my head, I can't breathe. I can't even move.

"Alex, are you okay? You look like you've just seen a ghost," Melissa asks.

"Um, I'm fine. I'm just a little tired that's all." I hope that sounds believable.

Suddenly the music stops again, and Mr. Wellington's voice booms throughout the room. "Ladies and gentlemen, there is about fifteen minutes until midnight. If you all would make sure you have some champagne and your masks, the countdown will begin shortly."

The wait staff begins moving through the room, carrying trays of champagne, just as the band starts playing again. Guests are scurrying around, gathering up their masks and taking glasses of bubbly from the closest server they can find.

The three of us turn to retrieve our masks as well, but before I can take a step toward the table, a voice from behind me says, "Here is your mask, Alex."

I turn to see who it is. My stomach drops when I see that it's Marcus.

"Might I have this dance?" he asks, handing me the mask.

Even though I have only known Marcus for a few of hours, I have come to feel the same way about him that Sasha does. His arrogance is so unattractive the last thing on earth I want is to dance with him, but I also don't want to be rude, seeing as though I'm the new kid, so I agree. Taking my hand, he leads me out onto the dance floor. Once we are exactly in the middle, where everyone can see us, he wraps his arm around my waist and pulls me in uncomfortably close.

"I am pleased that you are here this evening, Alex. My father has been looking forward to meeting you for quite some time. I was also very pleased to see how lovely you are." His words are wet in my ear, and it makes the hairs stand up on the back of my neck. "I'd like to get to know you better. I think we would make a good match."

His words sicken me. I pull back and try very hard not to laugh right in his face. All I can do is fake a small smile and try to wriggle loose from his tight grasp.

"What do you think?" he asks with a pompous tone in his voice. What he is really saying is I should consider myself lucky to have such a man interested in me and I should jump at his offer.

I try to think of the right words to say to him as to not offend him, even though I really want to tell him he is a deplorable human being and just having his arms around me at this moment makes me want to throw up. But then I think I should approach it with a little more tact.

Before I can open my mouth—and explain to Marcus that although it is a very generous offer, I have a boyfriend—a deep, sexy voice comes from behind me and asks, "May I cut in?"

Thankful that someone is saving me from this very uncomfortable moment, I immediately turn and say with maybe a little too much enthusiasm, "Yes, of course!" I turn back to Marcus and politely smile. "Thank you for the dance, Marcus. Happy New Year."

"Of course," Marcus replies with a disgusted tone. Releasing the hold he has on my waist, he nods to the man. Before he turns and walks away, he looks at me and hisses, "Happy New Year to you as well, Alex."

I watch for a moment as Marcus and his wounded ego exit the dance floor, then without a second thought, I look up to the face of the man who has so mercifully saved me from Marcus's clutches. He is wearing his mask, so I can't see what he looks, but what I can see is a smile of perfect white teeth, a dimple, and *breathtaking* blue eyes.

At this very moment, I know. I gasp, and my heart races.

"Hello, Alex."

"Hello, Seth."

And as though it had been scripted for a Hollywood movie, the lights dim, the band begins to play the Etta James classic "At Last," and Seth wraps his arms around me, and we begin to dance. It feels as though everyone else in the room has disappeared and we are there dancing alone together in the moonlight. It's perfect.

And for the first time all day, I feel safe.

I rest my head against Seth's shoulder as he tightens his hold around me. I can feel his heart beating as fast as mine. I take a deep breath and breathe in the way he smells. This makes my knees go weak. I feel him slide one of his hands gently up my back until it reached the exposed skin just below my shoulder blades. He softly caresses my skin, and instantly there are goose bumps all over my body. I let out a small gasp of delight.

I concentrate on how every curve of his body meets mine and how we no longer have two heartbeats. Both of our hearts now beat together as one. There is no one else in the world, just us, and I know at that moment *I love him*.

As we turn in time to the music, I open my eyes for a brief moment and see Nicole, Melissa, and Sasha watching us very closely. Sasha is standing with her arms folded across her chest and a scowl on her face as she stares at us. I know then Seth must be who she's in love with, but I don't care. I know he doesn't love her. I know, at least for tonight, he's mine.

One song leads into two and then three, but neither Seth nor I loosen up on the hold we have on each other. By this point, I can see Sasha has become much more animated as she stands glaring at us. Her arms are no longer folded across her chest. They are now flailing about, and she appears to be shouting at the other girls. It doesn't matter. The only two people in the room as far as I am concerned are Seth and me. I close my eyes again and tighten my hold on him.

He returns the gesture.

Snapping me back into reality is the roar of Mr. Wellington beginning the New Year's countdown. "Ten, nine…"

Seth and I pull apart slightly, and without letting go of me, Seth raises one hand and slides his mask up on to his forehead so I can see his face. *He is so beautiful.*

We stand there in the middle of the dance floor staring into each other's eyes as the rest of the room joins in on the countdown. "Eight, seven, six, five, four, three, two, one—*Happy New Year*!!!" the crowd shouts.

"Happy New Year, Seth," I whisper.

"Happy New Year, Alex," he replies. He softly places his finger under my chin, lifting it gently, and then he kisses me.

My knees go weak, and my body falls into his. I want this kiss to last forever.

Everyone around us has irrupted into a chorus of "Auld Lang Syne," and the sound of clanging champagne glasses accompany them in perfect harmony. But nothing can draw my attention away from kissing Seth. His lips caress mine tenderly, but with enough passionate force that my heart races uncontrollably and my stomach flips. His right hand cradles the back of my head, and as our lips part, I can feel the warm, soft touch of his tongue gently against mine.

There is no more music. The people and the commotion are gone. We're alone. His kiss has made the whole world disappear. It is *the* most amazing moment of my life, and I never want it to end. I never want him to stop kissing me.

With an abrupt *snap*, I am instantly thrust back into the crowded room as I feel a hand grab my arm and yank me away from Seth's embrace. It's a very irate Sasha.

"What the hell is going on here?" she shrieks, drawing the attention of the entire room. "This is who you keep blowing me off for—some outsider?"

Seth places his left arm around my waist, holding me tightly to him, and then very calmly, he says to her, "Sasha, you are being very rude. This is not the time nor the place to discuss this. You are making a scene. Now why don't you return to Sage and enjoy the rest of your evening."

His voice is like velvet, and my heart leaps as he speaks. The strength of his arm wrapped around me makes me feel so safe and relaxed. For the first time since this crazy day began, I feel as though everything is going to be all right.

"How dare you speak to me that way!" she snaps. Then turning her attention to me, she hisses, "And you pretending to be all shy and innocent and pretending to be my friend, *you* will pay for this."

"Sasha, what did I do?" I ask, even though I already know why she is so pissed off.

"You *will* pay," she growls again, pointing her satin-covered finger at me. Then turning dramatically, she stomps off. I don't care. The way I feel at this moment, I know Seth is someone I will fight for. And I'm pretty sure I can take Sasha.

I look up at Seth. He is smiling and shaking his head. "Don't worry about her, Alex. She's harmless. Don't let her ruin our evening," he says then kisses me on the forehead. "Come, let's take a walk."

As Seth and I make our way off the dance floor, everyone we pass makes a point of stepping out of our way. Even though everyone has begun dancing again, I can tell that all eyes are still watching us. We walk through the set of French doors at the northern end of the room and out into the cold, crisp air. My skin is covered with goose bumps instantly, but I don't feel cold. Seth's touch makes me warm.

Laid out in front of us is a long red carpet, like the one that led out from my cottage, with not a drop of snow on it, and as we walk across it, it feels as though its giving off heat, almost like we're walking down a long electric blanket. A short distance in front of us is a small gazebo laced with twinkle lights and green garlands. I can see a couple sitting inside, talking and holding hands. It's Amy and Nate. As we approach, Nate stands up and offers Amy his hand. She takes it and stands up to follow Nate's lead.

They exit the gazebo and walk halfway down the red carpet to greet us. The boys shake hands, and Amy smiles softly at me. "Hi, Alexandra. We're so happy you came tonight. It is such a pleasure to finally meet you," she says in a sweet voice.

"Thank you, Amy. It's a pleasure to meet you as well," I reply. "Congratulations on your engagement." I add, trying to sound like I'm "in the know."

She girlishly giggles and grabs a hold of Nate's arm. "Thank you so much. We are so happy. I hope you will be able to come to the wedding. It's going to be the party of the century! Besides, if you're with Seth, you'll have to be there—he's the best man!" she exclaims, winking at him.

"Well, then by all means, I wouldn't miss it for the world," I respond with a big smile.

"We'll leave you two alone. Come on, sweetie, let's get you inside," Nate insists, ushering Amy toward the Overlook.

We enter the gazebo, and I see there is a small fireplace to one side. The flickering glow, and the crackling sounds it makes, is very romantic. The heat it gives off fills the gazebo, and it no longer feels like we're outside in the snow.

"Please have a seat, Alex," Seth says.

The sound of his voice and the fact that we are alone suddenly make me a little nervous, and I can't speak, so I just smile at him and do as he asks. He joins me.

"You are so beautiful. Yvette had the perfect dress made to enhance your beauty. I haven't been able to take my eyes off you all evening." He smiles and brushes the back of his fingers down my cheek.

Embarrassed, I blush and look down to my lap. He places his finger under my chin, just as he had when he first kissed me, and lifts my face, so we are looking into each other's eyes. "Never doubt your beauty, Alex. You have a beauty far beyond just the physical. Your beauty is also in your soul."

The glow from the fire is flickering in his blue eyes, and with every word that comes out of his mouth, my heart stops. I feel as though I may be dreaming. *Is this really happening to me? Who is this amazingly beautiful man sitting here, saying these things to me?*

"I apologize for Sasha's little tantrum. She was completely out of line."

Finally finding the ability to speak I ask him, "Were you two together at one time?"

"No, never, but she has been holding onto the idea we will end up together one day. She's a silly girl," he responds with a chuckle.

"But she is so beautiful. Why wouldn't you want to be with her?" I can't help but ask.

"Yes, I suppose she is pretty, but I have known her all my life, and the person she is inside makes her very unattractive to me. To be honest, I do believe she and Marcus deserve each other. They are both very ugly on the inside."

"Oh, I see," I say, trying to hide my delight in knowing how he truly feels about Sasha. "She seemed perfectly nice to me, well, at least before the incident on the dance floor. She even confided in me about how she was trying to move on from some guy. I guess that guy was you. No wonder she was so angry when she saw us."

"Like the rest of us, she was brought up to have perfect manners, so it does not surprise me she came off very proper and polite to you. But trust me, it's all an act. Enough about her, I don't want our very first conversation to be about some crazy girl." When he smiles at me, all I wants to do was grab him and start kissing him again. It takes everything I have not to.

I nod in agreement and decide to change the subject. "When did you get here?"

"I landed on the island shortly before you did. I knew that as long as you were with Yvette, you were safe, so I spent time with the guys trying to get as much information as I could about what the plan was for tonight."

"Why are we just now meeting?"

"Because our fathers wanted to shield you from this world, which included me," he says with a somber tone. "But we have actually met before."

Knowing I would have definitely remembered meeting someone as gorgeous as Seth, I'm skeptical so I have to ask. "When?"

"Several times actually when we were young, but the last time was when you were three and I was seven. It was the day before your parents..." His voice trails off. "I'm sorry. I didn't mean to..."

"Seth, it's okay. It was such a long time ago, and I was so little I don't remember much about them. I need pictures to help me remember what they looked like." I hope that makes him feel better, but his expression doesn't change. People tread so lightly around the subject when they don't have to.

"I just can't imagine growing up and not knowing my parents. But I know your grandparents took wonderful care of you. They love you very much." His face lightens.

"Yes, they do but..." I pause for a moment, then knowing this is my chance to get some answers, I blurt out, "How do you know? How do you know so much about me?"

"I was waiting for you to ask me that. There is so much you need to know, Alex." He takes a deep breath and runs his fingers down my cheek, as he had done before, and then he begins. "Your father, Benjamin Shelley, and my father, Jackson Pierce, were best friends. They met at school freshman year and became inseparable. They spent the first two years as most college students do, partying and chasing girls and having a good time with an occasional class in between.

"The rumors about The Order have always swirled around the campus, and everyone knows each year fifteen men are chosen to become new members. But not just any fifteen men you see. The Order only chooses the best—men who come from prominent families and men whose futures are already mapped out for them.

"My father was a legacy, and it had been determined from day one he would be a Swordsman. Both his father and grandfather were Swordsmen, and in April of my father's junior year, he too joined The Order. Your father, on the other hand, did not come from a family of wealth or notoriety. However, he was incredibly brilliant and had a tremendous future ahead of him, and that is what drew The Order's attention."

Before he can continue, standing in the opening of the gazebo is a man I had not yet met, even though I thought I had met everyone. He stands there stone faced and waits for Seth to acknowledge him. Once he does, Seth's posture stiffens. His soft eyes harden.

"Pierce, the chairman wishes to speak to Ms. Shelley immediately. Come with me." The man's tone is harsh, and it frightens me a little.

Seth stands, offering me his hand. I take it and rise to my feet. I don't want to go back inside. I want to stay where we are and listen to Seth tell me his story. And I sure as hell don't want to go back inside and see Sasha again.

Seth turns his back to the man and whispers to me, "It's going to be okay. When we go inside, do not let go of my hand and whatever you do, do not let anyone near your bracelet."

Oh my God! My bracelet! Just then, I remember what Seth had said in his note about the "power" my keys have. I also remember Mr. Wellington taking an interest in my bracelet earlier. I begin to panic, and I grip Seth's hand tighter and begin to shake.

Placing his hand gently on my face, his eyes are soft again, and in a reassuring tone, he whispers, "I won't let anything happen to you I promise. Just breathe, try to relax, and do whatever I tell you to."

"Now, Pierce!" the man growls.

"Yes, we're coming," Seth snaps in response.

As we walk back inside people are still dancing and laughing and having a good time. And Sasha is nowhere in sight, which is a relief. I have enough to deal with at the moment. I sure as hell don't need another one of her temper tantrums. We follow the man who had so rudely interrupted our conversation over to the table where Mr. Wellington is seated. With him are six other men. Mr. Wellington is leaning back in his chair, sipping what I can only imagine is bourbon: after all, don't all rich, self-important men drink bourbon? His tie is undone and hangs limply around his neck. He appears to be a bit drunk. As we reach the table, he looks up at me and gives me a sinister grin.

"Ah, Alexandra, we thought perhaps you had gone off to bed. I am pleased to see you have not. Please have a seat. There are some people here I would like you to meet." Mr. Wellington motions for me to sit next to him. "Seth, you are free to go and enjoy the rest of the party."

Seth opens his mouth to respond to Mr. Wellington's demand, but before he can say anything, I speak up, "I would like Seth to stay if that is all right with you, sir."

"Anything you wish, my dear. Tonight is all about you," he replies with a cold smile and a tone that sends chills down my spine.

We take a seat, and as Seth instructed, I do not let go of his hand. Mr. Wellington takes notice.

"You two seem very cozy this evening. I was unaware you were so close. From what I had been told, the two of you have not even seen each other since Benjamin and Elaina's deaths." The sound of those words rolling off of his tongue enrages me for some reason, and my face gets very warm.

"We've kept in touch over the years," I snap.

Seth can sense my growing anger; he begins to rub the top of my hand, trying to calm me.

"Well, isn't that wonderful?" Mr. Wellington replies in a condescending voice. "Seth, we didn't think you were coming this evening. Since your father's passing, we haven't seen much of you."

I turn to look at Seth. His face does not show any emotional reaction to Mr. Wellington's words, but I can see sadness in his perfect blue eyes as he responds to the comment.

"I wouldn't have missed it, sir. It is always quite a party, and I promised Alex I would be here." He gives my hand a little squeeze.

"How is your mother?" one of the other men at the table asks Seth.

"She is fine, sir. She sends her regards."

After a brief pause in the conversation, Mr. Wellington breaks the silence. "Alexandra, I would like to introduce you to Preston Walker," he says, acknowledging the man who spoke to Seth.

I smile at the man but say nothing.

Mr. Wellington continues. "I'd also like you to meet Walter Abbott, Parker Ashcroft, Philip Chamberlain, Lowell Ferguson, and Edwin Hollister," he introduces each man going from left to right around the table. "We are The Swords and Skulls Class of 1985."

"Among others," Walter Abbott adds.

"Yes, among others. Thank you, Walter. But the seven of us, along with both your fathers, before they died, have always been a very close-knit group. Losing your father in such an abrupt way was very difficult for us. We vowed that you, Alexandra, would be taken care of and hopefully one day would become a part of our little *family*, for lack of a better word." His eyes are even colder now.

The polite and caring tone Mr. Wellington had used with me earlier is now gone. His warm, father-like qualities have been washed away by the booze. It is clear the honeymoon period is now over, and every word that comes out of his mouth not only frightens me but sickens me as well.

"Alexandra, we have watched you from a distance as you have grown up, and we are quite pleased with what a wonderful young lady you have become. And we feel it is time you get to know who your father really was. Not the Benjamin your grandparents knew and have told you stories about, but the Benjamin, Swordsmen Class of 1985," Preston Abbott adds.

"And who do you think he was exactly? And how dare you presume that person was so different from the son my grandparents raised?" My tone is sharp, and my anger now apparent.

"I'm not suggesting your grandparents didn't know who your father was, but by being a part of this group, there are certain things he was forbidden to reveal to them."

"Well, I think I prefer to remember the man my grandparents knew and loved and not a man who kept secrets and lied to the people he loved." I'm unable to hide my disgust any longer. "I don't want you to think I am not appreciative of all that you've done for me tonight, but there is something about all of this that makes me feel uneasy. Now if you will excuse us, I would very much like to dance with Seth again before the evening is over. It was a pleasure meeting you, gentlemen."

Feeling a bit nauseous but proud of myself, I stand up, and Seth follows suit. Still holding on to his hand, I lead him to the dance floor and wrap my arms around him.

"That was very impressive, Alex," Seth says, sounding surprised.

"I had to get away from them. There is something about the way Mr. Wellington spoke to me and the way Preston Abbott talked about my father that gave me the creeps.

"Ever since I stepped foot on this island, I have felt like there is something these people want from me. I am not naïve enough to think *The Order*," I say with mocking, "went through all the trouble to get me here and dress me up just to introduce me to their stupid club." I pause for a moment, fighting back tears of anger and rage. "They do want something—something they are willing to do anything to get their hands on. And now after meeting those other guys, I can tell they are all in on it." I look up at Seth, and the look on his face surprises me. "What is it?" I ask.

Speaking very softly, Seth answers, "You're right, Alex. You do have something they want, and they *will* stop at nothing to get it." He brushes his hand over my bracelet, and I gasp softly.

"Wait! My bracelet? This is what they want? Why?" I whisper.

Holding me very tightly, he kisses my ear and then whispers, "I can't tell you here. What I can tell you is that your keys hold a very powerful secret, and those men will stop at nothing to make sure that secret stays locked away forever."

Run!

I cling forcefully to Seth as we dance. My heart is racing again, but this time out of fear. I can see Mr. Wellington and the others staring at me. I know they have a plan, some way of getting ahold of my bracelet. Part of me wants to throw the bracelet in Mr. Wellington's face and put an end to all of it. But a bigger part of me knows that if my father thought it was important to keep it hidden from The Order whatever it is the keys keep locked away, then I must honor his wishes and do the same. Clearly, that is Seth's intention as well.

Seth's lips begin to move along my ear again. "Alex, I need for you to listen to me very closely. In about thirty seconds, we are going to walk over to the French doors leading out to the gazebo. When I tell you to, you are going to move as quickly as you can out those doors and into the gazebo. On the other side of the fireplace, you will find your bag." Seth pauses and subtly shifts us a few feet to the left, away from a couple dancing a little too close for Seth's liking. Once he feels as though they can no longer hear us, he continues.

"Now this is very important. You must do exactly what I tell you. It is extremely cold outside, but all you are going to have time to do is change into your boots and put on your coat. Once you have done that, I want you to quickly step out of the gazebo.

Directly behind the fireplace, you will see a path—I want you to follow it. Now I know it has been snowing, and it will be difficult to see, but I promise you it is there. I have put a flashlight in your bag, and once you reach the trees and are out of sight of the Overlook, I want you to use it." Seth looks down at me with intensity in his eyes that frightens me. "Alex, once you reach the woods, I want you to *run*."

I begin to breathe heavily, and my entire body begins to shake once again. My head is spinning, and it feels as though I may pass out.

Seth senses my fear and tightens his grip around me. "Alex. Alex. I need you to stay calm. I'm not going to let anything happen to you. I am going to get you out of here. You just have to do exactly what I tell you. Do you understand?"

I nod unable to speak.

"I need you to run as fast as you can, following the path until you get to the large stone fireplace at the northernmost part of the island. It is not going to be easy. With your dress and the elements, it will take you longer than it would if you were dressed properly, but I know you can do it. It is a little less than a mile, and it should take you about a half an hour to get there. I have also put a flare gun in your bag. If you get into trouble for any reason and cannot make it to the fireplace, fire the gun in the air, and I will come find you." He pauses again and then kisses me gently on the forehead. "I know I have just scared the hell out of you, but I need you to stay calm. Do everything you can to get there and wait for me. Do you understand?" he asks again.

"Yes," I whisper in a shaky voice. "But what do I do if you don't come for me?"

He places his hands on either side of my face, and with love and sincerity, he says, "I *will* come for you. I promise. My only purpose in life is to keep you safe. I will die before I let anything happen to you." Then he kisses me.

Taking me by the hand, Seth leads me toward the doors. We pause for a moment and look into each other's eyes. Seth smiles sweetly, and at the same moment, he reaches for the handle. I take one last look around the amazingly beautiful room that only hours ago was a welcoming place but now is the least safest place for me to be. Suddenly I notice there is a group of men heading straight for us, Marcus in the lead.

Seth gives me one last kiss and then opens the doors.

I step outside and take a few steps toward the gazebo. I stop and turn to take one last look at Seth. He steps back inside, closing the doors behind him, and I watch through the window as Marcus and his pack of Swordsmen swarm him.

I want to help him, but instead, I obey Seth's instruction. I swiftly make my way into the gazebo and find my bag exactly where he said it would be. I open it to find my boots, my coat, and the flashlight sitting on top. I quickly kick off my shiny pink heels and slide into my boots. I throw on my coat, grab my bag, and as quickly as I can, I begin to make my way down the snow-covered path.

I reach the edge of the woods, but before I can go any further, I take one last look at the Overlook to see if I can see Seth. I need to see if he is okay, but I don't see him. *I will come for you*, his words echo in my mind, and in my heart, I know he will come. I grip the flashlight and begin to run. The trees are thick and the snow has completely covered the path. I'm not sure if I am even on a path, but I know if I keep moving and didn't make any sharp turns, I will make it to the fireplace.

My gown makes it very difficult to run, so I gather up as much of it as I can, throw it over my arm, and press on. I can still hear the music emanating from the Overlook. I begin to remember the dream I had on the plane coming home from California and a strong sensation of déjà vu comes over me.

Over the sound of the music, I hear shouting. I can't hear what is being said, but I can tell it's Marcus doing the yelling. The arrogant tone in his voice is unmistakable. This gives me motivation to run even faster, anything to get far away from that guy.

I picture Marcus and his henchmen surrounding Seth, interrogating him, trying to find out where I've gone. I imagine them beating him, knocking him to the ground, kicking him until he caves in and tells them what they want to know. But the little I know about Seth, I know no amount of torture will make him talk.

Would Seth really die for me?

About ten minutes into my run, I hear someone following me. I know with the snow it wouldn't be difficult for someone to track my footsteps, and an overwhelming sense of fear washes over me. Forcing myself to be brave—so I don't let Seth down—I quickly duck behind a tree and wait to see if anyone approaches. Holding the flashlight like a club over my head, I wait in silence to attack. As the footsteps get closer, my heart begins to beat out of control. And just as I am prepared to jump out and start swinging, I see a deer standing there, staring at me. I let out a deep sigh and half a laugh then take off running again. Seth would be so impressed with my ability to scare off Bambi.

To my relief, about halfway through my journey, it begins to snow. I never thought, given the circumstance I find myself in, I would be happy for snow, but I am. I know the snow will cover up my tracks, so if Marcus and his goons come looking for me, they won't find my trail. Although, the fact I am on an island makes any chance of escaping without Seth's help slim to none, which doesn't help my anxiety.

I make it through the woods unscathed for the most part, and as I come into the clearing and catch sight of the large stone fireplace, I'm relieved. However, that relief is short lived once I realize Seth didn't tell me what to do once I got here. The only thing he said was to wait for him. But for how long? What do I do if he never comes? What if Marcus and his thugs do all the things I had imagined them doing to him and he can't get to me? It's cold and snowing, I won't last long out here by myself.

No! Alex, relax! I tell myself. He promised he would come for me, so I have faith he will.

The man is like a ninja. He came in and out of my dorm and my home without a trace and he has been following me for months, hell maybe even years and I never knew it. If anyone can get away from "The Order" it would be Seth.

I start to shiver as the snow falls around me and I can feel my hair beginning to dampen. I pull the hood of my coat up over my head and reach in and pull out the gloves that I have stuffed in the pockets. I try not to use the flashlight very often, in case there are people looking for me I don't want to draw attention to myself, but I quickly use it to scan the area to find some sort of shelter, there isn't any. The only place I can get relief from the snow is to go back into the woods. I walk back to the tree line and hunker down beneath a large tree. This allows me to see the open area around the fireplace, and it also keeps me from getting snowed on.

The adrenaline I had as I ran through the woods is beginning to wear off and fear is setting in, again. Every little sound makes me jump and it feels as though I have been sitting alone under this tree for hours. At times I can faintly hear the sound of the music coming from the Overlook as it catches a ride on the wind and travels out over the water. There are no stars in the sky and the moon only looks down on me when the wind blows the clouds out of its way.

Grateful for the many layers of my gown, I bunch them up around my legs to keep warm. I cringe at the thought of ruining my dress, but I know protection from the elements is much more important than preserving its beauty.

I have no idea how long I have been sitting under this tree, but the longer I sit here the more I begin to panic. What am I to do if

Seth doesn't come for me? I have faith in him, but there is always the possibility he won't or can't come.

I take off the pink glove covering my left hand and push up the sleeve of my coat until I find my bracelet. I twirl it around my wrist. And for the first time I wish my parents had never given it to me. I think about throwing it into the water and letting the current carry it away. Maybe then The Order will leave me alone and I can go back to my life the way it was before all this started. If I no longer have the bracelet, then they will have no use for me, right?

No! My parents entrusted me with their secret, so I have to see this through. I have to grow up, be the daughter who would make my parents proud and be the woman Seth is willing to give his life for.

I slide my glove back on and lean my head back against the trunk of the tree. My eyes are growing heavy, and I try very hard to fight the urge to fall asleep, but I am unsuccessful. With a sudden jerk of my head, I am thrust awake by the sound of a motor. I can see the outline of a small speed boat floating in the water. Not knowing if it's Seth, I remain perfectly still beneath my tree. I can hear the sound of someone splashing their way through the water, and then I hear someone whisper my name.

"Alex, where are you?"

It's Seth. I turn on my flashlight and wave it back and forth until I can see him walking toward me.

"I thought you'd never get here," I whisper.

"Come on. We have to get off the island," he says in a deeper tone. "They are looking for you. We have to go now!"

I rise to my feet and shake off the snow that found its way under the tree and on to my dress. I am so cold and scared that my entire body is shaking uncontrollably and Seth can't help but notice as he takes hold of my hand.

"You must be freezing, baby. I'm so sorry it took me so long to get to you. Come on, let's get you out of here." Sweeping me up into his arms, he carries me to the boat.

The Truth

As we speed away from the island, the wind feels like knives being thrown through the night sky, so I curl up on the floor of the boat and try not to freeze to death. Seth hands me a blanket; I wrap myself up in it and close my eyes. I must have fallen asleep because what seems like only seconds later, the boat has stopped and Seth is gently shaking me awake.

"Alex, we need to get off the boat," he says in his velvet voice.

"Where are we?" I ask groggily.

"There is no time to explain. We need to keep moving."

I stand and try to shake off the exhaustion that has taken over my body, but with everything that has happened in the past few hours, all my body wants to do is shut down. I look up at Seth as he stands patiently waiting for me to get acclimated to my surroundings. Then I ask, "So what now?"

"Now we get the hell off this boat before you freeze to death," he replies, reaching his hand out and taking hold of mine. "I know you're exhausted and cold, but I need you to stay focused. We will be someplace safe and warm soon, I promise."

I stumble over to the side of the boat, and with a graceful sweeping motion, Seth lifts me up onto the dock. And in an instant, he is on the dock next to me, carrying a couple bags over his shoulder. I look out over the dark water to see if I can see the island we left behind, but I see nothing, just a dark abyss that sends chills through my already frozen body. I drop to my knees exhausted, horrified, relieved, confused, angry—so many emotions.

"Are you all right, Alex?" Seth's is voice full of concern as he bends down, putting his arms around me and pulling me close to him.

"Honestly, I don't know," I whimper, trying to hold back tears.

"Come on, let's get you warm." Helping me to my feet, he leads me down the dock to a dimly lit parking lot. There waiting for us is a dark SUV with tinted windows and an Ontario license plate.

We're in Canada.

Without saying anything, Seth opens the passenger-side door for me, and I slide inside. I watch as he walks around the backside of the car, pausing to survey the area. Opening the back door, he tosses into the backseat the two bags he was carrying. Before closing the door, I see him take something out of one of the bags and put it inside his jacket, but I can't tell what it is. My eyes are so tired I can barely keep them open, so I can't be certain if what I'm seeing is real or if my eyes are playing tricks on me.

Seth climbs in the driver's seat and starts the engine. Before putting it in gear, he turns to me and places his hand softly on the back of my neck.

"It's going to be a long drive, baby. Lay back and try to get some sleep. We have a lot to do the next few of days, and I need you on your toes." He pauses, and with a sexy smile not even my sleepy eyes can miss, he says, "Dream about our kiss. I know it is what I will dream about once I am able to sleep."

I feel myself blush and am thankful we're sitting in a dark car so he can't see me. He caresses the back of my neck for a moment, then before I know it, we're driving. I lean my seat back and close my eyes, knowing I will fall asleep instantly. I want desperately to stay awake and ask Seth more questions, but the moment I close my eyes, I'm gone.

The sun is warm, and the ocean air is refreshing. I can see Barb and Danny swimming in the water. I reach into my bag and pull out some suntan lotion. "Let me rub some on your back," Chase offers.

"Thank you, baby." I reply, handing him the bottle.

Chase rubs the lotion on my back softly and seductively. He begins kissing the back of my neck. His soft caress gives me goose bumps. I lie back on the towel and close my eyes, waiting for him to kiss me.

As I feel the soft moist touch of lips to mine, my heart begins to race. His kiss is passionate and familiar, but I know it isn't Chase. I open my eyes, and the face in front of me is Seth. I gasp with pleasure.

With a jolt, I am awakened to find we're still driving. My sudden consciousness must have startled Seth. He reaches over and stokes my leg. "Bad dream?" he asks.

"No," I answer, not willing to go into any more detail. "Where are we?"

"We are just outside of Montreal," Seth replies.

"Are you hungry?"

Due to nerves and fear, I hadn't eaten much at the Gala, so I have to admit I'm starving, but what I really want to do first is get out of this gown—which now, by the light of day, I can see is completely ruined—and take a shower. Then I will worry about eating. So I reply, "A little, but I would really like to take a shower first if that's okay?"

"Of course," he answers with a sweet, sexy smile. "We are almost to the cabin. There you can shower and change, and I will make you some breakfast."

"Aren't you exhausted?" I ask. "You haven't slept all night, have you?" I can't be sure if he had stopped at some point to rest or even to get gas. Once I had fallen asleep, a bomb couldn't have woken me up.

"No, but I'm used to staying up all night and functioning on very little sleep. I've been trained to stay up for days at a time."

Trained? What does that mean? I have so many questions in my head that I don't even know where to start, and every time he opens his mouth, he just adds to them.

The sun is very bright as it shines in through the windshield, and it hurts my eyes. I flip down the visor to block some of it from shining in my face, and I catch a glimpse of myself in the mirror. I am horrified. I no longer look like a princess who had attended an elegant gala. I now look like the bride of Frankenstein, ready to jump out of the corner of a haunted house and scare the daylights out of someone's small child. My perfect hairdo now looks like a bird's nest, and my perfect makeup now looks like I am trying out for the circus. I'm a mess and unbelievably embarrassed. I cannot believe Seth is seeing me this way.

I reach into the backseat and grab my bag, hoping the things I had brought from home are still in there, and to my relief, they are. One thing I have always prided myself on is being prepared. I pull out my makeup bag, and inside is a small bottle of makeup remover and two cotton balls. I know, with the way I look, two cotton balls wouldn't do the trick, but I'll do what I can.

After I'm satisfied that I no longer look like a clown, it is time to brush out my hair. This is going to be painful. I begin pulling out what seems like an endless amount of bobby pins from my hair when I hear Seth chuckle.

"What are you laughing at?" I ask, knowing full well what he is laughing at.

"Oh nothing, you're just so cute when you're embarrassed."

"Gee, thanks, that makes me feel much more at ease." I hit his arm with the back of my hand. "I look like some kind of freak show. I can't believe you're seeing me this way."

"I've seen you look silly before." My eyes widen at his remark. "Remember the party Julie took you to last year where the two of you ended up going home covered in shaving cream and silly string?" he asks.

"Um…yeah."

"Yeah, well, I saw it all." He laughs. "And the time you and Barb dressed up like the Spice Girls for Halloween, yikes."

"Hey, we looked great!" I insist, smiling at the memory.

"Okay, well then, how about in the ninth grade when you were hit by a softball in gym class and you had a black eye for two weeks."

"Oh my God! How do you know all that?" I ask, staring at him in total shock.

"Alex, I've always been with you," he says, stroking my cheek. "But my point is, no matter what you look like, you are always beautiful to me."

My body tingles, and my face feels flushed. I can feel tears welling up in my eyes. I take hold of his hand and lift it to my lips. "Thank you," I whisper, just as a tear escapes and rolls slowly down my cheek.

Pulling off on to a long dirt road, Seth drives for several bumpy miles before finally coming to a stop in front of a small rustic log cabin. He shuts off the engine.

"We're here," he says with a sigh of exhausted relief. "Come on, let me get you inside." He comes around, opens my door, and offers me his hand. "There is an awful lot of snow on the ground. Would you like me to carry you?"

I look down at my dress and with a sigh reply, "No that's okay. My dress is already ruined—what's the point?"

As if I had said the exact opposite, Seth sweeps me up into his arms and carries me toward the cabin. "I'm not worried about your dress, Alexandra. I'm worried about you getting cold again walking through the snow, silly girl."

I smile. "Oh."

As we walk through the door, I can hear the sound of a crackling fire and I can smell the aroma of freshly brewed coffee. Someone knew we were coming. Seth sets me down and quickly goes back out to the car to retrieve our bags. I glance around the cabin, which looks a lot like the stone cottage from the island. There is a large main room with a sofa and a chair facing the fireplace. It has two doors across from the main entrance, which I assume are a bedroom and a bathroom. But unlike the cottage on the island, this cabin has a kitchen and dining area. It also has electricity, which the cottage did not have. I also notice there are fresh-cut flowers and a gift-wrapped box sitting on the dining room table. Before I can walk over to take a closer look at the box, Seth walks back through the door.

He has on a thick gray wool pea coat, and he is wearing jeans. I wonder when he had changed out of his tuxedo. It was too dark when we left the island, and I was too exhausted to notice what he was wearing.

So here we are—me in my ruined ball gown, winter coat, and boots looking like a complete freak and him in designer jeans and a perfectly tailored jacket, looking like he just stepped out of a Ralph Lauren AD.

Choosing to ignore the embarrassment of the moment, I ask him, "Who did all this?"

"My mother," Seth answers. "She will be back in a little while with some supplies. She is so excited to see you."

"Oh." I'm not sure how to react to meeting Seth's mother. Does she know everything about me too?

"Why don't you go ahead and take a shower? There are some fresh clothes for you in the bathroom. And when you're finished, we'll have something to eat." He gently slides my coat off of my shoulders and tosses in on the back of the chair that sits in front of the fireplace. He places his hand on the small of my back and guides me toward the door closest to the kitchen. He leans his head down and softly kisses me on my bare shoulder and then turns the doorknob opening the door to the bathroom. "Let me know if you need anything."

I turn and wrap my arms around his waist and lay my head against his chest. "Thank you."

As we stand there holding each other, I feel something sticking out of the top of his pants underneath his jacket. I can't tell what it is, but in my mind, I know. It's a gun. I look up into his beautiful face, smile, then turn and walk into the bathroom, closing the door behind me. I lean my back against the door and slowly slide down it until I am sitting on the floor. *He has a gun.* This isn't a game. No matter how much I would like it to be one, it isn't. My life and Seth's life are truly in danger. I need to know exactly what is going on.

I stand up abruptly and turn on the shower. I fumble around for a few moments trying to unzip my dress, and when I finally give in to the fact I need help, I crack the door and call for Seth.

"What is it, Alex?"

"I need your help."

He steps inside the bathroom with me, and I turn my back to him and pull my hair over my shoulder so he can get at the zipper. He slides the zipper slowly down my back, but the dress doesn't loosen. His fingers trace the top of the bodice, then I feel him undo the hook that is still holding the dress securely to me. It finally loosens; I have to use both my hands to prevent the gown from falling to the floor.

I stand motionless. With a tender touch, he begins running his fingers down the exposed skin of my back. *Ah!* It is so erotic it makes me quiver, and my entire body is instantly covered in goose bumps. I am definitely no longer cold. His soft, gentle touch sets my body on fire. I am so turned on. All I want to do is turn around, throw him to the ground, and make love to him right here on the bathroom floor. But I can't move. I can't even breathe.

He steps closer, and I can feel his body press up against mine. He wraps his arms around my waist, and in his velvety, smooth voice he asks, "Are you still cold?"

Holding tightly to my dress, I turn around in his arms so I can see his face. "No, I'm not cold at all. Quite the opposite actually," I reply in a whisper.

He smiles. The dimple on his left cheek makes my heart melt and his perfect smile makes me want to kiss him. But none of his godlike features can compare with his eyes. *His eyes!*

When Seth smiles, his eyes literally sparkle. I have never seen eyes so blue in all my life. Not even the most perfect sapphires can compare to the beauty of his eyes. He is so amazingly beautiful I can hardly believe he's real.

He leans his head down and kisses softly me on the lips. He raises a hand and gently cradles my head, just as he had done while we were dancing. His other hand is placed in the center of my back, pressing my body firmly into his. I let go of my dress and wrap my arms around his neck. I lace my fingers through his hair and let the moment take us where it may. What starts out as a soft, loving kiss quickly becomes one of passion and desire. The touch of his tongue to mine sends sparks through my body. At this moment, I am ready to give myself to him.

My breathing becomes rapid, and my blood races through my body. His hand grips my hair forcefully. The passion between us is unlike anything I have ever experienced. As his left hand slides through the open zipper of my dress and down the small of my back, I let out a gasp. *Oh my God! Is this really happening?*

His fingers lightly trace the lace of my panties, and just when I think he is going to sweep me up and carry me to the bedroom, a woman's voice calls from the other room. "Seth darling, are you here?"

The voice startles me, and I pull away from Seth, grabbing hold of my dress just before it can slide down and expose my breasts.

"Yes, Mother, we're here," Seth answers, smiling at me and giving me a little wink. "I will be out in a moment."

I just stand there, dying of embarrassment. I stare down at the floor, shaking my head, trying not to laugh. Almost getting caught—by his mother—making out is so ridiculous and comical, and we both know it.

Seth chuckles and kisses me on the forehead. "Why don't you take that shower? I'll be in the other room with my mother."

"Um…yeah. Okay."

"Take your time." He walks out and closes the door behind him.

I leave my gown crumpled in a pile on the floor, and I step into the shower. The warm water runs over my body; it feels wonderful. Despite the adrenaline that has been surging through my body, there is still a chill set deep in my bones. I can't be sure how long I had sat under that tree, but I know it was far longer than anyone should stay exposed to that kind of cold without the proper clothing. It won't surprise me if I ended up getting sick.

I wash my hair twice, just to make sure I get out all of the styling products Cynthia had used, then I turn off the water and reach for a towel. As I step out of the shower, I can hear Seth and his mother talking in the other room. They're speaking very low, so I can't make out what they were saying, but I think I hear her say my name.

I can't imagine how she must feel knowing her son is risking his life for a total stranger. If I were her, I would probably be trying to talk him out of it. I'd say, "Just let them have her" or "Tell her what she needs to know, give her a gun and the car, and let her find her own way out of this mess."

God, she probably hates me.

That thought brings tears to my eyes. A part of me wishes I had never gotten into that car with Patrick. I wish my parents had never given me my stupid bracelet. I wish I was at home with my grandparents. I let out a quiet sob as the thoughts wash over me.

But there is also a part of me that wants to be anywhere Seth is. I would risk the danger just to be near him. The way his touch sends sparks throughout my entire body, and knowing that he is willing to die for me is nothing short of amazing. I am completely in love with him. And I think that scares me more than the trouble I am in.

Overwhelmed by my thoughts, I begin to cry and cry hard. Sitting on the edge of the bathtub wrapped in a towel, I let my emotions overtake me. Seth must have been able to hear me from the other room because there is a sudden knock on the door.

"Alex, are you all right in there?" he asks.

Pulling myself together as much as I can, I answer, "I'm fine. I'll be out in a minute."

"Are you sure?" he presses.

"Yeah, Seth. Really. Just give me a minute, okay?"

He doesn't answer.

With a deep breath, I stand up and wipe the tears from my eyes. "Pull yourself together, Alexandra. This is no time to lose it," I whisper to myself.

I toss the towel over the edge of the bathtub and grab the jeans and the sweater laid out for me by Seth's mother. And to no surprise, everything fits perfectly. The steam from the shower has fogged up the entire room. With my hand, I swipe a path through the condensation on the mirror so I can see myself. I stare at my blurry image for a long moment. "Well, I look better than I did when I woke up this morning," I say out loud to myself, shrugging my shoulders.

I run a brush through my long wet hair and decide this isn't the time to worry about what I look like. However, with the way things are going with Seth, I don't want to look hideous, either. So I grab my bag and pull out my makeup. I apply just enough to look presentable. I take one last look at myself, tousle my wet hair a little, then open the door.

I stand in the doorway for a moment and watch Seth and his mother as they talk. They are sitting at the kitchen table, probably discussing what had happened the night before and sipping coffee. Once they notice me, they both stand up, and Seth walks over to me, putting his arm around my waist.

"Alex, I'd like you to meet my mother, Samantha Pierce."

"It's a pleasure to meet you, Mrs. Pierce," I say, extending my hand to her.

Ignoring my hand completely, Mrs. Pierce throws her arms around me and kisses me on the cheek. "I am so happy to see you again, Alex. It has been far too many years," she says, taking a step back. "And look at you! You are so lovely. You have grown up to look just like your mother."

"Thank you."

"Come sit down. You must be starved. Let me fix you something to eat." She grabs my hand, leading me to the table. Seth follows.

I sit down at the table, and Seth hands me a cup of coffee. I notice the gift-wrapped box has been moved and now sits at the other end of the table beneath the window. I make a point not to look at it.

I sip my coffee and watch as Seth and his mother dance around each other in the small kitchen area of the cabin. It is like watching a choreographed ballet. They anticipate each other's every move. When one needs a plate, the other is right there with it; when one is done with a pan or a bowl, the other begins washing it. It's amazing. It makes me smile.

Mrs. Pierce is incredibly lovely. Her long dark hair is pulled back away from her face and runs halfway down her back. She's tall and thin and also dressed as though she had just stepped out of a fashion magazine. The two of them together is a little intimidating. So much beauty in one place. I start fidgeting with my wet hair, trying to look a little more presentable, but I know it's a lost cause.

I look down, take another sip of coffee, and when I look up, Mrs. Pierce sets a plate of French toast and sausage in front of me. "I hope I make it as well as your grandmother does," she says, smiling at me.

There it is again. How did these people know so much about me? And how do they know things only the people who *really* know me can know?

"It looks delicious, Mrs. Pierce. Thank you."

Seth sits next to me with his plate full of food, as Mrs. Pierce poured herself another cup of coffee. We sit and eat without speaking for quite a while until finally Mrs. Pierce breaks the silence.

"So, Alex, tell me, how did you enjoy the Gala?"

I swallow hard. I quickly go over in my mind the best way to answer that question. I could tell her I had a lovely time until Mr. Wellington and his creepy band of Swordsmen cornered me at a table and totally freaked me out. Or I could tell her how Marcus Wellington thought he and I would make a good match and how the sound of his voice made me want to vomit.

Then again I could tell her how wonderful Yvette was and how much I enjoyed being transformed into a princess. And I could tell her how making out with her son on the dance floor was *the* most amazing experience of my life until psycho Sasha threw her temper tantrum and spoiled it. But before I can choose the correct response, Seth answers her question for me.

"Come on, Mother, how do you think she enjoyed it? It was stuffy and boring as it always is. And Marcus, of course, did everything he could to make her uncomfortable. Then, of course, there was Sasha. And how can I forget Mr. Wellington and the other men trying to intimidate her while completely wasted?" He takes a deep breath. "Oh yeah, and how about when I scared the hell out of her and made her run through the woods and sit under a tree for hours until I could lose Marcus and his merry band of idiots? I'm sure she had a blast," Seth snaps.

"All right, darling, I get the point. No need to get all worked up," she replies calmly.

"It wasn't all bad. There were some nice moments, although I have to admit most of it was pretty nerve wracking." I add, rubbing Seth's leg under the table.

"Well, I am just so pleased the two of you made it here safely," she says, smiling softly. "I'm sure you have a million questions, and Seth and I will do our best to answer as many as we can."

I look over to Seth, and for the second time since we met, I see sadness in his eyes.

I finish as much of my breakfast as I can, but the nervousness in my stomach doesn't leave much room for anything else. I thank Mrs. Pierce and carry my plate over to the sink.

"Just leave it in the sink, my dear. I will take care of it later. Why don't you have a seat near the fireplace? Would you like some more coffee?" she asks.

"No thank you ma'am," I answer walking over to sofa and taking a seat.

Seth too takes his plate to the sink and then comes over and sits beside me. He puts his arm around me, and I leaned into his chest. The sound of the fire crackling and the snowy view from the windows almost make me forget about everything that has happened.

Without warning, my mind suddenly focuses on my grandparents and then on Chase. I jump forward and gasp. "My phone! Seth, where is my cell phone?"

With an apologetic look on his face, he very calmly replies, "Alex, I had to dump your cell phone in the water. The Order would be able to track us if we kept your phone so I had to get rid of it."

"My grandparents! Barb! And—" I stop before I can say Chase's name. "I haven't talked to them since Patrick picked me up yesterday. I didn't even call them at midnight. They are probably worried sick about me. I have to call them!"

Pulling me back into his arms, Seth replies in a soothing voice, "My mother has called your grandparents and told them you and some friends decided to go skiing for the weekend and you accidentally left your phone behind. She assured them once you realized you didn't have your phone with you, you would call them from the ski lodge. She also asked that they pass the message along to Barb and Chase as well."

Great! He knows about Chase. What was I thinking? Of course, he knows about Chase. He was at Chase's Christmas party and saw us together, and I'm sure he followed me every time I went out with Chase and every time I went over to his apartment. I don't know what to do. I love Chase, I really do, but the way I feel with Seth is unlike anything I have ever felt before.

I lean my head back on Seth's shoulder and let out a deep sigh.

"What is it?" he asks.

"Nothing," I lie. I don't want to talk about Chase, especially in front of his mother. That is a conversation best left for another time.

"Tell me," he insists.

There are so many things going through my mind; finding something else to talk about, other than Chase, is going to be easy, so I start with important question number 1.

"What is so important about my bracelet?"

Mrs. Pierce is now sitting in the chair across from us, and as soon as I mention the bracelet, her face lights up. She asks, "Oh, Alex, may I see it?"

I lean forward and push up the sleeve of my sweater and hold my arm out to her. She takes my hand in hers, and with a soft touch, she examines each key slowly and deliberately.

"I have never seen all the keys together before. It really does make a lovely bracelet."

"Thank you," I say, leaning back into Seth's arms. "Now could one of you tell me what they mean?"

I look at Seth. He is staring at his mother. I turn my attention back to Mrs. Pierce. She is nodding to Seth as though she is giving him permission to explain. Or maybe it's encouragement, I can't tell.

I turn my focus back to Seth. Sadness is still in his blue eyes, and it breaks my heart. He softly caresses my face and fakes a little smile.

"Seth, please. Tell me what they mean," I beg.

"All right," he says, sounding defeated. "Do you remember the story I started to tell you last night in the gazebo?"

I nod.

"I told you how my father was a legacy so it was already determined he would become a member of Swords and Skulls. Well, now let me tell you how your father got involved. I don't know how much your grandparents have told you about your father, Ben, and I don't really know how much they really knew about him after he went away to college. But what you need to understand is your father was an incredibly brilliant man. He majored in biochemical engineering and was at the top of his class. By the time he was a junior in 1984, the government had begun to take a special interest in him.

"Due to your father's incredible academic achievements, and the fact he was my father Jackson's best friend, The Order had seriously began to consider offering him a place among the new class of Swordsmen. When they caught wind the government was interested in your father, well, that pretty much sealed the deal.

"Now what you need to understand is The Order isn't like a fraternity. It's not about keg parties and adolescent college activities. No. The Order grooms our nation's future leaders. Generations of men have been put into positions of power, whether in government, law, the military, and even the media, simply because they have been Swordsmen. For better or worse, our country is the way it is greatly due to The Order of Swords and Skulls."

How can any of what he is telling me be possible? Can millions of Americans really be blind to the fact that the freedom and democracy our forefathers fought for is nothing but a joke? My face gets warm with anger. The corners of my mouth turn down slightly, and my eyebrows pull together as Seth continues.

"To ensure that Ben would accept an offer from The Order, Jack was instructed to do everything he could to 'sell' Ben on the advantages of becoming a Swordsman. For months, Jack sang the praises of The Order and how he hoped, come April, the two of them would both get tapped and then they would become brothers for life."

"Wait. 'Tapped'? What does that mean?" I interrupt.

Without skipping a beat, Seth continues, "Every April 25th, the current Swordsmen class roams campus at midnight and taps prospective new members on the shoulder and asks them if they accept or deny. If they accept, a black hood is placed over their head and they are taken to the Crypt, the Sword and Skulls headquarters on campus."

Seth pauses for a moment, collecting his thoughts, then with a very serious and somewhat frightening look on his face, he goes on. "Alex, I want you to know what I'm about to tell you can easily get me killed. Revealing the secrets of The Order is an offense punishable by death. Most of the wives and the children of Swordsmen do not know what I'm about to tell you. Do you understand?"

Frightened, I just nod.

"Once the prospects are taken to the Crypt, they are led down into the dungeon. Once there, they are stripped naked and made to stand in a circle facing each other. Then the initiation ceremony begins. The chairman and as many alumni as are able attend, all dressed in black hooded cloaks, observe as the current Swordsmen class place the tip of a sword into each prospect's back, just between their shoulder blades. Then the chairman asks if they are willing to trust The Order with their lives. If they say yes, they are then instructed to take one step back. In doing so, the sword pierces their skin, and blood begins to run down their backs."

I gasp.

"Once each new member has been pierced, their wounds are then sealed by burning the Sword and Skulls crest into their skin. Once they are branded, they are Swordsmen for life. There is no going back.

"The fifteen men are then given red robes and taken to the confessional. There, each new member is asked a series of questions they are required to answer with complete honestly. The questions asked are about things that most people wouldn't even tell their best friend. They are incredibly personal and embarrassing questions. By answering the questions honestly, it proves the men have put complete trust in their brothers. They not only trust them with their deepest and darkest secrets, but they also trust them with their lives. If it is found out later someone has lied, no matter how small or insignificant the lie, the punishment is severe."

As I sit there nestled in Seth's embrace and listen to him tell me this story, I can't help but shudder. I know he can feel my body shaking, but I can't pull myself together enough to make it stop. What he is telling me is so outrageous. Who in their right mind would subject themselves to such madness?

I look at Seth's mother. She is just sitting there, holding on to her coffee and staring out the window. Clearly none of what Seth is telling me is news to her. Whether it is my uncontrollable shaking or the fact I have hardly said a word, Seth can sense I need a break. "Come on, Alex. Let's get some fresh air," he says, brushing a strand of hair from my face.

I slide on my boots and throw on my coat, watching as Seth leans down to whisper something in his mother's ear. He kisses her lovingly on the cheek then comes over and takes me by the hand. We walk outside into the cold Canadian air. Without a cloud in the sky, the sun is very bright. It bounces off of the snow as if it was a crystal blanket, creating millions of tiny rainbows. It is so beautiful. Seth puts his arm around my shoulder and pulls me close to him. I wrap my arm around his waist, and once again, I can feel the small bulge sticking up from his waistline.

He smiles at me and softly kisses my lips. "I want to show you one of my favorite places," he says, leading me towards the tress behind the small cabin.

We walk for a while without saying a word. My mind is still consumed with all the information Seth had just given me. I can't wrap my head around any of it. From everything my grandparents had told me about my father, becoming a member of some secret society seemed complete ridiculous, which makes me wonder, can anyone say *no* to The Order? Even if my father hadn't wanted to become a Swordsman, did he really have a choice?

We walk out of the trees and into a large clearing. Stretched out in front of us is the most breathtakingly beautiful winter wonderland I have ever seen. Hundreds of snow-covered trees lined the banks of an enormous frozen lake, which seems to go on for miles. Crystal icicles sparkle in the sunlight as they hang from their branches, and as if written by Dickens, two cardinals, one a deep crimson, the other a soft reddish brown, chase each other over the ice-covered water, coming to rest on a branch just a few yards away from where we stand.

Off to our left, about twenty feet from the water's edge, is a large tree trunk lying on its side, with its roots reaching up toward the sky. As we get closer, I can see that a bench has been carved into its side, facing the water.

Seth leans down, brushes off the snow, then asks me to have a seat. I comply with his request in silence and stare out over the water. The calm serenity of our surroundings can't slow my mind.

And there is not enough beauty in the world that can make what Seth is about to tell me any easier to hear.

"You're very quiet," Seth says, breaking the silence.

"I'm sorry. I'm just so overwhelmed by everything I'm not sure what to say," I reply.

"Alex, the reason I brought you out here is because I wanted to finish telling you the story away from my mother. It is too hard for her to hear what I am about to tell you, mostly because it involves one of her sorority sisters, and she blames herself for what happened."

The puzzled look on my face is enough for Seth to continue without a response from me.

"I told you how each new member is required to confess their deepest darkest secrets in the confessional. Well, one of the questions asked is about their sexual history. In the 80s, most of the men were pretty sexually active, especially the ones who had girlfriends, like our fathers. But there always seems to be one or two who have very little experience. So to help these guys increase their 'count,' The Order throws a spring barbeque.

"Now there is only one place in the Crypt where outsiders are allowed. That is the patio and barbeque area located at the back of the house. The inside of the Crypt is completely off limits to anyone who is not part of The Order or part of the staff. To make sure no outsiders make their way inside to snoop around, the entire house is wired with surveillance cameras. I mean every room—bathrooms, bedrooms, closets, everywhere. Maintaining the secrets of The Order is priority number 1."

The way Seth speaks it seems as though he has not only heard the stories about being a member of The Order, but he has personal experience with it as well. This bothers me, but I say nothing and let him continue.

"Preparing for the spring barbeque, each current member and each new member are required to invite five girls. This will increase the odds for the less experienced members to get lucky.

Since Ben and Jack both had girlfriends, they asked them if they would invite some of their single girlfriends to the party. My mother invited some of her sorority sisters. Now just so you understand, with the rumors that fly around campus about The Order and the unspoken notoriety that came with being a Swordsman, an outsider who was invited to one of these parties counts themselves as one of the privileged, and most people jump at the chance to attend.

"On the night of the party, it was made clear the priority was to make sure the less-experienced members were to get laid no matter how it happened. This meant a lot of alcohol was served, and if there was a girl who seemed to be of particular interest to one of the said members, if need be, the girl would be slipped something to, we'll say, get her in the mood."

My mouth drops open as I listen to what Seth is telling me. Basically, if the girls didn't go willingly, then they were drugged then date raped. I am horrified.

"I'm sorry I have to tell you this story but you need to understand everything." He takes both of my hands in his and raises them to his face, gently kissing them. I can see in his eyes it is difficult for him to continue. He wants to spare me the horror of what is left of the story but he forces himself to go on. "Do you remember the six men that Mr. Wellington introduced you to at the end of the evening?" he asks.

I nod.

"To the surprise of everyone, two of those men happened to be virgins when they were branded Swordsmen."

"Which two?" I ask.

"Parker Ashcroft and Lowell Ferguson."

I think back, trying to remember what the two men looked like, but I can't see them in my mind. There was a bald man with a mustache. Another was quite heavy and wore glasses. There was a very handsome man with salt-and-pepper hair. And there was one who had a very large scar on his neck I could only see because he had taken off his bowtie and unbuttoned his top button. I can't remember the other two.

"I can't remember what they look like."

"Lowell Ferguson was the bald man with the cheesy mustache, and Parker Ashcroft was the rather thin man with brown hair, and I'm not sure if you noticed it, but he had a scar on his neck."

"I remember him. I remember wondering how he got that scar."

"I will tell you how," Seth says cryptically. "On the night of the party, Parker had his eye on one of my mother's sorority sisters, Carolyn Peters. Carolyn was a very shy, very pretty girl who only came to the party because her best friend, Tina Mason, asked her to. Carolyn spent most of the evening alone, nursing a beer and watching Tina flirt with every man in site. Parker, being rather shy himself, found her lovely and tried to talk to her. She wasn't very receptive to Parker's advances, but he kept trying.

"By the end of the night, Lowell had 'encouraged' Tina to accompany him to his room. Lowell was given permission to take his 'date' to his room so he could complete his mission and also because Tina would not remember any of it the next day due to her intoxication. Parker, on the other hand, did not have the luck that Lowell did. Carolyn kept refusing the drinks Parker offered her, and by the time Tina had disappeared with Lowell, she was ready to go home.

"Most of the other Swordsmen had either gone off to bed or had left to get laid themselves. The Swordsmen that remained, Maxwell Wellington, Preston Walker, Walter Abbott, Philip Chamberlain, and Edwin Hollister, decided they were going to help Parker with Carolyn. So Max fixed Carolyn a drink, which she accepted.

"They invited Carolyn inside the Crypt to wait for Tina. They sat around with her, making polite conversation and waiting for the drug Max had slipped in her drink to kick in. Finally, Carolyn passed out."

My mind races with images of what those men did to that poor girl, even before Seth can tell me. I hide my face in my hands, fighting back tears, while Seth chokes out what happened next.

"They laid Carolyn down on the couch, lifted her skirt, and took off her panties. They all stood around and stared at her, waiting for Parker to complete his mission, but Parker froze. The guys started giving him grief and calling him a wuss and telling him he would be a disgrace to The Order if he didn't go through with it. Finally, Parker couldn't take it anymore, so he opened his fly and climbed on top of her." Seth pauses for a minute and lifts my face so he can see me. I'm crying. "Are you all right? Do you want me to stop?"

I do want him to stop, but I don't want to prolong this story any longer than I need to, so I tell him to keep going.

"Okay." He pulls me closer to him. "While Parker was raping the poor girl, the other guys stood around watching and cheering him on. With all of the commotion, Carolyn began to wake up."

I gasp.

"Once she realized what was happening to her, she started to scream and to fight back, but the guys won't let Parker stop, so they held her down and covered her mouth. When Parker finally finished, the guys loosened their grip on her. Carolyn managed to free one arm, and she reached for the first thing she could grab—the glass Max had given her. With the glass in her hand, she took a swing at Parker, and it broke across his neck, impaling him with a large shard. Carolyn took hold of the shard and tore it across Parker's neck, causing him to start bleeding uncontrollably.

"Walter Abbott was a premed student and immediately went to Parker's aid. Knowing because of what just happened they couldn't call an ambulance, it was imperative that Walter stop Parker's bleeding and stitch him up. While Walter was attending to Parker, the other guys tried to deal with a crazed Carolyn, who was trying to get free. She was kicking and scratching and biting with every opportunity. Philip decided to put a pillow over her face to stop her from screaming and biting. The others sat on her arms and legs to stop her from moving. And finally she did."

By this time, the tears are streaming down my face. I can't believe what I am hearing. I stare at Seth, petrified of what he was going to say next.

"She was dead."

With that one sentence, I completely lose it. I bury my face into his shoulder and begin to sob. Once I calm down, he kisses me sweetly on the forehead and asks me if I want him to go on. I nod.

"As soon as the guys realized Carolyn was dead, they began to panic. Walter had Parker's gash under control, but they still had a dead girl in the Crypt. So they did the only thing they could think of. They called George McAllister, The Order's chairman in 1984.

"McAllister was famous for living outside the law. He felt, because of who he was, and the connections he had the laws didn't apply to him. He made a point of instilling that ideal in the Swordsmen beneath him, so once he heard what had happened in the Crypt that night, he was on his way with his goons to clean up the mess.

"By this time Ben and Jack, were on their way back to the Crypt after taking their girlfriends home. And when they walked through the door, they walked right into the middle of a disaster. Max, who had always been the 'leader,' immediately took the two of them aside and told them what had happened. Neither Ben nor Jack wanted to have anything to do with what was going on, but once you are a Swordsman, what happens to one happens to them all, so whether they liked it or not, they were involved. A few of the guys had wrapped Carolyn up in a sheet and bagged up anything that belonged to her and anything that had blood on it. The others sanitized the room to get rid of Parker's blood.

"Now remember Tina, Carolyn's best friend, was passed out upstairs with Lowell. Tina had been given the same dose as

Carolyn, and she was still out cold. What the guys didn't realize was Carolyn didn't pass out because of the drug Max had put in her drink—she had passed out because she was tired. She had only drank a little of what Max had given her, so she didn't get the full dose. That is why she woke up so easily when Parker was on top of her.

"While everyone else was cleaning, Max had sent Ben and Jack outside to wait for McAllister to show up and keep a lookout for any other Swordsmen who might be getting back late. They wanted their secret known by as few Swordsmen as possible, and the count was already at eight.

"By the time McAllister and his men got to the Crypt, it was almost morning. The guys who were asleep in the Crypt would be waking up soon, and the guys who had slept somewhere else would start coming back, so they had to move fast. McAllister ordered Ben and Jack to stay outside and keep watch while he and his men took care of the crime scene. While Jack kept watch out front, Ben had made his way around to the back of the Crypt and watched as McAllister's men tossed Carolyn's body in the trunk of their car like it was nothing more than a bag of garbage."

Seth pauses again for a moment and studies my face. With a tender touch, he wipes away the tears that continue to roll down my cheeks and then kisses me gently.

"How are you?" Concern shows in his beautiful blue eyes. "Are you cold?"

"I'm all right," I reply nestling in closer to his chest.

Everything around us is so picturesque, and under any other circumstance, being here with Seth would be quite romantic. I wonder if we ever came back to this place if I would be able to appreciate its beauty or will it always remind me of Carolyn.

"Okay," he says, squeezing me tighter then continuing with the story. "When the sun finally came up, Ben and Jack were ordered back inside and they found Lowell had joined the group. Now the count was up to nine. Lowell had been told what happened and was instructed to get Tina, who was still passed out, out of the Crypt immediately and to take her home. Once he returned, all nine guys were called down to the confessional where McAllister was waiting for them.

"McAllister, in his most intimidating tone, instructed them they were to tell none of the other Swordsmen what had happened. When the police came around asking about Carolyn—and they would—they were all to stick to the same story: Carolyn left when the party ended and no one had seen her since. He also told them her body and all the evidence would be disposed of at an undisclosed location, so none of them could be persuaded or coerced into divulging the location. He warned them, once he left the Crypt that day, no one was to speak a word about what had happened—ever. 'This never happened,' he told them. 'I was never here.'

"He threatened that even years down the road, if any of them even so much as hinted at what had happened in his presence, there would be consequences. 'I have cleaned up your mess. Now it is up to you to maintain the integrity of The Order and keep your mouths shout! Clearly, I know how to make someone disappear, and I won't hesitate to do the same to one of you if you even think about opening your mouths!'

"Now what McAllister didn't know is while Ben and Jack were outside keeping watch, they decided they were not going to let being in the wrong place at the wrong time dictate the rest of their lives. Jack had grown up in the ways of The Order, so he knew exactly what the repercussions could be for knowing such a secret and what kind of blackmail could come their way down the road. So they came up with a plan to protect themselves.

"Although The Order was built on trust and loyalty, I don't think anyone in The Order has ever truly trusted another. It's more like a 'You scratch my back and I'll keep your dirty little secret' kind of mentality. It is really quite frightening." His arms stiffen a little around me.

"So after McAllister made his threats and was getting ready to leave, Jack and Ben slipped out and hid in Ben's car. When McAllister and his men drove away with Carolyn in the trunk, they followed them. Trying to keep enough distance between the two cars so as not to be noticed, they almost lost McAllister twice, but they managed to follow them all the way to the Swords and Skulls boat dock. They watched McAllister's men load Carolyn's body and the rest of the evidence onto one of the boats and then take off for the island."

"Wait! You mean Carolyn's body is buried on the island?" I interrupt him, horrified.

"Yes…it is, Alex." His voice is somber.

"Where?" I shriek.

"I'll get to that," he says. "Now they very well couldn't follow McAllister's men out to the island, so they decided to wait until the spring solstice, which was in just a couple weeks, to look for the body.

"On their drive back to the Crypt, they discussed how they would pull off their plan. They knew every room in the Crypt had video surveillance and that all the tapes were cataloged and kept in storage. So they decided that once everything calmed down, they would steal the tapes. They couldn't wait too long to make their move because they didn't want to give someone else the opportunity to come up with the same idea, so the decision was made to move on it that night."

He pauses again. I have begun to shiver. We have been sitting there for hours, and the sun had moved behind the trees. Without the direct sunlight the cold set in and it was time to head back to the cabin. And I think Seth can tell that I need another break from the story.

"Come on, baby. Let's get you inside. You're shivering."

"Okay," I whisper.

Walking back into the cabin, I notice it's empty. Seth's mother is gone.

171

"Where is your mother?" I ask.

"She had to go home. With you and me missing, The Order will be checking in on her to see if she has seen us," he replies, sliding my coat off my shoulders and tossing it on the chair. "They don't know about this place, so we should be safe here for a few days."

Days? I can't stay here for days! What about my grandparents and Barb? They think I'm away skiing with friends; I need to at least call them. And I really want to hear my grandparent's voices. I don't know what The Order will do to them to try to find me, so I need to know they're all right, and I want them to know I am as well.

And then there's Chase. I don't even want to think about how pissed off he must be. I know he is probably freaking out, and I don't want him to worry about me, either.

"Seth?" I say, in a soft voice.

He turns and looks at me. "What is it, Alex?" *God he's gorgeous.* Every time he says my name, butterflies fill my stomach.

"I need to call my grandparents so they know that I'm all right. And I need to call…" I can't let myself say his name. As long as we didn't talk about him then, for me, it's like Seth doesn't know he exists.

"Chase," Seth says, finishing my sentence.

I nod and stare at the floor. I can't look at him. Seth is risking his life to keep me safe, and I have to call my boyfriend. I feel like such a bitch.

"It's all right, Alex. I know all about Chase," he says, lifting my chin so we were looking into each other's eyes. "You've had a life all these years, and Chase has been a part of it. He's a good man, and he really cares for you."

I turn and walk away from him. Standing in front of the fireplace, I try to stop myself from crying again. I feel like that is all I've done since Seth and I met.

It is so confusing listening to him talk about Chase. Chase is a great guy and spending the past two weeks with him made me fall in love him all over again but being here and feeling the way I do about Seth makes me question my feelings for Chase.

In all the years I have known Chase, I have never felt for him the way I feel for Seth. I don't know what to do. A tear escapes the corner of my eye, and I shiver just a bit. Seth comes up behind me, wraps his arms around me, and pulls me into his body. It feels as though our bodies fused together and become one. We stand there for a long while saying nothing. The only sounds are the crackling of the fire and the swirling wind blowing outside.

I close my eyes and let myself become consumed by Seth's embrace. I wish we could stay in this place forever. I wish The Order and all the danger we're in would just go away, and Seth and I can stay in this cabin forever, shutting out the rest of the world.

Breaking the silence with his soft velvety voice, he asks me if I'm hungry. I'm not. I shrug then turn to face him. He kisses me gently on the forehead and takes my hand, leading me over to the kitchen table.

"Come on, you have to eat. We have a lot ahead of us, and you need to keep your strength up. Besides, my mother put a roast in the oven before she left. It should be done soon, and she makes the best roast in the world." He smiles his perfect smile, making my heart flutter.

He is like a little boy when he talks about his mom. It's so sweet. I can't help but smile back at him. "Well, how can I pass up the best roast in the world? Let's eat!"

Secrets

While Seth attends to the roast, I set the table. I glance at the gift that has been sitting there since we arrived. It's wrapped exactly like the box Seth had left for me on Christmas day—the one that held my twentieth key—except this box is much bigger than the key box. I assume the gift is for me, but not wanting to seem presumptuous, I decide to pretend as though it isn't there. If it is for me, Seth will give it to me when he's ready.

Everything looks and smells delicious, but I'm not hungry. I take a few small bites so not to appear rude, but for the most part, I just push the food around the plate. Seth notices.

"Please talk to me, Alex." His voice is sad, but his face is soft and sweet. "Tell me what you're thinking. I've been doing almost all the talking since we met. I'm sure you have a ton of questions."

He's right. I have a million questions running through my head, and I don't even know where to begin. I take a drink of water, clear my throat, and blurt out the first one that pops in my mind. "Why didn't our...err...Ben and Jack go to the police?"

With that one question, his sweet expression changes, his eyes darken, and his mouth turns down; it startles me a little. It's like it hurts him to answer my question.

"Alex, the one thing you *have* to understand about The Order is they are truly *above* the law. If they would have gone to the police, The Order would have had them killed the moment they stepped out of the police station."

I stare at him with my eyes bulging and my mouth wide open.

"The Order's brotherhood includes members of the CIA, FBI, military, and the police. All of whom have sworn an oath to put The Order above anything or anyone else. And if anyone should betray The Order, they are immediately punished. Punishments range anywhere from blackballing, removing a Swordsman's fortune, kidnapping loved ones, and, without hesitation, death.

"However, if you remain loyal to The Order, they will make sure your wealth grows beyond your dreams. They will make sure you reach high levels of power and influence and your family will be taken care of should something happen to you. For example, Parker Ashcroft is actually Senator Ashcroft from Maryland. And if he keeps in line, The Order will make sure he is president one day."

"Wait, the man who raped that poor girl is one day going to be the president?" I'm horrified.

"That's the plan," Seth replies. "Which is why we must keep you and your keys safe. The Order will stop at nothing to get their hands on what your keys are hiding. We have to get to it first."

"Seth, I don't understand. What do my keys have to do with Parker Ashcroft?"

He takes a deep breath and continues with the horrifying story he had been telling me earlier. "When Ben and Jack got back to the Crypt, they were immediately confronted by Max, demanding to know where they had been. They told him that with everything going on, they needed to clear their heads so they went for a drive. Max didn't really buy it, but he couldn't prove they were lying, so he let it go, but not without threatening them. He told them if they were planning on telling anyone, they better think twice because McAllister wouldn't hesitate to make them disappear along with Carolyn. And they knew he was right."

Taking a bite of food, he looks at my plate. "Don't you like it?" he asks.

"Yes, it's delicious. I just don't have much of an appetite," I admit.

"Please, Alex. You need to eat. Do it for me?" His eyes sparkle as they look deep into mine. I pick up my fork and do as he asks.

As I eat, he continues with his dreadful story. "Max, ever the alpha dog, barked at Ben and Jack to go get ready for dinner and to be sure they acted normally around the other Swordsmen. And of course, they did as they were told.

"With all that had happened, they had completely forgotten it was Sunday. That was going to make it harder for them to put their plan in motion. Sunday is the night all the Swordsmen come together for dinner to discuss upcoming events and just hang out.

"After dinner, all the guys were hanging out, having a good time. Even the guys who had just killed a girl the night before seemed to be in good spirits, but Max kept a close eye on Ben and Jack. He could tell they were having a problem living with the secret.

"Halfway through the evening, Ben and Jack went outside to 'get some air,' but really they wanted to talk about how they were going to get their hands on the video tapes. They knew doing it that night was out of the question, especially due to the fact Max was keeping such a close eye on them, so they decided to wait a few days to let things blow over a bit. It was obvious the other guys were not having the same difficulty with killing someone. Even though neither Ben nor Jack was directly involved, they seemed to be the only ones feeling guilty with what they knew.

"Shortly after they made their way outside to discuss their plan, Max appeared from the shadows. He was trying to gauge whether or not Ben and Jack were going to be a problem. Max knew Jack was fully aware of the consequences that came with crossing The Order, but he wanted to make sure Ben truly understood what would happen to him if he betrayed his brothers.

The First Time

By this point, I am so emotionally exhausted I can barely keep my eyes open. I have cried more in this one day than I had in the past ten years. I'm totally spent. I sit there in Seth's arms listening to the fire crackle until I feel myself starting to fall asleep. I let the feeling take me.

I slept for what felt like only seconds when Seth stands up with me in his arms.

"Where are you taking me?" I ask, in a groggy voice.

"I'm going to put you to bed. You need to get some sleep. We have a busy few days ahead of us," he answers, walking toward the bedroom.

"No, wait!" I demand, much more awake now. I want to spend more time with Seth. I want to stay in his arms. I don't want to go back to sleep.

"Alex, you really do need to get some rest as I do. We have a lot to do, and we are both going to need to be well rested." He kicks the bedroom door open with his foot, carries me inside, and gently sets me down on the edge of the bed. "Let me get the fire going in here so you don't get cold, then I will let you get some rest," he says, crouching down, striking a match.

"Where are you going to sleep?" I ask.

"I'm going to sleep out on the sofa. There are some pajamas for you in the dresser there and some fresh clothes for tomorrow. Is there anything else you need, Alex?"

As he stands up, the soft glow from the fire illuminates his face, and it takes my breath away. He is so beautiful. I shake my head in response to his question unable to speak. But what I really want to say is, *Yes, Seth. I need you. I need you to stay here with me. To hold me. To make love to me. To make everything else in the world disappear.* But I say nothing.

"All right then. Sweet dreams, my beautiful girl." He kisses me on the forehead and leaves the room closing the door behind him.

I lie back on the bed and stare at the ceiling for a while before finally getting up to change my clothes. I pull open the top drawer of the dresser and find a pair of pink fleece pajama bottoms and a pink cotton tank top. As I change, I look at myself in the mirror. All the crying has made my face look swollen and red. That's great. Seth looks as though he stepped out of GQ magazine, and I've spend the last day and a half looking like I stepped out of a horror comic.

I walk over and slowly open the bedroom door, praying it doesn't creek and startle Seth. I peek my head out. The soft glow of the fire illuminates the perfect lines of his face as he sleeps peacefully. I quietly walk the three feet from the bedroom to the bathroom and close the door behind me. I splash cold water on my face, hoping to reduce the redness and the puffiness. It helps a little. Then I brush my teeth and run a comb through my hair. I feel somewhat human again. After I'm finished, I walk over to the door and hold the knob in my hand for a moment. I don't want to go back into the bedroom. I want to lie down next to Seth on the couch. I want to feel his body next to mine, to kiss his perfect mouth, to touch his skin, but a part of me is also afraid to do any of those things.

Sigh! Slowly, I open the door and take a step back toward the bedroom.

"Alex, is everything all right?"

I gasp and jump at the sound of Seth's voice. "Oh! I'm sorry, did I wake you? I was trying to be quiet," I answer, trying to adjust my eyes to the darkness of the room.

"No, not at all." His voice is like silk.

As my eyes focus, I can see that Seth is no longer lying on the couch. He's standing over by the window in the shadows, looking outside. "Is there something out there?" I ask, afraid of the answer.

"No, I'm just making sure everything is as it should be. You can never be too careful."

Turning away from the window, Seth steps into the light of the fire. My heart races. He is standing there in nothing but a pair of sweatpants. I gasp again.

"What is it, Alex?"

I feel my face flush. The site of him sets me on fire. Embarrassed, I just shake my head and look down toward the floor.

Gracefully gliding over to me, he wraps his arms around my waist and holds me against his warm, naked chest. "Tell me what's on your mind," he says, kissing my forehead. I don't say anything. Placing a single finger under my chin, he gently lifts my face to look at him. As our eyes meet, he pleads, "Please, tell me." His voice is filled with worry.

I close my eyes and, with a deep breath, breathe him in.

"Do you even know how insanely beautiful you are? I mean, it's like you're not real. Look at you! Your body looks like it's sculpted out of marble. Your eyes are like sapphires, and your smile, oh my God, your smile is like a gift from God. And every time you touch me, I feel as though that if I died at that moment, my life would have been worth living just to feel your touch."

I slowly open one eye to see if he has any reaction to what has just spilled out of my mouth. I mean, none of what I just said has to surprise him. He probably hears it all the time. I'm sure Sasha has mentioned it before. There's no wonder she wanted to kill me when she saw us kiss. Who couldn't feel that way about him?

Seth bursts into laughter and kisses the top of my head, trying to muffle his amusement.

Was what I said funny? Does he hear things like that so often that it's comical to him? Now I'm a little annoyed. I open both eyes and stare at him as he tries to compose himself.

"I'm sorry, I don't mean to laugh" he says once his laughter subsides.

I scowl.

"Don't look at me like that. I'm not laughing because of what you said."

"Looks like it to me," I snap.

He lets go of my waist and places both hands on my face, no longer laughing.

"Alex, everything you see when you look at me and the way you feel when I touch you is exactly how I feel about you. You are the most beautiful woman I have ever seen. Your skin is like silk. You're eyes too are like precious sapphires. Your hair is like a ray of sunshine. You have the body of an angel. Your smile brightens up the room, and when you touch me, my life feels complete." He pauses for a moment, and just as a tear rolls down my cheek, he says the words that would change my life forever. "I love you, Alexandra."

I can't breathe. I close my eyes and feel his lips touch mine. Sparks fly through my body. Wrapping my arms around his neck, I run my fingers through his hair and let my body fall into his. As our lips part, the touch of his tongue to mine causes me to let out a soft moan. *Ah!* My body is screaming for him to touch me.

With one swift move, he sweeps me up into his arms and carries me back into the bedroom and closes the door behind us, never breaking away from our kiss. Our passion grows more intense as he stands holding me in his arms. I fisted his hair through my fingers, and the intensity of our kiss grows, making me shudder.

Pulling away slightly, he asks, "Are you cold?"

"No," I whisper. *Cold! Are you kidding me?* I feel as though my body is on fire, and all I want is for him to put the flames out with his kisses.

Setting me down so I am standing in front of him, he gently places his hand on the small of my back and pulls my body into his. I lay my head on his chest and wrap my arms around him, lightly tracing over the muscles of his back. This time, *he* shivers at *my* touch. This makes me smile. Tenderly, he begins running his hand up the back of my neck and into my hair. Gripping it softly, he pulls my head back and turns it so I'm looking up into his angelic face. He gently glides his thumb across my lips, and he stares intensely into my eyes, his desire palpable. I run my fingers down the curves of his chest then down his perfectly sculpted abs until I reach the top of his pants. I stop breathing, and my hands began to shake a little.

Releasing my hair, he places his hands on my waist. Never taking his eyes off of mine, he slowly lifts up my shirt. He stops just below my breasts. His breathing is heavier now. Without saying a word, I raise my arms above my head, and without hesitation, he slides my shirt up over my head letting it fall to the floor.

Softly, as though I might break, he traces the curves of my body just as I had traced his. With one hand on each side of my neck, he lightly slides his fingertips down, brushing them over my shoulders then down across the top of my chest. Pausing for a moment, he lets out a soft breath. Never taking his eyes off mine, he gently runs his fingers down my breasts and around my nipples. My body is screaming!

Continuing their journey, his fingers make their way down my belly. As he comes to the top of my pants, instead of stopping, he slowly slides both my pants and my panties down to the floor. Sweeping my naked body up into his arms, he kisses me sweetly and places me on the bed. I watch him as he stands for a moment admiring me. Lying naked in front of him is incredibly erotic. I feel sexy. I smile up at him then I reach out my hand and tuck one finger into the top of his sweatpants, giving them a little tug. A perfect smile spreads across his face, then he slides off his pants.

The light flickering from the fire dances off his perfect body and sends a surge of desire through me. It is unlike anything I have ever felt before, and all I can think is how badly I want to feel his naked body next to mine. I grab hold of his hand, pulling him toward me. His eyes burn into me as he slowly lays his perfect body on top of mine.

We make love for hours. Every touch, every kiss, is magic. Our bodies fit together like puzzle pieces as if we were created to fit together. I have never had an experience that has made me feel the way I do when I'm with Seth. He's not only my protector; he's my soul mate. He's what's been missing in my life.

I have always felt as though I'm half of who I'm supposed to be. I've never felt whole. I thought it was because I never knew my parents, but now I know that's not it. Seth fills the void I have lived with all my life. He completes me, and I know now my world has been changed forever.

As we lie naked next to each other, staring into each other's eyes, I can't help but smile. I am the happiest I have ever been. At this moment, no one is chasing us, no one wants to hurt us. There is no one else in the world but us. I finally know what bliss is.

"What are you smiling at?" he asks, smirking back at me.

"Nothing," I say, girlishly hiding my face in the pillow.

"You are amazing, Alex. Do you know that?"

"No. What do you mean?" I ask.

"I have watched you turn into this amazing young woman. You have so much beauty and grace, and I have always hoped that when we finally met as adults, you would feel for me the way I have felt for you for so long." He startles me as he gets out of bed and walks over to the door. "I'll be right back."

I stare as his amazingly beautiful body walks out of the light of the fire and into the darkness of the kitchen. When he returns, he is carrying a serving tray with a bowl of fruit and two glasses of water. Also on the tray is the present that has been sitting on the kitchen table since we arrived.

"I thought you might be a little hungry," he says. "Also, this is for you. It's from my mother." He hands me the beautifully wrapped box that I have been dying to open since I saw it.

I lift off the top and pull back the tissue. Inside is a beautiful silver picture frame that holds a picture of two families, our families.

"This was the last picture taken of us all before your parents died. It was your third birthday." He strokes my hair and waits for my reaction.

My eyes instantly fill with tears again. I try to fight them back, but one escapes and splashes down onto the glass before I can stop it.

"Don't cry, Alex. This should be a happy memory for you. Do you remember it?"

Brushing away another tear, I answer, "I don't know."

"Look closely." He points to the bear I am holding in my arms.

"That's Freddy," I announce with a smile of recognition. In the picture, I am sitting on my father's lap, clutching a small brown teddy bear I named Freddy.

Freddy has been my most favorite toy since as long as I can remember. I took him everywhere with me when I was a kid. I even thought about taking him to college with me, but I wanted to appear grown up and sophisticated, so I had left him behind at home. But whenever I'm home, other than Sam, Freddy is always next to me in bed.

"Freddy was my birthday gift to you. I picked him out and insisted I give him to you for your birthday. Do you remember why you named him Freddy?" He smirks as if the memory might be a bit embarrassing for him.

I think back for a long second but can't remember. I shake my head.

"On that day, while my parents were getting everything ready for your party, I had gotten into the refrigerator and snuck a little taste of your birthday cake. When my mother took it out so we could sing "Happy Birthday" to you, she saw the little fingers marks I had dragged through the icing. She yelled, 'Seth Fredrick Pierce, you are in big trouble!' And you busted out laughing.

"For the rest of the night, you kept calling me Seth Fredrick Pierce. You thought it was hilarious, and when you opened up my present, you insisted on naming the bear Seth Fredrick Pierce. Your father convinced you to shorten it to just Freddy. You reluctantly agreed. You thought the full name was much funnier. I told my father that very night I was going to marry you one day. That was the night I knew I loved you. And since I was seven years old, I've never loved anyone but you."

I set the frame on the nightstand. "Can you set the tray on the dresser please?" I ask.

With an odd expression on his face, he does as I ask. "Aren't you hungry?" he asks, lying back down next to me. Without answering him, I lay my body on top of his and begin kissing him.

"I guess not," he chuckles once he is able to catch his breath. We make love once more then fall asleep in each other's arms.

We Have To Move!

The sun comes up and streams in through the window, waking me first. Seth is lying on his stomach with his head turned toward me. Trying not to wake him, I turn onto my side and gazed at his angel-like face. I gently run my fingers through his hair then softly down his back, stopping abruptly when I feel a large scar in the center of his back. I remember feeling it last night as well, but I was too preoccupied to look to see what it was.

I prop myself up onto my arm and stare into the center of Seth's back. I let my fingers trace the outline of the deep, unusual scar, and I immediately know exactly what it is. "Oh my God," I whisper.

My voice startles him, and in one swift movement, he is on his knees, shielding my body with his and pointing a gun toward the bedroom door.

"Oh my God!" I gently place my hands on Seth's shoulders, trying to calm him. "Seth, it's okay, it's just me."

Once he has his bearings and realizes it is just us in the room, he lowers his arm and relaxes back down onto the bed still gripping white knuckled to his gun.

"I'm so sorry. I shouldn't have startled you like that. Are you all right?" I ask, running my fingers through his hair, wiping the sweat from his forehead, and trying not to be freaked out at the fact he is still gripping his gun as if his life—and mine—depend on it.

After a few quiet seconds, he looks at me then realizes he is holding his gun. He places it on the nightstand, turns back, and touches my face. "Baby, I'm sorry. I probably just scared the hell out of you. I'm a little on edge. I am never going to let anything happen to you."

"A little on edge? Really? That's what you're going with?" I can't help but laugh at him. "You were like a naked superhero standing over your damsel in distress, ready to shoot the first person who walked through the door. Thank God your mother isn't still here. That would have been something for her to see."

"Shut up!" he growls as he tackled me, pinning me down to the bed.

We are both laughing now and rolling around in the sheets. I look into his face as he smiles lovingly down at me, and I really do feel safe.

Once we stop to catch our breath, I remember what it was that started this free-for-all in the first place. With Seth still lying on top of me, I let my mind think about his scar, and my expression changes. I'm more serious now. But I'm afraid to ask the question.

"Alex, what is it?" Seth asks, noticing the change.

I say nothing. I'm not sure I want to know the answer to my question.

"Please tell me."

I turn my head and stare out the window. *How can this gorgeous, caring, and wonderful person I have fallen completely in love with be...* I can't even let myself finish the thought.

Rolling off of me, I can tell he's getting very concerned with my lack of response. He pulls my body close to his and turns my face to look at him. "Alex, please," he begs.

A tear escapes the corner of my eye and rolls down my cheek. I take a deep breath and in a whisper I ask, "Are you a Swordsman?"

He doesn't respond. He just looks into my eyes and strokes my face with the back of his hand.

"I saw your scar," I say after it is apparent he's not going to answer me. "I guess it shouldn't be a surprise to me, but…it is."

Still no answer.

"Why? Why would you become one of them knowing who they are, what they did? What they do? Why, Seth? Help me understand." I start to shake. I'm angry now. He holds me tighter. I struggle to get away, but he won't let me go.

Finally, he speaks. "It's who I am, Alex. Or who I was expected to be."

"What?" I scream, pushing harder to get away from him. "Who you are? That is *not* who you are! You are good, kind, and caring, and they are evil murderers! How can you lie here and say that is who you are?" I can feel my face getting hot and red. I struggle harder, but he has no intention of letting me go.

"It is who I was expected to be. If I hadn't become one of them, if I had chosen another path, it would have put my family in danger. It would have put you in danger. By becoming one of them, by being immersed in that life, I was given opportunities that have helped me learn the skills to protect you."

I stare at him so angry and even more confused. "What opportunities? What are you talking about?" I snap.

Seth gets out of bed, puts on his sweatpants, then sits back down next to me. I slide up, leaning back into the padded headboard, and pull the sheet up over my naked body. Clearly, the vulnerability of being naked is not going to make this conversation go any smoother.

"Alex, I am a legacy just as my father was a legacy. It was expected from birth I would become a Swordsman. And after the death of your parents, my father knew going against The Order would have most certainly gotten our family killed as well, and then there would have been no one left to protect you. My father made a deal with Max and the others involved with Carolyn's death. You were to be left alone to be raised by your grandparents, and I would be groomed to take over where my grandfather had left off." He pauses for a moment when he notices my mouth drop open.

"What are you talking about?" I ask again, my head now spinning. I can tell this is a story he does not want to tell me. But what could possibly be worse than the story he told me about Carolyn? I take hold of his hand and wait for him to continue.

"My grandfather is a Swordsman and a member of the CIA—a very powerful member."

"Wait! Your grandfather was a spy? Are you kidding me?" I chuckle for a moment until I realize Seth isn't laughing. He's serious.

"Yes," he replies, stone faced and more serious than I have ever seen him. It's sends a chill down my spine. "After he graduated, he was trained to be invisible. He was involved in covert operations all over the world and saved countless American lives in the process. He was also a trained assassin."

This is too much. In three short days, I have gone from average college student from suburban Detroit to a central character in a spy novel. I wish someone would pinch me—or slap me across the face, for that matter—to wake me from this insane dream. But the more Seth speaks, I know there is no waking up. This is real, and my life is never going to be the same.

I listen to Seth talk about his grandfather and how after he retired from the field he went on to work at Langley and train future CIA operatives to see and not be seen, and how to kill in ways even a medical examiner couldn't figure out the manner of death. Finally, he begins to tell me how he fits into the plan, and what the Swordsmen expected from him.

"My father was never the kind of man who could have been an operative. My grandfather said it was because he was soft. They never really did get along. They were very different men, and it pained my father that he could never live up to my grandfather's expectations. My father always said if he wasn't his father's son, he would have never even been considered by The Order.

"When I was born, they could tell at an early age I was much more like my grandfather than my father, and when The Order murdered your parents, the deal was made—if they left you alone, they could do with me what they wanted. With my IQ being as high as it is, I was accelerated through school and I entered college at the age of fifteen. And in April of my junior year, I was the youngest man ever tapped by The Order.

"My parents played their parts and attended every event and made sure I was properly socialized and groomed in the ways of The Order. For my father's obedience, he was given an executive position with one of the publications The Order owns, and for the most part, he was left alone. But his resentment of my grandfather and The Order grew so powerful it consumed him. Both he and my mother made sure I knew exactly who these people were controlling our lives and also made it clear there would come a day when I would have to protect *you* from them. And I promised I would never let anything happen to you.

"Once I graduated, I was sent to the farm for training. All the skills I learned made me a very valuable operative. But everything I learned I learned so I could protect you. You are the reason I am who I am. You are the reason I breathe. I love you, Alex."

He's quiet now. I know I should say something, but all I can do is throw myself into his arms and kiss him.

"So you're like my personal Jason Bourne?" I ask jokingly, trying to lighten the mood.

With one swift move, he has me pinned to the bed again, and I can't move. "You have no idea," he says with a devilish grin and a quick wink.

"My mother is here," he says suddenly then kisses me on the forehead.

"Seth, darling."

"Oh my God! Let me get dressed," I insist, struggling to get free from his grip.

"Relax," he says, laughing. "Take your time. I'll go out there and keep her occupied while you get dressed."

Seth goes into the living room to greet to his mother, and I take a moment to let the past three days flood my mind. How can I be so happy and so frightened all at the same time? Seth is the most amazing person I have ever met, and I am madly in love with him, but at the same time, if The Order wasn't trying to kill me, I wouldn't be here right now. I would never have even known Seth was alive. I don't remember him from my childhood.

I roll off the bed and throw on my jeans and a sweater. Before I go out to say hello to Seth's mother, I look in the mirror, run my fingers through my hair, and try not to look like I just spent the last several hours having sex with her son.

I take the frame from the night stand and gently glide my finger across the glass. I wish I had memory of that time we all spent together. I wish I had more memories of my parents. I can feel the tears welling up in my eyes, but before they can overwhelm me, I shake it off and head out into the living room.

"Alex, darling, how did you sleep?" Mrs. Pierce asks as I enter the room.

I glance at Seth who is standing behind his mother with a huge grin on his face. Trying not to burst out laughing, I answer, "Fine, Mrs. Pierce, thank you. I also wanted to thank you for this beautiful picture of us. I love it. I wish I could remember those days." I hold up the frame.

"Oh my dear you were so young. I wish we could have shared more special moments together," she replies in a somber tone then quickly changes the subject. "Let me make you both some breakfast. How about some bacon and eggs?"

"Let me help," I insist.

"Lovely. Seth, darling go put some clothes on, and we'll have breakfast ready shortly."

"Sure, Mom," he says, kissing her on the forehead then walks toward me kissing me the same way.

I can hear Seth in the shower as his mother and I prepare breakfast, and if I'm not mistaken, I swear I can hear him singing.

"Is he singing?" I ask.

A beautiful smile brightens up her face. "He always sings when he's happy."

I blush.

"He loves you very much, Alex," she says to me as she flips the sizzling bacon in the pan. "I hope you know that. He has loved you from the moment you came into this world. His father and I always thought it was a cute childhood crush, but the older you both got, I could see his love for you ran deep into his soul. He is prepared to die for you."

"I love him too, Mrs. Pierce. I can't explain it, but being with him, it feels like I'm home." I pause for a moment and try to think of a way to explain it to her. "My grandparents are wonderful and mean everything to me, but now with Seth, I feel complete. I always thought the emptiness I felt growing up was because I had lost my parents, but being here with him, the emptiness is gone. And if I lost him, I don't think I could go on. I can't explain it."

"I am so happy to hear you say that. He is my reason for being, and seeing how happy he is at this moment has made every ounce of pain and sorrow worth it." She smiles at me and wipes a tear onto her sleeve.

Just then, the bathroom door swings open, and Seth walks out looking so beautiful I drop the fork I am holding in my hand.

"What are you ladies talking about?" he asks, knowing full well we have been talking about him.

"You," I answer wryly.

"Well, that's just about enough of that," he insists, wrapping his arms around my waist and giving me a squeeze. "I'm starving. I've really worked up an appetite."

Immediately my face turns bright red. I elbow him in the gut, and he lets out a little "Ooof!"

We eat and talk about my parents and about my school. It's nice, comfortable. I have almost forgotten the circumstance that brought us together. Then without warning, a loud alarm goes off. Seth jumps to his feet and throws open the doors to an antique desk sitting next to the fireplace.

"Mom, were you followed?!" he asks with a note of panic in his voice.

"I don't think so," she answers.

"A car just triggered the alarm I set up at the entrance to the property. The one I showed you how to avoid."

"Maybe it was an animal," I offer, hoping I could be right.

"No, only a car is heavy enough to set it off." He pulls something out of one of the drawers and runs out to his mother's car. He walks around it slowly, holding a black box in his hand, when another alarm goes off. " They put a tracker on your car!" he yells up to us standing in the open doorway of the cabin. "*Alex, we have to go! Now!*"

Mrs. Pierce grabs my arm and pulls me back into the cabin and starts throwing my things into my bag. Seth comes running back into the cabin, gun in hand, and furiously begins to help. Not knowing what is happening, I'm frozen in place watching the two of the move around the cabin like a couple of tornadoes.

"Seth, I am so sorry. I didn't check the car before I left last night. This is all my fault." She's in tears.

"It's all right, Mom. We knew there was a possibility they could find us here. Just stick to the plan, and it will be fine." He turns and grabs me by my shoulders. "Alex, we have to go. Please, baby, put your boots and coat on now. We're out of time."

I blink and focus on his face then do as I am told. Everything is happening so fast, but I still feel frozen. I watch Seth run to the car with our bags and then back into the cabin. What only takes seconds to me happens in slow motion.

"Alex, now! We have to go!" Seth yells, trying to snap me back into reality.

I nod, and Seth grabs my hand pulling me towards the door.

"I love you, both!" Mrs. Pierce cries out, tears running down her face. "Come back safe to me!"

"We love you too!" Seth yells back to her as he pulls me though the open door and towards the car.

I am thrust back into my seat as Seth speeds the black SUV down the snow-covered road.

"Alex, it's going to be okay. My mother knows what to do once the men The Order sent for us get to the cabin. She will be able to buy us some time to get away," Seth says, trying to reassure me.

"Where are we going?" I whimper.

"We're going to use your keys to unlock their secret."

On the Run

I hold my knees tightly to my chest as we race away from the cabin. Trees blur past the windows, and I stare straight ahead, trying to process what is happening. Then as if someone or something enters my body, I take a deep breath, put my feet on the floor, and turn to Seth.

"Okay, so what now?" I ask, ready to take on The Order.

"Welcome back," he says, looking relieved I have finally snapped out of my fear coma.

"Sorry." I'm embarrassed I shut down the way I did. "Not sure what happened back there. I froze."

"That's okay, baby. You're handling all of this better than most people would. I'm proud of you," he replies, taking hold of my hand and giving it a little squeeze.

"Where are we going?" I ask, weaving my fingers into his.

"First, we have to make sure we're not being followed. As soon as whoever it is that made us at the cabin figures out we're not there, and that my mother isn't going to give them any information, they're going to follow our tire tracks. We're pretty deep in the woods, and we got a lot of snow last night, so following us until we get to a plowed road is going to be pretty easy."

"How long until we get to civilization?"

"About an hour."

"An hour?" A note of panic is in my voice. "Can they catch up to us?"

"My mother will stall them for as long as she can. And we got a pretty good jump on them. The alarm they set off was twenty minutes away from the cabin on a clear day. With all the snow on the road, it could take them thirty minutes or longer to get there." He turns and smiles at me. "Don't worry, Alex. I've done about a hundred practice runs. We're going to be okay."

I don't want to distract him, so I sit there silent as Seth races down the tree-lined road covered in snow. I'm sure the scenery is beautiful, and I probably would enjoy the view if we weren't driving at NASCAR speed and running for our lives. It's impressive though, watching him so focused. I somehow know that as long as I am with him I'm safe. The Order will never hurt me.

After what seems like hours, we finally speed out onto a clean, paved highway. My heart rate slows, and my grip on the safety handle loosens just a bit. I have faith in Seth's ability to drive in any condition, but it feels better to be on a road where all four tires are on the ground at the same time.

"How are you doing, Alex?" Seth asks.

"You've been awfully quiet."

"I'm fine."

"Talk to me. Tell me what's on your mind. We still have a pretty long drive ahead of us. I know you must have a million more questions." He takes my hand and gently strokes the top of it with his thumb.

"I do," I answer then hesitate for a moment.

"Go ahead," he insists.

I sigh just a little and look at his sweet profile as he concentrates on the road in front of us. "This is going to sound very stupid, considering everything that is going on and all the other questions I'm sure I should be asking first, but this has been making me crazy for months and really crazy since Christmas, and the more I try to figure it on my own, it just seems to make me crazier and—"

Seth interrupts me, "Whoa. Alex, take a breath. What do you want to ask me?"

Embarrassed, I look away from him and stare out the window. I collect my thoughts then ask, "How did you get in and out of my dorm room without anyone seeing you? And how long have you been coming in and out of my house?"

"I wondered how long it would take for you to ask me about that." He grins sheepishly. "I told you I have been watching you for quite some time now, and like I said before, my training has given me the skills to go around undetected. Sneaking in and out of both your dorm and your home is simple."

"What about Sam?" I ask. "Sam barks at everyone she doesn't know."

"Please." He laughs. "Sam and I are old buddies. I've been visiting you since she was a puppy. And I've trained her to be a pretty good guard dog."

"What do you mean you've trained her?" I'm so confused.

"I've been spending time with Sam, training her to detect intruders and teaching her to attack if you were ever in trouble."

"What? When? Do my grandparents know about this?" The tone of my voice is much higher now.

"Of course, not," He chuckles. "Whenever she was left home alone, and sometimes at night, I would take her and train her. She's a smart dog."

Why I'm surprised by any of this, I'm not sure. The more I learn about him, the more he amazes me. And the more I love him.

I sit silent again for a moment longer, trying to get the nerve up to ask him what else I really want to know. The butterflies in my stomach are moving around pretty fast, and the lump in my throat is pretty big, but I just have to get answers.

I turn and look at him again. He is so beautiful it takes my breath away every time.

"That can't be all you wanted to ask me. It's okay, Alex. Ask me anything," he insists.

I swallow hard and take another deep breath. I'm not sure I want to know the answer to my next question, but I have to ask. "So you know about Chase and…" I couldn't get myself to finish the question, but I know he knows what I'm trying to say.

"Of course. Chase is a good guy. I was sorry when you two broke up."

"Wait! What?" Now I am really confused. After the night we just spent together, he was upset I had broken up with my boyfriend?

"He made you happy. That is all I ever wanted for you. I was very proud of you when you didn't let him bully you into staying in Michigan to go to college. You are a very strong young woman. You don't let anyone tell you what to do, even if it means losing someone you love."

"But—"

He interrupts me again, "I know what you're asking, and yes it was, or is, very hard to see you with someone else. But you have to understand we were never supposed to meet again. If The Order hadn't decided to come after you, you still would not know I exist. You and I were never meant to be."

Now I'm pissed. "So I was supposed to go through my whole life feeling as though a part of me is missing? Never feeling whole? I always thought it was the loss of my parents that made me feel incomplete, but, Seth, it was you." I wipe away a tear that escapes the corner of my eye. "When I'm with you, I'm whole. The emptiness is gone. I never want to know that empty feeling again."

I turn toward the window and fight back the tears that have clouded my eyes. Doesn't he understand what it means for us to be together? Could he have really gone our whole lives without being with me? The thought is unbearable.

Seth raises my hand to his lips, gently kissing it. I turn back to look at him, and another tear runs down my cheek.

"Don't cry, my love. We're together now. That's all that matters." His silky smooth voice melts my heart.

"So you would have just kept keeping an eye on me forever if The Order hadn't..." I can't get the words out. "Would you have never let me see you or let me know you were there?"

"I *have* let you see me before. I've been mixed into crowds. We've even made eye contact once or twice."

"No way!" I insist. "I would have remembered seeing you. Do you honestly not know how incredibly gorgeous you are? You definitely stand out in a crowd."

He just smiles and ignores the question. "I've even held you while you've slept many times. You are so beautiful when you sleep."

"Oh yeah, I bet. Drool, snoring, messy hair. Sexy, I'm sure." I roll my eyes at the thought. "I can't believe I never felt you there."

"For the record, you don't snore," he says with a wink. "You even wrapped your arm around me once, thinking I was a pillow. I thought for sure you would wake up and scream, but you just snuggled up close to me, and once you rolled over again, I snuck out. That was our closest call."

"When?" I ask.

"The week before you left for USC. The breakup with Chase and the fact you were leaving home for the first time had made you pretty restless, and you weren't sleeping very well I thought for sure you were going to wake up, but you didn't. You held on to me for quite a long time that night."

"I remember that night. It was the best night sleep I had in weeks." I smile at the memory. "It was you. Just your presence calmed me. I slept through that whole night. Don't you see? My life is better because of you."

"And my life is better because of you."

We pull off into a gas station so we can fill up and get some supplies, which is good because I really need to stretch my legs.

"Alex, don't go inside without me," Seth calls to me as he pumps the gas. "Actually, stay in the car until I'm done. Okay?"

The tone in his voice scares me a little. I watch him through the window as he tops off the tank. He is surveying the area as if he is waiting for the people who are chasing to pull up at any moment. I sit patiently in the car and wait for him to finish.

After he's done, he walks around the car and opens my door for me. "Let's go inside and get some supplies," he says, offering me his hand.

"Bonjour, monsieur, mademoiselle," the man behind the counter says as we walk through the door.

"Bonjour," Seth replies, giving the man a little nod.

The French catches me off guard. "Montreal, right? Too bad I took Spanish in high school," I comment.

"Don't worry, babe. I'm fluent."

"Of course, you are." There is an unintended sarcastic tone in my voice. Is there anything Seth isn't an expert in? "So how many languages do you speak?" I ask, not really sure I want to know the answer. The more I learn about Seth, the more insignificant I feel.

"Five," he answers matter-of-factly, grabbing some lighter fluid off a shelf. "French, Italian, Spanish, Latin, and English, of course."

I knew I was sorry I asked. I took four years of Spanish in high school and retained very little. I may be able to go to Mexico and ask for the restroom and order a meal. I did well getting an A in every class, but for the most part, I wasn't too interested in really learning it. So of course, Seth, the superhuman, has amazed me yet again.

While he is snatching things off shelves, I grab some soda and some snacks. I figure we're going be on the road for a while, and stopping to eat probably isn't on the agenda.

By the time we are ready to pay for everything, Seth has three large bags full of stuff.

"$85.78, monsieur," the clerk says.

Seth hands the man a fist full of cash. "Merci. Conserver le changement."

"Merci, monsieur. Avoir une belle journée."

Seth pauses for a moment and then looks back at the clerk. "Si je pourrais vous demander une faveur?"

"Certainement," the clerk replies.

"Si certains hommes viennent ici et de vous demander si vous l'avez vu, pourriez-vous s'il vous plaît dites-leur que vous n'avez pas?"

The clerk looks puzzled.

"Je voudrais aussi en profiter votre vidéo de sécurité pour les dernières minutes."

"Monsieur?" I have no idea what Seth is saying, but from the tone of his voice, the clerk is very confused.

Seth reaches out and shakes the man's hand. With that one simple gesture, the clerk nods and steps away into the back room.

When he returns, he hands Seth what looks like a CD or DVD or some kind. "Vous êtes ici, monsieur."

"Merci."

The men shake hands again.

"Come on, Alex. We've been here far too long. We have to go." He grabs all three bags, and I follow him to the door. "Au revoir."

"Au revoir," the clerk replies.

Once we are back in the car, Seth races away for the gas station as if he just lit it on fire.

"What was that about back there?" I ask.

"Oh, that. That was just a conversation to ensure if the men following us stop there and ask if he has seen us, he hasn't." The corner of his mouth curls up as if he wants to smile but doesn't. "Let's just say I gave him financial amnesia."

"Ah. And the disc? I assume that was his security video?"

"You got it."

As Seth drives, he keeps one hand on the stirring wheel and holds my hand with the other. He gently caresses my knuckles with his thumb, and for a while, he tries to carry on a conversation with me. But after too many one-word answers, he gives up. Finally, he just turns on the radio, and we sit silent, listening to the music.

The landscape races by as I stare out the window trying to stay awake. I have millions of questions running around in my head, but I am already on information overload, and I don't know if I can handle anymore, and the music is helping me stay calm.

It's dark now, and I am standing alone at the edge of a dock, staring out over the water. Seth isn't with me. I am cold and scared. It's snowing again, and I'm not wearing my coat.

"Seth?" his name floats out over the water into the dark nothingness. I shiver and wrap my arms around myself. There's no answer. I turn to walk back down the dock, and an uneasy feeling washes over me. Then I see it—a dark shadow off in the distance. I stop walking.

"Seth!"

Where is he? How could he have left me here alone in the dark? I don't know what to do. If I turn around, I'm faced with the cold, dark water. If I keep going, I will walk straight into the arms of whomever it is waiting for me in the shadows. *What do I do?*

"Seth!" I scream. "Where are you?!"

Then I hear it. A voice I know all too well. "Alex, it's okay. Come to me. I'll keep you safe."

"Chase?"

There he is, stepping out of the shadows and walking toward me.

"Chase, what are you doing here?"

How did he find us? Seth and I have been driving through God knows where in Canada for two days. How could Chase have found us? How the hell did he get here?

"It's okay, baby. I'm here to take you home." He's smiling at me and holding his arms open, inviting me in. I want to run to him and let all six foot three of him wrap me up in his embrace and take me home. But something keeps me from moving.

"Alex, what's wrong? I'm here to take you home. You're safe now. Everything can go back to the way it was. They told me so." He waves at me to come to him.

They? Who's they? I stand motionless. Chase takes a few steps closer.

"All you have to do is give them your bracelet, and everything will be just fine. Trust me. It's for the best." He looks to his right, and my eyes follow his. Standing there is Marcus Wellington and two other men I remember seeing at the Gala.

"Chase, what have you done?" I shriek in horror.

"I'm making sure you are mine forever." His sweet smile is gone. "Just give them the bracelet, and let me take you home. He can't help you anymore. Only I can."

"He? You mean Seth? Where is he?" Dread fills my heart. What have they done with him? I look toward Marcus.

His cold stare and evil grin sends chills down my spine. "We have taken care of Pierce. He won't be interfering anymore, and unless you do as your boyfriend says, you will suffer the same fate as your fallen hero. The Order always gets what it wants, and if you know what's good for you, you will get with the program and give us that damn bracelet."

"No!" I scream, holding my wrist against my chest.

"Fine! Have it your way." Reaching around his back, Marcus pulls out a shiny silver handgun and, with one quick shot, puts a bullet in Chase's head.

I watch as Chase's lifeless body falls into the pure white snow. Instantly, the snow turns bright red as Chase lays there in a pool of his own blood.

"Oh my God! No!" I spin around and run as fast as I can to the end of the dock stopping just before it drops off into the water. Marcus and his men are immediately behind me. I don't turn around.

"Alex, just give me the bracelet. Chase and Seth are dead. Your parents are dead all because of you, and if you don't give me that damn bracelet, your grandparents will be next. Can you live with that?"

His voice burns into my soul. *No, I can't live with that. I can't live with any of it.* I turn to face him. "No, Marcus, I can't." I take a deep breath, threw my head back, and let myself fall into the cold, dark, icy water.

"*No!!!*"

"Baby! Baby! Wake up! Please wake up!"

Opening my eyes, I see Seth's angelic face full of panic staring down at me, his hand softly caressing my face. He kisses my forehead.

"Baby, you were having a nightmare. It's okay, you're okay. You're safe." His tone is soft, but I can tell he's frightened. I have never seen Seth frightened before.

I wrap my arms around his neck and start to cry.

"Shhh. I'm here, Alex. Everything is all right. Please stop crying."

"I don't know if I can do this," I say between sobs. "I don't think I'm strong enough."

He pulls away and holds my face gently in his hands. "Alex, if I thought for one minute you couldn't do this, I would have taken your keys and given them to The Order a long time ago. You *can* do this. You are the strongest, bravest person I know. You just have to believe in yourself." His sweet words don't calm me.

"What about my grandparents and my friends? They are in danger because of me, I know it. I've had a glimpse of who these people are and what they are capable of. What if they go after the people I love? What do I do then?" I cry harder.

We are parked outside of a small office building that looks to be closed for the holidays. Seth unbuckles his seatbelt, gets out of the car, then walks around and opens my door. "Come here," he says, holding out his arms.

I unbuckle myself and step out into the cold winter air and let Seth wrap my up in his arms. He kisses my hair, and I press my head into his chest. I'm still shaking from my dream, but there is something about being in Seth's arms that finally calms me.

"Let's get you inside before you get cold." He shuts the car door and leads me toward the back door of the office building.

"Where are we?" I'm puzzled by our location.

There is a buzzing sound, and Seth holds the door open for me. "We're meeting a friend of mine so we can switch cars."

"How long have we been driving?" It felt as though I had been asleep for just a few minutes. Just long enough for Marcus to kill Chase.

"About six hours."

Six hours? Jesus! I'm still so tired. Could I really have been asleep for six hours?

"Seth, I really need to talk to my grandparents and Barb and..." I can't say his name, but after my very graphic nightmare, I have to hear his voice so I know he's okay. "I need to know that they're all right, and I know they must be worried about me too."

"Of course. Let's get inside, and we'll take care of that." He leads me down a dimly lit hallway to a large oak door. Scrolled out in gold leaf on the door are the words:

STEPHEN STANTON
FOUNDER, PRESIDENT AND CEO

"Who's Stephen Stanton?"

Turning the door knob and pushing the door open, Seth answers, "He's an old asset of mine."

"Asset? I would hope I'm more than that, Pierce?" Standing up from behind a large oak desk is a tall, lanky man wearing baggy jeans and an old, beat-up Toronto Blue Jays sweatshirt. He has salt-and-pepper hair and what looks to be about three day's worth of stubble on his face. He's rather handsome. "I would say more like friends these days, wouldn't you?"

Walking out from around the desk, he and Seth do the handshake, man-hug thing, and Seth smiles. "Yeah, okay. I guess we're friends." Both men laugh, and I roll my eyes as I witness male bonding in its rawest form.

"Would the two of you like to be alone?" I chime in, feeling ignored.

"Sorry, baby. Stevie this is—"

Stephen cuts Seth off before he can finish his sentence. "Alexandra, of course. It's a pleasure to finally meet you. Seth talks about you constantly. To be honest, I was beginning to think he made you up. The way he talks about you I fully expected you to be able to walk on water." He laughs and punches Seth in the shoulder.

Men!

"Hardly. I'm pretty sure I'd sink like a stone." I roll my eyes again, and Seth wraps his arm around my waist.

"Well, one thing he was right about is how lovely you are. If he turns out to be a jackass, give me a call. I'd treat you like a princess."

He makes me blush. Who is this guy? A silver-tongued devil for sure.

"I'll keep that in mind. Stevie, is it?" I smile wryly, trying my best to be a woman of sophistication and mystery.

"Stephen Stanton at your service," he replies, taking my hand and kissing it softly. This makes Seth tighten his hold around me.

"Knock it off, will ya? Stop hitting on my girl." Seth's tone is light, but his grip around my waist tells another story. "Do you have everything I asked for?"

"Of course," Stevie says, tossing Seth a set of keys. "It's the silver Mercedes out back. It's has all your supplies and is gassed up ready to go."

"Perfect. What about the sat phone? Alex needs to call home."

Stephen walks over to his desk and pulls open the top drawer. "This will scramble any tap your guys have placed on her families phones, but just to be safe, no calls over five minutes." Stephen hands Seth what looks to be a cell phone, only bigger with a large antenna. Then he hands Seth a thick manila envelope. "All the documents you need to get out of the country fast."

Seth nods and slips it into his back pocket. "Thanks, man. I owe you big time for this." Seth offers Stevie his hand.

"Let's call it even. You've saved my ass more times than I care to remember." He grabs Seth's hand and pulls him in for another man hug. "You two be careful. Keep this pretty girl safe."

"I intend to."

"Alex, it has been such a pleasure to finally meet you and to find out you weren't just a figment of his imagination." He laughs at his own joke and leans in kissing me on the cheek.

"Thank you, Stevie."

Closer

We transfer all our bags and supplies from one SUV to the other, say good-bye to Stevie and set off into the darkness. Our little encounter with Stephen Stanton has snapped me out of my funk and I'm ready to start talking and listening again. There are still so many questions I need answers to.

I gaze at Seth as he drives, the soft glow of streetlights illuminating his perfect features. He notices. "What is it, baby?" he asks, in his honey-sweet voice.

"I still have so many questions," I answer, running my fingers through the back of his hair.

He sighs. "That feels nice. My body has the most amazing reaction when you touch me."

I blush. *Mine too. You have no idea!*

"Ask me anything." He's like an open book. I know that no matter what I ask, he will tell me the truth.

"How did your father die?" As soon as the question comes out of my mouth, I wish I could take it back.

He takes his eyes off the road for a moment and glances at me. The corners of his perfect mouth are turned down, and there is deep sadness in his sapphire eyes. "Cancer."

"I'm so sorry." I slide my fingers from his hair and run them gently down his cheek. He leans into my touch. "How long ago?"

"May."

My heart hurts for him.

"May I ask *you* a question?" he asks, changing the subject.

"Of course."

"What were you dreaming about when I woke you up at Stanton's office?" He turns his eyes back to the road as if he doesn't want to see my face when I answer.

I hesitate trying to figure out the right way to tell him about my nightmare. "I was dreaming that Marcus was killing everyone to get to me and my bracelet." That's an accurate summary.

"Killing who in particular?" he presses harder, unsatisfied with my answer.

Does he really want me to go into detail? I avoid his question by asking another. "What do you mean?"

"You talk in your sleep, Alex. I'm sure Julie has probably told you that." He pauses waiting for my response.

What the hell did I say? I'm afraid to ask, but I have obviously said something that upset him. "Um, yeah. She's mentioned it. I have since I was a little girl. My grandparents told me I used to cry out in my sleep for my parents, but from what Julie has told me now, I just say random things that don't really mean anything."

"You still call out for your parents on occasion, but for the most part Julie's right. You still haven't answered my question." He turns his eyes back toward me and it feels as though he's staring into my soul.

"Why don't you tell me what I said? That might help me remember." Remember Marcus putting a bullet into Chase's head.

He's staring straight ahead again. He takes a quick right turn and pulls the car into a dimly lit parking lot. Throwing the car in park, he turns so his full attention is on me. This makes me nervous and my throat goes dry.

"You were calling out for Chase. You kept screaming his name over and over again. Please tell me what your dream was about."

His eyes are sad like before when he had been talking about his father.

I don't remember screaming Chase's name in my dream. I remember calling out for Seth, wondering where he was and why he had left me alone. I remember Marcus saying that he had taken care of Seth, and I remember him shooting Chase. Maybe I screamed out for Chase then. *Okay I can explain that.*

I give him the details of my dream and wait for his reaction. Surely, he can't be jealous. Doesn't he understand how I feel about him? For crying out loud, it was just a dream.

"That's why I told you I need to call my grandparents and Barb. And yes, I need to call Chase as well. I need to know that they are all okay, and I'm sure they are all worried sick about me too. I haven't spoken to any of them since early Friday." I take his hand in mine and raise it to my lips gently, kissing his knuckles.

My explanation doesn't take the sadness from his eyes however. Without saying anything, he pulls the phone Stephen had given him out of his pocket and hands it to me.

"This is a satellite phone. Stanton's company makes them. It is designed to bounce the signal off of random satellites around the world while you talk on it. It is also equipped with a scrambler that should interfere with any taps The Order may have on your family's phones. Make the calls you need to make, but keep each call under five minutes. No longer, do you understand?" His tone is harsh. "The Order has state-of-the-art equipment and may be able to override the functions of this phone, so the shorter the better. Tell me you understand."

I nod. I'm getting a glimpse of CIA Seth, and it intimidates the hell out of me.

"I'm going to step outside and give you some privacy."

Without so much as a smile, he steps out into the cold air and leaves me sitting in the car alone. It feels like he just slapped me across the face. My feelings are hurt, and I'm not sure why. *What did I do?* I look at him through the windshield, and a tear runs down my cheek. Why is he being so cold? So I said Chase's name in my sleep. What's the big damn deal? I explained my dream to him; why is he so upset by it?

I stare down at the satellite phone, slowly dial the number, and hit Send.

"Hello?"

I can't speak.

"Hello? Alex, is that you?" His tone sounds panicked.

Taking a deep breath I try to make my voice sound upbeat. "Hi, Chase!" *That was way too chipper. I need to tone it down a bit.* "Happy New Year."

"Jesus Christ, Alex! Where the hell are you?" Chase is angry—very angry. "We have been worried sick about you. What the hell were you thinking going off without your phone and not calling anyone for almost two days? You had us calling hospitals and police stations all over the state. Your grandparents even called Julie in Georgia to see if she knew where Amber lived. She doesn't even know Amber. Where the hell are you?"

Chase ends his rant long enough for me to finally say something, but I'm at a loss for words.

"Damnit, Alex! Tell me where the hell you are. I'm coming to get you right now."

Yeah, that can't happen. My voice returns, and I answer him. "Chase, relax. I am perfectly fine. I decided to go skiing with Amber and some of her friends for a few days. It's no big deal."

My response makes it worse. "No big deal! Are you freaking kidding me? Tell me where you are right now!"

"Chase, stop yelling at me. I'm fine, and I'm having fun—that is all you need to know. I just wanted to call and let you know that I'm all right and that I'll see you in a couple days. You don't need to worry about me." I pause to take a breath when I hear Barb's voice in the background.

"Oh my God, is that her? Let me talk to her right now!"

Good, I can kill two birds with one phone call. This is convenient.

"Alex, what's going on?" Barb's voice is panicked but sweet, unlike Chase who just sounded pissed.

"Hey. I'm just having some fun. What is the big deal?" I ask, trying to sound nonchalant.

"It's not like you to just run off and not tell anyone where you're going. You had us all worried sick." I can hear Chase in the background trying to get the phone back from her.

"Would you tell him to calm down please?" I demand. "I am not a little girl. I can take care of myself. I've never reported my every move to him before, and I'm sure as hell not going to start now."

I need to calm down. I knew he was going to be angry, but this is ridiculous. "Barb, listen. I have to go. This call is probably going to cost a fortune. I'm fine, really. Just having fun with some new friends. No big deal. I love you, and I will see you in a few days."

"But—"

I cut her off before she can say another word. "Seriously, I have to go. See you soon. Bye."

I hit the End button before she can respond. *Well, that sucked! Who the hell does he think he is?* Now I'm pissed! I take a few deep breaths to calm myself then dial my home number.

"Hello?" Grandma's sweet voice is a welcome sound.

"Hi, Grams. It's me."

"Alex, sweetheart! Are you all right?" she asks, sounding relieved.

"I'm fine. I just forgot my phone at Amber's. No big deal." I have to convince her that I'm okay. I don't want them to worry about me. I have never gone off without telling them where I was and who I was with, but for their own safety, this time I have to be vague.

"We've been so worried. We called Julie to see if she had Amber's number, but she doesn't know Amber." I can tell she's confused and wants answers.

What can I say? I hate lying to my grandparents. I've never had to before. "Alex? Thank God." Grandpa picks up the extension to join the conversation.

"Hi, Papa. I'm fine. I'm so sorry I worried you. The ski trip was a last-minute decision. We're up north in the middle of nowhere, and I left my phone at Amber's house. This was the first chance I had to call. Please don't be mad." I hate this so much. Lying to them is so hard and makes feel like crap.

"We're not mad, sweetheart. We were just worried." Grandma sounds less anxious now but still confused. "Alex, who is Amber? Why doesn't Julie know her?"

Crap! Another lie coming right up!

"Oh, Amber is in one of my art classes. We don't hang out in the same crowds at school, so Julie has never met her." *Please believe me! Please believe me and stop asking me questions!*

"Well, that would explain it, I guess." Grandpa's deep voice chimes in again. "You better call Chase. He's been going out his mind with worry."

"Um, yeah. I know. I already talked to him. He's being ridiculous." I try to stifle my annoyance. "I don't have to check in with him every time I want to do something without him. I'm not his girlfriend anymore, no matter what has happened between us over the past couple of weeks."

"Alex, he's just worried, that's all. No need to get so upset." Grandma knows how easily Chase can get under my skin.

I huff. "I'm sorry. He just makes me crazy sometimes. I'm living my life the same way I have for the past year and half we've been apart, and I'm not about to change anything. Not for him."

But I *am* willing to change everything for Seth. *Seth!* I can see him watching me through the window.

My five minutes are up. "I love you, guys. I just wanted to call and say Happy New Year and to let you know I'm okay. I'll be home in a few days." *Hopefully.*

"Okay, sweetie. We love you too. Have a good time." Her voice is sad now. She knows something is wrong.

"I love you both so much. I'm sorry I worried you." My voice cracks a little as a lump grows in my throat. "I've got to go. Bye."

"Bye," they say in unison, and I press End.

Unable to stop myself, I begin to weep uncontrollably. Suddenly Seth's arms are around me, and his lips are pressed into my hair. "Shhh…It's all right, baby." He pulls me onto his lap and closes the door. I sit in his lap in the passenger seat of the silver Mercedes and cry for what seems like hours. Seth says nothing. He just lets me get it out.

Finally, when I calm down, he wipes my face with his hand and kisses my forehead. "Talk to me," he says softly, looking into my eyes. His face is soft again, with no sign of CIA Seth.

I sniffle and wipe my nose with the back of my hand. *Hot!* "I've never had to lie to my grandparents before, and I could tell they were so worried. What if I never make it back to them? What if I never see them again?" The thought overwhelms me, and before I can help it the tears start again.

"Alex, I am not going to let anything happen to you. You *will* go home."

"How can you be sure?"

"Because once we use your keys, I am going to take the evidence and use it to ensure your safety. The Order will never touch you or your family. This I promise you." There is no doubt in his voice. He believes what he's saying to me.

"How?" I ask.

"What do you mean how?" His eyebrows wrinkle in an incredible cute way when I confuse him. It makes me want to smile, but I don't.

"How will you ensure that?

"You let me worry about that." He kisses my forehead again. "First, we have to get out of this parking lot, get a good night's sleep, and then tomorrow, we will use your keys to unlock The Order's deep dark secret."

Sliding out from under me, he gently touches my lower lip with his thumb, smiles, then closes the door, leaving my body on fire. How does that one touch send my body into fits of desire? I want to forget about everything that has happened in the last few hours and just make love to him right there in the back of the Mercedes.

Jumping back into the driver's seat, he throws the car in Drive, and we're off again.

"So it looked like you got into a pretty heated conversation with Chase," he says casually, like it's no big deal.

What? All I want to do at this moment is jump his bones, and he wants to talk about Chase? Ugh! Why?

"Yeah, I guess so." I'm irritated by his comment, and I really don't want to get into the details.

"What did he say?" he presses.

"He's mad because no one knows where I am and he wants to come get me." My annoyance for both Chase's behavior and Seth's questions is apparent in my voice.

"Yeah, I'd like to see him try." He laughs.

I raise an eyebrow and smirk at him. "What's so funny?"

"Oh nothing." He chuckles again.

Men are so annoying. So what? If Chase tried to come to find me, would Seth go all super CIA ninja on him or something? That's all I need. Two alpha dogs getting into a pissing contest over me.

"Can we not talk about Chase anymore please?" I grumble. "He's pissed. I told him to get over it, and that's the end of it as far as I'm concerned."

With a huge ear-to-ear grin on his face, Seth touches my bottom lip again with his thumb and says, "That's my girl."

Oh my God! I want you right now!!! My face flushes, and I turn my head toward the window and rest my forehead against the cool glass.

"Are you okay?" Seth asks.

"I'm fine, just a little warm." *My body is on fire, and if you don't make love to me soon, I may explode!* "I'm pretty sick of being in the car too. Are we stopping somewhere for the night?" *Oh please! Oh please!*

"We're almost there, baby. About twenty more minutes."

Thank God!

This is ridiculous. Our lives are in danger, and all I can think about is getting my hands on his perfect body. *What the hell is wrong with me?*

Seth finally pulls into an underground parking garage at the back of a large apartment building. It has to be at least seventy-five stories high.

"Where are we?" I ask, awed by the enormity of the building.

"This is one of Stanton's crash pads. We're going to stay here for the night." He switches off the engine. "Stay in the car. I need to make sure this place hasn't been compromised." Getting out of the car, he pulls his gun from his coat and gives the parking lot a once-over. Satisfied with what he sees—or doesn't see—he slowly walks around the car and opens my door for me. "Come on, I need to get you inside."

"But what about the bags?"

"Don't worry about the bags." He grips my hand tightly pulling me next to him. "Stay close to me," he insists.

As we enter the building, we are greeted by an older gentleman wearing a doorman's uniform. "Good evening, Mr. Campbell. It's a pleasure to see you again. It's been awhile."

"Yes, it has. How are you, Stewart?" Seth replies. "This is my wife, Alexandra."

"Hello, Mrs. Campbell. It's a pleasure." Stewart smiles at me and offers me his hand. "You are just as lovely as your husband said you would be. It's so nice you are able to join your husband on this trip. He always seems so lonely without you."

What is going on? Who is this guy? Mr. & Mrs. Campbell, really? A little heads up would have been nice.

"It's a pleasure to meet you as well, Stewart." I smile and shake the man's hand.

"Will you be staying the week?" Stewart asks Seth.

"No, just the night. Our visit is a short one." We take a few steps toward the elevator then pause as Seth turns his attention back to Stewart. "Could you get our bags from the car please, Stewart?"

"Of course, sir. My pleasure." Seth tosses Stewart the keys then presses the button to call the elevator. Within seconds, the doors opens, and we step inside. Seth enters a code into the keypad, and the *P* button lights up. My stomach falls, and I feel a bit queasy as we are immediately thrust toward the sky at warp speed... *69; 70; 71; 72; 73; 74; P—penthouse.*

We step out of the elevator into a modest foyer—white walls, black marble tile on the floor, and a small black table with a vase of white roses in the center. Seth leads me toward a large metal door. He pulls a shiny silver key from his pocket and inserts it into the keyhole, turning it to the right. I expected the large metal door to open, but instead, a smaller door slides up. Seth places the palm of his right hand flat against the palm reader then leans forward, allowing the retinal scanner to scan his right eye. After a few beeps and buzzes, the large door finally opens.

Well, this is new. High-tech security at its finest. I take a step toward the door, but before I can go any further Seth sweeps me up into his arms.

"What are you doing?" I squeal, kicking my legs, trying to get down.

"I'm carrying my bride over the threshold," he jokes with a grin. His smile perfect and completely cheesy.

"Are you kidding me? Put me down!" I insist, kicking my legs some more.

"Absolutely not!"

"This is ridiculous! Put me down right now!" I'm trying hard not to laugh, but I can't help myself.

"Why, Mrs. Campbell, you wouldn't deny your husband one of the oldest marriage traditions, now would you?" His sexy smirk drives me crazy.

"If you don't put me down this instant, I am going to scream bloody murder!"

"Oh, I'm sure I can keep you from doing that." Suddenly his perfect lips are on mine.

I tangle my fingers into his hair and kiss him with everything I have. I open my mouth and let his tongue caress mine. The taste of him is so sweet. Sparks fly through my body, and I ache for him. I have been longing for this without even knowing it. All of the stress and exhaustion from the day is gone. All I want to do is make love to this amazing man.

Keeping one arm securely around my waist, he slowly lets my legs drop so my feet are just barely touching the floor. He holds my body as tight as he can, fusing us together. He weaves his fingers through my hair, grabbing hold, then deepens the intensity of his kiss. The taste of him drives me wild. This man is mine, and I am his. Come what may, I will never let him go.

"Excuse me, sir." Stewart's voice startles us both, and in one quick second, I go from total exhilaration to total embarrassment. "I apologize for the interruption. Where would you like your bags?"

I try to pull away from Seth's embrace, but he just smiles, not loosening his grip on me. "Just there is fine, Stewart. Thank you."

"Very good, sir. Will there be anything else?" Stewart asks, looking a little embarrassed himself.

"Actually"—he smiles sweetly down at me—"Alex, why don't you go into the kitchen and see if there is anything to eat? I need to speak with Stewart for a moment."

"Um, okay," I reply, confused.

"It's through there to the left." Seth points down a long hallway. I nod, smile at Stewart, then make my way to the kitchen.

The last thing I am is hungry. *Are you kidding me? I was seconds away from crazy, hot sex on a cold tile floor. Now I have to downshift into "Let's have dinner" mode. Ugh!*

I open up the refrigerator and stare blankly inside. It is fully stocked with anything and everything one could want or need, but I don't want any of it. I want Seth. In a huff, roll my eyes, close the door, and wander out into the living room. My footsteps echo as I walk across the shiny hardwood floor. The soft glow of the fire is all that illuminates the pristine and elegant space. The tiffany-blue walls are accented with white-crown molding and decorative trim. Expensive works of art are strategically placed throughout, and a large crystal chandelier hangs in the center of the enormous room. Two large over stuffed white sofas sit facing each other on either side of the fireplace, and between them is a plush snow-white rug that gives the room warmth.

The warm glow of the fire flickers as I take in the beauty of the room. Across the room from the fireplace are a set of French doors. I make my way over and peer through the glass. It's dark, but to my delight, I see they lead to an outdoor patio. I turn the knobs and throw open the doors, allowing the cold night air to rush through me. The crisp air cools my scolding-hot skin. I stare out into the city and suddenly realize where we are.

"Toronto," I say out loud.

"Yes, Toronto." Seth's voice startles me, and I spin around quickly, almost losing my balance.

"Did I really sleep long enough for us to have made it all the way from Montreal to Toronto?" It didn't feel like I had slept that long. It's like a five- or six-hour drive when the weather is good. It's been snowing for days and the roads were horrible, so it must have taken us at least ten.

He smiles his sexy little smile. "You were out for a while, babe."

"I'm so sorry. I should have tried harder to stay awake. Maybe then I could have driven for a while." I feel horrible. "It felt like I was only asleep for a short time."

"I'm not surprised. The way you were tossing and turning, it didn't seem like a real restful sleep, but I didn't want to wake you. Besides, I wouldn't have let you drive, anyway."

I roll my eyes at him then walk toward the railing. The view is breathtaking. Seth is behind me. He engulfs me in his strong embrace and nuzzles his face in my hair. I lean back into him and close my eyes.

"So what now?" I ask.

"Now we get a good night's sleep, then tomorrow we retrieve what we came here for."

I shiver a little, and he leads me back inside. The warmth from the fireplace is welcoming.

"Are you hungry, baby?" Seth asks.

I shrug. I watch the fire as it hisses and dances before my eyes. It's almost hypnotic. Even though I had slept for hours, according to Seth, I am still exhausted and not at all hungry.

"Stay there and get warm. I'm going to make us something to eat."

I hear him walk from the room, but my eyes remain locked on the flickering fire.

My mind begins to wander, but I can't hold on to my thoughts. It's like a slide show flashing through my mind. Images of Maxwell Wellington, Marcus, Nikki, Parker Ashcroft. Then there's Carolyn. I have no idea what she looked like, but my mind creates an image of her faceless, lifeless body. It makes me shiver again.

I hear Seth's velvet voice. "Alex, are you still cold?"

"No."

He sets a tray full of food on the white rug then sits down next to it. "Sit with me," he says sweetly.

I join him and smile as the glow from the fire lights up his beautiful face. He brushes the back of his hand down my cheek. "What is it, baby? Please tell me." His eyes are soft and full of concern. I kiss his fingers as they pass my lips, but say nothing.

We sit in silence, staring into each other's eyes for a long time. I don't know what to say to him. Part of me wants to tell him how much I want to go home. Another part wants to tell him how much I can't wait to stick it to Wellington and Ashcroft and all the other assholes that hurt that poor girl. Then there's the part of me that is screaming, wanting to say to him, "Make love to me! Help me forget why we're here! I love you!"

But what comes out of my mouth surprises us both. "Did The Order murder my parents?"

Seth's eyes widen, and his posture stiffens. He doesn't answer me.

"I don't remember if it was you or your mother that said it, and I think I was in too much shock for it to really sink in at the time, but one of you said that my parents were murdered." I pause, waiting for him to respond, but he doesn't. "I was told it was a car accident."

Seth looks toward the fire. The flames dance and flicker in his perfect eyes, and I can swear I see tears forming. I kiss his hand again. I want him to know that no matter what the answer is, I am ready for it, that I can handle it.

"Please," I whisper.

Not turning his eyes from the fire, his velvet voice answers yes.

I am immediately filled with rage. I jump to my feet, walk across the room, and glare out into the dark Canadian night. I want to scream! I thought I could handle knowing the truth, but evidently, I was wrong. Deep down, I think I knew, but just that one word from Seth made my blood boil.

"Alex." Seth's voice is almost a whisper. He's stands behind me now but doesn't touch me. I wait for him to wrap his arms around me, but he does nothing. I can see his reflection in the window, but I can't make out the expression on his face. I ache for him to hold me, but I am too angry to move.

We stand in silence for what seems like an eternity until I can't take it any longer. Why won't he touch me? I turn on my heels and gaze into his eyes. He looks so sad it melts my heart; all my rage and anger is gone.

"Seth?"

He doesn't answer me.

I place my hand on the side of his face, and he leans into my touch. "Why do you look so sad?" I hate the look on his face. I want to do any anything I can to make that look go away. "Please talk to me."

He places his hand over mine, and with the other, he finally pulls me into him. "Alex, I love you so much." He opens his mouth to say something else but stops himself.

"I love you too." I lay my head against his chest and wrap my arms around him, holding him to me as tightly as I can.

Pressing his lips into my hair, he whispers, "I'm sorry."

"Why?"

Tightening his hold around me, he kisses my hair again then lets out a painful sigh. "I'm sorry because you were never meant to know any of this. You were supposed to go on with your life not knowing this world existed. You were always supposed to think your parents died in a car accident. You were never supposed to know about Carolyn, about The Order"—he pauses—"About me."

It feels like someone just stabbed me in the heart. I pull away and stare him in the face. "Knowing you is the best thing that has ever happened to me. There is nothing you can tell me, nothing I have to run from that will ever make not knowing you better." A tear rolls down my cheek. "You make me whole. All the emptiness I've felt my entire life is gone when I'm with you."

He has to understand! There is no danger great enough, no secret horrifying enough to make me let him go. I will run forever as long as he is with me. I refuse to live my life without him.

"Seth, don't you understand what you mean to me? Can't you feel how much I love you?" The tears are falling faster now. My heart aches with the thought that he doesn't know how much I need him—how much I love him.

"Alex, you are my world. Everything I have done, all my training, every breath I take, is for you. If anything ever happened to you I couldn't go on living. And it kills me to know that you are in danger now because of my family." His eyes are filled with so much pain.

"Wait! What do you mean?"

He takes my hand and leads me over to one of the overstuffed sofas. "Sit. Please."

Without hesitation, I do as he asks. He sits next to me but far enough away so we aren't touching. *Why is he pulling away from me?* This isn't like him at all. I have only known him a few days, but there has hardly been a time that he wasn't touching me in some way. I am so confused. I want to reach for him, but I don't. I sit there quietly, waiting for him to explain to me what he meant.

He takes a deep breath and runs his fingers through his hair. He can't even look me in the eyes. "Alex, the reason you are here, the reason The Order sent for you, is because of my father."

What!

"When my father found out that he had cancer, it had already progressed to stage 4. There was nothing the doctors could do but make him as comfortable as they could. He declined very quickly, and the medication they had him on made him very paranoid. He started going off on these rants about Carolyn and about what happened. He would wake up from a deep sleep hysterical and want to go to you to protect you. My mother and I tried to reassure him you were fine, that the secret was safe, but it didn't matter. The worse he got, the more out of control he became.

"We tried to limit his visitors because we were never sure what would come out of his mouth and to whom. One night, my mother was sitting with him and he was going off on one of his tirades about keeping you safe and keeping The Order away from your bracelet. But what my mother didn't realize was that Maxwell Wellington and Edwin Hollister had stopped by to see my father and they had been listening to everything my father had said from the hallway.

"Once my mother realized they were there, she tried to convince them that what my father had been saying was nothing more than ravings of a very sick man, but they didn't buy it. When they left, she immediately called me.

"It didn't take me very long to figure out what they had planned, and there was no way in hell I was going to let them touch one hair on your head. So that's when I started following you 24/7 out in California and plotting out what I needed to do to keep you safe."

There is so much pain in his voice. All he can do is stare at his lap and run his hands through his hair over and over again. He won't look at me.

I slide closer to him and lace my fingers in between his. He thinks what is happening is his fault. He's blaming himself. But I didn't understand why.

"Baby, I am so sorry." His velvet voice is soft, almost a whisper.

I want him to look at me. I need him to look into my eyes and know this isn't his fault. "Seth, you have nothing to be sorry for. This is not your fault. Look at me, please." I beg.

He lifts his sad eyes, and they meet mine.

I place a hand on his face. "None of this is your fault. You—"

He interrupts me, "If I had kept a better eye on my father, if I would have prevented Wellington from visiting him, none of this would have happened." He is so angry with himself. He pulls away from my touch and stumbles over to the window. It's as if the sight of me cuts into him like a knife.

I feel helpless.

I go to him. Quietly, I stand behind him so he can see my reflection in the glass. I close my eyes and try to think of the right words. "I want you to listen to me." I place a hand in between his shoulder blade, over his scar.

He flinches, and his breathing becomes heavy.

"You have spent your entire life carrying the weight of someone else's burden. You sacrificed you own happiness to protect everyone you love. You are the bravest, most amazing person I have ever met. The fact that Wellington found out about me and my bracelet just shows that it's time to finish this. You don't have to protect me anymore. We're a team. Let me carry some of the weight now. I'm ready."

I mean every word. I *am* ready. Those seven men who murdered that poor girl—and my parents—have gotten away with it for far too long. It's time they pay for what they did, and I am going to do whatever it takes to make that happen.

I step around and stand in front of him. I gaze deeply into his eyes and smile softly. He doesn't smile back.

"Seth, your father was a sick man. There was nothing you could do about that. And to be honest, I'm glad all of this has happened."

"What?" His eyebrows pull together, and his eyes narrow in confusion.

"If Wellington wouldn't have found out about me then I wouldn't be here... with you. Nothing else matters as long as I'm with you. I love you!"

"But you're in danger because of me. Because I didn't keep Wellington away from my father. If I had only kept a closer eye on Wellington's movements, I could have—"

I press my fingers to his lips, cutting him off. "Would you rather have gone through life never being able to be with me? That's how it would be if none of this had happened."

"I know but—"

"Shhh." I stretch up and kiss him softly on the lips.

He wraps his arms around me; all the tension in his body is gone. He draws me into his body and kisses me so passionately it makes my knees buckle. I loved him so much. Sweeping me up into his arms, Seth carries me down a long, dark hallway and into a dimly lit bedroom; a single candle flickers from the nightstand and the soft sounds of a piano plays in the background. Stopping at the foot of a king-size bed, still holding me in his arms, he smiles sweetly, lovingly down at me. My heart surges in my chest, and my stomach does flips. I want him so badly.

"What is that smile for?" I ask.

Playfully kissing the end of my nose, he whispers, "I love you."

There is still a hint of sadness in his voice, and it brings a tear to my eye. "I love you too." I weave my fingers through his hair, bringing his face to mine and kiss his lips. Nothing else matters as long as I am with him.

The hole has faded away. Our lips never part as my feet touch the floor and Seth begins slowly taking off my clothes. The kissing stops only when he pulls my sweater up over my head. Tossing it to the floor, he reaches around and unhooks my bra, slowly sliding the straps off of my shoulders. Before I know it, he has removed all my clothes and I am standing in front of him naked.

"You are so beautiful."

His velvet voice makes my blood race. For the first time in my life, I feel sexy. This amazingly gorgeous man thinks I'm beautiful. This amazingly gorgeous man loves me.

With his eyes locked on mine, he gently touches my bottom lip with his thumb, and instantly I'm on fire. That one touch is all it takes to drive me crazy. I reach out and begin unbuckling his belt, but when I go to unbutton his pants he stops me.

"Wait," he whispers.

Reaching behind his back, he pulls out the gun he has in his waistband. I had forgotten he had it. He places it on the night stand, then taking my hands, he places them back on his pants so I can finish what I had started. As his pants slide down to the ground, I lift up his shirt and tug it up over his head. His body is amazing. I gently trace the curves of his muscles down until I reach the top of his boxers, and without stopping, I grab hold of and pull them down to the floor.

Now it's my turn to stare. He is so incredibly sexy. My body is screaming out for him to make love to me. I have to touch him.

"Don't move," I whisper.

Starting at his shoulders, I begin caressing and gently kissing his body—his chest, his abs, his hips, but I stop just before kissing and touching him *there*. I want to tease him a little. With a devilish grin, I look up into his eyes and wait for his reaction.

Nothing. He stands perfectly still watching me—eyes dark, no smile. He just waits for my next move.

Without thinking, I lift my hand and gently brush his lower lip with my thumb.

Snatching me up into his arms, he tosses me onto the bed and is instantly on top of me, kissing me like he has never kissed me before. His rock-hard body forms to mine, and all of our desire and lust for one another explodes.

As we make love, Seth whispers in my ear, "I love you."

Just the sound of his voice saying those three little words makes my body burst into complete and total ecstasy. That is all it takes to make me lose complete control, and he keeps saying it over and over again until my body can't take anymore.

"I love you!" I shout, as my body is pushed again into ultimate pleasure. His body shudders around.

We lay motionless, Seth on top of me, my arms and legs still wrapped around him, our hearts beating rapidly as one. I can feel his breath in my hair, and his lips are lightly touching my ear. I gently caress his back with my fingers tips but stop when I brush over his scar. I stay still for a moment and wait for Seth's reaction. He does nothing.

I slowly begin to trace over the deep mark with one finger, picturing it in my mind as I do. I think about a young eighteen-year-old boy giving his freedom over to a group of men who intend to control his every move for the rest of his life. The whole idea of what Seth went through and is still going through and everything he had to give up to become the perfect Swordsman breaks my heart.

A tear escapes the corner of my eye, rolling down the side of my face, coming to a stop when it reaches Seth's lips. He slowly rolls his body off of mine and lays on his side, facing me, our bodies still touching.

"Alex, what is it? Why are you crying?"

I turn toward him and nuzzle my face into his neck. I hate crying again. It seems like that is all I've been doing since we've been together. He wraps his arms around me and tangles his legs into mine. I know I should be terribly frightened, but as long as I'm with Seth, I'm not. I know he will protect me. I know I'm safe with him.

"Please, Alex, tell me why you are crying." His voice is sad again. I know it hurts him to know I'm upset.

"Your scar. It made me think about all the things you've been through, all the things you've had to give up. I hate them."

I'm angry again. Angry for what they have done to Seth and angry for what they had taken away from me. My body stiffens. Pulling away slightly so he can look into my face, Seth's blue eyes sparkle as he smiles at me.

"What's so funny?" I ask, annoyed at his amusement.

"Nothing," he says, surprised by my reaction. "I just love your passion. It takes a lot for you to let people in and for you to trust them, but once you do, you do anything and everything you can to make sure no one hurts them. The way you love is a gift, and I hope the people you love value it as much as I do."

I stare into his beautiful face unable to respond. I *won't* let anyone hurt him. He is right about that. He told me once he would die for me, and I want him to know I feel the same way. "I will die before I let The Order or anyone else hurt you. I know you are here to protect me but I'm here to protect you too. I may not have your ninja skills, but I will throw myself in front of a bullet if I have to. Those assholes already took my parents from me. I will be damned if I let them take you too."

He chuckles at my bold statement and kisses me on the forehead. "Easy, tough guy. I would like my lady bullet-hole free if you don't mind. Every inch of you is perfect, and I would like to keep it that way." He traces his finger down the length of my body, giving me goose bumps, and I can't help but smile.

"Don't make me laugh," I demand, trying to get serious again.

"Yes, ma'am."

His sarcasm makes me giggle. *Damn it!*

Taking me by surprise, as he usually does, Ninja Seth pins me to bed so I can't move. I struggle to free myself, but there's no use. He smiles down at me then kisses me firmly and passionately. I think perhaps he is ready for "round 2," but before the urge can overwhelm us, Seth is off of me and putting on his clothes. Disoriented by the sudden blood rush, it takes me a second to figure out what he's doing.

"Come back to bed," I insist.

Shaking his head at me, he pulls a sweatshirt out of the top drawer of the dresser and tosses it to me. "Nope. Get up. There's something I need to teach you," he says, pulling his t-shirt over his head.

"What are you talking about? It's the middle of the night." I am totally confused.

"Just get dressed and meet me in the kitchen." Before I can argue, he disappears through the bedroom door.

Reluctantly, I do as I'm told. I slide on my blue jeans that are lying on the floor next to the bed. Leaving them unzipped, I reach for the sweatshirt Seth threw at me. I unfold it and hold it up. *Toronto Maple Leafs! Absolutely not!* Disgusted, I wad it up and toss it on a chair. I throw on my bra, take a quick peek at myself in the mirror, and run my fingers through my hair. I feel sexy. Maybe my appearance will entice Seth to want to come back to bed. But if not, I have a t-shirt in my bag that is still in the foyer.

Brimming with self-confidence, I make my way down the hall and venture to the kitchen in just my bra and unzipped jeans. Seth is staring into the refrigerator. He doesn't hear me come into the room. *His Spidey senses must be off.*

I stand silent and watch him push things around, trying to decide what he wants to eat. Finally, he turns around, carrying a jug of orange juice. As soon as he notices me leaning up against the wall, his eyes widen and the jug slips out of his hand. But just before it can hit the floor, he snatches it up and sets it on the counter.

Oh! His Spidey senses are back! I laugh out loud; he smiles.

"Excuse me, miss. I think you may have forgotten something in the bedroom."

"Why, sir, whatever are you referring to?" My face flushes as his eyes are no longer looking at my face but at my breasts.

"Ms. Shelley, are you trying to distract me from my mission?" he asks, still staring at my chest, a sexy grin on his face.

"Perhaps."

Keeping his eyes locked on mine, Seth glides around the counter in the center of the room. Aggressively pulling my body into his, he runs his hand up the back of my neck; tangling his fingers into my hair and pulling my head back, he whispers, "You're trouble." I giggle; he kisses me. *Maybe my plan has worked. Round 2.*

My lips part, and our tongues meet, shooting sparks through my body again. My knees buckle, and I fall into him, waiting for him to snatch me up into his arms and carry me back into the bedroom.

But to my surprise and disappointment, he pulls his lips away and says, "Get dressed, baby. This is important."

He slaps me on my bottom, making me jump, then pours himself a glass of orange juice. I scowl at him with a frustrated look on my face, then in a huff, I turn to retrieve my bag from the foyer. I zip up my pants then throw on the USC t-shirt I had packed for the trip. I manage to find a hair tie that had fallen to the bottom of the bag, and I walk over to the mirror that is hanging to the left of the elevator. The light is better in the foyer than it had been in the bedroom, and as I look at my reflection, I almost don't recognize myself. Somehow, I look different. Older.

As I pull my long hair back into a ponytail, I notice Seth walking up behind me. He engulfs me in his gentle embrace, kisses my neck, and then looks at me in the mirror.

"You are so beautiful."

I blush, and he kisses my neck again.

"You better stop that, or I'm going to drop you right here on this cold marble floor and make love to you again," I threaten.

"Promises, promise," he muses.

Just as I turn to make good on my threat, he takes a step back, hands me my coat, then walks toward the elevator doors. "Sorry, baby. Things to do," he says, waving me to him. I shuffle over to him defeated and sulk as he helps me on with my coat.

The doors open, and we are back at the entrance to the underground garage. Stewart stands up from his small security desk to greet us. "Mr. and Mrs. Campbell, is there anything I can help you with at this late hour?"

"We're just running out for a bit, Stewart. We shouldn't be more than a couple of hours. You know how to get a hold of me if anything comes up."

"Yes, sir," Stewart nods and holds the door open for us.

It's about two in the morning as we speed through downtown Toronto, and I have no idea where we're going. I let my mind wander as building after building flash by my window. I start thinking about making love to Seth on the foyer's cold marble floor, and it makes me smile. Seth notices.

"What is that grin for?" he asks, brushing his fingers down my cheek.

"I was just thinking about how I would rather be making love to you on the foyer floor." I can't believe I said that out loud. I know I must be blushing, but it's too dark for Seth to notice.

"Oh trust me, I'd rather be doing that as well, but what we are about to do is important."

I frown.

"I'll make it up to you later, I promise," he adds, skimming my lower lip with his thumb.

He knows that drives me crazy!

We pull into the parking lot of a small, concrete, windowless building. Seth turns off the engine and opens his door. "Ready?" he asks.

Ready for what? Where the hell are we?

Always the gentleman, Seth makes his way around the car and opens my door, offering me his hand. I take it without asking any questions and walk with him toward the eerie-looking building. As we approach, I notice a small security camera aimed at the entrance. Encased in the thick gray cement is a large steel door. Seth reaches out and presses a small white button that is discretely hidden within the concrete. If you didn't know it was there, you would never notice it. After a few seconds, there is a loud buzzing and a click. Seth opens the door, and we walk inside.

"What's up man?" a tall, stocky man dressed in camo cargo pants and a khaki shirt asks Seth, offering him his fist.

"Need to give my girl a lesson," he replies, giving the man a fist bump.

The man just nods.

"Alex, this is Bill."

"Ma'am," Bill says, giving me the once-over then offering me his hand. "You've got the place to yourself tonight. Eyes and ears are inside. Let me know if you need anything."

Eyes and ears? What?

"Thanks Bill," Seth says just as Bill leaves the room, closing the door behind him.

"Talkative guy," I joke.

"Well, it is two in the morning, so we probably woke him up. Besides, he's a military man. They're generally short on small talk."

"Got it."

To our left is another large steel door and, next to it, a keypad. I watch as Seth presses a series of numbers into the pad, then just like the front door, there is a loud buzz and a click. As the door swings open, I immediately understood what we're doing here.

It's a gun range. Seth is going to teach me how to shoot.

"Scared?" Seth asks, with a small smirk.

"A little…"

Hell yes! I've never held a gun in my life. To be honest, they scare the hell out of me. My grandpa owns a gun for home protection, but it's kept in a safe, and I have never seen it, so as far as I'm concerned, it doesn't exist. It's only in the last couple of days that I have been anywhere near one.

"Don't be scared, baby. Knowing how to shoot a gun properly is important."

Seth leads me by the hand to the center shooting lane. Sitting on the counter are two sets of glasses and two pairs of earmuffs. *Eyes and ears. Now I get it.* Seth reaches under his coat and pulls out his gun. He releases the magazine, pops out the remaining bullet from the chamber, and sets everything on the counter. I glare, intimidated by it, even though it isn't even loaded. My mind races with images of Seth "in the field," and I wonder if he has ever killed anyone with it. Seth slides my coat from my shoulders, and I remain motionless, unable to take my eyes off the gun.

"Put these on." Seth hands me a pair of protective glasses and a set of earmuffs. "The earmuffs are electronic. You will be able to hear me talk, but once you begin shooting, they will deaden the sound."

Hypnotized by the deadly weapon sitting in front of me, I just nod, put on the glasses and earmuffs, and wait for his next instruction.

"First, I'm going to show you how to hold it. It's not loaded, so you don't have to be afraid of it." I take little comfort in that.

Standing directly behind me Seth takes my right hand in his and places the gun into my palm. He then wraps my fingers around the grip. "Extend your index finger. Keep it out straight alongside of the gun until you are ready to shoot." His words are stern, but I can feel his warm breath next to my ear, and I do as he instructs.

"How does that feel?" he asks.

I say nothing. My entire body is shaking. Wrapping his left arm around my waist, he pulls me close into his body; this calms me—a little.

"Now I want you to pick up the mag and slide it into the frame. Push it in hard enough so the button here on the side pops out." Releasing my waist for a moment, Seth points to a small button on the left side of the gun.

I hesitate, but as soon as his arm is back around my waist, I do as I'm told. I push the bullet-filled magazine into the handle of the gun as hard as I can, and just as Seth said it would, the small button on the side pops out.

"Good, baby." Seth's voice is soothing. "One last thing, I want you to rack the slide."

Do what?

"Pull back on the top of the gun as hard as you can, then let it go."

Being right handed, my instinct is to switch the gun over to my left hand and pull back with my right, but Seth stops me. "Try it with your left hand. In an emergency situation, you need to be able to make it hot then fire right away."

Make it hot...rack the slide... All his crazy lingo is making my head spin. With my left hand, I pull the slide back then release it, loading a bullet into the gun's chamber. I just made it hot.

Oh my God!

"Breathe, baby! You're not breathing." He almost sounds amused. This annoys me.

"I am breathing," I snap.

He chuckles. "All right. No need to get snippy. Now I want you to stand with your feet shoulder width apart and your chest square to the target."

He releases his hold around my waist. "Don't let go," I whisper.

"I'm right here, Alex." He is only inches away, but as soon as he lets go of me, and I'm standing there holding the gun alone, I'm terrified. The shaking grows stronger, but I take a deep breath and square myself toward the target.

"That's my girl. Now point the gun at the target. Wrap your left hand around the frame, keeping both thumbs forward." He leans around, examining my grip, adjusting it slightly. "Good. Now widen your stance just a bit." He taps the inside of my feet with the toe of his shoe. "Now slide your right index finger around the trigger, and when you're ready, with both eyes open, aim at the center of the target and squeeze."

I can do this! This is important. Seth wants me to be able to protect myself, and I want to be able to protect him if I need to. Taking a deep breath, I square my shoulders, straighten my posture, then pull the trigger.

Oh my God!

The recoil is stronger than I expect. I stumble back into Seth's arms. "Did I hit it?" I ask in a tone several octaves higher than my normal speaking voice. The surge of adrenaline is unexpected, and I want to fire it again.

Seth chuckles at me then presses the button recalling the target. "Let's see."

As the faceless silhouette makes it way down the line, I can see the small hole my single shot made through the paper. It's to the left off center. If it had been a real person I would have winged him. I smile at my accomplishment.

"Not bad for your first shot. Not bad at all." Seth kisses me on the top of my head like a proud father. "Want to try again?" he asks.

I nod enthusiastically.

He replaces the target with a new one and folds up the other, stuffing it in his pocket. "We'll save this one for posterity," he jokes.

As he sends the fresh target sailing to the end of the lane, he gives me some pointers and has me adjust my stance just a bit. This time, I stand with my right foot slightly behind my left and instead of stopping after one shot, I keep going until the mag is empty. It is such a rush. I fire eleven shots, and all eleven hit the target. My aim isn't great; I meant to hit the target in the center all eleven times, but at least they all went through the paper.

We spend the next hour or so working on my aim, and I improve. I learn to control the weapon better the more I fire it.

We go through two boxes of ammo between the two of us, and when it's Seth's turn, I watch in awe at his precision and accuracy.

By about three thirty, my adrenaline has worn off and I am so tired I can hardly keep my eyes open. I need sleep. Seth wasn't kidding when he said he could go days without sleeping. It's so late—or early, however you want to look at it—but Seth still looks amazing and acts as if he has just woken up from a long night's rest. It's annoying. I sit slumped in a chair and start to doze off while Seth cleans his gun. I am cold but too tired to get up and put on my coat.

"Are you cold, baby?" he asks, sitting down next to me, pulling me into his chest. He is so warm. "Why didn't you wear that sweatshirt I gave you back at the apartment?"

"You're joking, right?" I scoff at the idea.

"What do you mean?" He doesn't get it.

"It was a Toronto Maple Leafs sweatshirt!"

He raises an eyebrow at me then rolls his eyes. "Right. What was I thinking?"

"I honestly don't know, but don't ever let it happen again." I giggle. "Besides, I prefer keeping warm this way." I nuzzle my face into his neck, and he squeezes me tight.

Answers

I wake to the sound of shouting coming from the other room.

"You are going to stay the hell away from me and my family, or I will take you and all those other assholes down! You can bet on it!" a man's voice says sternly and forcefully.

"You're loyalty is expected. If you try to come after us, we will make you pay. We own you, and don't you forget it!" The second man's voice sends chills down my spine. It's a voice I vaguely recognize but can't place. One thing I do know, neither voice sounds like Seth.

I know I shouldn't, but curiosity gets the better of me, so I get up to go see what's going on. Groggy and a little disoriented, I trip over something that is lying on the floor and realize I'm not in Stevie penthouse apartment. I don't know where I am. A single lamp spins a kaleidoscope of colorful shapes around the room, and as my eyes adjust, it becomes apparent that I am standing in the middle of a little girl's room.

As the lamp spins and illuminates different areas of the room, I can see dolls and stuffed animals, ruffled pink bedding, and butterflies painted on the walls. A sense of comfort and familiarity washes over me until I hear shouting once again. Trying not to make any noise, I creep down the hall toward the sound of the voices.

I reach the end of the hall and peer around the corner. Standing there are two men—one tall with dark hair and a face I vaguely I recognize, the other a bit shorter with dark-blond hair and eyes that look like mine—standing toe to toe, threatening each other.

The blond man growls, "You listen to me, Max."

Max?

"With what I have on you and the others, I can send you away for the rest of your lives. Do you really want to test me? Leave us alone, and I will consider keeping what I have on you buried. That way, you all can go on and lead the pampered little lives The Order has planned for you." He pauses, taking a long drink from the glass in his hand.

"You are going to leave Jack and his family alone as well. He wants nothing more to do with the ways of The Order. The men in his family have given up everything to be who they were expected to be, but that all stops now. You will leave him and his son alone. Do you understand me?"

"You have no idea who you're dealing with," the dark-haired man hisses. "As for Jack, his father will never allow him to just walk away. You can be sure of that!" A menacing grin spreads across his face, and it makes the hairs on the back of my neck stand up. "You think you've won your life back, Ben? You couldn't be more wrong."

Ben? I gasp, then one little word escapes my lips. "Daddy?"

The blond man turns and walks toward me. "Alex sweetheart, you should be in bed." Sweeping me up into his arms, he kisses my forehead, and I begin to cry.

"Shhh...it's all right, baby. Daddy's here." He wipes away the tears from my cheeks and kisses me again. "Mr. Wellington and I are just talking. Everything is all right. I'm sorry we frightened you."

I throw my arms around his neck. "Daddy! Oh, Daddy!" I cry harder.

"Wake up, baby."

I can hear Seth's voice in my mind, calling me back to reality. His warm chest presses against my back, and his lips are kissing my neck. I lean into him as the safety of his embrace soothes my anxiety.

"Alex?" He waits patiently for me to say something, but the pain and sadness from my dream leaves me longing for my father and unable to speak. Instead, I roll over and nuzzle my face into Seth's neck. "Did you have a bad dream?" he asks sweetly.

I still don't answer him.

Pulling his head away from mine a little, he lifts my chin so he can look into my face. My eyes are full of tears and my breathing is shallow. I know I should say something, but the images of my father and a young Maxwell Wellington are all I am able to focus on.

"Baby, please. You're scaring me."

With a deep breath, I gather myself enough to finally speak. "Did my father and Wellington ever have an argument in the living room of my old house?" I ask.

"I'm not sure. Why do you ask?"

I roll onto my back and stare at the ceiling. Seth props himself up on his elbow and gazes down at me. We stay silent for a moment while I process my thoughts. "Seth, I don't think my dream was so much a dream, but more like a memory."

"What do you mean?"

"I think I was remembering a night from my childhood. A night when Maxwell Wellington came to our house and threatened my father." I look into Seth's face, but he doesn't say anything. I continue. "My father was telling him that what he had on him and the others would put them away for life and that if The Order didn't leave our family and yours alone, he was going to use it. Max screamed back that loyalty to The Order was expected and if he turned his back on them they would make him pay. Then the conversation ended when they noticed me standing there."

Seth scratches his head, like he is searching for the memory in his own mind. "It's possible," he says finally. "What else do you remember?"

I close my eyes, trying to recall more details. "I remember waking up in my room with a kaleidoscope lamp flashing images on the walls then—" Seth interrupts me.

"Wait. A kaleidoscope lamp—you're sure?"

"Yes, why?"

"The kaleidoscope lamp was one of the gifts you received for your third birthday."

"Okay?" I'm confused.

"Alex, your parents died the day after your third birthday."

My body stiffens. If my dream was truly a memory, then that was the last time I ever saw either one of my parents alive. The day after my third birthday, my grandparents had come over to babysit me while my parents went out. When I woke up that morning, my parents were already gone and Grandma was there to get me ready for the day.

"Tell me how my parents really died."

"Alex..."

"Please!" I beg.

Unable to look me in the eyes, Seth stares blankly out the window into the cold Toronto morning. "I've already told you more than you were ever supposed to know, and in the past three days I have watched you cry more than anyone should ever cry in a lifetime. It kills me to watch you hurt." His blue eyes are the darkest I have ever seen them, and I know his heart breaks with what he is about to tell me.

"Alex, what you know about your parents' death is true. They did die in a car accident, but the circumstances released to your grandparents and the media were false. It's true they were struck head-on by a semitruck, but the driver was not intoxicated as the police reports states. The driver, Gus Jones, was hired by

Wellington to hit your parents while they were driving to meet with my parents.

"He was instructed not just to hit them but to keep accelerating until the truck had completely crushed your parents' car. In return, he was promised the best legal representation and more money than he could make in a lifetime. Due to heavy gambling debts and hefty child-support payments, Jones was in debt up to his eyeballs, with no relief in sight, so he jumped at Wellington's proposition.

"Now Max being Max, he, of course, couldn't get his hands dirty, so he made Preston Walker handle the heavy lifting. On the morning of September fourteenth, Walker sat outside your house and waited for your parents to leave. Following them on to the highway, he radioed ahead to Jones that they were coming. Speeding ahead, Walker made sure he was several car lengths ahead of your parents, and once he saw Jones's truck coming from the other direction, he flashed his lights, signaling to Jones to pick up speed and cross over the median. Once his truck made impact, your parents had no chance. Their car was demolished, and from what the coroner said, they both died instantly. Jones walked away with only a few minor injuries.

"Jones was taken into custody and charged with a DUI and two counts of vehicular manslaughter. But before he was arraigned, Jones was allegedly murdered in his holding cell by another prisoner. Max never had any intention of fulfilling his end of the deal, and I am convinced to this day he had one of the officers on The Order's payroll kill him. And now you know everything."

Tears overtake me, again. Caressing my face, Seth eyes are pained, and I can see that he is searching for the words to comfort me. He kisses my lips gently and whispers, "I'm sorry."

I try to breathe, but the air catches in my throat and pain rushes through my stomach, like someone has just punched me in the gut. I'm filled with anger and hatred. Hatred for Maxwell

Wellington, hatred for the other men who participated in causing so much pain and hatred for The Order.

Seth holds me and lets me cry until I have no more tears left. In his arms, I'm home. Because of his love, I'm strong. It's time to finish this!

Proof

The water is soothing as it cascades down from the oversized showerhead, washing away the salty tearstains from my face and massaging my skin. But it can't wash away my anger. The rage and hatred I have for The Order is only temporarily pushed aside when the sadness and pain of knowing the truth floods my mind—the truth about how my parents really died and why and the truth about poor Carolyn Peters. I want to make Maxwell Wellington and the other men pay for what they did, not just to me and my family, but for what they did to Carolyn and hers. I want to give her family closure, and I want her to be able to rest in peace, knowing that her killers have finally been brought to justice. But can Seth and I make this happen? Or will The Order kill us as well just for trying?

There's a snap, and the shower door opens, startling me. "May I join you?" a naked Seth asks, a boyish grin spread across his lips.

Taking his hand, I pull him in under the water, and he draws me into his body. I rest my face against his chest and listen to his heart as we stand in silence, letting the water pour over us. There is something about being in his arms that calms me. I never knew I could love this deeply.

"How are you?" he asks, breaking the silence.

"Angry, sad, and just all around pissed off."

"I'm sorry."

His words cut into me like a knife. It pains me to know that he thinks this is somehow his fault. "Stop saying that," I snap.

My harsh tone takes him by surprise. "What did I say?" he asks, looking down at me wide eyed.

I reel in my anger and soften my tone. It's not him I'm mad at. "Stop saying you're sorry. None of this is your fault."

"I know, but—"

"But nothing. You can't take the blame for something that happened before either of us was even born. I know you did everything you could to protect me from what is happening, but the truth is, if Wellington and those other assholes hadn't killed Carolyn in the first place, none of this would be happening. Our lives would have been totally different. I would still have my parents, and you and I wouldn't have had to grow up without each other." The thought of that life brings tears to my eyes. A life with my parents, a life always knowing Seth, is a life I can only dream about. But now, a future with Seth is all that matters to me.

"You're right," he agrees.

"I know," I reply, a triumphant smile brightening my face.

His eyes narrow, then he brushes his thumb across my lower lip, shooting sparks through my body and making me shudder. "You think you're cute, don't you? Even as a little girl, you always had to have your way, and I was always more than happy to indulge you. Looks like things haven't changed."

"Glad to hear it," I snicker, throwing my arms around his neck, kissing him deeply.

Once dressed, we make our way to the kitchen, and I force myself to eat a bagel and some fruit while Seth scarfs down three eggs over easy, five strips of bacon, toast, a huge glass of orange juice, some fruit, and a cup of coffee.

"Hungry?"

My sarcastic tone makes him smile. "We have a big day ahead of us, so I need to fuel up. Besides, I've had a lot of extra physical activity over the past few days that has made me pretty hungry."

I blush, thinking about our most recent escapade in the shower.

"You're so cute when you're embarrassed," he gushes.

Trying to ignore him, I take our plates over to the sink and turn on the faucet to wash them.

"Don't worry about those, baby. Stanton has people to take care of that. Besides, we need to get moving."

"Where are we going?" I ask.

"It's time to unlock the secret."

I don't know why, but his words make me nervous.

We make our way down to the parking garage, and I see that Stewart has been relieved by another man, a younger man. As we exit the elevator, the man stands to greet us. "Mr. Campbell, sir. How are you?" the man asks.

"I'm fine, thank you, Jeffery. I'd like you to meet my wife, Alexandra." He calls me his wife so casually as if it's the truth. I smile.

"Hello, Mrs. Campbell, it's a pleasure to finally meet you," Jeffery says, extending me his hand.

"And you," I reply, returning the gesture.

Jeffery looks to be in his mid-thirties, not very tall but very muscular. And the way he carries himself, I figure he is probably ex-military.

"I assume Stanton has briefed you as to the situation?" Seth asks Jeffery in a very stern manner. He's CIA Seth now.

"Yes, sir. The perimeter has been secured, the building has been searched floor by floor, and the men are in position," Jeffery answers, looking serious and ready for his mission.

"Excellent. We shouldn't be gone long, and if by some chance we are followed, I need the men alert and ready."

"Copy that, sir. I understand."

Whoa! This just got intense.

Seth nods then takes me by the hand leading me to the car. "What was all that about?" I ask.

"There's intel that our location may be compromised, so Stanton has his security team on high alert just in case," Seth replies calmly, like it's no big deal.

My eyes widen. "Wait, The Order may know we're here? When did you find this out?" I can't hide the panic in my voice.

"Shortly before I joined you in the shower."

What the... "You mean to tell me that when we were doing... whatever...in the shower, and while you were so casually eating half the contents of the refrigerator, you knew Wellington's goons could be on to us?" I shriek, baffled by his casual demeanor.

"Relax, Alex. This place is like Fort Knox. It's while we're out that we have to keep our eyes open for trouble." He presses the button on the keyless entry then opens the passenger side door. "Hop in," he insists.

I feel like I might throw up. How in the hell can he be so calm? If Wellington and his men found us, trapping ourselves in a seventy-five-story high-rise doesn't sound like a very smart idea. How will we ever get out? And what if they get to us while we're out driving or, worse, when we're using my keys to unlock the evidence? What will we do then? I know Seth is trained for this kind of situation, but I'm not. Sure, I've spent an hour firing bullets at a paper target, but that certainly doesn't make me qualified to engage in a gunfight. My head is spinning.

Seth puts the Mercedes in gear and heads out of the underground parking lot. But instead of driving with one hand on the wheel and the other holding my hand or rubbing my knee, this time he is driving with one hand on the wheel and the other gripping his gun. He pauses before pulling out on to the street and nods to a man dressed in black standing to the left of the exit. The man nods back, then Seth pulls out, hitting the street well above the speed limit. To my relief, it didn't snow last night, so the roads are dry and clear of slush and ice. As Seth races through the streets of downtown Toronto, I glare at every car we pass, every person that exits a shop or is just walking down the street. Everyone looks suspect to me.

Our drive is a relatively short one, and when Seth parks in front of a cigar shop, I stare at him completely confused. "Why have we stopped here?" I ask.

"You'll see," Seth answers cryptically. "Don't get out of the car. Wait for me to come around to get you."

All I can do is nod. There's now a huge lump in my throat, and my mouth is so dry it feels like my tongue is wearing a sweater. I do as I'm told and wait as Seth slowly makes his way around the car, surveying the area, and even though I know he's there, I still jump when he opens the door.

"Put your hood up," he orders me with a stern tone.

Without asking why, I pull the fur-trimmed hood up over my head. Seth takes my hand and urges me out of the car. Wrapping his left arm around my waist, securing me to his side, he then casually slips his right hand into his coat, concealing his weapon. He leads me toward the door of Fitz's Cigar Shoppe. As we enter, there is an overwhelming aroma of tobacco and herbs with a hint of leather and grape. It's an odd sensation, and my sense of smell is immediately stimulated. Behind the counter is a tall, thin man with dark-rimmed glasses and curly brown hair. He looks to be in his late fifties. Not at all who I thought I'd see in a cigar shop. I was expecting a short, fat man with thick stubby fingers and yellow teeth.

"Seth, how are you?" the man asks sullenly, a hint of an Irish accent in his voice. He seems annoyed to see us.

Seth ignores the question.

The man gives me the once-over. Then the corner of his mouth twitches. "And who do we have here?"

"Fitz, this is Alexandra Shelley."

Shelley? He used my real name.

"Shelley." From his tone, I can tell that my name has piqued his interest.

"Yes, Shelley." Seth is stone faced and more serious than I have ever seen him.

Fitz gives me a half smile. "And how are you, Ms. Shelley?"

I open my mouth to speak, but Seth answers his questions for me. "Not very well, seeing as we are standing here in your shop. You know why we're here," he snaps.

"Indeed, I do." Fitz's voice sounds worried now.

Sliding the hood from my head, I give Fitz a little smile, trying to ease the tension in the room.

Fitz smiles back at me. "I can see your father in your eyes, but you are definitely your mother's daughter. Very beautiful."

"Thank you," I reply quickly before Seth can snap at him again.

"I'm sorry we are meeting under such circumstances, but I'm sure our boy Seth here is making sure you are kept safe."

"He is, Fitz." I look at Seth; he is glaring at Fitz, irritated by our conversation. I lightly brush my fingers down his cheek, but he doesn't smile; he just tightens his hold around my waist.

Fitz walks out from behind the counter toward the door, locking it and flipping the sign that hangs in the window from Open to Closed. "Well then, if you two would follow me."

Seth finally releases me from his vice-like hold and we make our way behind the counter, following Fitz down a narrow hall that is lined with box after box of cigars from all over the world. Seth has me walk in front of him, but I can sense that he is no more than an inch behind me. I turn my head to look at him and see that he has taken his gun from his coat and is keeping a close watch on the door, making sure no one comes in.

Fitz comes to a stop when the hallway suddenly dead ends. I glace to the right and then to the left and realize there is nowhere to go from here. We are surrounded by nothing but shelves of cigar boxes. There's no door or entryway to go through, just boxes.

Confused, I stand silent as Fitz draws a dirty, old skeleton key from his shirt pocket. Then removing a box that reads Dona Flor-Brazil, he exposes a small keyhole in the wall. Before he inserts his key, Fitz turns to me and asks, "I assume you have *your* keys, Ms. Shelley?"

Before I answer, I look to Seth. He nods, letting me know it's okay. I push the sleeve of my coat up until the bracelet is set free and slides down my arm. "I believe these are the keys you are referring to," I answer, looking Fitz dead in the eye.

"Indeed, they are." Lifting the lid to the small cigar box he pulled from the shelf, Fitz reaches in and takes out a single cigar, offering it to Seth. "This is a token from your father. He told me that if the two of you ever showed up here together, I must make sure you do not leave without it."

Seth's eyes narrow, and his forehead furrows, but he takes the cigar from Fitz and examines it briefly. "Thank you," is all he says.

"You remember how to get out once you are finished, yes?" Fitz asks Seth.

"Yes."

"Good." Turning his attention back to me, Fitz takes my hand and gently kisses my knuckles. "It was a pleasure to meet you, Ms. Shelley. God be with you on your journey."

I smile politely, unable to respond. He's words, although kind and sincere, make my scalp prickle and my stomach turn.

Inserting the key into the keyhole, Fitz gives it a quick turn to the left, and suddenly the wall of boxes slides to the right exposing a large steel door. "Key number 1 please, Ms. Shelley." I lift my arm to him, and he spins the bracelet around until he finds key number 1. He guides my hand toward one of two keyholes in the large door. Removing a shiny silver key from his pants pocket, he inserts it into the second keyhole then turns both keys in unison.

There is a loud click, and the large steel doors pops, opening slightly. Fitz removes both keys, allowing me control of my arm, then hands the other key to Seth. "Once you are inside, you are on your own. No one will be able to get through this door, not even me. Retrieve what you came for. I sincerely hope you do remember how to get out; if not you will be trapped in there."

Seth nods, offering Fitz his hand. "Thank you."

"Seth, I am grateful to your grandfather and everything he has done for me, but I have fulfilled my end of the agreement. I have kept this room and its contents safe and secure for over twenty-five years. It's time my life is mine again. Once you leave, please do not return." Fitz's plea saddens me.

What could Seth's grandfather have done for him that would have been so great that this man would put himself in danger by keeping the evidence of Carolyn's murder hidden from The Order for all these years?

"You have my word," Seth assures him.

We step into the darkness that is behind the large steel door, and as Fitz closes it behind us, my body stiffens and I grab hold of Seth's arm trying to find some sense of security. The air begins circulating around us, and it is cool against my face. As my eyes adjust to the darkness, I see the floor is illuminated by a soft glow leading us down another narrow hallway. Seth urges me forward.

"Where are we?" I ask, trying to hide my fear.

"We're in the vault," Seth says matter-of-factly.

The vault?

"Okay. I'm going to need a little more than that. You forget I wasn't brought up in the supersecret world of the CIA," I grumble.

I can't really see his face, but I think he's smiling at me. "Sorry," he chuckles. "My grandfather had this place built when he brought Fitz over from Ireland and got him set up in business here."

"Yep, still confused."

He takes my hand leading me further down the hall and then down a long flight of stairs. He continues, "Fitz is one of my grandfather's old assets. They met while Fitz was a member of the British Secret Intelligence Service. You probably know it better as MI6. That's usually the way it's referred to in the movies. Anyway, in the early '80s, Fitz was sent back to Ireland on a mission to infiltrate the Irish National Liberation Army during a time known as the Troubles.

"There was intel that the group was going to try to bomb locations where casualties would include high-ranking members of the British government. Fitz's job was to find out when and where and relay the information back. For three years, he was successful. MI6 was able to stop bombings at several locations and arrest numerous rebels. But something went wrong, and Fitz's cover was blown. The army beat and tortured him for months, trying to get him to talk, but he wouldn't. He would never tell them who he was and who he worked for. All they knew is that he had sent information back to Great Britain and he was a trader.

"My grandfather got word of his imprisonment and decided he needed to rescue his friend. Now keep in mind that my grandfather is CIA through and through, and making friends with an asset is forbidden. You cultivate a relationship with them that gets you what you need, nothing more. They are disposable. But for whatever reason, my grandfather cared for Fitz, and he was determined to save him. And he did.

"He and two other operatives went into Northern Ireland and successfully executed a mission rescuing Fitz and two other prisoners. He brought them all here to Canada and set them up with new lives, but he always made sure that Fitz knew he owed him one. So when Fitz opened his cigar business, my grandfather had the building turned into a secure location where, if need be, top-secret information could be stored and not gotten to unless you had all the keys."

I stare down at my wrist. *All the keys.*

"When Ben and Jack had retrieved all the evidence of the murder, they knew that hiding it out of the country would be the only way to keep it safe. So Jack convinced Ben that they should tell my grandfather what happened and see if they could keep all the evidence here.

"Now my grandfather's loyalty is not just to the CIA. It is also to The Order and, betraying The Order was something he was not willing to do, but he respected Ben's need to free himself from the hold that Wellington and the other's had on them, and he also hated McAllister, so he allowed them access to the vault under one condition: they were never to let the evidence go public. They were only to use it to get control of the situation."

"Wait! Did they ever get control of the situation?" I ask.

"In a way yes, but in a way no."

"What the hell does that mean?" His cryptic answers irritate me.

We reach the bottom of the endless staircase. Seth punches a code into a small keypad, opening another steel door then we enter a large hollow room. Our movement activates a motion sensor, and the room is immediately brightened. On the wall to our left are several squares with keyholes. On the wall to our right are several security monitors and on the wall directly in front of us is the Sword and Skulls insignia carved into the stone at least eight feet high. The sight of it makes my blood boil.

In the center of the room is a large stone rectangle with several items neatly arranged on top and not an ounce of dust. Seth walks over to it, picks up a remote control, then points it at the monitors. The nine square boxes flicker then come to life. Seven of the screens show us different views of outside the building, and two show us a view inside Fitz's shop, all in black and white. Fitz has returned to his post behind the counter, but his expression is nervous, and he's fidgeting with something.

"Wow, that's some high-tech equipment," I joke, trying to lighten the mood and calm my nerves.

Seth snickers. "Yeah, well, this was state of the art in the '80s when it was installed, and since you and your family have had the key for the past twenty-plus years, we couldn't really get in here to update things."

"Oh, right." I roll my eyes. Then Seth's cryptic comment pops back into my head. "Tell me what you meant by 'In a way yes, but in a way no.'" I used my quote-unquote fingers as I return his words.

Seth sighs. "What I meant was that Max knew my father would never betray The Order because he knew my grandfather would never allow it, but he never really trusted your father. After they all graduated, Ben went to work for BioMed, a company that had no Order affiliation. This did not go over very well with The Order. Wellington and some of the other high-ranking members tried to strong-arm your father into going to work for the government and engineering chemical weapons, but he refused, and when Max pushed harder, Ben threatened to go public. That's when Max knew he had to get rid of him."

He takes a step toward me, reaches out to touch me, but in anger, I step back out of his reach. There is something about being in this room and having that ugly skull staring down at me. I just want to get the hell out of here.

"Can we just get this over with?" I snarl.

Seth's eyes widen at my outburst. "Yes, of course. Will you please come stand next to me?" His voice is tender, and I immediately feel awful for snapping at him.

I stand quietly next to him, and he takes hold of my hand. Gently, he places it on the stone table then removes my bracelet. He picks up a pair of what look to be tin snips and begins removing each key from the links of the bracelet. My heart sinks deeper and deeper with every snip.

Fighting back tears, I need to take my mind off of what he is doing. "How is it there is absolutely no dust in this room? If no one has been in here for over twenty years, it should be covered in dust and filth.

"This room was vacuum sealed. All the air was sucked out, keeping the evidence free from moisture and anything else that could contaminate it. This is probably one of the most sterile places in the world," he answers, concentrating on his task.

"Wow, you CIA guys don't miss anything, do you?

"Nope." His voice is childlike, and it makes me smile.

With one last snip, the final key is free, and all twenty keys now lay independently in front of us. "What now?" I ask.

"Well, you already know what number 1 unlocks. Let's see what the others have to show us." He takes the other nineteen in his hand, and we walk over and stand in front of the boxes mounted in the wall to the left. "It takes three keys to open each box, so we need to do a little trial and error to figure out which ones open which box."

It takes us about twenty minutes, but we finally figure out each key combination. We stand and stare at the wall, three keys in each box, but neither of us makes a move to open them. I look up into Seth's face and see sadness again. We both know there is no turning back now.

I make the first move. Turning each key in box 1, I open the door and pull out a metal container. I place it on the counter. Without opening it, I walk over and open box number 2. Seth stands perfectly still and watches my every move. Once I have emptied them all, I take him by the hand leading him to the six metal containers I have laid out on the stone counter.

"Shall we see what's inside each?" I ask.

He says nothing.

I flip the latch on the first box, and inside is a cardboard box. Using the small blade that is lying on the counter, I cut through the tape and open the flaps. Inside are five Betamax videotapes. "Looks like we're going to have to find a dinosaur to be able to play these," I joke. Seth remains quiet.

Opening the second container, I pull out a manila envelope labeled Photos. I turn it over and begin to tear open the flap when Seth stops me. "Don't!" he says loudly startling me.

"What?" I ask.

"Don't open that," he insists.

"Why?"

"Those have to be the photos that Ben and Jack took when they found Carolyn's body on the island."

"Okay." I look at him puzzled.

"I know what seeing those images did to my father. When he was ill, he would wake up screaming her name and it would take my mother and me hours to calm him down. Even when I was younger, he told me that the image of Carolyn's lifeless face haunted him whenever he closed his eyes. I don't want you to have to go through that. Please, Alex, don't open that envelope."

The horror and panic in his voice take me off guard. I didn't think anything could affect him that way. I place my hand on his face and gently caress his cheek. "Thank you," I say with a smile.

"For what?"

"For loving me so much." I lean up and kiss his lips then place the envelope on top of the videotapes.

Flipping the latch on container number 3, I pull out a brown paper bag. Inside are what appear to be Parker Ashcroft's bloody clothes and the shard of glass Carolyn cut him with. Container number 4 also holds a brown paper bag, but in this bag are Carolyn's clothes, which I'm sure has Parker's DNA on them. DNA wasn't available in the '80s, but I'm sure my father knew that someday, the fluids on her clothes would be able to be used to identify her rapist.

In container number 5 is a small cloth pouch. I untie the strings holding it closed and empty the contents into my hand. In my palm is Carolyn's gold cross necklace. The one my father took so he could one day return it to her family. "We have to get this to Carolyn's family," I say, looking at Seth.

"Okay," he whispers.

Placing the necklace back into its pouch, I slip it into my pocket for safekeeping.

"One box left," I say out loud. I flip the latch of container number 6, and inside I see a small letter-size envelope with my name on it. I freeze immediately.

"What is it?" Seth asks.

Slowly, I take the envelope from the container and examine the perfect swirls that spell out my name.

Alexandra

I look to Seth as he waits patiently for me to answer, but I can't speak. I just hand him the envelope. He sees my name scrawled across the front then asks, "Would you like me to open it?"

I nod.

Gently, Seth tears open the flap and pulls out a pale-pink sheet of stationery. I watch as his eyes skim the content. "It's from your mother."

My mother?

Tears start to well up in my eyes, and my hearts races. Seth shows me the letter, but I do not take it. This is the first time I have seen my mother's handwriting. It's lovely. Perfect calligraphy, not like my chicken scratch. I stare, unable to reach out for it. I look into Seth's eyes.

"Would you like me to read it to you?" he asks.

I nod once again.

Smoothing out the creases in the paper, Seth clears his throat and begins.

My darling Alexandra,

If you are reading this letter it means your father and I are no longer with you and for that I am deeply sorry. The thought of leaving you has haunted us for so long. There is nothing in this world that either of us love more than you, my sweet girl. Every moment with you has been a blessing. You are perfect in every way and you are the reason I was put on this earth.

By now you must know that your keys hide a hideous secret and it is now up to you and Seth to make sure Carolyn gets the justice she deserves. You have a strong, brave heart my daughter and I know you will do whatever you can to make the men who killed her pay for what they did.

Trust Seth. Trust his father. And most of all, trust your heart.

Always know that your father and I love you with all our hearts and what we've done is the right thing, even if that means being taken away from you. Live life to the fullest. Love with all your heart. And never forget that your parents love you.

All my love,
Mom

Seth looks into my eyes, and a deep sob escapes my throat. Wrapping his arms around me, Seth holds me as I cry into his chest. Losing my parents at such a young age, I never really felt the pain of what I had lost. Or at least I don't remember it. But now, listening to Seth read my mother's words, I feel it. I feel it as though they died yesterday. I feel the pain of what was taken from me.

I can feel Seth's breath in my hair as I cry. He holds me not saying anything, letting me work through my pain. Suddenly his arms tighten around me and his body stiffens. I look up at him, and the look on his face frightens me.

"Alex, we have to go *now!*" he barks.

I turn and look toward the security monitors. There standing in Fitz's shop, holding a gun, is Marcus Wellington and two other men. My breathing accelerates, and I begin to shake. "What do we do?" I ask.

Without answering me, Seth moves to the stone counter and begins stuffing all the evidence from each container into a bag. He grabs the one remaining key from my bracelet that we haven't used yet then pushes everything else off onto the floor. Metal containers and tools hitting the stone floor echo loudly throughout the hollow cavern. The noise is deafening.

Once he is finished, he grabs hold of my hand. I am staring at the monitors watching Marcus and his two goons as they are beating the hell out of Fitz. The two men I don't know are holding Fitz up while Marcus repeatedly punches him in the face and in the gut, and I can tell that Fitz is not giving him what he wants. From what Seth has told me about Fitz, I am sure he can withstand the beating he is taking from a guy like Marcus Wellington.

Seth tugs at my hand. "Baby, we have to go."

I nod and walk back toward the door where we entered.

"We can't go back that way," Seth calls to me.

I glance quickly around the room but see no other way out. *How the hell are we going to get out of here?*

Seth extends his hand. "Come with me."

He leads me back to the stone table and lifts me up on to it. "What are you doing?" I ask.

Jumping up on to the table with me, Seth turns and stares at the monitors. Pulling out his gun, he takes aim and fires at the two screens that show images of Marcus, shattering the glass and making the screens go black. "God, I really hate that guy," he growls.

Shocked at his outburst, I sit paralyzed on the stone slab. Taking the one remaining key, Seth places it into a small keyhole in the center of the stone. Something must have been covering the hole before because I did not notice it until Seth put the key in.

"Sit on your knees then lay your chest on your lap and keep your forehead pressed to the stone," Seth instructs me.

I do as I'm told, and Seth mirrors my position. With a swift turn of the key, the entire stone begins to lower into the floor. "It's going to get hot, baby, but we're going to be fine. Just stay on your knees and follow me."

"What do you mean it's going to get hot?" Just as the words leave my lips, the stone comes to a stop and a thick steel plate seals off the room above. Instantly, the temperature rises to an unbearable heat.

"Oh my God!" I scream.

"Follow me, quickly," Seth yells back.

As fast as I can, I crawl away from the intense heat, trying to keep up with Seth. He's fast. He's several yards ahead of me now, and I'm starting to hyperventilate. The tunnel is too narrow and dark. I've never been very good in tight spaces.

"Seth!"

"Faster, Alex!" he yells back to me.

"I can't!"

Claustrophobia is setting in, and I'm beginning to panic. I'm paralyzed. The heat is making it hard to breathe, and I feel like

I'm going to lose consciousness. I try with everything I have to move forward, but I can't. I lay my chest on my knees and fight to stay in the now.

"Seth..." My voice is a whisper.

Insurance

The cold air on my face and the soft tone of Seth's voice bring me back to reality. Disoriented, I struggle to get my bearings and am very relieved once I realize I am no longer trapped in that heat tunnel.

"What happened?" I ask Seth once I was able to speak.

Kissing my forehead softly, he lets out a sigh of relief. "You scared the hell out of me, baby! Why didn't you tell me you were claustrophobic?"

"I didn't know." It's the truth. I know I freak out in small spaces and don't like being in big crowds but I had no idea my phobia was so intense. "I'm sorry. I think it was a combination of everything. The heat, the small space, the darkness, Marcus, everything. Why was it so hot in there?"

"Once the evacuation mechanism was triggered, the room was fire sanitized."

"Fire sanitized?" *This is another CIA thing I'm sure.*

Seth nods. "The room has been consumed by fire and will burn at a temperature even higher than a crematory. Everything that was left inside will be complete destroyed."

"How long will it burn for? And what about Fitz's shop?"

Seth smiles a little. "Don't worry about Fitz. His shop will be fine. The fire will burn for a few hours, then the air vacuum will trigger, sucking out all the air, causing the fire to go out. It will be like the room never existed."

"Wow," is all I can say.

"Well, now that you're back in the land of the living, we have to get the hell out here! Can you stand?" Seth asks.

"I think so," I answer. Slowly, I stumble to my feet and breathe in the cool air. I look around and notice we are in an alley. "Where are we?"

"In the alley behind the stores that are across the street from the cigar shop," Seth replies. "I need you alert. We need to make it to the car without Marcus and his thugs seeing us."

What? The Mercedes is parked directly in front of Fitz's shop. Why are we going to risk trying to get back to it? Can't we just steal another car or something?

He takes my hand and kisses it softly, and I notice that the sleeve of my white winter coat is filthy. I look down to find so is the rest of me.

"We are wasting too much time, Alex. We have to get to the car and get the hell out of here. Do you understand?" He waits for me to answer.

I nod.

"Okay. Do not let go of my hand for any reason until we are in the car." He's staring me square in the face. The blue of his eyes are dark and intense, but still beautiful and hypnotic. I nod that I understand and weave my fingers tightly around his.

We walk casually from the alley then make our way down the sidewalk past the row of shops that are across from the Mercedes. Pausing for a moment, Seth takes his gun from his coat and holds it against his thigh. He surveys the area then pulls me toward the car. Just as we are halfway across the street the door to Fitz's shop opens and out walks Marcus and the two men.

"Damn it!" Seth growls just as he and Marcus make eye contact.

In unison, all four men raise their guns. We're outnumbered three to one. I don't have a gun.

Releasing my hand, Seth pushes me behind him.

Wait! Don't let go of my hand, remember!

I peer over his shoulder and glare at Marcus.

"Alex, I want you to slowly reach under my jacket with your right hand and take the gun that is holstered in the back of my waistband." Seth's voice is soft so only I can hear him.

I slide my hand up under his coat until I feel the leather holster. Gripping the receiver, I pull the gun free and lower it, keeping it concealed behind Seth's back.

"Good girl. Now take hold of the gun the way we practiced and wait for me to tell you what to do." I obey his instructions. I hold the cold black Glock 19 in my hands and wait.

Seth has not taken his eyes off of the men across from us, and I can't take my eyes off Marcus. The arrogance on his face is sickening. I have an overwhelming urge to raise my gun and try to shoot the look off his face. Never in my life have I thought about shooting another human being, but there is something about Marcus Wellington that makes me want to rid the world of his very existence.

"We don't have to do this Pierce," Marcus says, breaking the silence. "Just give us what we need to end this, and you and the girl can go."

"You know that's not going to happen," Seth responds, his voice cold and low. "This is going to end, but not the way you and your daddy want it too."

Marcus laughs at Seth's words. "You really think you can stop us? We've got you outnumbered, and all I have to do is put a bullet in the leg of that pretty little girl of yours, then you will really be at a disadvantage."

"Alex." Seth's voice is soft again and draws my attention back to him. "I want you to move out from behind me and raise your gun. Then when I tell you to, I want you to take aim at the cigar in the center of Fitz's window and pull the trigger."

What? Is he insane? What if Fitz is still in there? I can't shoot out his window!

As if he read my mind, he says, "Don't worry about Fitz or anyone else. Just hit the window. Tell me you understand."

"Okay," I whisper then take two steps to my left and raise my gun, aiming at the window directly behind Marcus's head.

He smiles. "Oh, isn't this cute. You taught your girlfriend how to hold a gun, but I'm pretty sure she doesn't know how to use it. I bet it isn't even loaded." Marcus's words enrage me, and I want to shoot him even more now.

"Really? Would you like to test that theory, you arrogant son of a bitch?" Seth's hatred for Marcus oozes from his tone.

The adrenaline coursing through me is causing tunnel vision. All I can see is the cigar that is painted on the window behind Marcus's head. Everything else around me is black. I can hear Seth's voice, but I can no longer see him. I can't see Marcus's men, either, and I think I've stopped breathing.

Just then a woman exits the flower shop that is next to Fitz's. As soon as she sees all the guns, she screams at the top over her lungs and drops the vase of flowers she's holding, shattering the glass all over the sidewalk. This grabs the attention of Marcus and his men.

"Now!" Seth yells.

Without hesitation I pull the trigger, and as if in slow motion, I watch as my bullet flies past Marcus's ear and embeds itself into the cigar painted on Fitz's window.

Bullseye!

My shot causes Marcus and the other men to fire back. Seth pushes me to the ground, and I crawl toward the Mercedes using it for cover. Seth fires back, and all I can hear are the screams of the woman who was only there to buy flowers.

I can't let Seth do this alone!

My need to protect him kicks in, and I make my way to the back of the car. Craning my head around, I can see one of

Marcus's men. His attention is on Seth, so I take aim and fire one shot that hits him directly in the shoulder, spinning him around and knocking him to the ground.

"Alex, get in the car!" I hear Seth shout.

I do what he says and crawl into the backseat, closing the door behind me. Moments later, Seth is in the driver's seat and we are speeding away. I look out the back window, and I can see the man I shot lying on the ground, holding his shoulder. The other nameless man is at his side, and I can see blood flowing from his leg. Marcus appears to be uninjured.

Figures!

I crawl into the front seat and look at Seth. He is intense and focused as he races through the streets.

"Where to now? Back to the apartment?" I ask.

"I'm not sure. Open this, and let's find out," Seth answers, handing me the cigar that Fitz had given him.

Confused, I hold the cigar in my hand and stare at him. "Okay, what am I supposed to do with this?" I ask.

"Break it in two. There should be some coordinates inside."

Why am I not surprised?

I snap the Brazilian cigar in half, and sure enough, sticking out of one end is a rolled piece of paper. I pull it out, read off the numbers to Seth, and he enters them into the car's GPS. Within seconds, the generic voice is telling us to turn left at the next intersection.

We drive in silence for a while, then out of nowhere Seth says, "That was some pretty good shooting back there, baby. Two direct hits, I'm impressed."

I blush a little then reply, "Yeah, well I've always been a fast learner. I really wanted to shoot Marcus in the face."

"What stopped you?" he asks.

"Taking a life isn't something I'm prepared to do. Besides, if I did I would be just like one of them."

"You're an amazing girl, you know that?" Seth takes my hand and caresses it softly. "Every day, I love you more and more."

His words give me butterflies in my stomach. I love him so much. More than I have ever loved anyone. I lean over, kiss his cheek, and whisper, "I love you too."

We drive for what seems like hours, turning every time the GPS commands. We are deep into the Ontario countryside. Farms, some active and some dilapidated and abandoned, are scattered throughout our drive. Finally, we turn onto a dirt road with no name.

"Your destination is on your right," the voice says.

Destination? All I can see is a small shack with a tin roof surrounded by trees. Seth pulls the car around to the side of the hovel and parks it where it can't easily be seen from the road, even though I can't imagine who else would drive down this road to nowhere. It dead-ends, and this is the only building on it.

"Wait here, and keep your eyes open," Seth barks.

Yes, sir! I know he's only trying to keep me safe, but all of his orders are starting to bug me. I can obviously take care of myself. If he didn't think so before, the bullet I put in that guy's shoulder should be a good indication.

Within a few minutes, Seth is back and opening my car door. "Where are we?" I ask.

"I'm not really sure. I knew my father had another safe house, but I had no idea this is what it was. What a dump." Seth looks annoyed.

"How do we get in? Do we just kick the door down?" I ask jokingly.

Seth snickers. "No, I have a key. Besides, it might look like a dump, but I'm sure the walls are re-enforced steel. Come on." He takes my hand, and we walk up to what appears to be the only door. Pulling a ring of keys from his pocket, he spins them around until he comes to the one he wants.

Unlocking the door, Seth takes one last look around, making sure we are still alone, then ushers me inside. Instantly, both of our mouths drop open. The shack is not a shack at all. The space is no bigger than my dorm room, but it is beautiful. Oak-paneled walls, a stone fireplace, and a dark-green leather sofa and matching recliner. It's like we stepped into Jackson Pierce's man den.

"Nice dump," I say to Seth, bumping him with my elbow.

Seth's face is priceless. Dumbfounded, he makes his way around the room, lighting oil lamps and placing fresh logs in the fireplace to start a fire. It had gotten dark on our drive, and it also had started to snow. The temperature had also dropped quite a bit, and it looks as though we're in for a lot of white powder.

"Stay inside while I go to the car to get our things. I have a feeling we're not getting out of here tonight." Seth closes the door behind him as the wind whips around outside.

I toss my now ruined coat on the sofa and take a look around the cabin. I can't really call it a shack anymore. There is no electricity, so the only light comes from the lanterns and the flickering of the fire, but it's enough. On the back wall is a bookcase filled with books and tarnished silver picture frames. To the left of that is the only other door. Curious, I turn the knob and look inside. To my relief, it's a bathroom. Grabbing one of the oil lamps, I take it inside with me and close the door. A small mirror hangs on the wall, and I can see that I am a mess *again*!

"Alex?" Seth's voice sounds panicked. I open the door and step out so he can see me. Dropping everything that he is holding, he rushes over and wraps me in his arms. "You scared me," he whispers.

"I'm sorry. I just wanted to freshen up a bit. I'm a mess again," I reply, embarrassed that he's seeing me like this again!

"Don't worry about that. Let's get you something to eat. I know I'm starving and you must be too."

We sit together on the floor in front of the fire and Seth pulls a loaf of bread and some peanut butter and jelly jars from a brown paper bag, along with a box of plastic silverware. These are the supplies we bought back in Montreal. Also in the bag is a family-size bag of Doritos, six cans of soda, and a bag of marshmallows.

"Marshmallows?" I ask.

Seth smiles. "I don't know why I grabbed them. You used to love roasting marshmallows when you were little. I guess I thought we could roast them at the cabin in Montreal, but we didn't get to stay there long enough, but I think this place is even better."

"I agree." The things he remembers about me as a child blows my mind. It's like he set every little detail to memory, in case he never saw me again.

I make us each a PB & J sandwich and crack open two cans of soda. It's like we're on a picnic. The shootout in front of Fitz's shop is a distant memory. It's just us again. There's no one else in the world.

After we finish eating, Seth puts a kettle of water on the fire so I can freshen up once it's warm enough. I watch his every move, once again mesmerized by his grace and beauty. He empties the contents of his pockets on to the small oak table by the door, and a shiny object catches my eye. *My key.*

I get up and stand next to him, taking the key in my hand. It's key number 19.

"All the other keys are gone aren't they?" I ask, staring at the single key in my hand.

Seth hesitates then answers, "Yes."

His answer cuts me like a knife. The one thing that made me feel close to my parents was that bracelet, and all that's left is key 19 with its perfect blue sapphire.

"I'm sorry, Alex. Once the keys were inserted, there was no way of getting them out. They only key I was able to save for you was the evacuation key. The others were all disintegrated." He runs his finger down the length of the key in my hand.

I close my hand around his finger and lean my head against his chest. At least I still have one, and as long as I have Seth, nothing else matters.

"Why did your father send us here?" I ask.

"I'm not sure. There must be something here he wanted us to find. Care to have a look around?" He kisses the top of my head, and I release the hold I have on his finger.

The room is small, but it has plenty of places to hide a letter or small object of some kind. And neither Seth nor I know what we are looking for. I start at the bookcase. I thumb through novels by Ernest Hemingway and William Shakespeare, short stories by Edgar Allen Poe and books written about Mickey Mantle and Jackie Robinson. But the books that peek my interest most are the ones about the Freemasons and the ones about The Order of Swords and Skulls.

Seth is on the other side of the room, looking through the drawers of a small desk that sits next to the fireplace. I can hear him grumbling to himself, irritated that he is coming up empty. The last book I come across is a leather-bound photo album. I flip quickly through pages of black and white photographs, and on the last page, I find a letter addressed to Seth. I call his attention to it.

Seth takes the envelope over to the sofa and turns one of the oil lamps up higher so he can see better. Unlike me, Seth is not intimidated by the letter written by his father, just the opposite. Without hesitation, he tears open the flap and pulls out the paper. Joining him on the couch, I sit quietly as he reads.

Seth,

You are here because there is one more thing that will help you bring down Maxwell Wellington. It is hidden under one of the floorboards in front of the fireplace. Find it. Listen to it, and do with it what is best for you and Alex. Keep our girl safe. I am very proud of you my son.

Be safe.

—Dad

Immediately, Seth is on his hands and knees, knocking on each of the floorboards, trying to find the right one. The fifth board he hits sounds different from the others. Grabbing the fire poker from the stand, he uses it to pry up the loose board. From underneath, he pulls out a small wooden box.

Before he opens it, Seth looks at me and takes a deep breath. "Open it," I encourage.

Inside the box is a small silver tape recorder with a tape still inside. Again Seth looks to me as if he needs my permission. I nod to him, and he presses Play.

"Why did you do it, Max?" a deep voice asks.

"I don't know what the hell you're talking about, Jack," Max replies.

"Don't lie to me. You've won. Your secret is safe. Just tell me why you had to kill Ben and Elaina. They have a daughter. All they wanted was to be left alone. Now that beautiful little girl has to grow up without her parents. How can you live with yourself?" Jack's voice is distressed and angry.

"I told him not to screw with me, but he didn't listen. Now he's dead. His wife was just collateral damage. And no one can prove that I had anything to do with it. That gambling junkie truck driver is dead, so he can't talk, and you know damn well

275

your father won't let you say anything. And you know what, I could care less if that little girl has to grow up without her parents. When I close my eyes at night, I sleep like a baby."

Max's voice makes my blood run cold. How can anyone be so callous? Is this what being a part of The Order does? It makes their men stone-cold killers with no regard for anyone other than themselves and their brothers. The longer the tape goes on, the more I start to feel sick.

"You are an unbelievable bastard, Max, and one day, you will pay for your crimes. This I can promise you." Jack's voice was almost a whisper. You could tell talking about the death of his best friend hurt him deeply, but he achieved his goal. He got Max to admit that he was the one who arranged the death of my parents.

Seth presses the Stop button and waits for my reaction. But I'm not sure how to react. I'm angry and sad and full of rage, but the sound of Maxwell Wellington's voice on that tape does something to me. It makes me driven. I know what I have to do. He has hurt far too many people, and his time as Sword and Skulls royalty is over, and I'm going to be the one to take him down!

The Last Night

"Alex?"

Seth's voice pulls me out of my own mind. The thoughts of revenge and justice take a backseat to the calming feeling I get from just hearing his velvety voice. I smile at him.

"The water is ready. Would you like to freshen up and change your clothes?" Seth asks.

I am covered in dirt and have been dying for a shower, but I guess a sponge bath will have to do. I nod. Seth removes the kettle from the fire and carries it into the bathroom, filling the copper sink with steaming hot water. I take off my sweater and jeans, leaving them in a pile on the floor, and join Seth in the tiny room.

He blushes a little when he notices I am wearing nothing but my bra and panties. "I'll give you some privacy," he says, taking a step out of the room.

"Stay with me?" I ask in a soft sultry voice, taking him by the hand. "I'm sure you could use a little freshening up too."

Without saying a word, he turns around and stands within an inch of my body. I lift his shirt up over his head and toss it to the floor. The soft glow from a small oil lamp is all that illuminates the tiny space, but by now, I know every inch of him by heart. Every curve, every muscle, every part of his perfect body, has been set to memory.

I dip a small washcloth into the steaming water then gently begin wiping away the day's dirt and stress from his body. I savor the moment—every minute we have together is a gift. I love him more than I can ever express with mere words. I want him to feel my love with every touch, with every kiss. I lean up and press my mouth to his.

"My turn," he whispers, tickling my lips.

I smile again and step back, allowing him to take over. Placing his hands on my shoulders, he turns me around so I am facing away from him. Seth brushes my long blond ponytail to one side and kisses the back of my neck, igniting my skin and sending sparks through my body.

Only he can wash away my pain and anger.

"I love you," he whispers.

Sweeping me into his arms, Seth carries me over to the fire. Holding me tightly, he slowly drops to his knees, never taking his eyes off mine. "Make love to me," I whisper.

The next few hours are the most passionate hours of my life. The love we make is the love that can only be made by soul mates. But it also feels a little sad.

We lay naked in front of the fire, and I watch as the flickering light dances across his body. Seth is quiet, too quite. "What's wrong?" I ask, breaking the silence.

He doesn't answer.

Propping myself up onto my elbow, I look down into his face. He's staring up at the ceiling, and he looks like he's about to cry. "Talk to me," I beg, brushing my fingers down his cheek.

He turns his head to look at me just as a tear escapes the corner of his eye. I can't imagine Seth crying. He is the strongest, bravest man I know. He's a CIA operative for God's sake—men like that don't cry. What could possibly bring a tear to his eye? He's making me nervous.

"Please." My voice is soft, and now I have tears in my eyes.

One glides down my cheek, then finally, Seth says something. "Don't cry, baby. I'm sorry."

I brush the tear away and try desperately to hold back the rest. "Why are you always saying you're sorry? And why all of a sudden do you look like your dog just died?"

Seth reaches up and grabs the blanket that is on the end of the sofa. He spreads it out over our naked bodies then turns onto his side and faces me. I mirror him and wait for him to speak.

"Alex, there is something I want to tell to you, and I don't want you to say anything until I am finished, all right?"

"Okay."

Seth pauses and takes a deep breath. The pain on his face breaks my heart, and I am terrified for what he is about to tell me.

"You are the love of my life. I have loved you from the moment you were born and every second after. I will love you until my last breath, and I promise I will never let anyone or anything hurt you. The reason I am always saying that I'm sorry is because none of this should have happened. You should be at home with you grandparents enjoying your carefree life. All the pain you have experienced over the past few days is what I have spent my entire life trying to keep you safe from, and I failed."

I open my mouth to argue, but I stop myself.

"Don't get me wrong. I would not trade these past few days with you for anything. I have been the happiest I have ever been just being with you. I would run with you forever, but I am determined to get you home safely and to get The Order out of your life for good. They will never hurt you or your family again. You have my word." His lip quivers as he finishes, and I can tell he is fighting back tears. There is something else he's not telling me, but I don't want to push him.

I need to say something. Something that will make him understand that as long as I'm with him, life is perfect. But all I can do is kiss him and hope that he can feel how much I love him.

Good-bye, Marcus

I wake to the sound of Seth moving quickly through the tiny cabin. The fire has gone out, and I have the blanket pulled up over my face to keep warm.

"What are you doing?" I ask, peeking over top of the blanket.

"You need to get dressed," Seth replies sternly.

"Why? What's going on?"

Seth is fully clothed and is staring out the lone window, holding his gun. "There's someone out there," he tells me.

"Are you sure it's not just an animal or something?" I ask, getting up and grabbing fresh clothes from one of the bags Seth brought in from the car last night. "We are in the middle of nowhere. Besides, didn't we get a ton of snow last night? The roads must be a mess. There's no way Marcus could have found us already. Could he?"

The question is out there, but I already know the answer. These guys are good. They found us twice before, so it is very possible they found us again. I walk over and stand next to him and look out into the white nothingness. It must have snowed at least two feet last night.

"Keep clear of the window, baby. Don't give them anything to aim at." He has his CIA voice again. The mission is on, and he's ready for it.

But what if Marcus and the other men are out there? There is only one door and one window. They are sure to have both covered. How are we going to get out of here?

I move around the cabin, stuffing things in bags and making sure all the evidence is secure in one place—videotapes, two bags of clothes, photo envelope, voice recorder, etc. Carolyn's necklace—it's in the pocket of my other jeans. I find the pile of clothes I left on the floor the night before and pull the small cloth pouch out of one of the pockets. I don't know why, but it's important to keep this one item close to me.

In the same pocket is the one and only key I have left from my bracelet. I open the pouch and drop the key in with the cross for safekeeping. Putting it back in my pocket just doesn't seem like a safe-enough place, so I reach up under my shirt and stuff it inside my bra. It's a little uncomfortable, but it's also close to my heart, and that is where it needs to be.

Seth is still staring out the window like a caged animal. I hesitate to speak, but I need to know what the plan is. My stomach is in knots again, but I'm not as scared as I probably should be.

"Baby," I whisper and wait for his response.

The sound of my heart beating in my ears counts off the seconds until Seth finally speaks. "They're out there." He's angry. "How the hell did they find us? *I* didn't even know about this place. The Order sure as hell couldn't have known about it. Somebody is feeding them information."

"Stanton?"

"No. I trust him with my life. He would never betray me."

"Then who?" I ask, not knowing who else would be privy to such classified information.

He growls, "I don't know, but when I find out, they *will* pay."

He means that. He has spent his entire life keeping me safe, and if someone is responsible for putting me in danger, he will not let them get away with it. That I'm sure of.

"Maybe they put a tracker on the car like they did your mom's car?"

"That's possible, but there is no way they knew which car was ours, so they would have had to put trackers on every car in front of Fitz's shop. That's unlikely. No, someone tipped them off." He taps his gun on his thigh, and I can see him getting angrier by the second.

"Okay, so how do we get out of here? There is only one door." My tone is strong and confident. Yes, I'm scared, but I am also ready. Firing that gun yesterday gave me strength I didn't know I had. I only took two shots, but I hit my target both times. I'm ready for more.

"Put your coat on," he orders.

I grab my dirt-and-soot-covered coat, frown at the sight, and pull it on over my shoulders. *Damn, I loved this coat.*

Seth is messing with something on the table, and as I walk up behind him, I pull the gun from the back of his waistband. This startles him. "What are you doing?"

"Getting ready," I answer.

"I think I've created a monster. One good hit, and suddenly we're Bonnie and Clyde." He's joking, but I can see pride in his eyes. "Grab the evidence bag." I throw the strap over my shoulder and wait for my next instruction.

"Take this." Seth hands me a piece of paper with an address scrolled across it.

"What's this for?" I ask.

He glances out the window again then back to me. "I don't know what's going to happen once we get out there. The only thing I want you to do is get to the car."

"What's the address for?" I ask again.

"If for some reason I am unable to get there with you, that is the address to Stanton's apartment. Punch it into the GPS, and get there as fast as you can. Don't stop for anything or anyone."

"I'm not leaving here without you!" I protest.

"Yes, you will." He's stern, but the idea of leaving without him is too hard to imagine. "If something happens, you have to get yourself and the evidence back to Stanton. He knows what to do if something happens to me. He will take care of you and get you home safely. Tell me you understand."

No, I don't understand! I will not leave here without him. I don't respond.

"Alexandra, please! Tell me you understand!" He's pleading with me now.

We have come too far to turn back now, and I know the most important thing is to keep the evidence out of the hands of The Order, so I just nod. But if he is not in the car with me I don't know if I can do this without him.

Seth hands me the key to the Mercedes.

"I don't know how many men are out there. You and I took out the two Marcus had with him yesterday, but I'm sure he has plenty of backup. Max would not send his son up against me without a small army." He has a hint of arrogance about him as he says that, and I am confident it will take more than three guys to take Seth down.

"The car is only twenty yards behind us in that cluster of trees. When we walk outside, I want you to keep your back up against the cabin and stay behind me. Marcus was instructed not to hurt you, and I am a Swordsman, so killing me is something they will do only if they have to. Once we reach the end of the building, I want you to keep your head down and run as fast as you can to the car. If you are shot at, shoot back. Don't look back. If I'm not there with you in a minute or less, leave without me. Do you understand?" He places his hand on the side of my face. It feels like he's saying good-bye.

I swallow hard and whisper, "Yes." Throwing my arms around his neck, I kiss him as hard as I can. I kiss him as if it's our last kiss. The thought makes me want to cry, but I hold back the tears and tell myself that we will both make it out of here together.

"I love you," he says.

"I love you too." I kiss him again.

"Ready?"

No!!! I take a deep breath and check my gun, making it hot. "Ready."

With my gun ready and a pit in my stomach, I follow Seth to the door. I take one last look around the tiny cabin and see a picture frame on the mantel I hadn't noticed before. It's a picture of our fathers, Ben and Jack, arms around each other and smiling as if they did not have a care in the world. It was clearly taken before The Order—before Carolyn. The image gives me a surge of adrenaline. I am determined to finish what they started, what they died for.

Seth cracks the door, and instantly a shot is fired toward the cabin. He closes it quickly. He looks around then grabs the bag that held our clothes and throws it over his shoulder.

"What are you doing?" I ask.

"Put the bag down and take off your coat," he orders.

Confused, I do as he says. He tosses my coat to the table then takes off his own coat.

"Put the bag back over your shoulder, then put my coat on over it." He hands me his gray pea coat. It's huge but conceals the bag nicely. I think I understand what he's doing. He wants them to think *he* is carrying the evidence, not me. But now that I am wearing his coat, he is going to freeze. Then I think about his "training." The CIA probably conditioned him to be able to withstand extreme cold or heat.

"Now what?"

"I am going to exit carrying this bag, drawing their attention. Wait thirty seconds, then open the door and race toward the car. Get in, lock the doors, and wait another thirty seconds. If I'm not there by then, leave. Drive as fast as you can, and don't look back."

"I can't leave you to fight Marcus and his men alone. I can help." My voice is pleading.

"Don't argue with me, Alex, please. I will be fine."

Fighting back tears, I nod that I understand, but in my heart I know that I'm not leaving this place without him.

"It's time."

He doesn't look at me. He places his hand on the door handle, and before I can stop him, he's out the door. Shots ring out. One, two, three, four—there are so many coming from all different directions.

Thirty seconds, I remind myself then pull open the door and run like hell toward the Mercedes. I catch the attention of two of the gunmen hiding in the trees.

"She's over here!" one of them calls out.

"I got her!" shouts another.

The next voice I hear I will never forget as long as I live. It's Marcus's voice. "Don't let her get away! One in the leg! I need her alive!" he shouts.

It seems the faster I run, the farther away the car gets. I feel a bullet fly past me, and without hesitating, I turn and fire back in the direction from where it came. Another ricochets off a tree about three feet from me. Again I fire back. I reach the car just as another bullet is embedding in its side.

"Don't let her get in that car!" Marcus screams. But it's too late. I'm in.

I fire up the engine and quickly survey the area looking for Seth. Two men are closing in on me. I throw the car in Reverse and hit the gas, but the car doesn't move. There is too much snow on the ground. *Son of a bitch!* I reach down and put the SUV in four-wheel drive and try again. This time, it moves a little. I throw it into Drive and floor it. The car leaps forward and nearly hits a tree, but I am able to navigate around it, only scraping the side along the bark.

Where is Seth?

Bullets fly at me from every direction, and I see Marcus running toward a dark SUV parked along the snow-covered dirt road. But I don't see Seth. My adrenaline is pumping, and I am determined to find him. As the Mercedes gets traction, I see three men facedown in the snow. Blood flowing out of them, and the contrast between red and white is striking. Suddenly I see someone taking aim at Marcus, now in his SUV. It's Seth. He's holding his side, and I can see that he's been shot.

Oh my God! I slam on the gas and race toward him. By this time, Marcus is speeding toward him as well. But I'm closer. I get to him just as Marcus is about to fire his gun from the driver's side window. "Get in!" I scream, throwing open the passenger-side door.

"I thought I told you to leave!" Seth growls as he climbs in the car.

"Seriously? You really thought I was going to leave you here? Have you met me?"

"Okay, sarcasm. Shut up and drive!"

I speed through the snow as fast as I can with Marcus hot on my tail. I try to keep my eyes on the road and not the blood flowing out of Seth's side.

"Baby, are you okay?" I ask.

"I'll be fine, just keep driving." His voice is weak, and I can tell he's losing too much blood.

I can see Marcus gaining on us in the rearview mirror. I'm out of practice driving in the snow, and in this kind of situation, I'm a little out of my league, but I keep the gas pedal to the floor and aim toward civilization. Suddenly we're hit from behind, and it causes me to lose control momentarily. As I regain control Marcus slams into us again. Seth moans in pain, and I press the pedal deeper into the floor.

"Baby, put your seatbelt on," I yell to Seth, but I don't think he's hears me. "Seth, can you hear me?"

His weak voice grumbles, "What?"

"Put your seatbelt on, please. Do it now!" I yell again.

"Why?"

The pain is evident, and I can tell moving hurts. He's losing so much blood, and if I don't get away from Marcus, I'm afraid Seth is going to die.

"Trust me. Please, baby, do as I say."

What I am about to do is going to hurt him so much, but it is the only thing I can think of, so I have to try. Finally, he does as I ask. As his shaky hand clicks the belt in place, he calls out in pain. I speed forward toward a sharp curve in the road. Marcus has fallen behind a little, and this is my only chance.

"Hold on, baby!"

Just before we hit the curve, I slam on the brakes. The back end of the Mercedes starts to fishtail, and we begin to spin, but I am able to get control, stopping us just before plowing into a huge snowdrift. My sudden and unexpected move causes Marcus to react. He swerves to avoid colliding with us and hits the curve too fast to control what happens next. I watch as the black SUV spins out of control and slams head first into a large tree, crushing the front end in on Marcus, pinning him behind the wheel.

"*Oh! Uh! Jesus!*" Seth's agonizing screams pull my attention away from the horrific crash. "*Alex!*"

"Oh my God! Seth, are you okay?" I shriek, reaching for him and placing my hand over his wound.

"What happened?" he groans.

"We stopped." That's the best answer I can come up with.

He stares at me with wide, pain-filled eyes. "Stopped! Why? We have to keep going! Marcus is coming for you!" His urgency and protectiveness is still there. He's the one who's injured, and he's still trying to protect me.

"Shhh…" I stroke his face and try to calm him, but he's still so agitated.

"Marcus!" is all he can say between moans.

"Baby, can you sit up?" I ask him.

"Why?"

"I need you to see something." I help him slide up in his seat then point to the wreckage that is Marcus's SUV.

"Who is that?" he asks.

"Marcus."

"Marcus! I have to…" Unbuckling his belt Seth tries feebly to get out of the car.

"Where the hell are you going?" I yell.

"I have to see—"

"The hell you do! You have been shot. We need to get you to a hospital." I reach over to put the car in Gear when Seth raises a bloody hand to stop me.

"Alex, please," he's pleading with me again. "I may hate him, but he's my brother."

"What the hell are you talking about? He tried to kill us, and you want to see if he's all right? Are you crazy?"

This is insane. How deep can loyalty go? Marcus is probably the one who shot him! Seth is not getting out of this car!

He just stares at me, knowing that no matter what he says, I won't understand.

"Fine! I'll go." I reach for the door handle.

"Take your gun."

"This is ridiculous!" I open the car door and step out into the deep snow, gripping my gun. Slowly, I make my way toward the pile of scrap metal that once was a beautiful black BMW X5. I can hear Marcus moaning as I get closer. There is no way he is getting out of that wreck without being paralyzed or losing a limb. The front end is completely sandwiched in on him. I raise my weapon and approach the driver's side door. The window was blown out by the crash, and between what the airbag and the steering wheel did to Marcus's face, his is almost unrecognizable. There is blood everywhere.

"Alex." Blood is pouring out of his mouth, and he gurgles as he says my name.

Where's your arrogance now?

"Alex," he calls out again, this time reaching a bloody hand out to me. "I'm sorry."

"You're sorry?" *Is he freaking kidding?*

"I'm sorry," he says again, this time in a whisper.

I keep my gun pointed at him, but a part of me wants to go to him—to help him. If I didn't detest him so much, I would be trying to save his life. But the image of Seth bleeding out in the other car stops me.

"It's too late for sorry." I open my mouth to say more, but the smell of gasoline stops me. Bending down, I can see gas leaking from the undercarriage. *Oh God! I have to help him.* I tuck the gun into the back of my pants and run to his door and begin pulling as hard as I can. "Hang on, Marcus, I'll get you out."

I pull and pull, but it just won't give. I climb, throw the back window, and try to pull him out that way, but every time I touch him, he screams out in agony. I don't know what to do.

"I'm going to go see if there's a crowbar or something in our car. Something to pry this door open."

Just as I turn to run back to the Mercedes, Marcus yells, "Alex, stop!"

His command surprises me. I turn around to face him.

"There's nothing you can do, not by yourself. Just go. Get Seth to a hospital. Tell him I'm sorry. Tell him I was just trying to protect my father." He's starting to spit up blood again, and I can see it running from his ears as well. I have to do something.

"I'll get to a phone and send help. Hang in there, and I will get someone out to you, I promise." The tears are flowing down my face again. I'm crying over a man I can't stand. A man who tried to kill me. But right now all I see is a helpless little boy who loves his father. It breaks my heart. I take hold of his hand and promise again, "I'll send help."

I run back to the Mercedes and find a semiconscious Seth slumped over in the passenger seat. "Baby, look at me."

He is so pale, and his breathing is shallow. Not only do I need to get help for Marcus, but if I don't get Seth to a hospital, I'm going to lose him. I activate the GPS in the car and start typing in *hospital*.

"What are you doing?" Seth groans.

"Trying to find the closest hospital." *What does he think I'm doing?*

"No. Just get me to Stanton's."

"What? No! You need a doctor." He's completely delusional now. I continue the search for the closest hospital.

He raises a limp hand, trying to stop me. "Stanton is a doctor."

What the hell is he talking about? Stanton is a military tech designer, not a doctor. The loss of blood is making him crazy.

"Please. Take me to Stanton." He can barely speak now, but he is so insistent. I grab the crumbled up sheet of paper out of my pocket and type in Stanton's address.

Before I pull away, I take one last look at Marcus. He doesn't appear to be conscious. As quickly and carefully as I can, I begin driving, following the GPS directions.

I have to get to a phone. My thoughts float between keeping Seth awake and making sure I get help for Marcus, but really, all I want to do is scream and cry. Once all of this is over, I'm probably going to need some serious therapy.

"Turn left in one quarter of one mile," the GPS lady interrupts my train of thought.

Without warning, a tremendous explosion rocks the sleepy Ontario countryside, and I know help for Marcus is too late.

"Good-bye, Marcus."

Don't Look Back

"Seth! Baby! Wake up! Stay with me! We're almost there!" He doesn't answer me.

Seth has been in and out of consciousness the entire drive back to Stanton's, but this is the first time I am unable to bring him back by calling his name. I reach over and touch his face. He's cold, and he's barely breathing. We are only minutes from the apartment. I step on the gas, blowing through a red light, and receive several irritated honks and finger gestures from the drivers that have to swerve to avoid hitting us. My heart is in my throat, and all that matters is that I get Seth to the apartment.

As we reach the entrance to the underground parking garage, I begin honking my horn, furiously grabbing the attention of the armed guard keeping post. He recognizes the Mercedes and quickly opens the security gates, allowing me access. Once inside, I am met by Jeffery and two other armed men. As soon as they take control of the situation, I completely lose my composure.

"*Help him!*" I scream in between sobs. "*Help him!*"

"Man down. Gunshot wound to the abdomen. Massive blood loss. Nonresponsive," Jeffery barks into his radio. "Smith, you take her. We've got this."

Two strong hands grip my shoulders and pull me away from Seth. "*No!* I have to stay with him." I struggle to free myself from his hold, but I have no strength. I'm hysterical. Seth won't wake up and I'm helpless. If he dies, I don't think I can go on living.

I fall back into Smith's arms.

"Come, Mrs. Campbell, let's get you up stairs. They will take good care of him. He's going to be just fine," he says.

His words are sincere, but there is no way he can be sure of that. We had been driving for over an hour. Didn't he see all the blood in the car? No one can lose that much blood and survive.

"Seth," I whisper then everything goes black.

"Welcome back," a deep, soothing voice says as I slowly open my eyes.

"Seth!" I sit up quickly, but it makes my head spin, and I have to lie back down.

"Easy, Alex."

I focus on the face that is looking down at me. It's Stephen Stanton. "Stevie, where's Seth?" I ask, almost afraid to hear the answer.

"He's resting."

Resting! He's alive! I have to see him! I try to get up again, but Stevie holds me down.

"Alex, please. Let me take a look at you. You've been through quite a trauma." He takes hold of my wrist and begins taking my pulse.

What is he talking about? Seth is the one who was shot, not me. I'll be fine just as soon as I can see for myself that he's okay.

"You're pulse is a little fast, but that is understandable. Now I want you to sit up slowly." He offers me his hand and helps me upright. The rooms spins a little. "How do you feel?" he asks.

I furrow my forehead. *I don't know how I feel.* "I don't know," I answer.

"Can you tell me what day it is?"

To be honest I have no idea what day it is. The past few days have blended together, and I've lost track. My lack of response doesn't seem to faze him.

"Can you tell me where you are?"

"Your apartment in Toronto," I answer.

"Good. How about your parents' names?"

"Benjamin and Elaina Shelley."

"Excellent. I think you are going to be just fine." He hands me a glass of water and two small white pills. "Here, take these," he insists. "Just something to help you relax. You've had quite a day." He smiles like it's no big deal.

I hand the pills back. "I'd rather not if that is all right. I'm fine. I'd just really like to see Seth now." I take a drink of water.

"He's sedated. I was able to remove the bullet. He was very lucky it missed hitting any vital organs. The only major concern was the amount of blood loss, but he's doing fine."

He's proud of himself. I can see it in his face. He's saved his friend's life. I want to hug him.

"May I see him?" I ask again.

He smiles. "Of course. Please." He offers me his hand.

Stevie escorts me down the hall past the room where Seth and I made love and into another bedroom where Seth is sleeping peacefully. I rush to his side but hesitate.

"May I touch him?" I ask Stevie.

"Yes, of course."

I lean over his angelic face and kiss his forehead. He doesn't wake. "Is he in pain?" I ask.

Stevie chuckle, "Not with the drugs I gave him. But he will be later once they wear off."

I smile at his relaxed demeanor. I haven't known him long, but he seems like a man that is always calm in stressful situations. "Stevie, may I ask you something?"

"You may ask me anything, my dear." He takes a step closer to me, but I keep my eyes on Seth.

"Forgive me, but I thought you owned a tech company. But after Seth was shot, he insisted I bring him here because you are a doctor." I look up to see his reaction.

He's smirking at me. "I don't believe that was a question."

I roll my eyes at his sarcastic response. "Okay, how's this. Stevie, are you a doctor?"

"I used to be."

What? I narrow my eyes and just stare at him, waiting for him to elaborate.

After a long pause, he continues. "I was a military doctor. That is how Seth and I met—under very bloody circumstances. But if you want more details, I'm afraid you will have to ask him. I have put that part of my life out of my mind." He runs his fingers through his hair and looks down at his friend.

I can see in his eyes that he truly cares for Seth. Whatever happened between the two of them must have brought them very close. Although Stevie is old enough to be Seth's father, I can see that their bond runs deep.

"Once my military service was up, I decided my skills would be better used working for the Peace Corps, so I joined Doctors Without Borders. The pain and carnage I experience traveling through third-world countries took it out of me, and I couldn't do it anymore."

"So you quit?" I can't help the tone of surprise in my voice.

He sighs. "No, I just turned my focus to something else."

I don't know how to respond to that. I look down at Seth lying there all bandaged up and alive and can't imagine why someone who has such a gift would choose not to use it. But I am so grateful that he was able to save the love of my life. Before I can stop myself, I throw my arms around his neck and squeeze him tightly. "Thank you," I whisper.

He wraps his arms around me and returns the sentiment.

"Would you stop hitting on my girl?" Seth's weak voice startles us, and I release my hold on Stevie and immediately throw myself onto Seth.

"Seth! I was so scared!" Tears stream down my cheeks and splash onto his bare chest.

"Oh, easy, baby," Seth moans, pushing me away from his wound.

"I'm sorry!" I gasp, realizing what I've done. I pull away but he stops me.

"Hey, man!" Stevie smiles at the sight of his conscious friend. "You can't blame a man for trying. She's quite a catch." He reaches down to examine the Seth's bandage. "You're a lucky man."

"I know," Seth replies, squeezing my hand and smiling his perfect smile.

Stevie laughs. "Yes, her, but I was referring to your injury. The bullet managed to miss all vital organs, and other than a hole in your gut, you only have two cracked ribs, which appear to have been caused by a seatbelt."

Damn it! That's my fault.

"How about my girl here? She check out okay?" Seth asks.

"She's no worse for wear. She doesn't have a scratch on her." He sounds almost surprised. To be honest, so am I.

I lie down on the bed next to Seth and nuzzle my face into his neck. Everything is going to be all right; I know it. He turns his head and kisses me on the forehead.

"I'll leave you two alone." Stevie turns to leave the room then pauses. "Oh but, Alex, our boy needs his rest, so don't stay too long."

I nod in agreement.

"Would you just get out of here?" Seth insists.

Stevie chuckles as he exits the room.

"I should be very angry with you," Seth says, trying to hide a smile.

"Why is that?" I ask.

He narrows his eyes at me. "Because you didn't do as you were told."

I prop myself so he can see my face. I want him to understand, to really see what he means to me.

"Seth, I would have never left you there. I would have fought to my last breath to get to you. If you had died there, I would never be able to forgive myself or go on living without you."

He places a weak hand in my face. "I know," he whispers.

His eyes start to get heavy, and I can tell he's fighting to stay awake. "You need to rest, baby. I'm going to go and let you sleep."

"Don't go," he insists, stopping me before I slide off the bed. "Stay until I fall asleep."

His requests warms my heart, and I lie back down next to him. I run my fingers through his hair and down the side of his face and watch as he slowly drifts off. He looks so young and helpless. CIA Seth is so strong and confident, which makes him appear much older than he really is. It's easy to forget that he is only twenty-three. But right now, he looks even younger than that. He's a boy who needs to be taken care of, and I plan to do just that for the rest of our lives.

Stevie is on the phone when I enter the living room. His conversation is intense, and it makes me uncomfortable eavesdropping, so I go into the kitchen and pour myself a glass of juice. A few moments later, he joins me.

"Sorry about that," he says, leaning up against the island.

"Is there anything wrong?" I ask.

He looks down to the floor and rubs his fingers across his forehead.

"What is it?" I press.

He looks at me and sighs. "We found out who leaked your location, and it's not going to make Seth very happy."

"Who?"

He doesn't answer.

"Stevie, who is it?" I have to know. He must tell me.

"His grandfather."

What? "His grandfather? I thought..." My mind doesn't know how to process this information. "The way Seth spoke of him I thought he was dead." I think back to all the conversations we had about his grandfather; not one gave me the impression he was still alive.

"To Seth he is dead." Stevie's tone is cold. "Seth may have been molded in his grandfather's image, but he has never loved or respected the man."

Apparently Stevie doesn't respect him either.

My head is spinning. "Are you sure he is the one who told Marcus..."

He nods.

"What the...why would he...he almost got us killed! Why..." I've lost the ability to finish a sentence.

Seth's grandfather sent Marcus and those other men after us. He's the reason Seth is lying in that bed. He's the reason Marcus is dead. Who would do such a thing? My stomach starts turning, and the acidy juice now burns as it pushes its way back up into my throat. I lean over and heave into the sink.

Stevie walks over and places a gentle hand on my back. "Are you okay?" he asks.

No! I heave again.

Once there is nothing left in my stomach, I wipe my mouth with my sleeve and pull away from Stevie's touch. I run from the kitchen and throw open the doors to the patio. The cold air rushes through me, sending goose bumps across my body. I stare out into the Toronto Skyline. The sun is shining, and I can see the CN Tower glisten. My anger stops me from truly appreciating its beauty.

"Alex." Stevie's voice is behind me again. "It's very cold. Please come back inside." I feel his hand on my shoulder, but I don't move. The cold air is all that is keeping me from exploding. My blood is boiling so hot I feel like my skin is melting.

"I need a minute," I snap, and I immediately feel guilty for my tone.

He removes his hand, and I hear him walk back into the apartment. I gaze into the sky, but my eyes can only see Seth covered in blood and seconds from death. Then I see Marcus. The boy who loved his father. The boy who died in the most horrific way.

I begin to shiver. I don't know if it's because of the cold or because of my thoughts, but I finally walk back inside. Stevie is sitting on one of the sofas, waiting patiently for me to regain my composure.

"Stevie, why would Mr. Pierce do this?" I ask.

He shakes his head. "From what my contact has told me, neither of you were supposed to get hurt. You were supposed to be brought in with the evidence, and things were going to be worked out internally." He pauses for a moment and looks me in the face. "Clearly, he underestimated both of you."

"Clearly," I growl. "Now Marcus is dead, Seth is in that bed, and they still don't have what they want. And they're not going to get it!"

I can tell that Stevie is surprised by my outburst, but he's smiling at me.

"Seth said you were tough."

"Are the bags we had with us still in the car?" I ask.

"No. They are in my office. Why?"

"Could you take me to them please?"

Stevie stands. "Of course. Follow me."

He leads me through a door just off the living room. As we enter, the lights brighten. Stevie's office is a nerd's fantasy: high-tech devices and gadgets everywhere. Flat-screen monitors on every flat wall surface and a computer unlike anything I have ever seen before.

"They're here," Stevie says, drawing my attention to the bags on the floor near his desk.

I rummage through the evidence bag and pull out the five Betamax tapes. "Do you have anything that can play these?" I ask, showing him the archaic bricks of plastic.

He laughs so hard I think he may fall down. "I haven't seen one of those in a million years. May I?"

I hand him one of the tapes, and he examines it like it's from another planet. This irritates me. *Can you play it or not?*

He walks over to a black metal cabinet and pulls open the doors. With a few flips of switches and a loud hum, Stevie slides the tape into a machine then turns toward one of the huge monitors. I follow his gaze. After a few seconds of snow, a black-and-white image finally appears on the screen.

I glare at the silent images of young men moving about a large room. And I gasp when I see a woman enter the picture.

"Is there sound?" I ask, not able to tear my eyes from the screen.

"There doesn't appear to be," Stevie's voice says from behind me.

It doesn't matter. The image of Carolyn, with her knee-length skirt and sweater set is enough to break my heart. I move closer to the screen. Why I need to see what was about to happen I don't know, but I have to see it for myself. I have to see what those men did to her. I have to know that everything that has happen over the past few days happened for a reason.

I watch in horror as Wellington and the other men tear at Carolyn's clothes. As Parker Ashcroft violates her. As the men cheer him on. And I gasp as she wakes and realizes what is happening to her. I want to scream, "Stop!" I want to look away, but my eyes stay glued to the screen.

Just as Carolyn plunges the shard of glass into Parker's neck, the screen goes black. I turn to Stevie and am taken back by a very pale and angry Seth standing next to him.

"Why…" I don't finish my question. I know why Seth made Stevie stop the tape. He never wanted me to see any of this, to have this in my memory. He wants to protect me.

"Is everything ready?" Seth asks curtly.

Stevie nods. "It'll be here within the hour." The two of them exchange a knowing glance, then Stevie leaves the room.

"You should be in bed," I remind Seth.

"I'm fine. Just a little sore." He holds his hand out to mine. "Come with me," he says.

I take his hand, and he leads me to the bedroom where we spent the night. Lying on the bed is a fresh pair of jeans and sweater just my size.

"Jump in the shower, and get cleaned up. I'll be right here when you're done." He kisses me gently, and I can see sadness in his eyes.

As quickly as I can, I wash all the dirt and blood from my body, wash my hair, then wrap myself up in a towel and go back into the bedroom to be with Seth. Something is wrong, and I have to find out what it is.

Seth is on the bed lying on his back and holding his hand over his wound. He's in a lot of pain I can tell.

"Are you okay, baby?" I ask. "Should I go get Stevie?"

He shakes his head no. I grab the clothes off the bed and quickly get dressed. I want to take care of him. Whatever he needs. I sit down next to him and place my hand gently over his. He flinches a little.

"Sorry," I mouth.

"We need to talk," he says, trying to sit up.

I try to hold him down, but he fights me. "You need to rest. We can talk later," I insist.

"No. We need to talk now."

His sense of urgency frightens me. "Okay," I reply, helping him sit up.

He takes my hands in his and looks me in the eyes. "I love you so much."

"I love you too."

He puts his fingers to my lips, silently telling me not to speak. My heart starts to race, and I can feel tears welling up in my eyes. I'm not going to like what he's about to say.

"Alex, I love you, and in a few minutes, Stevie is going to take you home."

Home? No! We haven't finished what we started!

"You are going to go home to your family, and I am going to finish this. But once I do, there is no coming back for me. I will be on the run for the rest of my life. I won't let them take away *your* future too. You are going to go on and graduate. You are going to have a career. You're going to get married and have a family—everything you deserve. And The Order will never come near you again. I promise"

"No!" I scream through tears. "I don't want any of that without you!"

He pulls me close to him, and even though it hurts, he holds me tight. "You have people who love you. People who would be devastated if you didn't come home. You know you can't hurt them like that, not for me. I need you to promise me that you will go home and continue your life and forget about me."

"No!" I scream again. I'm weeping uncontrollably. *How can he be saying this to me? How can he think I can just go home and carry on as if none of this has happened? Does he think I can just stop loving him?* I feel like I'm dying.

He raises my face to his and kisses me firmly. I want to beg him to stop saying these things, to take it back, but I can't speak.

Jen McCombs

I can barely breathe. I wrap my arms around his neck. I refuse to let him go. I won't let go until he changes his mind.

"I'll run with you," I whimper.

He tries to pull me off, but for the first time he's not strong enough. I cling to him as if my life depends on it. I won't let him go! I can't let him go!

"Alex, you need to let go. You're hurting him." Stevie's voice is behind me now, his hands on my shoulders trying to pull me away. Trying to pull me away from my only reason to live.

Seth moans in pain, and I finally set him free.

"I'm...sorry," I say between sobs.

Stevie is holding me back as Seth catches his breath and the pain subsides. "It's time," he tells Seth from over my shoulder.

My knees give out, and I fall to the floor. *Why is this happening?*

Stevie helps me to my feet. Seth comes and stands in front of me. He gently takes my face in his hands and kisses my lips. "You are my life, Alexandra. I will love you until the day I die. Good-bye." He kisses me again then leaves me standing there alone with Stevie.

"*No!*" I scream. "*No! Seth! No!*" I try to follow him, but Stevie restrains me. I fight with everything I have, but I can't get free of his hold. I crumple to the floor again. I lie there holding my knees to my chest and cry harder than I have ever cried in my life. It feels as though a train has ripped through my chest. I want to die.

Unable to stop him, Stevie lifts me in his arms and carries me down the hall to the elevator. Once inside, I feel like I'm about to pass out. Within seconds, the doors open again, and Stevie carries me out on the roof of the building, where waiting for us is a helicopter.

My mind is telling me to fight. To struggle to get free and run back to Seth and beg him to change his mind, to take me with him, but I can't. I've lost the will to live, and as Stevie places me inside the helicopter, my body begins to shake.

302

Jeffery is behind the controls of the massive vibrating machine, and once Stevie is inside, I feel us ascend into the air. A part of me wants to throw the door open and jump. Jump to my death. Death is the only way to make this pain go away. Instead, I think about what Seth said about my family and how they would feel if I never came back. My grandparents have already lost their son; I can't leave them too.

I look back at the mile-high apartment building and watch as it grows smaller and smaller.

"Don't look back, Alex," Stevie says. "It will only make it hurt more."

Life after Death

When the helicopter finally touches down, Stevie slides open the door, lifts me into his arms, and carries me to the black town car that is waiting for us. I know he's talking to me, but I cannot hear a word of what he is saying. All my senses are gone. I don't feel, I don't hear, and I can't even see. My body has shut down. My heart has died, and the rest of my body is prepared to join it.

I have no idea where we are, and I don't care. I just lie curled up in the fetal position, numb to the world.

"Alex!" Stevie is shaking me. "Alex, look at me. Please."

I try to focus on his face, but he's just a blur.

"What do we do?" I hear Jeffery ask.

"She's in shock. She's shutting down. I told him this was a bad idea."

Stevie's voice is concerned for me, but I can hear his disappointment in it as well. But disappointment in whom I'm not sure. Is he disappointed in me that I'm not stronger? Disappointed that I'm not handling this better, or is he disappointed in Seth for doing this to me? I hope it's the latter. How did Seth think I would handle this? Just smile and understand that he's doing this for my own good? Why would he think being apart would ever be the right thing?

"Alex, I need you to focus. To listen to me now." Stevie's voice is low and soft. He's trying to pull me into the present. "Can you hear me?"

I nod.

He sighs. "Good. You're home."

Home! I crane my neck to look out the window, but I don't get up. I can't get up.

"Do you understand?" he asks.

I nod again.

"Good. I have assigned Jeffery to you. He will be your protection detail until we know you are no longer in danger." He pauses then asks again, "Do you understand?"

Protection detail? Just let The Order have me. I don't care anymore.

Again I just nod.

"Your family and friends won't know he's here, but he has been instructed to follow your every move. To keep you safe. You are to return to school and continue your life as if the past few days have not happened." He takes hold of my hand, gently caressing it. "Alex, Seth is doing this because he loves you."

Loves me? If he loved me, he wouldn't have sent me away. He doesn't love me!

I try to pull my hand away, but he stops me. He flips my hand over and places a small business card in my palm. "Take this. I am available to you 24/7. Anything you need, just call or email." He slides a bag in front of me. It's the bag I started my journey with. "All your things are inside. We have replaced your cell phone as well. I have programmed my number and Jeffery's number into it. You may want to go through your messages."

Messages. Right. There are probably a million messages from my grandparents and Barb and... of course, Chase. How am I supposed to just go back to my life? Nothing is ever going to be the same. I will never be the same, and the people who know me and love me are going to notice.

I feel Stevie place something over my shoulders. "Please put this on."

I force myself to sit up and slide my arms into a brand-new white winter coat. The same coat that I had ruined the day before. Stevie is sending me home exactly the way I left it.

I can see my house now. We are parked just a few doors down. Part of me wants to run to it, throw open the door, and wrap my arms around my grandparents and never let go. But another part of me is afraid. I'm not the same person I was when I left. Will I disappoint them? Will the secrets I now know change our relationship? That thought is like a punch in the gut. The Order changed my father from the son they knew, and now it has changed me. They don't deserve any of this.

Stevie's voice pulls my attention. "It's time, Alex."

I can see him now. The blurriness is gone. His handsome features are soft and kind, fatherly. "Tell him I love him," I whisper.

He glides his fingers down my cheek. "He knows," is all he can say.

Jeffery opens the car door, and a burst of cold air rushes through me. Stepping out slowly, I turn back to Stevie. "Thank you."

"Anything you need, I'm here."

I stumble toward my house, and as my knees weaken, I'm not sure I can even make it. As I reach the end of the driveway, I hear the high-pitch cry of my grandmother.

"Alex! You're home."

The two of them race toward me, and just as I'm overtaken by my grandfather's embrace, I collapse.

"Alex!" he shouts. "What's wrong?"

I spend the next two weeks in bed, unable to eat or sleep and barely able to speak. Sam never leaves my side. My grandparents are beside themselves with worry. They bring in doctor after doctor, trying to figure out what is wrong with me, but they can find nothing. Physically, I'm fine. I am a medical mystery.

Chase comes to see me every day and begs me repeatedly to tell him what's wrong. He brings me flowers and food. He even tries bringing over DVDs. He watches them while I stare off into space. Barb is the only one who doesn't push me. She stays with me for days and lets me cry when I need to cry, lets me scream when I need to scream, and even though I don't tell her what happened, she knows me better than anyone, and she knows I will come around when I'm ready.

Two days before I am scheduled to return to school, I overhear my grandparents discussing sending me to a hospital.

"We can't send her back to California like this," Grandpa says. "She needs help."

"Maybe we should just keep her here," Grandma suggests.

"I think a hospital is the only place that can help her."

Both of them sound so distraught. I have to put an end to this. I can't let them send me away, and I need to go back to school. I need to pull myself together.

I get out of bed and make my way downstairs where my grandparents are sitting at the kitchen table, discussing what to do with me. The sight of me takes them by surprise.

"I'm fine," I say matter-of-factly to both of them.

Immediately, Grandma is by my side, weeping. "Alex, you've had us so worried."

I hug her and once again say, "I'm fine."

Grandpa joins her embrace, kissing my hair, and I can tell he is fighting back tears. "You're not fine. I think you need help, sweetie."

I pull away from his hold and snap coldly, "I said I'm fine. I'm going back to school in two days. End of discussion."

They both stare at me, shocked by my tone. I feel guilty for my abrasiveness, but I need to make sure they understand me. And I need them to see that I'm fine. Strong enough to continue with my life.

"I'm hungry."

With those two small words, Grandma's face lights up, and she insists on making me something to eat. Grandpa, however, is still skeptical. He watches me closely. The three of us sit at the table as I eat the eggs and toast Grandma prepared for me, and I can hear that the television is on in the other room. What the news is reporting catches my attention.

"Senator Parker Ashcroft, rumored to be the top Democratic front-runner in the next presidential election, and six other men were arrested today for the rape and murder of a college coed over twenty-five years ago," a woman's voice announces.

I immediately push away from the table and run to the TV.

Images of Maxwell Wellington, Parker Ashcroft, Preston Walker, Walter Abbott, Philip Chamberlain, Lowell Ferguson and Edwin Hollister flood the screen. Each man being lead away in handcuffs and trying to hide their faces from the cameras.

"All men are being charged with murder in the second degree, sexual assault in the first degree, and illegal disposal of a corpse. There are few details at this time, but a source within the State Police department tells us that this gruesome crime was caught on videotape. It is our understanding that the tapes and other evidence were delivered to the police by an anonymous source."

"How awful," Grandma says from over my shoulder.

I ignore her and continue to glare at the television as the anchorwoman continues, "We have learned that all seven men are members of an elite secret society, a group that has been using its influence to protect these men since their time in college when the crime occurred.

"No other names have been released at this time, but we have been told that others affiliated with this secret society will also be charged. We will bring you more on this breaking news as it becomes available."

The screen goes black. "You don't need to be listening to that kind of thing," Grandpa says, irritated by my interest. "Let's sit down and talk."

Overwhelmed by what I just saw, my mind races with thoughts of Seth. *He did it.* He brought Wellington and the others down. But now what happens to him? Where will he go? His grandfather must be furious, and the rest of The Order will certainly want his neck. I try to pay attention to what my grandparents are saying to me, and I answer them the best I can. I desperately try to convince them that I am fine and that I am okay to go back to school. My grandfather is not so sure. Finally, I can't take it anymore.

"Listen!" I snap. "I am nineteen years old. I am not a child. I love you both, and I'm sorry I worried you, but I am fine now, and I am going back to school whether you want me to or not. Now if you will excuse me, I want to take a shower."

With that, I leave my stunned grandparents speechless and race up to my room, slamming the door behind me. I grab my cell phone and frantically type in Stevie's name and hit Send.

"Hello Alex." The sound of his voice pains me a little. It makes me yearn for Seth.

"I just saw the news. Is he okay?" I can't hide my panic.

"He's fine. How are you?" he asks, changing the subject. "Jeffery says you have not left your house since you got home. Is everything all right?"

Who gives a damn about me! Seth is the one on the run! Irritated, I reply, "I'm fine." I push a little harder. "Stevie, where is he?"

He lets out a deep sigh. "You know I can't tell you that. It's for your own safety and his." He pauses for a moment then says, "Alex, you have to move on with your life. If something happens that you need to know, I will contact you, I promise. But now, you just have to let it go. I'm sorry."

His words are like acid on my heart, slowly and painfully melting it away in my chest.

"Stevie." My voice cracks. "Tell him I'm proud of him. Tell him I miss him."

"I will. Good-bye, Alex." The line goes silent, and Stevie is gone.

I turn on the shower, sit on the floor, and let the water wash over me as I cry. I am so proud of what he has done. He finished what our fathers started, but at what cost? He will never be able to return to his life. What about his mother? What will happen to Mrs. Pierce now? Is she running with him?

I finish my shower and get dressed. I head downstairs, grab my coat, and announce to my grandparents that I'm going out. Before they can stop me, I am already out the door on my way to Barb's. I spot Jeffery in a black sedan and give him a little nod as if to tell him I'm all right.

"Oh my God!" Barb shrieks when she sees me standing at her door. "Finally! Come in."

She steps aside allowing me room to enter, but instead, I say, "Take a walk with me."

She grabs her coat, and we start walking through our quiet little neighborhood.

"Are you going to tell me what happened to you?" Barb asks after a few blocks of silence. "It was him, wasn't it?"

We walk and walk, and I tell her everything. I tell her about my father, about The Order, about poor Carolyn Peters. I tell her about the island and the Gala. I tell her about running for our lives and about shooting a man, and I tell her about Seth.

In a most unlike-Barb manner, she just listens to me. She doesn't say a word. I don't know if it's because everything is so unbelievable or if it's because there's just nothing she can say. But once I'm finished, she throws her arms around me and hugs me as tight as she can. She even starts to cry.

We stand alone on the snow-covered sidewalk and just hold each other. The relief I feel from finally telling someone what happened is such a weight lifted off of me I can hardly contain myself. She promises me that she will never breathe a word of what I had just told her to anyone. And I know I can trust her.

Once I get back to school, Julie notices immediately that something is wrong. She tries for weeks to get me to tell her what's going on, but I can't. It's only when she notices I've stopped getting "love letters" that she thinks she knows what's up. She thinks I've had my heart broken, which I guess in a way is true.

It's only when I return to California that I truly allow myself to grieve. And I hit all five stages of grief like a sledgehammer.

Denial. For weeks I convince myself that once all the hype surrounding the trials of Wellington and the other men dies down, Seth will come for me. I keep a bag packed and hidden under my bed, just so I am prepared when it happens. But he never comes.

Anger. Once the anger sets in, my art work changes dramatically. I've never been one to verbalize my pain, so it comes out when I draw and paint. Black and gray, along with blood-red cover piece after piece with no discernible rhyme or reason. Just heartbreak and hatred splashed across canvas. Not one of my professors knows what to make of my work. They grade me well, but don't understand where my focus comes from.

Bargaining. After a while, Stevie becomes my lifeline. I bombard him with calls and emails. I beg him to let me see Seth just one last time. I swear to him that I will never contact him again if he will only let me see him. Let me speak to him. Something. He takes it all in stride but never gives in to my pleas. He assures me every time that Seth is fine, but for our safety, this is the way things need to be.

Depression. Just about spring break time, I turn into a zombie. I had promised Barb that she and the boys could still come out to LA. We spend the week by the ocean. My body is there, but my heart and soul are not. I sit in a chair and gaze out into the water, while Barb and Danny frolic in the sand. Even Julie and Chris tag along—Chris has turned out to be a keeper. Chase is amazing. Day after day, he just sits quietly next to me and holds my hand. When the silence gets to be too much, he starts to talk aimlessly about school and hockey and what's been happening back home. He does everything he can to bring me back, but there is nothing he can do. He never gives up, though.

Acceptance. By the end of the semester, I make it to acceptance. I am ready to go home and face my friends and family and get on with my life. And I do just that. I spend the summer trying to make up for my behavior. I am the perfect granddaughter and friend. I still think about Seth almost every second of every day, but I have pushed the pain to the back of my heart. There are so many people who love and care about me I can't let them down. This includes Chase.

Before I return to school for my junior year, there is something I have to do. I have to see Stevie.

Jeffery still follows me every day. But he's not like Seth was. I know he's there. We even have lunch once a week. He's sweet. He gives me as much information as he can, which isn't much, about what has been happening with the trials and The Order, and it does make me feel safe having him around.

One week before I am supposed to go back to Cali, I leave my house and tap on his car window. "What can I do for you, Ms. Shelley" He stopped calling me Mrs. Campbell the day I came home.

"I'd like to go see Stevie. Would you drive me?" I ask, opening the car door and climbing inside.

"Of course."

We spend the four-hour drive to Toronto making idle chit chat, but once we pull into the underground parking garage of Stevie's apartment building, I have a reaction that I didn't expect.

"Are you all right?" Jeffery's surprised by my reaction as well.

I'm shaking. Taking a deep breath, I pull myself together and get out of the car. "I'm fine."

Jeffery quietly follows me into the lobby. "Allow me," he says, pressing the button calling the elevator.

The doors open, and before we can step inside, Stevie steps out. "Alex, what a pleasure to see you. Please come up." He ushers me into the elevator, leaving Jeffery in the lobby.

The ding announcing our arrival to the penthouse floor makes me jump. I follow Stevie into the apartment, and immediately, images of Seth flood my mind. I fight with everything I have not to break down and cry.

"To what do I owe the pleasure?" Stevie asks.

"I need you to do something for me," I reply, pulling two padded envelopes from my purse.

He eyes me with curiosity. "What do you have for me?" He reaches out, and I hand him one of the envelopes.

"I need you to find Carolyn Peter's family and return this to them. It was what my father wanted, and I need to make sure it's done." He flips the envelope around in his hands. "I figure that with your resources, you will be able to get this done."

"Of course," he replies. "My I ask what is inside?"

"It's the necklace she wore every day. It's important they get it back."

He smiles at me the way a proud father smiles at his child. "I will be sure to get it where it needs to go." He pauses then asks, "And the other?"

He points to the second envelope, the one I still hold in my trembling hands.

A lump rises in my throat, and I glance down at the unsealed parcel. Tears rolls down my cheeks as I look into Stevie's eyes. "This is for him." I can't say his name. "Please tell him that I am finally doing as he asked. I am getting on with my life. Tell him that I will always love him and that I want him to have this." I hand Stevie the envelope.

"May I?" he asks.

I nod.

Stevie lifts the flap of the envelope and empties the content into his hand. Resting in his palm is the remaining key from my bracelet. He looks to me.

"I want him to know he will always have the key to my heart." Tears are now flowing down my face.

I lunge forward and throw my arms around Stevie's neck. He holds me close.

"Thank you for everything. I won't bother you again," I say, pulling away.

He stops me and hugs me tighter. "You have never been a bother. It has been my pleasure to look after you, and I will continue to do so. If you ever need me for anything, please promise me you won't hesitate." He kisses the top of my head.

"I promise," is all I can say. I break free from his hold and rush to the elevator.

Once the door opens in the lobby, I am a mess. Jeffery rushes to my side. "Is everything all right?" he asks a little bit panicked.

"Please take me home," I whimper.

I'm as good as my word.

My third year at USC, Julie and I rent an apartment off campus on the beach. I throw myself into school, I get a job working at an art gallery, and I commit to making a long-distance relationship with Chase work.

There is one other thing I become dedicated to: fitness and self-defense.

Between classes and work, I've become obsessed with taking martial-arts classes and working out. I run along the beach every morning and every night, and I also go to the shooting range once a week. I am licensed to carry a small handgun, and I've become pretty good at firing it. Seth promised that The Order would never come after me again, but in case they do, I am going to be prepared.

A part of me died the day Seth sent me away, but life goes on, and I'm going to make the most of every day.

Forever

It's been five and a half years since those few days with Seth, and not one day has gone by that I haven't thought about him at least a hundred times. I wonder where he is. If he's safe. And I wonder if he thinks of me as often as I think of him.

The media frenzy that came from the trials of Maxwell Wellington and the other men drew a lot of unwanted attention to The Order. But from what I can tell, it is still going strong, recruiting fifteen new men every April and leading them down a path they can never return from.

Jeffery stayed assigned to me until I graduated, and we actually became pretty good friends. I would email with Stevie on occasion, but I never asked him about Seth. I knew that as long as we didn't talk about him, he was all right.

After graduation, Julie married Chris and decided to make LA her home. Not me. Once my time at USC was up, I came home to Michigan. Home to my grandparents and home to Chase.

Chase made good on his promise. He did everything he could to prove to me that I was the girl for him. He flew out to LA to see me at least once a month, and every time I went home, he catered to my every need. I did my part as well. I forced myself to put Seth behind me and really tried to be the best girlfriend I could be. And for the most part, I was happy.

I got a great job at one of the top advertising agencies in the area, and after about a year, Chase and I moved in together, and we've been taking things one day at a time. It is everything I thought I always wanted.

"Alex, it's time. Are you almost ready?" Barb's voice is soft as she enters the room. I can hear violins and a piano coming from down the hall.

I take one last look at myself in the mirror.

Barb smiles. "You are the most beautiful bride," she gushes. "Chase is going to die when he sees you."

I stare down at the two-carat diamond ring that has weighed down my left hand for over a year now. My hand is shaking.

Barb notices. "Sweetie, sit down." She leads me over to the pale-pink sofa that is next to the only window in this small cramped room. She slides the window open to give me some air. "You don't have to do this," she tells me, knowing exactly why I'm having second thoughts. "You just jump out the window, and I'll take care of everything else. I promise."

I smile at her and wrap my arms around her shoulders, holding her tightly. "You are the best friend in the whole world. What would I do without you?"

"Back at ya, baby!" she giggles.

She pushes me away and, with a very serious look, stares me dead in the face. I know what she's about to say. I stop her.

"I'm getting married," I tell her. "Chase is a good man, and he loves me. I have to stop wanting something I can't have." I pause and wait for her reaction, but she says nothing.

I furrow my brow at her, confused by her silence. She rubs her fingers over my forehead, smoothing out the lines. "Don't do that. It will show up in the pictures," she insists. We both laugh.

"How do I look?" I smooth out the lines of my simple but elegant wedding gown. Barb tried so hard to get me to buy a dress that had more "sparkle" (her word), but every dress I tried on reminded me of the dress I wore to the Gala. I couldn't get myself to wear a dress that reminded me of *him*. Besides, this dress was more Chase—simple and uncomplicated. "You mean boring." Were Barb's words the first time I tried it on.

"You look perfect," she answers. "But how about me? How do I look?" she asks jokingly.

"You are the most beautiful maid of honor ever!" I insist. "No one will be looking at me at all." I wink at her.

"Alex?" My grandpa's voice takes us both by surprise. We turn to see him standing in the doorway.

"I'll be right outside," Barb says, slipping out behind him. "You are so beautiful, Alexandra."

He never calls me Alexandra. That one word makes me feel all grown up. And I guess I am now. I'm not the three-year-old little girl who came to live with him lost and confused by the death of my parents. I'm a woman. A woman who went through hell and back to set things right. A woman who is about to start the next chapter.

"Thank you." I blush as I smile at him.

He hands me a small velvet box. "Your grandmother and I know how hard it was for you when you lost your bracelet, and we know this cannot take its place, but we wanted you to have a part of your parents with you today."

The hinge snaps as I open the small box, and inside is a new charm bracelet, but instead of keys, there are five small lockets. Grandpa reaches out and opens each one. Each holds a picture of my parents. One of my mother by herself, so lovely. One of my father by himself looking very regal. One of them together laughing. Another of them together kissing and finally one of the three of us as a family. It's perfect. I do everything I can not to cry. Barb will kill me if I mess up my makeup.

"It's perfect," I tell him, wrapping my arms around him and hugging him close.

"May I?" He places the bracelet around my wrist and fastens the clasp.

"Thank you for making my life perfect. You and Grandma have meant everything to me I am the luckiest girl in the world." I'm fighting back tears again.

"No, Alex, thank you." A tear slips down his cheek. "You have been a blessing from God. You are the reason we were able to go on after..." He can't finish his sentence. We hold each other, and for the first time, I realize that I held his life together just as much as he did mine. The death of my parents could have destroyed us all, but instead, we grew stronger together.

"Let's get out of here before we both end up a blubbering mess," I tease.

"Good idea."

Barb is waiting for us as we make our way to the chapel doors. She pulls me aside, fluffs up my dress, and as she brings my veil down over my face, she whispers one more time, "You don't have to do this."

"Yes I do," I whisper, glancing toward Grandpa.

"Okay, but if you change your mind, just give a look, and I'll cause a scene or something, and you can haul your ass out of here."

We both laugh. *God, I love this girl.*

With a deep breath, I take hold of Grandpa's arm and watch as Barb gracefully makes her way down to the altar. Once she is in her place, the musicians begin to play *Canon in D Major.* Everyone stands, and my stomach begins to churn as Grandpa leads me down the aisle.

All eyes are on me, but my eyes are on Chase. With Danny at his side, he is grinning from ear to ear. He looks so handsome in his tan suit, and the closer I get to him, the more the panic begins to set in. *I'm doing the right thing,* I keep telling myself with every step. *I'm doing the right thing.*

With a firm handshake, my grandfather gives Chase his blessing then offers him my hand. He lifts my veil and kisses me gently on the cheek then turns to join my grandmother in the front pew.

"You look beautiful," Chase whispers to me.

I blush.

The minister instructs everyone to sit down, and then he begins. "Dearly beloved…"

The room is spinning. Everything is blurry. I can no longer hear what the minister is saying. My heart is pounding in my ears, and I've stopped breathing.

"Alex?" Barb's voice breaks through the pounding. I turn to look at her. She's reaching for my flowers. I hand them to her but don't let go. "Okay?" she whispers.

My eyes burn into hers. What I'm about to do will change everything. I swallow hard then whisper, "Barb…I can't."

She nods and mouths, "Okay."

I turn my attention back to Chase who is patiently waiting for me to rejoin the ceremony. Slowly, I slide my engagement ring from my finger.

"What are you doing?" Chase asks.

I try desperately to look him in the eyes, but the pain I am about to cause is too much to bear. I place the beautiful ring in his hand and whisper, "I'm sorry."

"Alex, please. Don't do this. I love you so much." The pain in his voice cuts me to my core.

His words cause a stir from our guests, and I hear my grandmother say my name. I turn back to Barb.

"Just go. I'll explain to everyone. Find him. Find your heart."

I throw my arms around her. My best friend. My confidant. My rock. "I love you," I murmur.

"I love you too."

I can't look back at Chase. He's never going to understand.

Grabbing handfuls of my dress, I take one last look at my grandparents then sprint as fast as I can toward the doors of the tiny church. Shrieks and confusion spill out from the crowd as I make my way past them. Chase is yelling out my name, and I can hear Barb trying to stop him from coming after me.

"Chase, you have to let her go!" she yells. She's talking to him, but it's also her way of telling me she's not going to be able to hold him back for long.

I push through the doors with all that I have and rush out into the summer sunlight. I have no idea where I'm going or how I'm going to get there; I just know that I have to find *him!*

Suddenly and out of nowhere, he's there! Seth! My soul mate, my life. Just as beautiful, just as perfect.

We race toward each other, and I throw myself into his arms. I'm whole again. The hole that had been punched through my heart when he left me is full. All my fears, all my doubts, are gone.

"Baby, I'm sorry!" He hugs me tightly to his body. "I came here to stop you. To tell you that I can't live without you. To—"

I kiss him before he can finish.

Fire burns through us.

"I love you!" I say against his lips. I pull away and gaze into his sapphire eyes. The eyes that haunted my dreams for all these years. The only eyes that can see me for who I truly am. "I tried. I tried so hard to forget you. To lead a life without you but that life is an empty life. You make me whole. You are the reason I live."

"You are the reason I live." He kisses me again passionately. My heart swells with happiness. I know in this moment he will never let me go again. No matter what happens, we are in it together.

I lay my head on his chest. Something hard presses against my cheek. I unbutton the top two buttons of his shirt, and there, hanging from a silver chain, is key number 19.

"I've worn it every day since Stanton gave it to me," he says, answering my unspoken question. "The key to your heart."

"You've always had my heart."

"Just as you've had mine." He holds me so tight as if he's afraid to let me go. "You are so beautiful. Every time I closed my eyes, I saw your face. You've haunted me, Alexandra. I will die before I ever leave you again."

"Promise?"

"I promise." He smiles. *Oh God, his smile!*

The crowd from inside the church has started to gather outside, and I can hear Barb trying to get control of the situation.

I smile up into Seth's angelic face, letting him know that I'm ready, ready for *our* life to begin.

The corners of his mouth turn down slightly, and I can see a touch of sadness in his eyes "You know you can never come back," he says somberly.

"I know."

"Are you sure?"

"With a doubt," I assure him, placing my hand over the key that hangs over his heart.

His smile returns, and he places a gentle hand on my face. I lean into his touch. *Heaven!*

"We should probably go," I urge.

He nods. "But first…" He pulls something out of his pocket. "This is the ring that will forever be on your left hand." He slides a perfect princess-cut diamond ring onto my finger then brings it to his lips, kissing me gently. "Forever…Mrs. Pierce."

"Forever…Mr. Pierce."